THEY WILL SURPRISE YOU

VB SCOTT

No Barrier Publishing

Contents

Dedication

To Diamond Lake, a jewel in the Oregon Cascades and the site of decades of memories. May it forever remain a peaceful haven away from modern, hectic times.

CONTENT ADVISORY

The following book contains:
    Graphic, bloody violence and gore
    Sexual content (consensual, non-graphic)
    Threat of rape
    Homophobic slurs
    Drug use, alcohol consumption, and sex by minors
    Child and canine peril
    Cannibalism
    Forced drug overdose
    Brief suicidal ideation

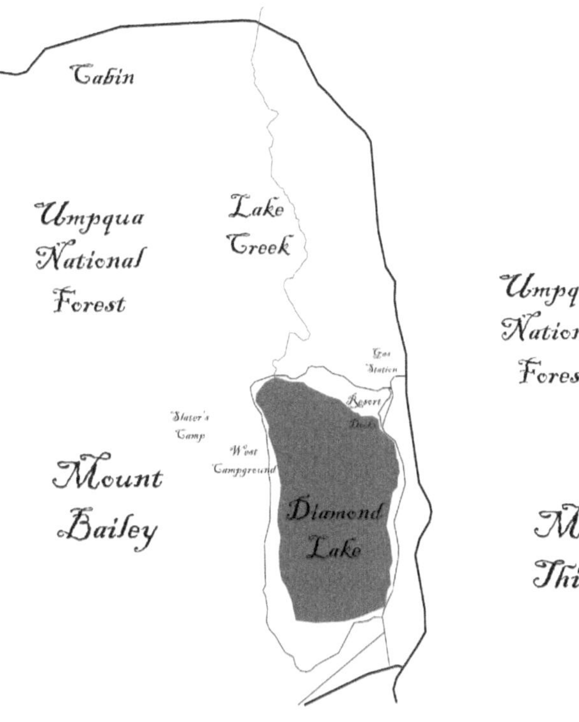

Cabin
Umpqua National Forest
Lake Creek
Umpqua National Forest
Gas Station
Resort
Dock
Slater's Camp
West Campground
Mount Bailey
Diamond Lake
Mount Thielsen

CHAPTER 1
NATURE

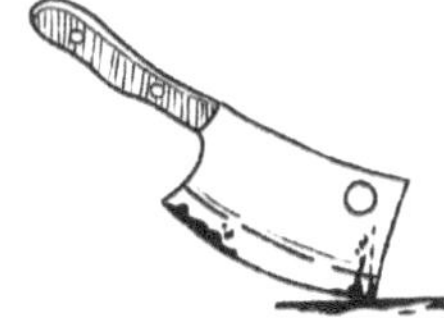

KILL COUNT: ??

WHERE SOME PEOPLE SHRINK in the cab of an F-350 truck, Slater was a man that filled it, both in body and the air about him; a man that feared no task or evil. He drove through the menacing gate, up the long driveway covered in foreboding foliage, to his farmhouse with the same paint from its original construction a century and a half ago. Its dank, dangerous vibe drew him and his family to its occupancy. Where some parents fretted over school districts, Slater valued privacy. Their previous house always had looky-loos—they couldn't resist wandering onto his property, getting in his way, trampling his wife's flowerbeds, making a mess of his collections, leaving his doors and windows open, spraying their bodily fluids everywhere...

Slater stepped out of the truck onto his new property and stalked over to a college-aged idiot looking through a window of Slater's home. The man didn't pay attention to what he trampled, or consider that *maybe* if the homeowners didn't come to the front door when he knocked, he should have moved on to bother the neighbors.

Once, in the old place, two teenagers peeped on Slater's wife, Killian, from a tree as she undressed in their bedroom. They'd shuffled to another branch as she progressed to the master bathroom, and it was hard to say which sight had startled the one so bad he lost his footing—Killian's glorious body or the luxuriously deep red that washed off of it. Regardless, the fool that had broken his leg on the fall exposed their location with his wailing, and made it all the easier for Slater to catch them. Killian volunteered to teach them a lesson, then she spent the following week pressuring Slater to find a new house. She didn't like work coming home to them—not with their sixteen-year-old daughter and eight-year-old son not quite ready to leave the house.

So, they packed their things and took the neighbor's F-350 and whatever they could fit into the bed. Ol' Todd didn't much appreciate Slater "borrowing" the truck, but Slater convinced the ornery gossip to look the other way. It was 180 degrees the other way, but he certainly stopped protesting after getting a new view of the living room window from his rocking chair on the front porch.

The owners of the new house in central California weren't too keen on handing over the keys to the property, either, but Slater preferred to take possession without the messy business of lawyers and real estate agents anyway. Slater and Killian were two of the greatest teachers in the country, and they always got what they wanted, one lesson at a time.

Slater seethed behind the back of the guy leering into Lynn Chelsea's room—all that work relocating, and they still couldn't escape the prying eyes of people who thought a man's house was a beacon for their drama.

Lynn screamed as the young man cupped his hands around his eyes and pressed into the glass. Slater loomed behind the man while she covered herself with a towel and pulled the blackout curtains closed.

"Woof. Bangin' bod, fugly face," the man said to himself before turning into Slater's bouldery chest.

Slater grabbed him by the neck and lifted him into the wall.

"What are you doing on my property, frat boy?"

"I— We're just—" the man gasped under Slater's tightening grip.

"There are more of you?" Slater dropped the man to allow him to speak.

"We investigate...paranormal activity. Looking for...abandoned houses..." the man managed while regaining his breath.

"This isn't abandoned. Are your idiot friends running around my property right now?"

"Not that I...know of. We split up to—"

"Daddy! *Why* is he still here?" Lynn screeched as she rounded the corner from the back yard, fully clothed in a preppy outfit she knew her parents hated. They had acquired a closetful of appropriately distressed and disturbed apparel she refused to wear. "He saw me naked!"

"I didn't *mean* to—"

Lynn slapped him and grabbed his neck, pushing him into the wall. She got him a few inches off the ground. Slater crossed his arms, proud to see her growing strength. Like father, like daughter.

"Your mother doesn't appreciate us bringing work home. She hates cleaning up the mess," Slater reminded her.

"I don't care! *I'll* do it and clean it up myself!"

"Like how you clean your room? Raccoons would do a better job."

The man struggled to remove Lynn's grip from his neck as the two lazily mused over what to do with him. A white Mercedes pulled up next to the F-350. Lynn dropped the man and put her hands behind her back, looking innocently away from Killian's angry expression as she exited the car. Her business suit looked great; the white blouse accented with dapples of red that Slater loved seeing on her.

"Classes went well today, I see?" Slater asked his wife, kissing her on the cheek as she took in the frat boy, her hands on her hips.

"What did I say about—?"

"We *know*, Mom. We were just talking about it."

"Well? What's the deal? Is he selling something? Why haven't you escorted him off the property?"

"Because he's a peeping tom! He watched me come out of the shower!"

"I didn't mean to—!"

"Honey, I'm sure he didn't know that was your room. Does he have binoculars? Was it premeditated?" Killian asked as she put her arm around Lynn's shoulder.

"No! I didn't know, I swear!" the man pleaded.

Slater caught the man's eyes with his gaze and shook his head, letting him know interrupting his wife wasn't a good idea.

"Alright, young man. If you promise to refrain from future acts of trespassing, you can leave our property," Killian said, pointing down the long driveway. "Chop-chop!"

The man took off. Lynn shrugged out of Killian's arm and skulked away, mumbling about never being able to help with the family business. Killian ran her hand across Slater's chest as she made to walk back to her car, then paused halfway. She glared at the flower garden she had painstakingly lined along the outside of the house when they moved in.

"Who trampled my flowers?" she asked with an edge that made Slater's heart melt.

"*We* all know how important your flowers are to you, dear."

Killian kicked off her heels and ran down the driveway at full speed after the traipsing trespasser. Slater chuckled. Although his wife's flowers were sacrificed for the greater good, he was pleased with the outcome: the guy had never properly apologized. He'd gotten off far too easily in Slater's opinion.

Slater entered the house to find their boy Murdock playing with toys in the living room, tearing off limbs and putting them onto the torsos of other toys. Killian preferred nature to take over the property and enjoyed watching wild animals roaming around. To that end, she'd procured for Murdock as many toys as needed to keep him occupied so he wouldn't go after the animals. It was a horrible experience trying to get Lynn to stop "playing" with the wildlife. Luckily, she lost interest in it long before they moved into the new place, her focus shifting with her hormones.

"Hey, little man. Was your big sister a good babysitter today?"

"No. She just stayed in her room the whole time. Probably whapping it to those stupid boy-toy posters she has in there. Why do you think she was in the shower before dinner?"

"That's a horrible thing to say about your sister. Where did you even learn about that?"

"From the neighbor's kid. He showed me his tablet and all the sites his older brother forgets to close after whapping—"

"Alright, I've heard that word enough today. Don't let your mother hear you talking like that."

Slater tousled his boy's hair and went into the walk-in freezer off the kitchen to grab dinner from one of the meat hooks. He nearly tripped over the ice block that kept the room cold. Almost time to get a new one… Killian already had the antique wood stove fired up when Slater dropped the slab on the counter. He took in her disheveled business suit and her blouse, no longer neatly hinting at cleavage, but almost entirely undone—buttons popped—beneath the navy-blue jacket.

"Mmm, you look so…" Slater said, trailing off as he wrapped his arm around her lower back. He pulled her close for a passionate kiss. Her soft lips melded perfectly with his, as they had for decades. Her heavy breathing from her little run tingled his senses further. When he knocked on her lips with his tongue, inviting hers to meet his, she pushed him away, leaving a red handprint on his white T-shirt.

"Not here, Slater. Murdock's right outside the room. Tonight, though, after the kids go to bed…" she teased, knowing how much her low voice stirred him.

She cupped her hand between his legs and gave him an infuriating, single pull that almost finished him right there. She turned to the stove and bent over in her tight skirt, torn from the run. He watched her slowly stoke the flames of the kindling before reaching for a piece of firewood. Her perfect heart-shaped butt almost gave Slater a heart attack, so he re-entered the freezer to cool off his veins—he didn't want to be pushing that down during dinner. He could already hear Murdock making another inappropriate comment.

At dinner, Lynn was in one of her typical moods, pushing the lightly charred meat around on her plate, hardly eating at all. Murdock pointed at her plate after clearing his. She let him take it, then rested her chin on her palm and sighed.

"Your father worked on that for an hour, Lynn. You need to eat so you can be strong when you get into the family business."

"I had the chance to do that today, but you two killjoys won't cut the umbilical. I haven't been off the property since we moved!"

"You haven't learned everything yet," Slater said after hard swallowing a hunk of meat. "How to blend in, move silently, never get caught..."

"So, when are you going to teach me?"

"With the move and needing you to watch your brother, it's been hard to find the time," Killian said. "Your father and I are working all the time. There are a lot of deviants around this town that need lessons."

"*I* need lessons!" Lynn cried. "I'm sick of being stuck at home! I want to be in a real high school, teaching the mean students lessons like you do to their parents!"

"You're not *ready!*" Slater pounded his fist on the table.

Murdock rolled his eyes at the family's melodrama and started playing with his knife, pretending a meat blob needed emergency surgery.

"Can I be *excused*, please?" Lynn pouted.

"Your mother is still eating, and your brother—"

"He's just playing with his food! And Mom eats too slow. I want to go to my room!"

"Probably going to *whap it* again," Murdock smirked without looking up.

Lynn reached over to slap at his face but couldn't reach. She swiftly rose from her seat, lifting her knife up over her head, ready to plunge it into her brother's.

"Young lady, you drop that knife and leave the table!" Killian yelled.

"That's what I wanted all *along!*" Lynn stabbed the knife into the table halfway up the blade, then ran off to her room. She slammed the door, knocking dust off the fan above the kitchen table and seasoning the remaining food.

Killian leaned her cheek on her palm and sighed, cocking her eyebrow at Slater, who smiled and shrugged.

"Alright, little man, either finish that or go play with your toys."

"When can I get a tablet, Dad?"

"It wouldn't do any good out here. There's no cable for the Internet, and no company will work on this house to install one. No electricity, either. Guess I should have led with that."

"Can't you *make* them? Teach them a lesson?"

"Teaching them a lesson won't always get you what you want, champ. Sometimes we need other people to actually do *their* work, you know."

"But Billy's house has Wi-Fi! They're just across the field! Why does the cable company help them and not us?"

"You need to learn to be happy with what you have, young man," Killian said. "And stop antagonizing your sister. She's having a hard enough time adapting to the new place."

"I don't *care* about her! I just want a tablet! I'm tired of playing with these stupid toys all alone!"

"Your mother and I go out of our way to take those toys, Murdock. I don't appreciate your attitude right now. You can go to your room, too."

"This isn't *fair!*" Murdock cried as he ran to his room and slammed the door. His sister screamed through her own door for him to shut up.

Killian sighed again. Her ponytail band had loosened after the day's events and she hadn't straightened her mussed up black hair, nor washed her hands, tucked her blouse back into her jacket, nor changed out of her torn skirt. Her feet were filthy from ditching the heels and running down the dirt driveway.

"Tell me where you want to do it right now, Killian," Slater said as he tore away his shirt and unbuckled his belt. "I'm about to explode."

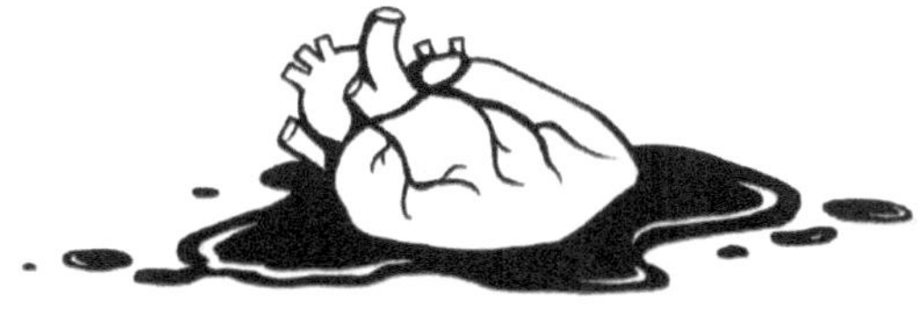

Killian snuggled into Slater's chest beneath his heavy arm as they lay together on a bed of their clothes over moldy hay in the barn.

Absorbed by their exchange, Slater hardly noticed the smell from the dark corners of the building or the trickling sound of little rivulets of blood flowing towards the center of the barn.

"I'll be carving up that mess all day tomorrow," Killian said while running her fingers through Slater's chest hair.

"I'll do it for you. You've got a lot of work still, right?"

"No rest for the wicked. Too many lessons to teach. Not enough time in the day…"

"Maybe if you took Lynn with you…"

"Yeah… But you had a point. She's not ready."

"She's got to start sometime, dear."

"You know, I don't like it when you call me 'dear.' It makes me feel like my best years are behind me."

"Sorry, sweetheart. Come here. Let me show you I don't believe that for a second."

Hay clung to their damp, sweaty bodies after their second romp, their heavy breath the only sound left in the barn. Slater held his wife against his torso.

"Why don't we make more time for this, hon?" Killian said.

"Two kids and two jobs. Kids want independence. The move's been hard on them and us."

"Have you ever thought about a vacation?"

"What, like Disneyland? Do you know how many lessons we'd be teaching there? Unruly kids, inattentive parents, horny teenagers, rude staff, lines as far as the eye can see? Murdock wouldn't be able to control himself. *I* wouldn't be able to—"

"What about a vacation from *lessons?* We could go camping, miles away from the nearest town. Bond with each other in nature. Get three tents…set ours up out of earshot of the kids'…"

"I love this side of you, sweetheart. It's the best idea since cooked meat! I'll get that mess carved up and on ice in the morning, then go into town for camping supplies. You can get the kids ready to go and we'll leave in the early afternoon."

"This'll be so great, Slater. I can't wait. I'll start packing tonight."

Killian stood up, her naked body even dirtier than before after the multiple rolls in the hay. Slater couldn't resist grabbing her elbow and bringing her in for another.

Slater and Killian sat miserably in the front seat of the F-350 while their children complained and fought the entire trip to the Oregon Cascades. More than once, he wanted to teach *them* a lesson, but his wife calmed him with a soft touch on his arm every time he started to turn around.

They didn't often travel together—or *leave the house* together, for that matter. Slater's concentration on the road gravitated to his wife's calm silhouette more than once. Despite the kids, it brought him happiness to be on the trip since they'd pulled out of town. He hadn't expected such a renewed attraction for Killian once their work interrupted their home life the previous day, seeing her before she'd had a chance to clean up.

Only recently he'd been coming up with lame excuses to avoid intimacy with her, even when she was making a half-hearted effort to engage on his behalf. Even with her own maternal milieu sapping the spark from her once-insatiable appetite, Slater had been the one skipping meals.

Now all he wanted was a week of having their own tent and large sleeping bag, a welcome change of pace from searching for odd places to fool around to avoid their kids hearing them. It was a long way to go to rekindle his fire for Killian, but after the previous night, he knew every mile would be worth it.

Slater drove around the northern shore of Diamond Lake, ten miles north of Crater Lake. Campgrounds were set up on all sides of the lake, but since they planned to avoid too much contact with other campers, not any site would do. He parked the F-350 in the west campground, with its spectacular view of Mt. Thielsen. No one was more excited to exit the vehicle than Slater. Everyone grabbed their tents and sleeping bags, and they trekked across the highway from the campground to a more isolated spot within the Umpqua National Forest between the lake and Mt. Bailey.

After helping the kids set up their tents, ignoring their grumbling, Slater and Killian pitched their tent over a hundred yards away from the other two. The sweat from the hiking and clearing the sites attracted dirt to their skin. Killian looked as ravishing in nature as she had in the kitchen. Slater knew she'd only rebuff him if he tried to start something with so much daylight left. She would be right to: better to save his energy for the night, knowing the kids would be asleep and far away, but showing restraint in the presence of such a primal beauty proved taxing.

Slater hiked up the slope of the mountain for thirty minutes and stood on a small rock outcrop that offered a better view of Diamond Lake. He took a deep breath and contemplated taking property nearby if the farmhouse didn't work out. Surely, there'd be no looky-loos out in a perfect place like this.

Chapter 2
Paper

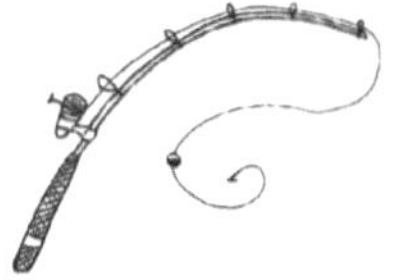

Kill Count: 4

TIMOTHY HUNT EXITED THE family Nissan Rogue and stretched his legs after eight long hours of driving from San Jose, California. Jessica followed not long after, climbing out of the passenger side. She yawned and stretched from her two-hour nap over the final leg of the trip. Timothy hadn't minded letting his wife sleep. He played I Spy and Twenty Questions with his bored sons, TJ and Corey. Corey gave half-assed answers to everything, still irritated he couldn't hang out with his friends. It was the week after his sophomore year of high school ended and they'd all be going on their own family vacations by the time Corey returned home from the trip. The poor kid would be alone during the peak summer goof-off weeks.

Timothy had apologized a dozen times, but his work needed him the most during the summer, and if the family was going to do anything together during the kids' long breaks, it would have to be that week. TJ hadn't minded. He would play with his portable gaming device at home or in nature. Almost nothing outside of that tiny screen mattered. Jessica didn't like him bringing it along, but Timothy knew he'd complain the whole time if they didn't let him, and Timothy needed the relative quiet more than anything. His batteries required more recharging than TJ's handheld after the car ride.

He convinced the family to put their phones in a bag that they'd keep in the car for the whole week to cut off the outside world. They all grumbled, but the service was bad anyway, and really it was more of a social experiment to see how long any of them could last (TJ's handheld notwithstanding—that would be like amputating a limb).

Magnolia, their golden shepherd mix who got her name from the butterfly magnolia tree in their backyard, scrambled out of the car as the boys exited and made a beeline for a chipmunk. Easily distracted, she gave up on the critter pursuit before she'd even gotten to it and bolted for Diamond Lake's muddy western shore past several empty campsites.

"Corey, TJ, bring Maggie back here, please. I'm not sure what the leash rules are yet."

The boys grumbled but did as asked. Jessica removed tents from the back of the midsize SUV. Timothy helped her set up camp while the boys played with Maggie down by the water. Initially annoyed that they didn't come back and help, Timothy let it go. They looked like they were already having some fun, so he took the small victory. Save for a white-F-350 with no tents around it, the rest of the west campground lay empty.

After setting up the smaller tent for the boys and Maggie, they erected the larger tent. Jessica brought in two sleeping bags and unfolded them. Timothy nodded at the bags and raised his eyebrows.

"Two, Jess? You don't want to...you know...use *one*? Like we used to?"

"Sorry, Tim. This wasn't the best week for me—if you had that in mind."

"Oh, yeah, of course. We don't necessarily... I mean... It's fine. This is about the whole family, not just you and me."

Timothy couldn't hide his disappointment. He meant to reconnect with her after the busy school year. Weeks would go between "date nights" and during one frustrating stretch of two months Jessica didn't seem all that interested, even when they could squeeze in a solitary fifteen minutes together without either of the boys around. He felt stupid for not planning that aspect of the trip better. Not that he could have. With the whole year being so off-kilter, he'd forgotten the cadence of her cycles.

Jessica's butt taunted him while she smoothed out the sleeping bags on her hands and knees. She sat back on her feet and mock-pouted at his downcast look, then crawled to him as he unpacked his hiking gear. She surprised him by putting her mouth to his ear and tugging at it with her lips.

"That doesn't mean *other* things can't happen," she whispered.

Timothy's heart nearly beat out of his chest. Before he could respond she pulled away from his ear and brought their lips together. He almost passed out before Jessica mercifully released him and crawled away towards the tent flap, wiggling her butt the whole way.

"After the boys are asleep," she said without looking back.

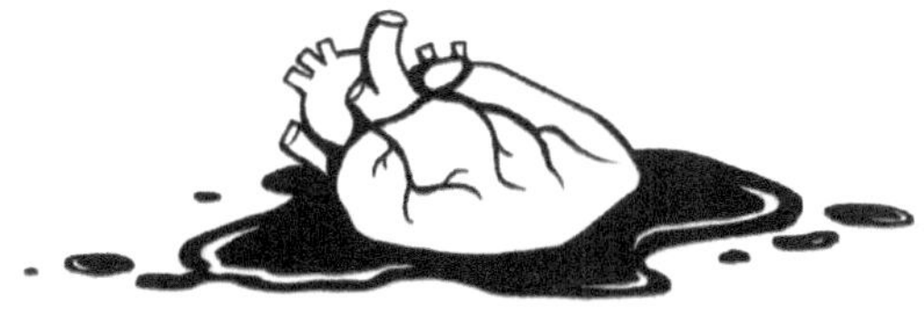

The boys cast their lines off the shore of the northern area of the campground while Maggie dried off in the dirt behind them, resting after a couple hours of swimming and running around. Jessica lay on top of their site's picnic table, reading a trashy paperback and bobbing her leg over the other knee. Timothy watched the boys from a foldout chair, well away from their casting radius.

He turned to see Jessica switch her legs to the opposite side, reminding him of the Sharon Stone interrogation scene in *Basic Instinct* even though Jessica wore shorts. His mind wandered to imagining what Jessica might have in store for him once the boys were asleep, and his heart sped up again.

He considered himself the luckiest guy to come out of their high school. Timothy and Jessica were best friends since the ninth grade but she never showed an interest in taking it any further. It would have been a "smart match" but not a passionate one.

Neither of them had many other options for dating due to their acne problems and awkward social skills, but didn't want to complicate things just because they could. They'd developed a tight bond, otherwise, that carried them to graduation without any extra messy teenage drama. Unfortunately their connection weakened once they went to Stanford. Her beautiful face cleared up, making her popular and bringing out her personality for everyone else to adore; a treat that only Timothy had been privy to before.

He couldn't really blame her for forgetting about him.

An acquaintance of his talked him into being his wingman at an off-campus party, and Timothy saw Jessica for the first time in three years since they'd drifted apart freshman year. His acne problems had cleared up by then, but he'd never gotten over his social awkwardness. He wanted to leave the moment he walked into the house party, but his friend had pulled him along.

Timothy owed the acquaintance: he'd gotten him an internship at a Silicon Valley start-up, but *his* social skills weren't that much better than Timothy's. However, Timothy made a great wingman play that resulted in the acquaintance leaving in the car that brought them there with a pretty, buzzed girl. The play left Timothy alone at the party, awkwardly nursing cheap beer and watching all the youthful horniness permeate around him.

Thankful to have a reason to move once his beer was gone, he went into the kitchen to find Jessica crying with another girl rubbing her shoulder. Not sure if she would even recognize him, he snatched the last beer from the fridge and turned to leave. His ears caught fire when Jessica called his name from behind; the searching in her voice...

Though he knew she only used him to forget her very-recent breakup, he was okay with that. He cared about her more than any other guy she might have picked up in desperation, but his initial chivalric motivations met an ultimatum when they found out he'd accidentally gotten her pregnant. If they hadn't been such good friends in high school, it would have been impossible for him to dream that the pregnancy would be anything beyond regrettable.

Now Timothy was up in the Oregon wilderness with their boys and family dog, and his soulmate was going to happily "take care of him tonight." Not even the boys' sullen attitudes could ruin the trip for him, even if it started raining every day for the rest of the week. Timothy considered himself the luckiest guy in the world.

"Afternoon, sir."

Timothy jolted out of his thoughts. A Forest Ranger stood beside his chair, wearing an ugly beige uniform and holding a clipboard at the ready. He pushed aviator sunglasses up on his nose.

"Hello!" Timothy greeted him. "How's your day?"

"Just fine, sir. Can I see your fishing licenses and park receipt, please?"

"Oh! Yeah, they're in the car. I'll be right back."

Timothy ran his fingers lightly over Jessica's arm as he passed the table, then retrieved the three fishing licenses he'd purchased in Klamath Falls. The Ranger looked them over and marked the info down on his clipboard.

"Limit's five per day, sir."

"Yeah, that's what they told me. The boys haven't caught anything yet."

"Better luck in the morning. They're leaping out of the water right before dawn."

The Ranger carried on along the shore towards a hulking man standing behind a boy as they cast a pole into the lake together. Timothy had never seen a man that large before. He wore jeans and a tight white T-shirt, and even from such a distance he saw it was spotty with dust from the volcanic basalt that covered most of the area. They weren't "glampers," certainly.

The Ranger seemed to ask them for the same information, but it was obvious that the man didn't have a license from his reaction. He gestured aggressively in a number of directions while the boy stood with his hands on his hips, scowling at the Ranger. More out of concern for the Ranger than out of the kindness of his heart for the man, Timothy jogged towards them, waving his arm in the air.

The enormous man dropped his aggressive posture and took a step back from the Ranger when he noticed Timothy approaching.

"Hi! Sorry! Uh, I'm assuming this gentleman doesn't have a license? Can he take one of mine? I don't really like fishing, I'll just keep the two for the boys. No reason to let this one go to waste, right?"

Timothy smiled at the man, pleased that the aggressive frown gave way to puzzlement. The Ranger looked at both of them and sighed, then took the license and handed it to the man after marking more notes on his clipboard.

"These licenses are *per pole*, sir. I don't want to come back here tomorrow and see you both fishing, and I *will* be back to see the receipt for the camp site you said is 'in your tent.' Kill all the chub you want, but the limit for rainbows is five per day. Are we clear?"

The large man's eyes flashed something akin to...rage? Timothy hardly caught it. Maybe it was a reflection from the lake...

"We're clear," the man said before the Ranger went back towards the west campground parking lot.

Timothy smiled at the man, then rocked back on his heels, feeling that old awkwardness come back on him.

"Oh, uh, thanks," the man said, scratching the back of his head with his meaty hand.

"Sure thing. I'm Tim. This your first time at the Lake?"

"First time...yeah. Not at *other* lakes, but this one, yeah."

"Da-a-a-d. This is boring!" the young boy whined.

Timothy smiled again at both of them.

"You know, I've got a son that's about your age. Maybe he'll show you his game console?" He hooked his thumb back towards the direction of the campsite.

The boy's eyes lit up and he looked excitedly at his father. The man frowned again, but a look crossed his face that seemed like he remembered he was supposed to be having fun, and nodded. The boy ran off down the shore, dropping the pole near his father's feet. The man sighed and picked it up.

Tim offered the stranger his hand. The man looked at it like the gesture was foreign to him. He stared down at it for a moment, but eventually he reached out and took it, nearly crushing Tim's hand with an iron grip.

"Name's Slater," he said after casting the line out. "I've been to many lakes, as I was saying, just not here. Sometimes the wife likes to work with me at the other lakes, but the kids are tagging along for the first time."

Timothy found it hard to believe the man had a wife and kids. His face was asymmetrical. He looked like a distracting background monster in a horror movie. His wife must be just as...

Timothy cut off his rude thoughts. Who was he to judge other people's looks? He was so plain as to border on ugly, if he was being generous to himself. Hardly worth someone of Jessica's caliber...

Slater cocked his eyebrow at Timothy's strange silence and furrowed brow.

"You said 'kids?' Got another boy?" Timothy asked, hoping to hit the right note of friendliness.

"Teenage daughter. Never leaves her room at home. Now she says she's never leaving the tent. Drove hundreds of miles for all this open space and she's 'not coming out.'"

"Yeah, yeah. I know exactly what you mean. Corey doesn't like all this, either. He'd rather be at the movies, or anywhere with air conditioning, really, hanging out with his friends. So, uh, where are you camping?"

Slater gave a look that Timothy interpreted as one to stop asking questions. Timothy shut up and put his hands in his pockets.

"Well, I better get back to my family. Almost time to start cooking dinner. I'll send your boy back to you. What's his name?"

"Murdock. It's okay. I'll come get him myself."

Slater reeled in the line and slipped the hook through one of the hoops, then they walked towards the campsite, Slater taking the lead.

"I think you're going to like this lake," Timothy said, unable to stop blathering, "It's pretty quiet, even during peak times. All the people are over in the northeast part of the resort. They've got a bar and grocery store over there. You, uh, ever feel like getting a drink this week, come knock on my tent. I'll buy you a cold one."

Timothy couldn't read Slater's neutral expression, so he didn't press the suggestion. Murdock protested being pulled away from TJ's game console, but TJ sweetly offered that he could use it tomorrow if he came back down to the campsite. That placated the boy, and Slater guided him back towards the road. He tossed the pole noisily into the bed of the white F-350 and they crossed the highway into the unmarked forest.

Jessica put a hand on Timothy's arm with concern as he watched after them. He didn't understand camping away from the campsite, but then he shrugged and asked his wife what she wanted help with besides starting the fire.

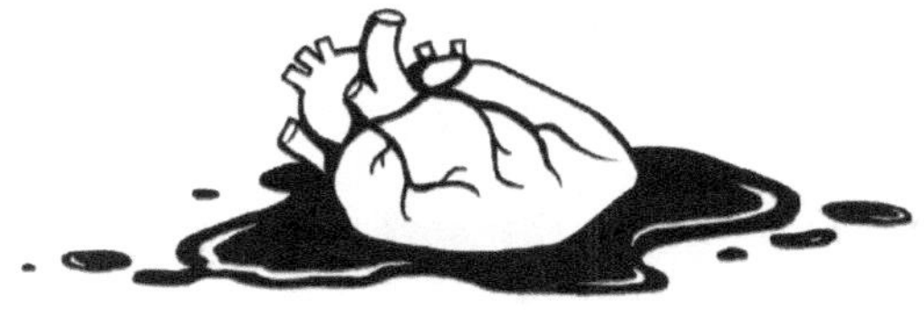

Halfway through their meal, Timothy noticed movement from the other side of the highway. Slater came lumbering out of the trees in the diminishing light of the sun, setting over Mt. Bailey's rounded peak. He looked angry as he walked towards the truck.

Against his better judgment, Timothy waved and called out to Slater before he could get into the vehicle.

"Everything all right, Slater?"

Slater appeared to ignore him, then paused with the truck door opened and dropped his head. He shut the door and came towards the campsite.

"Oh, it's stupid. I thought we'd catch fish for dinner so I talked everyone out of bringing food. Now they're all mad at me for not catching anything and want me to go to the grocery store before it closes."

Jessica raised her eyebrows to Timothy and motioned to their picnic table of leftovers. The boys hadn't brought their best appetites for the generally healthy food their mother was prone to cooking. Even though the plan had been to "rough it," they'd been disappointed to learn that didn't mean "hot dogs at every single meal."

"Say, Slater, that'll take you a while to drive over and back. We've got plenty to share and we can't exactly store it all in a fridge."

Slater stared at the two of them as if no one had ever been kind to him in his entire life. Timothy felt pangs of sympathy fire off in his chest. He decided to make the decision easier for Slater.

"Here, I'll help you carry some of it to your site. Corey! Come help me with this food."

"This is completely unnecessary. I don't want to bother—"

"It's no problem at all! It's my wife's vegetarian lasagna. She's famous for it. You'll *love* it!"

Corey sighed and thrust himself out of his foldup chair next to the fire.

"What do you need, four plates?" Timothy asked.

"Really, it's too much. We're not vegeta—"

"Would you rather starve your family?" Timothy nudged Slater with his elbow. "Come on, it's really good. We'll bring the food over with you then head right back. We won't take up any of your time with the wife and kids."

Slater frowned once he realized he wasn't going to win the fight and led them across the highway to the hiking trail he seemed to have made himself.

"Dad," Corey whispered from several paces behind Slater as they scrambled up the dusty non-trail. "You're being pushy. I don't think that guy's telling the truth about the food. He was probably going to the resort for beer."

"Why lie about it? You're being paranoid. Besides, he said he has a teenage daughter."

Timothy nudged his son while sing-songing "daughter," which earned him a scowl. It was barely perceptible in the increasing darkness, but Corey's "looks" were as predictable as they were withering.

"So, what, you're trying to set me up? I do *not* want to get involved with this guy's family. He looks like he cracks open coconuts with his bare hands. And, *hello!* They aren't camping in the designated areas. We're being led to our deaths at the end of a machete. Or *those hands.*"

"You watch too many movies. When did I raise you to be so distrustful?"

"I'm just putting two and two to—"

Slater stopped and turned to face both of them. Corey took a step back.

"I can take these the rest of the way. I see the fire."

"Are you a waiter? You can hold four plates full of food at the same time? Come on, shy guy! We'll be out of your hair in no time!"

Corey sighed pointedly behind Timothy.

Slater huffed and continued through the trees. They came to the crackling fire. A woman and two kids startled as they parted from the evening shadows. The dirty but gorgeous woman with black hair was spitting a squirrel and resting it near the fire with some chipmunks and other skewered rodents. A large, unidentifiable hunk of meat sizzled alongside the animals.

"Wow, Slater, you weren't kidding about the scarcity of your food situation. Heh. Um, hi, you must be Slater's wife. I'm Timothy, this is my son, Corey. Your husband said you... Well, here's some food my wife made and my ingrate sons hardly touched."

The woman looked at her husband and communicated something with her eyes, then picked herself up off the dirt and brushed the dust from her shabby wilderness garb.

"Well, thank you so much, Timothy. Corey. That's so thoughtful of you to come all the way up here. I'm Killian. I thought my husband was joking when he said we'd be 'roughing it,' but, *here we are!*"

She waved her hands around and took the plates from Timothy's hands, handing one to Slater before sitting back down in the dirt next to the fire.

"Oh, um, Corey, was it?" Killian said. "I heard you met Murdock. And this is our daughter, Lynn Chelsea, pouting and trying to keep the dirt off her shoes in the dustiest place on Earth."

Corey handed a plate to Murdock and Lynn Chelsea. She looked out-of-place in the sort of outfit girls wore to Corey's private high school. She was a sight of sophistication among her three dirtier, unkempt family members. She smiled shyly and ran a strand of hair behind her ear at Corey. She reminded Timothy of Jessica when they first met. She was...a little hard on the eyes, to put it gently, but her smile lit up her face.

"Thank you again, so much. What nice young men," Killian said brightly. "Tell me where you sleep—I mean, where you're *camping* and I'll bring your plates back tomorrow and thank your wife. It smells so...just *so* good."

Slater reached out and nearly crushed Timothy's hand again in a parting shake, then did the same to Corey, making him wince with the same force.

"Thanks, Tim. We'll see you tomorrow, yeah?"

"Sure thing. Good to meet you all. Don't be strangers!"

Timothy nudged Corey again on the way down.

"What'd you think, eh? She was pretty stacked, wasn't she?"

Corey scoffed in the way only teenagers ever do.

"Cut it out, Dad. She looked more like her dad than her mom. And no one's saying 'stacked' anymore. Also, are you going to nudge everyone from now on? That's really annoying."

Timothy put his arm around his son, knowing how much that annoyed him, too, even though literally no one else on Earth could possibly see the exchange of affection. He still acted embarrassed and shrugged out of the gesture.

They hiked the rest of the way back down the hill in silence. When they returned, Corey zipped himself into the tent with TJ and Maggie while Jessica read by the campfire light. Timothy sat in his fold up chair and let the fire warm his hands and face.

"That was so nice of you, Tim. Were they friendly?"

"Oh, yeah. I think you'll like Killian. She had this really cheery quality. She's bringing the plates by tomorrow."

"Really? Those were paper plates..."

"I guess that didn't occur to me when she said it. Oh well. That hike wiped me out a little bit."

"That's too bad," Jessica said, flipping a page in her book without looking up.

"Nah, it felt good. It was a nice workout. Just tired is all."

Jessica tilted her head at him, then tossed the book into the campfire. Timothy looked at her wide-eyed as the fire intensified in brightness for the short time it took to devour the paperback.

"That book sucked."

She got out of her chair and surprised him by straddling her legs through the sides of the chair and putting her arms around his neck. She kissed him as she had in the tent earlier, but deeper and longer, then pulled back to look into his eyes.

"I don't want to hear any excuses on this trip already. I know this last year's been...less exciting. But up here..." she kissed him again before continuing, "get into that tent, shut the fuck up, and take off your pants."

Chapter 3

Pairings

Kill Count: 4

TERA SPENT MOST OF the three-hour bus trip from South Umpqua High School staring at the back of Shawna's head. Her cascading black curls bounced and danced off her shoulders whenever she talked with the other girls or watched the passing greenery, creeks, and canyons. Tera would have given anything in the world to kiss the ears peeking out from her hair. Whenever any of the boys talked with Shawna, it reminded Tera that Shawna wasn't into girls and never would be. It made for a dismally long drive, especially knowing what she had to look forward to once they reached their destination.

Shawna had transferred to their bumpkin high school from Portland early in the year, and became a lightning rod of popularity and prejudice—the only Black student in a small, white, conservative town. Tera had been the only student brave enough to sit next to Shawna at lunch on her first day, drawn to her big-city fashion and the cool way she talked when she introduced herself during First Period.

It wasn't lost on Tera how many of her acquaintances stopped being acquaintances when that happened. She didn't care, though.

She had enough cache with the cheer coach and the Queen Bee of the squad to get Shawna a tryout, and they became fast friends. The rest of the cheerleaders took to Shawna soon after, and that brought its own sort of popularity with the jocks.

Shawna didn't let her growing social status affect the special bond she and Tera had, but the more Tera fell in love with her, knowing in her heart that nothing would ever come of it, the more Tera involuntarily distanced herself.

Halfway through the trip to Diamond Lake, one of the football players sat behind Shawna and playfully pulled on one of her curls. Shawna laughed it off, but Tera knew she was only doing that to avoid a big confrontation before they'd even reached their destination. Tera stood up from her hunter's perch at the back of the bus and boxed the wide receiver into his seat.

She grabbed him by the shirt and whispered, "Teddy, if I see you pulling hair or snapping bras or any other horseshit during this trip, I'll make sure you won't be able to fuck around with Sarah the whole week."

Teddy scoffed and started to push Tera out of the way. She thrust her hand between his legs and squeezed tight.

"Start showing some respect, asshole."

"*Okay*, Tera," Teddy said through clenched teeth.

She let go and pinched her fingers in front of his face.

"That was only a fraction of the pain. Don't be a douchebag. Count your lucky stars we invited you guys up here at all."

She let him out and he moved gingerly to the front of the bus, pretending nothing had happened as he reconvened with his teammates. Shawna turned in her seat.

"Thanks, T," she said as they bumped fists. "I hope you're not going to hover over me like that all week."

"Of course not. But what better time to set a precedent than on the stolen bus before we take over half a campground?"

Chase, the Queen Bee, had bribed one of the burnouts with the promise of booze and "maybe more" if he could pull off a heist of a rival school's bus. He could invite anyone else who helped him accomplish it. Along with the three guys he brought along, the bus carried eight cheerleaders and six football players.

Tera had protested to Chase that the imbalance of boys to girls would lead to trouble, especially after what Chase had "implied/promised" them. Chase teased Tera that if she was so worried about the imbalance, Tera could work on double-soda-shaking. Tera rolled her eyes and told the Queen Bee to get double-stuffed herself. Chase was a good sport about it—her relationship with the school's varsity quarterback was strong enough to handle light sexual teasing. They didn't have the melodramatic blowups a lot of media portrayed of the head cheerleader and quarterback duo; they seemed genuinely in love. Tera admired them for that, even though she didn't like how they looked down on everyone around them, and in Chase's case, bossed them around.

Still, Chase respected Tera's cheer skills and minimized strife among the girls when it arose. Chase's goal above all else was to make them the best cheer squad in the county, and they got along fine under that pretense.

Several of the boys in the front, unable to hide their horny desires, kept asking Ian, the head burnout who masterminded the bus theft and drove it, when they would get to the campsite. The sun was setting, and they were already "pitching tents."

If the sex imbalance had been reversed, Tera could have relaxed. It would have left all the boys "taken care of" and she wouldn't have to hide which team she actually played for. Nobody knew Tera's secret except for her best friend Peter, who had his own secret. They'd pretended to date all four years of school, fooling their parents and everyone else in town. Unfortunately, Peter had been dragged to the coast that week and had no way to get out of it, so Tera was left to stew over her love for Shawna and, apparently, be the Queen Bitch keeping the boys in line.

Without Peter there to keep up the act, if she were approached by any of the boys, she planned to toss out the excuse of being on her period. Hopefully, in their current numbers, hurt feelings would be the least of Tera's worries.

Tera caught two of the burnouts almost always looking in her direction. Perhaps if they tried to make a move, they'd respect her relationship with Peter once she brought it up. If that didn't work, she'd pull out the period excuse. If they still didn't get the hint, they'd be clutching their junk for a different reason all week.

Worries of socially awkward shutdowns aside, she found it fascinating how the three groups sized each other up over the bus trip. Chase and Darren, Molly and Garrett, and Tera were off the board, leaving five girls and eight boys. Tera had a feeling, if the boys were choosing, they'd likely skip Darleen, or cruelly play Rock, Paper, Scissors for her when she was inevitably the last to choose. She had a cute face and the best personality of all of them, but in a huskier body.

Chase wasn't shy about her "allowance" of both a heavier girl and a Black girl in her squad and how it would earn them "hidden points" in competitions. Tera considered creaming Chase's spankies with the knowledge they had a lesbian in the group, too, but nothing was worth outing herself in their country-ass town.

Tera wouldn't mind helping a homegirl out by wing-manning if she didn't already know that Darleen pined for Jason, the linebacker-slash-tight end. Unfortunately, he had an eye for Misty, who seemed to already be gunning for Luke. Only Amber dug any of the burnouts. Assuming Darleen was in for a lonely week, that left two girls and five boys, three of those being the undesirable burnouts. Tera wondered what any of them felt for Shawna. They were likely as afraid of interracial dating as Tera was of outing herself.

She couldn't wait to get to Oregon State University in Corvallis after her last summer of fear.

Once the football team demonstrated their value by pitching their tents and erecting most of the girls' tents by lantern light, they all sat around the fire the burnouts had started. Chase gathered everyone's phones in a bag and put it on the bus, claiming they couldn't truly appreciate each other with those in their pockets. Everyone complained, but knew Chase would get her way in the end. The cell reception was nonexistent, anyway.

Darren opened a twenty-four-pack of Pabst and gave a can to each person.

"Sorry, guys, this was all my brother would buy for me. One of you will have to get more from the store tomorrow."

"Who's got the fake ID?" Misty asked.

Everyone looked around the circle, hoping someone would raise their hand.

"No one thought to get one?" Ian asked. "Did you lie to me about booze for the bus, Chase?"

"...No, I thought Darren would come through with more than this."

"I got this," Jason said after shotgunning his beer and catching the next one from Darren. "I went into Ray's once and bought beer. They didn't even card me."

Tera rolled her eyes. "That's because Darleen was working and she didn't card you, bro."

Most of the group laughed. Ian hunched his disgruntled shoulders, but one of his accomplices shuffled around in the duffel bag that he'd kept close to his person since they'd gotten onto the bus.

"If you pussies and ladies can't figure out the booze situation, I brought enough weed to bomb this whole campsite," he said as he produced several baggies of flower and edibles.

Most of the cheerleaders and jocks were straight-laced when it came to drugs. A few of them perked up while the rest scowled at the guy.

"I'm not risking my scholarship, bro," Luke said. "We have drug tests next month."

"No one's forcing you, *bro*."

Ian put his hand on the guy's arm. "More for us, Nick."

Tera wanted to stop thinking about who would take Shawna into their tent, or vice versa, and Darren's shitty single beer wasn't doing the trick.

"I'll have one of...whatever, Nick," she said, ignoring Chase's quick scowl.

Darleen and Amber requested some, too. Chase scoffed dramatically and pulled Darren away from the campfire to their tent. The rest of the party broke up to their separate tents.

Tera coughed at her first "inhale," then listened to Nick and Ian tell her what she had to do to make it smoother. Darleen and Amber followed as they passed it around the fire. Tera leaned back on her hands on the picnic table as she waited for her turn to come back around.

"So, you're Ian and Nick. Who are *you guys?*" she asked the other two burnouts.

"I'm Tony, this is Zack. We stole the keys from the bus lot."

"Ooh, I want to hear how this all went down," Tera leaned in after passing the joint to Darleen.

The boys talked out their heist while tent zippers opened and closed with the movement of bolder boys and girls making their pairings. Tera smiled wider as the joint got shorter. Zack seemed to be into Darleen, to her delight. She was less sure about who Amber was eyeing between Tony and Nick. After having one of the remaining beers and a long inhale, Amber made everyone's eyes pop out of their heads as she grabbed Tony *and* Nick's hands and took them to her tent.

Darleen and Tera sputtered laughter. Ian rolled another joint as the dwindling group finished the first one. Tera whispered into Darleen's ear and stifled a snort as Darleen took an extra-long drag, then worked up the courage to grab Zack's hand and go to his tent.

Ian did a great job seeming disinterested in Tera as they shared the last joint. Halfway through, he stood up. Tera prepared to shoot him down.

"Come take a walk with me, up on the highway," he said, surprising her into silence instead.

He walked carefully to avoid loose rock and tree roots with a dim, nearly useless flashlight leading the way. They passed a Forest Ranger vehicle parked near the entrance of the west campgrounds with no occupant.

Ian stopped in the middle of the empty highway and flicked off the flashlight, then craned his neck up. Tera did the same. The Milky Way spun around them in its purple, white, red, and black majesty. There wasn't a single trace of light pollution over one of the only spots in the west campground they could look up without trees blocking the view.

"I've got a girlfriend," Ian said, startling Tera from the celestial dizziness she'd been absorbed in. "She's with her family in Texas for a month."

"Ah. I was getting ready to tell you I'm on my... Never mind. So, what are you doing up here, then?"

"Honestly, I was just trying to get those guys laid. They've had a long, lonely couple of years..."

"Well, you succeeded spectacularly."

"You working out all the pairings still?" Ian asked.

"...Yeah. With you and me off the table it's Jason, Bobby, and Shawna left."

"I saw the way you looked at her from the rearview mirror the whole trip. You're hoping neither of them make a move on her, huh?"

If there were any light, Ian would have seen Tera's face burning red. "It's none of your—"

"Whoa whoa. It was just what I observed. I could see the way everyone looked at everyone else with that giant bus mirror. I played a little game, guessing who would pair up and who would sleep alone. I got three right besides the obvious ones."

"Mm."

Tera passed the joint back. "Would you do Shawna?" she asked.

Ian sputtered and coughed. "I said I have a girlfriend."

"Not what I meant. Jason and Bobby probably won't touch her because she's Black. They come from red stock in a red town. If you *didn't* have a girlfriend, would you date a Black girl?"

"Yeah, I don't give a fuck what other people think."

"Easy for you to say, but... I envy that."

"You, uh...you ever just *ask* her?" Ian prodded as he passed the near-finished joint back.

"She's not bi, if that's what you're getting at. Found that out early on with some lame Truth or Dare shit at one of our hotel stays during a competition."

They stood in silence, not noticing in their hazy state and with the hypnotic trance the galaxy put them in that they'd gravitated to leaning back on each other's shoulders for balance.

Approaching lights got them to move off the highway and to lazily walk back toward their site. On the way, Tera noticed the passenger side door of that Ranger's vehicle hung open. She paused, and Ian came back to her when he couldn't hear her footsteps anymore.

Tera went to the vehicle and found a clipboard along with a mess of papers all over the front seats. Ian walked around the vehicle, understanding what gave Tera pause without her having to explain.

One of the papers lay face up, and she observed handwriting scrawled outside the official columns of the government document. It said: "Check in on aggressive, creepy guy and his son in the morning. Bring backup."

A hand on her shoulder caught her off guard. She cocked her fist back reflexively. Ian winced and backed up.

"Sorry, dude," she said. "Find anything?"

"Big footprints that don't match the hiking boots belonging to the Ranger."

"You know what kind of patterns Ranger hiking boots have?" Tera asked with awe in her voice. It'd sound astounding even if she weren't baked out of her gourd.

"No, just guessing based on the driver side prints, and following them over here."

"It's just so weird he'd leave the door open and this mess behind. Think a bear chased him?"

"Hmmph. Don't know. And, sorry, don't really care. I'm getting ready to turn in after I eat half a bag of marshmallows."

Tera took one last look around the interior of the vehicle, then closed the door and followed a few paces behind Ian. Their group's tents were all spread among adjacent sites. Tera sighed at the sounds coming from some of them as they passed. Once Ian safely climbed into his tent and zipped it behind him, Tera stopped outside Shawna's.

At another competition in Portland, she and Shawna shared a hotel room and they'd gabbed all night. Tera had been elated to discover that her bed had the *perfect* angle against the closet door's mirror to afford an unhindered view of the bathroom sink. Shawna changed into and out of her uniform several times over the stay, with several accompanying showers.

Tera had felt like a peeping tammy, but Shawna's obliviousness demanded Tera take advantage of something she never thought she'd get close to otherwise. Using the hotel blanket for cover, she took in Shawna's sumptuous curves, then pretended to be napping when Shawna came around the corner.

The weed almost gave her the courage to walk up to Shawna's tent, unzip it, and crawl into her sleeping bag. There was a one-in-a-billion chance Shawna would allow it, but that was still *a* chance. Tera even took a couple of steps in that direction before she realized someone's hand held her arm.

She made out Jason's silhouette.

"You think I got a shot with her, Tera?" he whispered.

Asshole!

"Sure, man..."

She sniffed back a few bitter tears on the way to her tent. Tera zipped the sleeping bag over her head and pressed her hands to her ears to block out all the rustling fabric, grunts, and moans seeping out of all the tents around her. If she ever heard the sounds of Shawna's pleasure, she didn't want it to be like that.

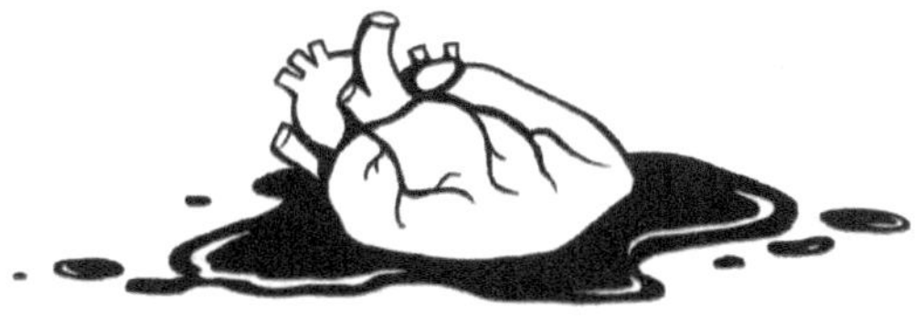

Tera's auburn hair was mussed up when she crawled out of the tent in the cold morning. The smooth-as-glass lake surface caught her eye, along with a breathtaking wall of fog a perfect distance from the shore. Occasionally a fish plopped out and disturbed the tranquility, but only for a moment. Towards the middle of the campground, most of her friends chatted and stood in line with all their sundries for the one working shower stall and bathroom on the site.

Ian crawled out of his tent and stretched, then lifted his head in her direction. She returned the gesture with a small smile. She felt too gross to go over and talk to him, though, especially after the rough night of tossing and turning before she managed to get to sleep. Her heart sank when Jason stooped out of Shawna's tent and went to his own. Shawna came out with her towel and shower caddy. She stopped by Tera's tent to share the experience.

Tera had faked happiness for her boy-infatuated friends most of her life, but she almost snapped at her best friend to shut up and leave her alone. It would have been one thing if they were all at home, but at the lake it was too close in proximity. Tera's unrequited misery would have to live alongside Shawna's gleeful conquest for the rest of the week.

After Shawna parted to stand in line, Tera crossed her arms and made her way to the fire Bobby started. He already snagged a few trout and had them roasting in tinfoil on large rocks close to the fire.

"Mornin', Bobby. Guess it's easy to be productive without all the distracting hormonal nonsense... Sorry. What's *my* excuse for not helping, right? I'll make the coffee."

"Thanks. The stuff's on the bus."

She noted the Ranger's vehicle hadn't moved, then something more puzzling—the bus's hood partially opened. She climbed onto the front tire and lifted it the rest of the way. The sight within froze her.

A body materialized next to her, rubbing against her shoulder and thigh as it struggled to peek in as well. Tera gave a jolt like she'd touched the battery.

"Jesus, Ian! Stop sneaking up on me."

"Sorry, I was wondering what you were doing. This is... I mean, what the *fuck*?"

Most of the cables in the engine compartment were cut and several components had been removed.

"Good thing you guys stole a rival's bus..." Tera quipped, and Ian couldn't help himself to a little smile.

CHAPTER 4

LEGAL

KILL COUNT: 5

KATIE SCRUNCHED HER NOSE at the rancid smell blowing past as she opened the motel room's door—something akin to a hundred wet dogs and fish rotting in the sun. She didn't have much food in her stomach but she almost threw up anyway; she'd been driving for twelve solid hours, and most of that in the dark, hopped up on multiple energy drinks. She wouldn't let her clients drive her car, and, thankfully, they'd all agreed to rest at the Diamond Lake resort motel on their way to Bend.

"What did you expect on a fishing lake?" Samantha said as she brushed past Katie to take in the room, then shuddered. "God, I *hate* this smell!"

Katie closed her eyes when she felt a presence behind her. He'd been pushing her buttons the entire trip, thinking his payment for her services was enough to put up with his poking and prodding.

"You're good at blocking things," Randall taunted. "Like an actual d—"

Katie turned and swung at his head. He caught her fist with his free hand, while the other lay casually over the shoulder of his current drug-addled conquest. Randall laughed and pushed her aside, following Samantha into the room. His lackey Trent was the last in before Katie closed the door behind her.

"Brilliant fucking idea, Randall. I can't believe I let you idiots talk me into this trip," Katie said.

"Who's the more...idiot? The idiot, or you for following—" Trent said.

"You butchered that, moron. And *yes*, I'm just as much an idiot for getting into this with you people."

"Come on, Katie," Samantha said. "We're paying you good money."

"You said there'd only be one guy to deal with in San Francisco, and nothing about being armed, or a fucking shootout!"

"I've heard enough of your whining, dyke," Randall said. "That's all you've done since Sam brought you in. You're lucky your driving skills saved the day, or we'd have ditched you back in Medford."

The door opened behind Katie and another one of Randall's lackeys, Boyd, came in carrying two bags. He dumped their contents on an open bed—stacks of cash and bags of drugs. The girl that was otherwise adhered to Randall's side reached for a baggie. Randall slapped the back of her head and pulled her away by the neck of her jacket.

"That's *not* for you, Kelly! That's to start our new life in Portland."

"Randy-y-y, I *need* it!"

"We've got our own shit in the car. Katie, go get some. It's in that hole in the side of the passenger seat."

"Get it yourself, asshole. All you're paying me to do is drive."

Randall pushed Kelly to the bed to get her out of his way and closed on Katie, pulling his handgun from the back of his waistband. He pressed the barrel up beneath her chin and forced her into the corner of the small, shabby room. The wallpaper was sticky against her palms as she pressed into it. She noticed Samantha look away.

"You'd better cut out the attitude, bitch. I have half a mind to kill you and steal your car. But everything will be much easier if we do this in your legally-owned car, without a murder tailing us to our new life. And all you gotta do is make another...stop in Bend, then drop us off at my cousin's in Portland, then you're home free. *Until* then, stop being a killjoy, get the drugs, and get high with us."

He put his gun back and rejoined Kelly on the bed. All but Sam stared at Katie, waiting for her to go back to her car for their shit. Her face still burned from the adrenaline of Randall holding his gun on her, so she decided she needed the cool morning air to calm down anyway. She slammed the door behind her and retrieved their personal drug supply from the car.

Back in the room, she dropped it onto the unoccupied bed.

"Enjoy, friends," she said through gritted teeth. "I'm going to see if I can get the rattling beneath the hood fixed. Try not to overdose while I'm gone."

Randall pulled out his gun and pointed it at her again. She shrank back and held her hands in the air next to the door.

"You still want the other half of the payment?"

"Yes, *of course*," she muttered.

"Obviously if you ditch us, you won't get it, but in case that thought is running around in your head, I'll kill Samantha if you don't return."

"I *get* it, Randall! You want to get to Portland? I need to fix the fucking car! I'm not *ditching* you!"

"Hand over your phone. Then you can do whatever you think you need to do to get the car working right."

Randall returned his gun and pocketed Katie's phone, then snorted a line off Kelly's thumb. Katie slammed the door and descended the stairs. Samantha caught up with her in the middle of the parking lot.

"I'm sorry, Katie. When I brought you the job I— I thought this would be easier. He made it sound so—"

"—Simple? Spare me. I fell for your sob story. You knew I hated my job and needed to start over myself. I never would have agreed if—"

"I know. The guns and drugs. Randall bungled that royally."

"No shit. So, are you coming with me or getting high with them the rest of the fuckin' day?"

"As soon as you left, they forgot I was there. Kelly took her shirt off and all four of them—"

"Gross. Proves how stupid they are, though, letting their leverage walk out the door. I really wish I didn't need the rest of the money..." Katie sighed, resolving her plan of action. "Alright. Well, maybe we can arrange for a second room while I ask around for the closest place to get parts. I'm not sleeping on either of those beds when we get back... It's really weird none of you have phones, you know that?"

"Part of cutting away our old life. We'll get new ones in Portland."

They made their way into the small general store on the other side of the main resort lodge. Several teenagers wandered around. Some of the girls held up overpriced sweaters with local logos while the boys milled around the beer fridge and snack aisles. A boy a bit younger than the others stood with his little brother at the boat rental counter, in front of a gorgeous couple that looked like the prom queen and king from central casting. Katie stood in line behind them as Samantha searched for snacks of her own.

Katie noticed a girl in the opposite of "camping" clothes hiding behind some display stands and racks. She seemed to be watching the boy at the front counter—unless he casually glanced around, then she pretended to be absorbed with something else, nonchalant. Besides her attire, the girl seemed out of place in a store full of some of the most attractive upperclassmen Katie'd ever seen. Still, the shy, totally-not-spying-on-anyone girl's body was enough that Katie would have no trouble showing her a good time, if she didn't so obviously appear to be on the wrong side of eighteen.

A commotion from the beer fridge area caused everyone to look in that direction. The shop's cashier yelled at the guys to take the beer out of their jackets and put them back in the fridge. Their faces turned bright red as their female counterparts laughed at them and they put the beer back. The abashed scoundrels left the store and went out to the small beach while the girls finished perusing clothes.

The younger boy and his brother took the mandated lifejackets from the boat clerk and went outside to the canoe they rented. The prom royalty inquired how many people fit on a party boat, then rented two. Katie blew air overhearing the rental price for the week, but they paid like it was nothing to them.

Beautiful and *rich. Little bastards.*

When it was Katie's turn and Samantha joined her side, they asked where they could get car parts. The clerk said the nearest place was forty miles away and expensive due to its remoteness, but if she wanted to pay less, the next closest was in the opposite direction in Roseburg. When Katie thanked the man at the counter and turned to leave, one of the guys who hadn't been trying to steal anything stared at her. She ignored him and exited the building.

"Uh, miss?" the guy called, following them out the door.

"Yeah?" Katie responded, expecting him to ask if she'd buy them all beer.

"I overheard you need car parts? We, uh… We have an issue with our bus, and we need some, too. How are you planning to get to Roseburg?"

"Was just gonna drive my car."

"Will it make it? I mean, it needs something, obviously, but it'll get you there before blowing up?"

"Sure. I don't think it's a big deal, I just need an excuse to get away from…*our* travel companions for a while."

"Can I go with you to pick up the parts? You'd be saving our lives."

"Dramatic much?" Samantha said, but smiled at the cute guy's reluctant request, as if he'd never talked to women older than his fellow high schoolers before.

"What's your name?" Katie asked.

"Bobby, ma'am."

"Ma'am? Jesus, *already*? Well, I'm Katie, this is Samantha. You ready to go? I'm planning to leave right now."

"Oh, can you swing us by the campsite? There's a few still there working on the bus right now and they could give me a list of what's needed."

"Sure, let's—"

"Hey, Shawna!" Bobby yelled suddenly, causing Katie and Samantha to jump. "I'm getting a ride to the campsite. I'll see you on the other side!"

A pretty Black girl waved at him before getting onto one of the two party boats with the rest of the teenagers. The younger boy and his brother from the shop had already slipped the canoe into the water and were well on their way beyond the docks. The home-ly, overdressed spy girl emerged from the store and watched the canoe paddle away. Katie glanced at her, at the canoe, at the party boat, then back to her.

"Is that girl with any of you?" she asked Bobby.

"Her? I've never seen her before. No idea who she is."

Katie approached her since she looked a little too young and out of place to be on her own. The girl shrank away when she noticed Katie coming over.

"Hi! Did your friends forget you? Do you need a ride?"

Up close, the girl wasn't *quite* so ugly, but the dirt haloing her face wasn't doing her any favors. The longer Katie stood there, the more fidgety and self-conscious the girl acted. Her eyes darted back and forth, unsure of the situation.

"It's alright, we're not abducting you. We're going to that campground over there. Can we give you a ride?"

"Uhh, no. Thank...you. I've got some...work to do on this side."

"Oh, you're working? I wouldn't have guessed. You're so young and you're dressed a hundred times better than anyone else up here—except those kids getting on the party boat. Uh, well, we're going to take off. Last chance for a free ride..."

The girl dropped her eyes down and away, avoiding Katie's gaze.

"Okay. See you around, then."

They got into the car and drove around the north end of the lake to the west campground. Katie parked close to the yellow school bus. Four boys who seemed like they'd be at home in the motel room doing drugs with her clients perched around the open engine compartment with their shirts off in the rapidly warming late morning sun. One girl was right there among them with marks on her face and arms where she'd brushed them with her own oil-covered fingers. Her auburn hair was pulled back in a ponytail, and she wore a dark pink athletic bra.

One of the boys made a lewd joke while she bent over the engine block, and her well-honed abs tightened as she shook with laughter. Her smile was the cutest thing Katie'd seen all day, even after the glamazons in the general store.

"Hey guys, I got someone who'll take me into town for parts. Can one of you make a list of what we need?" Bobby said as they approached the bus.

The obvious mechanic of the group, the only one with his hands deep beneath the hood and didn't appear to only be standing around to shoot the shit and impress the girl, nodded and hopped down from the front tire. He and Bobby boarded the bus. Katie pulled herself up on the tire to peek into the engine compartment and gasped.

"I know, right?" the auburn-haired girl said.

"You as good with cars as Tera is?" one of the boys asked.

"I—"

"They're just fuckin' around. I have no idea what I'm doing," Tera said.

"You're the dirtiest of the three of them, except for the guy with Bobby," Katie observed.

"Just distracting myself. It's been more fun than I thought, working around an engine. These guys are pretty funny...*sometimes.*"

One of the boys sidled next to Katie. Cheap weed emanated from him, even without a shirt.

"So...you ladies gonna join our party when you get back?"

Katie admired his boldness.

"She's not into it, Nick," Tera said as she blackened a rag with her hands. "Besides, you've got Amber to look forward to... Oh?"

Nick's confident posture slackened. One of the other boys scratched his arm and looked away, his face turning red as a radish.

"That was...not what we expected..."

"Like most things seen in movies, too good to be true, huh?"

Katie liked Tera's teasing attitude, along with the bit of empathy behind it.

Bobby and the other boy came around and flashed the list.

"Hope they stock this stuff," Bobby said.

Samantha took the list from him and started walking, unsubtly letting Katie know she wanted to get back in the air-conditioned car. Katie waved at the teenagers hovering around the engine compartment. Before getting into the vehicle she looked back to see

Tera smiling at her while she talked to the boys. Katie returned the smile, then put the car onto the highway.

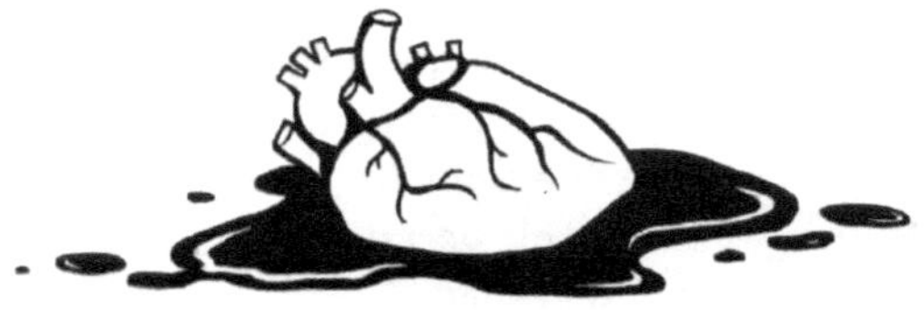

In Roseburg, Bobby offered to pay Katie when they returned to the camp. He had no money on him, but he knew some of the other kids carried cash. Normally Katie wouldn't have bought the story, but she saw what the prom couple had been packing when they rented the party boats. He also convinced her to stop at the liquor store. Not that she bought for him and his friends, but his stuttering request to buy *her and Samantha* booze did pique her interest. She'd want to drown out whatever Randall and his crew planned on doing that night if she got stuck shacking with them. God forbid if the room available was next door and they had to listen to the "festivities" on the other side of the wall.

She and Samantha bought a bottle each of tequila and whiskey.

After picking up a quick bite and a cooler filled with ice cream for the teens, they made it back to the resort as the sun began to set. As the car approached the southern entrance of the west campground, the car swerved and tilted unnaturally. She got control of the vehicle and parked it next to an empty Forest Ranger's vehicle.

The teens sat around the campfire and Bobby went to meet them with the ice cream cooler. Katie walked around the vehicle and stared at the back tire in disbelief. A twenty-inch crossbow bolt stuck in the side of the tire. Someone must have fired it from the other side of the road, but all Katie could see was a thick embankment of trees, rocks, and no camp sites.

Katie went out into the highway while Samantha caught up. The forest didn't move, but it would have been hard to see even with better light. Goosebumps rose as a breeze swept past her from the direction of where the car swerved.

"What do you want to do?" Samantha asked, snapping Katie from her concentration and increasing her raised skin to the point of discomfort.

"I don't really want to change a tire in the dark, and… What happens if we drive back in that direction to get to the motel? Besides that, I'd rather not go back to the motel anyway. It's a few miles to walk back, too. All signs point to sleeping in the car and walking when it's daylight. That or we could bum a ride on one of these guys' boats in the morning back to the resort. They owe us one."

Samantha looked at the campfire and the laughing teenagers.

"Go ahead," Katie sighed. "I'm sure they're looking for a couple twenty-five-year-olds to talk to, especially knowing we have liquor thanks to Bobby."

"I mean, no phones, no TV… Talking with them would be better than sitting in the car alone with you… No offense."

"None taken. The last thing we need is to become friends."

Katie thrust the tequila bottle towards Samantha before she could respond.

"Have fun, Sam."

Samantha sighed and walked to the campfire. A little cheer came from some of the ones who saw her bottle of tequila as she sat next to Bobbie. Katie pulled out the spare tire from the trunk and laid it and the tools next to the damaged tire, then sat down and leaned against the fender. She took a pull of the whiskey and grimaced. The trip was already eating into what they'd given her up front. She imagined the damage and hassle of whoever took out her tire doing it again tomorrow.

Maybe she could convince Randall to come over with his gun and do a little hunting. Maybe he'd take a crossbow in the chest for his effort. *Win-win, either way.*

"Hiya!"

Katie had been relishing the image of Randall dying at her feet and didn't notice the exquisite pair of legs shooting out from wonderfully short shorts standing in front of her. She peered up to Tera's cute smile and returned it. Then Tera noticed the tire and her expression turned.

"Oh, shit! I thought you were just being anti-social. How the fuck did you get a bolt in your tire?" Tera lowered herself to get a better look, and Katie helped herself to a better look of the back of Tera's shorts.

"Not sure. I might investigate tomorrow, but for now, I'm going to get a little buzzed and try to change it. You want to help me out, grease monkey?" Katie rethought changing the tire on the fly, at the possibility of fumbling around in the dark.

Tera snorted and shook her head. "It took me forever to clean all that off. Why don't you come join us?"

"Are you angling for this whiskey bottle?"

"*I'm* not, I hate liquor. We've got J's, though, if you prefer..."

"Maybe I'll join Samantha, in case she gets lonely."

"I don't think that'll happen. I saw her put her hand on Bobby's thigh and laugh at one of his dumb jokes. Like, the incredibly *dumb* jokes you'd only laugh at if you're trying to get some."

"Jesus Christ," Katie shook her head. "That's all we need—a statutory case on top of..." Katie dragged her sentence off before the whiskey made her say something stupid.

"Oh, we're all eighteen. Just graduated last week. This is our last time together before we all go our separate ways."

Tera sniffed and slid her fingers over her eyes and up into her hair, trying to hide her seemingly unexpected rush of emotion. Katie offered the whiskey bottle and shook it a little bit when Tera balked. She sniffed again and took it, then tried to drink way too much for someone who hated liquor. The whiskey sprayed out in a fine mist that covered Katie and the side of her car, then she coughed violently.

Katie laughed and got up to rub Tera's back and grab the bottle. When Tera's coughing subsided, Katie felt a strong urge to slide her arm from Tera's back to her shoulders but thought better of it. One of the boys could be her boyfriend, and making a move might cause a scene. Then she remembered something Tera had said in the afternoon.

"Tera, how did you know I 'wasn't into it' when that boy invited me to the party?"

"All those boys with their shirts off, me in my sports bra. I, uh—*noticed* where your attention was."

"Maybe dark pink is my favorite color…"

"Mm-hmm. Goddamn, that still burns. I need water."

"After you, Tera," Katie said before following her to the campfire. As she admired Tera's fine silhouette in the glow, Katie thought the trip had finally trended in a positive direction.

Chapter 5

We're On Vacation

Kill Count: 5

IN THE SHADOW OF Mt. Bailey as the sun set, the work-avoiding couple made their way from their tent down to the highway. Slater held Killian's hand as they tromped over rocks, dirt, and desiccated fallen logs, both managing with ease. He noticed the large campfire at the south end of the campground, a couple of cars, and a school bus with its hood open. His grip tightened, and Killian matched it.

"Why are you taking us over here?" Killian asked. "The Hunts' camp site is the other way."

Slater didn't answer as he changed their movement pattern from a casual walk to stealthily weaving behind trees and large boulders, as if—

"Slater!" Killian whisper-yelled. "What do you think you're doing?"

He let go of her hand and pointed towards a tree across a near-by site, signaling Killian to follow his lead, then got behind his own tree, quietly seething over the horrid laughter of unsupervised teenagers. Several of them passed around the herb that smelled like skunk. Slater normally liked the smell of a skunk; it was one of the few things he and Lynn could agree on. But coming from those little white papers... Slater's eyes narrowed to a red tunnel.

His rage intensified as he took in the totality of the debauchery before him. Two bottles of liquor made the rounds. Several of the teens made out in the open, and hardly any of the others reacted in disgust as they went about their hedonistic behavior.

It would be *so easy:* there were several metal spears holding hot dogs and marshmallows near the fire; some of them had sharpened the end of branches for the same purpose; he could tear some of the metal from the foldout chairs, snapping it into a jagged end with his knee; the hot rocks near the fire pit could bash in plenty of heads; zipping them into their sleeping bags and roasting them inside; broken liquor bottles; flaming firewood...

The old standby—his hands.

His knuckles and neck cracked as he loosened up the joints.

One of the girls closest to him looked up at the snapping sounds, likely worried it was an animal walking on branches. Her ponytail flung around her shoulder as she frowned into the darkness. She stood up and walked towards his tree to investigate.

"That's right, girlie," Slater whispered. "Time to *learn.*"

He licked his lips and curled his fingers into claws when he was tackled from the side, driving him into the dirt. Killian straddled him and twisted the fabric around his shoulders, scowling and hissing.

"No! We're on *vacation!* We're not *working!* You *promised!*"

Slater almost protested when they both looked up in unison to the ponytail girl's voice.

"Are you guys okay?"

Killian glared at her husband one more time and shook her head tightly, then stood up to address the newcomer.

"Why, yes, dear, we were just out for a stroll and my husband here tripped over a tree root."

"Oh, I'm sorry! Here, let me help you up."

The girl reached out her hand and stooped over. Slater recoiled, aware that his instinct would force him to crush her hand and pull her down, either ripping her arm out of its socket or twisting her pretty little head off her body. Killian recognized the look in his eye and positioned herself between the girl and Slater.

"Oh, thank you so much. He's okay, though."

Killian helped him up, then brushed off his clothes like she would for Murdock in the off chance he ever had to be presentable in front of normal people.

"Now, run along, dear, back to your sinner party. Don't worry about us."

"Excuse me?"

"I said, 'don't worry about us.' We'll just be on our way."

"Before that... You said—"

"What did I—"

"Dinner. *Dinner* party," Slater said, barely hiding the contempt in his voice.

"Oh, yeah, I gotcha. Well, I hope you're okay."

The girl returned to her party. Killian pulled at Slater's arm while he dragged his feet, finding it hard to look away from the scene. Halfway through the campsite, Killian steered them towards the small building that housed the site's only bathroom and shower.

"You already went before we left our site; you need to go again so soon?" Slater asked.

Killian grabbed his shirt and pushed him into the building. She pressed him into the wall and jumped up onto his hips while he grabbed her sides. She kissed him noisily, causing his red rage to turn to red passion as blood rushed to his head.

"I wanted...to teach those fucking...kids a lesson...so much!" Killian said between explorations of each other's mouths. "I'm so sorry I had to...stop you...but you..."

"Promised, sweetheart. I did."

Killian hopped down from his hips, ripped the buttons of her plaid shirt open, then slipped off her hiking pants. Slater leaned her back and covered her exposed, sweaty mud-caked cleavage with his face.

"Get the rage out. Quickly, Slater. They're expecting us."

Disheveled appearances shocked Tim and Jessica into silence when Slater and Killian finally arrived for their designated double date. Killian smiled and apologized.

"Ol' Mister Klutz here tripped over a root near our campsite and pulled me down with him. I'm surprised two buttons survived, to be honest. It was a *wreck*!"

"A-are you okay?" Jessica said, approaching Killian with a wet hand towel.

Killian seemed unsure what to do in the face of sincere concern. She took a step back and held her arms up.

"We're fine. I'm sorry we didn't go back and change but we knew we were going to be late anyway. And I think we've run out of clothes already..."

"After the second day—?" Tim started.

"So! Tim," Slater interrupted. "Did Murdock give you any trouble today?"

"Not at all. He's been glued to the game console. He didn't want to go fishing with the boys on the canoe, so he stayed on the shore playing. I'm going to see if there's a place we can plug in the portable battery next time we're at the resort."

"Sorry for the trouble, Tim," Slater said.

"It's not any trouble," Tim gave a genial smile, much happier to be useful than annoyed by having to expend extra effort.

Jessica finally stopped staring at Killian's mussed hair, dusty makeup, and torn, crumpled wardrobe, then opened a cooler close to the fire where they'd set up a grill.

"I've got all the veggies prepared. Next is the fish. The boys caught them shortly before dusk, so I haven't had a chance to clean them yet."

"Ooh, let me help you with that," Killian said. "Where's your fillet knife?"

Jessica handed it over gingerly to watch Killian flip it in the air and catch it with blind expertise. Tim and Jessica's mouths dropped. Slater nudged Tim and shrugged in his wife's direction, hoping he'd appreciate that Slater was using the same gesture Tim liked so much. Tim didn't seem to notice, though, as Killian cleaned the fish with smooth, surgical flicks of her wrist. She even tossed the last fish in the air and gutted it before catching it at her hips.

"Where's your foil, dear?" Killian asked.

Jessica pointed at the picnic table, mesmerized by Killian's display. She retrieved a sheet and placed the guts, tails, and heads on top, then folded the edges up. She put the foil on the grill next to the filets and turned around to see Jessica stifle a heave.

Killian froze, puzzled. Slater shrugged when she looked to him for an answer.

"Um, you know, people don't usually eat those parts..." Tim explained in his wife's stead.

"Really? All the vitamins and nutrients are in there! Why would anyone waste the best parts?"

Tim looked at Slater for an answer as well.

"She ain't lyin', Tim. If you don't want'em, we'll eat'em all."

They sat around the fire while the food cooked. Tim passed around cans of beer that Slater didn't recognize, even from all the high school sleepovers and college parties he'd broken up over the years. He sniffed at it and wrinkled his nose.

"This beer won a local microbrew award," Tim said. "Infused with organic Oregon oregano, mint and a yuzu married with a Valencia orange, it was handcrafted with Washington cherry bitters in a musty 19th-century basement in the Ghost District of Portland's slave-built underground, brewed in old brothel tubs by free-range, deodorant-abhorring men with the longest mutton chops and handlebar mustaches you've ever seen. It's low ABV, high IBU, quadruple IPA, and GMO-free. Once you try it, you'll swear off every other beer in the world, and become violently offended when someone offers you anything else."

Slater and Killian stared at him, dumbfounded. "Violently offended" was moments away from coming to fruition. Tim and Jessica looked at each other and burst out laughing.

"I'm *kidding*, guys. Jeez. My college roommates and I liked to do Mad Libs, and pretentious beer descriptions was one of them. I have no idea what these taste like; we picked them up because the sea otter on the case was cute."

Slater took a cautious sip while eyeing Tim to make sure not a single thing he said about the beer was true, or Tim would be swallowing the can. Killian brightened up as the tension dissipated and they all knocked back a can.

While the fish sizzled on the grill and the guts' aroma made Slater's mouth water, the four of them made awkward small talk that hadn't become any less awkward since they met. He could see his poor wife struggling to find the best words to use, ones that wouldn't scare the couple whenever they asked a question. Slater's nature didn't make it any easier for her.

"Tim mentioned you have a daughter that's the same age as Corey, but I haven't seen her yet. When can we meet her?" Jessica asked.

"Whenever your boy isn't around," Slater said.

"Excuse me?" Tim tilted his head with a frown.

"What he means is," Killian said with an edge towards Slater to warn him off, "they're both sixteen and we'd rather... You know, their *hormones*, and..."

"Uh, yeah, we get that they're teenagers," Jessica said. "Isn't your daughter around them at school?"

"She's...homeschooled," Killian said. "We're...*very* insistent that she doesn't touch a boy until she's married."

Jessica and Tim exchanged looks and shrugged.

"We're not trying to set up our kids on dates," Tim said. "We're just...you know...*realistic* about things. And they've got to interact sometime, right? This is when they get to be awkward and figure things out before they take on more responsibilities as adults and become only *slightly* less awkward."

Slater arched his eyebrow at his wife. Her look calmed the rage building in the back of his throat. Tim meant well, but he was also casually promoting blasphemy under the guise of underage "innocence." Slater let it go. He'd made his stance clear. So long as they didn't try and overrule their parenting methods, he wouldn't discipline them for theirs.

Between the women's light chattering while they ate, Slater's ears pricked up at the occasional loud noise coming from the opposite end of the campground where those teenagers were still up. Soon they'd be breaking up into their tents. Oh, how that always made it easier...

"—a real drink?"

Slater shook the lessons running through his mind away and opened both eyes wide in question over what he just missed from Tim.

"I said, do you want to get a real drink? At the bar? We can take the Rogue. I'll let Corey know to keep an eye on the boys while we're gone."

Slater made an excuse to grab something from the truck when he spotted Lynn skulking around the F-350. Lynn popped her head out and jumped back into cover when her father was clearly making a beeline to her location.

"What are you doing down here? You're supposed to be up in your tent."

"This is *my* vacation, too, Daddy. Why can't I join you?"

"You can't come to the bar, and I don't want you near their boy. I saw the way you looked at him when he handed you that disgusting veggie mash. Now get your ass back to camp and stay there."

"Let me stay with Murdock, at least. I'm his babysitter, right?"

Slater sighed. She wasn't wrong. He didn't worry about Murdock finding his way back to his tent on his own—he was largely fearless. But he also didn't want the boy killing every animal between there and their site. Or one or both of the Hunt's boys, even.

"Alright. Stay with him and take him back to the camp site soon. Don't let him kill anything on the way."

"Thank you, Daddy."

"Don't get near their boy or talk to him unless it's to say, 'good night.'"

She reached up and kissed his cheek, then stalked closer to the shore where Corey sat with TJ and Murdock, the glow of the gaming console lighting up the boys' faces. She'd gotten much better at approaching people without them noticing until she was right on top of them.

It nearly brought a tear to his eye.

The back of the Rogue was a tight fit for Slater, but it gave him an excuse to have Killian snuggled extra deeply into his side without annoying Tim and Jessica in the front. When they exited the vehicle in the resort's parking lot, two men argued loudly outside one of the motel rooms. Slater could tell they were drug-users based on their outfits, aggressive behavior, and other little details he'd picked up from teaching lessons to punk junkies. Two more came out of the motel room to attempt to calm them down.

Killian tugged on Slater's arm. She gave him a sympathetic look, then a murderous one to the group of loudmouths as they walked by. He realized he might have to reciprocate and take *her* rage out in the bathroom again. But first, Tim and Jessica waited for them at the bottom of the stairs to the bar.

Shortly after they ordered their drinks and sat down at a side booth, the four loud junkies came in and took seats at the bar. For thirty minutes they spoke noisily about their criminal acts, providing Slater with a laundry list of well-deserved lessons. The ruffians drowned out their conversations and made Jessica and Tim pause several times. Slater loved watching the contours of Killian's jaw set and clench. She wanted to teach them a lesson as badly as he did.

Two of them began arguing again. There would probably be a fist fight, and many nervous patrons actively cringed away from their presence. The shorter one broke out of the taller one's grip and stomped out of the bar. Killian started to get up, but it was Slater's turn to bring her back to the moment by placing a hand on her thigh. She composed herself and sat back in the booth.

Jessica offered to buy another round and walked up to the bar. As she leaned on the counter waiting for the drinks, the tall junkie reached down and gave Jessica's butt a squeeze. Rage nearly blinded Slater, both at the situation and at Tim, who didn't immediately jump out of the booth to save her. Before Slater could reprimand him, Killian had cleared his lap and crossed the room with the punk's hair pulled back and her hand around his throat.

The junkie's whorish girlfriend slapped his face and stormed out of the bar while Killian threatened him with unimaginable violence. Unimaginable to anyone but Slater, anyway

Tim finally went to his wife and pulled her away from whatever Killian planned to do. Slater sensed her restraint from across the room. He could hear Killian's voice chanting *"we're on vacation"* over and over in his mind. Surely it was doubled for her, deafening against the rush of blood in her ears.

She let go of the punk and grabbed him from behind, then pushed him out the door and down the stairs. When she returned, Slater thought the bar would go silent in horror, but to his surprise all the patrons but the fourth remaining deviant burst into applause. Killian was as surprised as Slater, but after a moment she milked it with a wave and bow, then returned to the booth with Jessica and Tim.

The couple shook with adrenaline, while Killian projected a picture of calm. Jessica thanked her and they downed the second rounds quickly. Their tongues loosened the more they drank, and it seemed like Killian might even like the sloppy way Jessica fawned over "her hero." The alcohol had almost no effect on Slater, though, due to his size.

Before ordering a third round, the last junkie, who'd been sulking at the end of the bar, came to the table with a sheepish expression.

"Um, I'm sorry for my friends. We're all worried about a couple of our other friends who haven't returned since they left for car parts earlier this morning, and we have no way to reach them. We're just on edge. Can I buy your next round?"

"What's your name, young man?" Tim asked.

"Boyd, sir."

"Well, Boyd, I appreciate your boldness. Tell the bartender we want the same as the last round, then tell *your* friend if he tries that again with my wife, he'll wish he was back in the clutches of *my* friend."

Slater rolled his eyes at Tim's empty threat, but it did the trick as far as the free extra round was concerned. It struck him then that Tim had called Killian his friend. Of all the things Slater thought to get out of their vacation, friends were the absolute last thing he would have imagined.

They went outside after the third round and stood around the entrance with looser tongues and chummier conversations. Killian slipped on saying some things, to which Jessica would react with a horrified look that turned into laughter, infecting Killian in turn, then they got handsy with each other in their drunk, humorous fits.

Tim could hardly stand, so Slater took his keys and the initiative to get them back to the other side of the lake himself. Not wanting to interrupt their conversation while Killian seemed to be enjoying it so much, he took a walk around the building. A bright fluorescent light came from a separate building next to the bar. He peered inside the window of the front door to see a wall of large industrial laundry machines beside some smaller, consumer-sized ones for guests to use.

Most of the machines churned with white towels and sheets. One machine caught his eye for all the red sloshing against the window. A small splash of it smeared on the outside, near the buttons.

Slater entered the building, and a trail of blood led him from the door to the machine. He forced the door open after pausing the cycle, and the soapy, red mixture spilled out on the grungy linoleum floor. Inside housed the body of the first punk who'd left the bar after fighting with the taller one, bent in half from behind in order to fit into the machine.

Slater backed away from the machine and left the building in a stride that could be considered quick, but not in a hurry. The scene hadn't frightened or horrified him in the slightest, but he didn't want to be seen near that mess of a lesson on his vacation. The thought darkened his mood: someone like *him* was around the resort, and they *weren't* on vacation.

Chapter 6

Experience

Kill Count: 6

Chatting in the cool night air and the ride back to camp cleared Timothy's mind for the most part, but the buzz from the bar encounter hadn't completely faded. It took him a moment to realize TJ was sitting at the picnic table alone without Corey as they pulled up. When they exited the vehicle they could make out TJ's crying. Timothy's blood boiled at the thought Corey had left him there. That wasn't like him, though. He may be a sullen teenager most of the time but he always looked out for his little brother.

TJ told Jessica what happened while Timothy circled the edge of the fire light, surveying for Corey. Slater and Killian also volunteered to look around. They both had an uncanny way of looking, though. They moved from cover to cover, almost like they were hiding, too. Timothy knew where they were and he *still* lost track of them a couple times.

Corey walked into the campsite from the direction of the highway. Jessica confronted him for leaving TJ alone by the picnic table as Timothy came back. Corey explained what happened, showing immediate regret for how the scene looked to his parents.

"Murdock took the game from TJ, so Lynn and I chased after him. When he ran across the highway, Lynn told me to wait while she flushed him out."

"Lynn was down here?" Killian asked.

Corey shrugged, unsure why there was an edge to her voice.

"It's okay, sweetheart," Slater said. "I told her it was alright as long as they didn't touch. She wanted to keep an eye on Murdock. A lot of good that did…"

Slater gave Corey a look, and after the conversation at dinner about their overprotectiveness of Lynn, Timothy pre-empted Slater's question.

"You…didn't touch her, did you, son?"

Corey gave an overdefensive, shy answer in the negative. Slater and Killian visibly cooled off and relaxed their postures, which in turn relaxed Timothy.

"I'm so sorry Murdock took your game," Killian said to TJ. "I promise we'll find it and get it back for you."

"I don't think he cares about the game, ma'am," Corey said. "He was more shocked by Murdock pushing him to take it than anything."

"I'm, uh, sorry, Tim," Slater said while scratching the back of his head. "We don't have electronics at home. I probably should have realized something like this would happen. Kid's been begging me for a tablet for a while now."

"Well, TJ's alright," Jessica said. "I'm sure they can make it up once we're all safe and accounted for. Where do you think Murdock ran off to?"

"I'll be surprised if Lynn doesn't find him," Killian said with a hint of pride. "Her tracking has improved a lot this year."

"Can I help you look?" Timothy asked.

"We've got this, Tim. We're sorry for all the trouble. Thanks for taking us to the bar. We should do that again, right, sweetheart?"

Killian peered out into the forest, distracted, but she murmured her assent. They walked across the highway, then split ways and disappeared up the slope.

"No electronics, huh?" Timothy said. "Must be pretty rough for a kid to grow up that way in this day and age."

While Jessica escorted TJ to the bathroom facility in the center of the campground, Timothy sat next to Corey as he poked a long stick into the fire without purpose.

"You really didn't touch her, did you?" Timothy asked.

Corey gave him an annoyed look, then shook his head.

"Her folks are a little protective of her. I just want to be sure we don't cause more issues for them. Between you and me, if you *did* find a girl you liked..."

Corey's scowl shut Timothy up and he put his arms in the air, a little relieved that Corey didn't seem receptive to having a more grown-up conversation about sex. Timothy was an unwilling virgin throughout high school and wasn't a fan of the meaningless sex in college until he'd found Jessica again. He didn't think he had the best experience to talk to a sixteen-year-old confidently on the topic. Knowing himself, he'd bungle the interaction and come off like he encouraged it, or expressly forbade it, or both. That's all a confused boy would need—mixed messages with little in the way of conviction.

"I...liked talking with her," Corey said, breaking Timothy from his long stare into the fire. "She fumbled her words a lot and didn't really know what to talk about. She made a lot of random observations about the lake and camping. I guess I always assume girls know what they're talking about, since they steer every conversation. That's what they do at school anyway. It was nice seeing one act as awkward as I feel."

You're definitely my kid, Timothy thought.

Jessica brought TJ back, then found the s'mores ingredients while Corey located the metal skewers.

"Those kids at the other end were pretty loud," Jessica said. "I'm glad the sound doesn't carry this far, or we'd have to say something. Have you talked to any of them, Corey?"

"Only saw them in the store. They're all seniors. Or were, anyway. None of them are interested in talking to a sophomore..."

"I'm not going to push you to socialize, but maybe when you see them again—"

Corey cut her off with his patented scowl. Timothy shrugged at her sympathetically. After Corey headed off to the bathroom, Timothy explained how he'd almost started an awkward conversation about contact with the other kind. Jessica also confirmed Timothy wasn't ready for that job.

A couple s'mores consumed later and four teenagers materialized from the darkness at the edge of the campfire light. Maggie barked once, then approached the four. They held out their hands for her to sniff, then she returned to TJ's side.

"Good evening, folks," said a handsome boy chiseled from pure NFL-quarterback stock. "Apologies for any of our noise reaching you over here. There's no one else in the camp and we've got trouble with our bus."

"Oh, that's horrible," Jessica said. "Have you called anyone?"

"Our cell phones were stolen, ma'am," the unfairly attractive girl on the quarterback's arm said. "We had them all in a bag so we wouldn't be tempted to use them while we're up here, and whoever messed up our bus also took the bag. We have some guys that took auto shop who might be able to fix it, but we don't have some of the tools they need. You wouldn't happen to have a toolbox we could borrow?"

"I'll check the back of the car," Jessica said.

Timothy thought it was both cute and embarrassing how TJ's gaze affixed to the chests of the beautiful girls.

"I wish I could say I'm handy, kids, but I've never so much as changed a car battery. Or tires. I don't even know which is the easier of the two! We've got another friend camping nearby that might know more, though. I'll ask him tomorrow morning."

"Thank you, sir," a pretty, huskier girl said. "We're sorry to be a bother. We just don't have a backup plan to get home since the bus broke down."

"Understandable," Timothy smiled.

Jessica came back with a small ratchet set that they kept in the storage compartment above the wheel well.

"Thank you so much, ma'am," the quarterback said. "How long are you in camp? So we know when we need to return it..."

"Don't worry about it. We can always get a new one back home."

"Thanks again," the larger girl said as they turned around.

"Wait, kids," Jessica said. "You guys don't happen to have any...younger friends with you?"

"We all just graduated, ma'am," the burnout on the arm of the large girl said.

"Oh, okay. Our boy's sixteen and he's looked pretty bored since we got here. I was hoping..."

"Was he off to the bathroom a bit ago? We passed him on the way over, but he didn't say anything," the quarterback said. "He sure didn't look bored with that girl holding his hand, though."

Jessica looked at Timothy, confused. The quarterback's girlfriend came forward.

"We're having a party tomorrow night. Out on those two boats tied to the dock. No alcohol, no drugs. We'll stop by tomorrow to see if your son wants to join us. If that's alright with you, of course."

"Uh, sure, yeah, that'd be fine," Timothy said after attaining agreement from Jessica's eyes.

"Thanks for the tools again, sir. Ma'am," the quarterback said as they disappeared beyond the campfire light.

Timothy and Jessica sat down and skewered fresh marshmallows.

"Get a good look, there, son?" Timothy frowned at TJ, who's marshmallow had caught fire due to his inattention. "It's very rude and inappropriate to—"

Corey came back into view and held out TJ's game console. TJ jumped up to grab it, but was disappointed when it didn't turn on. Timothy pointed him towards the extra battery and looked at Corey as he sat down without saying anything.

"Where did you find that?" Jessica finally asked.

Corey fidgeted but seemed to conclude that lying about it wouldn't help.

"Lynn found it and brought it for TJ."

"Where is she?" Timothy asked.

"She said she needed to get back to her camp and disappeared."

"Anything else...happen?"

"No, Mom. She surprised me and left quickly."

"Corey," TJ said as the console glow illuminated his face. "What's this on the screen?"

Corey shrugged and shoved his hands in his pockets. Timothy grabbed a flashlight off the picnic table to examine what TJ pointed at. It was dark red and dripping.

"Son, are you bleeding right now?" Timothy asked Corey.

"No. Not that I know of."

Timothy shone the light on him and gasped. Five red finger-prints stained the chest of Corey's white shirt.

"Did something happen to you? What's going on, Corey?" Jessica asked as she moved closer to inspect the prints.

Corey peered down at his shirt, then shrugged.

"Maybe she fell down on the way over here and scraped up her hand. That route up to their camp wasn't exactly the safest, and she didn't have a flashlight. I don't know if she was hurt. She didn't say anything, anyway."

"Let me see *your* hands, son," Timothy said.

Corey pulled them out of his pockets and held them up to the light. They had blood on them as well, consistent with the image of Lynn and him holding hands like the teenagers said earlier. Timothy sighed.

"Look, Corey, it's not that we don't think that's cute or any-thing, but we need you to steer clear of that girl. Her parents are—"

"Overprotective. She told me. She said she didn't care—"

"At her age, what her *parents* say goes. Especially...*those* par-ents," Timothy said as he recalled Killian's threats to that ass-hole who cupped his wife's butt. "If she had just given you the console, that would have been fine, but you can't touch her *or* let her touch you."

"Jesus, Dad, make up your damn mind!"

"Don't talk to your father that way, young man!" Jessica said.

"No! Last night he tried to set me up with her, and you both allowed her to hang out with us and Murdock while you went to the bar. I can't help that she came out of nowhere with the stupid game—"

"Okay, son. That's understood. That was before we talked with her parents and understood how important and, well, different they want to raise their kids. Please be respectful of their wishes. Lynn doesn't call the shots just yet. Anyway... We got you invited to hang out with those kids across the camp tomorrow. Maybe it will help keep your mind off Lynn."

"Trying to set me up again? Then you'll tell me I can't hang out with them after that, right? I've had enough of your mixed messages, both of you! Just leave me alone!"

Corey crawled into his tent and zipped it closed with a little too much aggression, getting the zipper caught twice on the follow-through.

"What can I clean this with, Mom?" TJ asked, holding up the console.

"I think we have some hydrogen peroxide in the first aid kit," Jessica said before fishing the kit out of a bag on the picnic table.

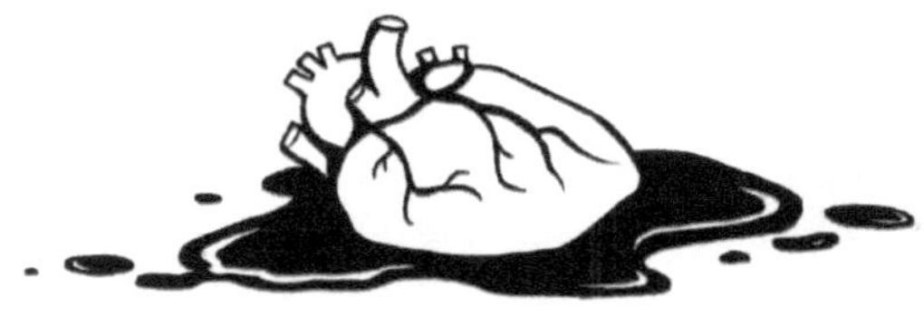

Jessica shut down Timothy's mild protestations that taking care of him two nights in a row wasn't fair to her, or that the previous night was more than he'd bargained for the whole week. She planned to get a little more *experimental* on her second quest and she wasn't about to let her determination be dampened. It was difficult to keep his pleasure at a low volume, so he bit down on the back of his index finger.

Timothy's head swam, and his eyes fluttered so fast he almost didn't notice a shadowy figure growing in the light cast from the dying campfire onto the side of the tent. He blinked several times before realizing the figure was huge, as big as Slater, and it carried a long object in its hand.

Fear pushed his wife's blessed efforts out of his mind, and it left him frozen in inaction. His mind raced for where to find a weapon, or if he should do anything at all—wouldn't it be better to *avoid* grabbing the attention of whatever lurked out there?

Jessica raised her head after a moment of Timothy being unresponsive.

"Losing stamina alre—?"

"Shhh," Timothy shushed, and pointed at the shadow as it moved back and forth, searching for something around their site. If it started moving towards the boys' tent, Timothy determined he would spring out and grab the flashlight or a metal skewer, whichever he got his hand on first. He *would* act to save his boys, wouldn't he? *Yes, of course!*

Maggie barked from the boys' tent. Corey cursed at her to shut up. The figure stopped moving and looked in the direction of the barking. Timothy put a hand on Jessica's shoulder to stay put, then unzipped the tent flap in one swift yank and burst out.

By the time he rounded the tent, the figure disappeared into the darkness. Corey unzipped their tent flap and Maggie charged out, running off along the northern path out of the campground. Timothy searched the site for anything missing. A large hand grasped his shoulder. He swung around and up. An iron fist caught Timothy's and lowered it.

In the dying fire's light, Timothy recognized Slater.

"What the *hell* are you doing here? Was that *you* in my campsite?"

"No, Tim. But someone was rooting around our camp, too. I followed them down here. I'm glad to see you're okay. If you'll excuse me..."

With that Slater followed in Maggie's direction. Timothy only briefly thought about taking the flashlight and joining the search if nothing more than to bring back Maggie. But there were black bears and mountain lions, and someone large running around with a dangerous object. Maggie would either come back on her own or he'd go out in the much safer morning light to look for her.

Timothy returned to the tent and answered all of Jessica's concerned questions. After she seemed relieved enough, he laid down in his sleeping bag.

"What are you doing?" Jessica whispered.

"Hmm? Going to bed?"

"We're not finished."

"Are you for real? Some strange guy with a—"

"Is it your opinion that we're safe now? Slater's on the case, after all."

Timothy mulled it over. What could he do at midnight to be any safer? He felt it was safe enough to go to sleep…

"I guess so."

"Stop hedging, Tim. Get back out of that sleeping bag."

Maggie hadn't returned by morning. Jessica was busy cursing about their stolen cell phone bag from the car. Timothy pored over the four slashed tires of the Rogue with Slater, whose F-350 was in the same state. Once Jessica joined them, they agreed to go to the lodge in the canoe to call someone, or perhaps get a ride.

"Oh, wait," Jessica said, "those kids have that bus over there. Maybe we can help them fix it and they can get us to Roseburg."

"You handy with vehicles, Slater?" Timothy asked.

He shrugged in response, as if only half-hearing the question. Slater appeared deep in thought, much like Timothy's college friends during their weekend chess matches. Almost nothing brought them out of those trances.

"TJ, honey, don't wander off, please. Get back here and I'll make breakfast," Jessica called as TJ walked toward the northern path out of the campground.

"I'm looking for Maggie, Mom!"

"We'll look together soon! Get back here first!"

TJ moped back to the picnic table and sat next to Corey, who had been staring into space since he woke up. He perked up the moment Lynn approached from the northern path. It was odd to Timothy that her hands still bore dark stains of the blood she'd smeared on Corey, but, then again, their family seemed *really* into the idea of "roughing it." Although admittedly less bloody than Lynn, they were all growing increasingly dirty in their appearances.

As Lynn came by the picnic table, Timothy witnessed her brush a hand against Corey's shoulder. The interaction left behind another stain and a smile from the boy. Slater thankfully had his back turned to the scene. Lynn then put her hand on TJ's back and said something to him. TJ got up and ran to Jessica to hug her. Corey got up from the picnic table to join the gathering.

"Lynn said Maggie's safe! She's tied up at the lodge!"

Slater regarded his daughter as she and Corey came to the group, standing about a foot apart.

"How come she's tied at the— Oh, Lynn! Your arm!" Jessica held Lynn's arm up. It had several bite marks radiating out from her elbow.

"*That's* why, Mrs. Hunt," Lynn explained calmly. "Dogs and cats don't react to me very well. I endured the biting while I tied her up. It was the only way I could think to get her back to you today safely. She wasn't going to come on a nice walk with me, so..."

"Yep. It's like a family curse," Slater confirmed, not seeming at all worried about his daughter's wounds. "I think we give off strange pheromones or something. Always growling and snapping at us if we get near."

"I can't believe you put yourself in harm's way like that, dear." Jessica was frantic with worry. "Let me get the first aid kit. My god, Maggie has *never* bitten anyone in her life! I'm so sorry, Lynn."

While Jessica tended the wounds, TJ and Corey thanked Lynn and went to retrieve Maggie themselves, via the canoe.

"Shall we go talk to those kids about their bus, Slater?" Timothy asked.

A shadow crossed Slater's face, then he shook his head and it disappeared.

"Sorry, Tim. I've got more tracking to do. I lost the trail last night. Maybe I can pick it up again in daylight."

"I tracked him all the way to the resort, Daddy," Lynn said. "It's all paved over there, though, so when I lost him I went after the dog."

Timothy puzzled over that. He'd only seen Slater that night. When had Lynn gotten involved?

"Lynn, I want you to check in with your mother and wait for me to return. Am I clear?"

"I want to help, Daddy. I need to learn how to track on pavement, too."

Jessica exchanged a look with Timothy at the strange turn the conversation had taken.

"Fine. Get your mother and meet me at the resort," Slater said, then turned to Timothy. "Sorry I couldn't catch the guy, Tim. We'll see what we can do about these tires. See you this evening."

The two parted ways from the campsite, leaving Timothy and Jessica alone.

"Is it just me, or are they getting a little weirder?" Jessica asked.

"'Oddly nice' is how I'd put it. Oddly nonchalant, too. Am I the only one kind of freaking out over all this?" Tim turned to his wife for support.

"No, I mean... Tim, her arm was clear when she left with him. Like, healed? No medicine works that fast."

"Maybe the bites weren't that bad? It could have looked way worse with all the blood and dust?"

"...Maybe. I'm getting a shower in, then let's walk to the resort for coffee and a phone."

"Sounds like a plan," Tim agreed, although he would have liked some additional affirmations. Maybe he *was* the only one freaking out.

Chapter 7
Best Friends

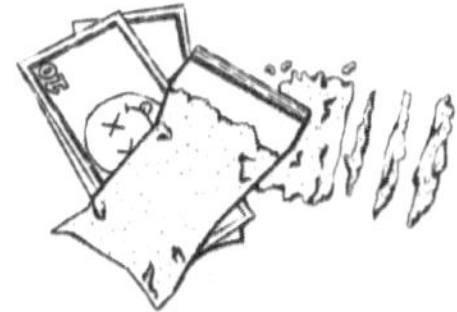

Kill Count: 7

Tera knocked on the back window of Katie's car, waking her with a start. Katie blinked a few times, then stretched along the back seat. Her brown wolf cut was all mussed up as she yawned and climbed out of the car. The messiness actually enhanced the look.

"Sorry to wake you, Katie. Thought you'd want to see what they did to your tires."

"What who di—? God-*damn* it!"

Katie walked around the vehicle—even the spare she'd left out was slashed.

"Got us, too," Tera said as she motioned to the bus's flats. The vandals got the Ranger's vehicle as well.

"Why would anyone—?"

"Good morning," an older man waved and approached them, then paused when he saw the tires. "Damn, looks like they got you all as well. Guess that allays any suspicion one of you kids did it."

"Don't know that for sure," Tera started, "we were pretty—"

"Pretty tired!" Katie interjected. "We were all pretty *tired* from trying to fix the bus, then we went right to bed after washing up."

Tera arched her eyebrow at Katie's unnecessary coverup, in *no way* less suspicious than what Tera was going to say.

"Well, my wife and I are going to make some calls from the resort. We'll let them know of your problems, too," the man said.

"No need to do that on our behalf," Katie said. "My friend and I will go with you. Hey, Tera, can we borrow one of the party boats? Sir, you and your wife can ride along. Sound good?"

"Sure. She's finishing up in the shower, then we'll meet you at the dock in about thirty minutes."

"See you there."

Tera put her hands in the pockets of her letterman jacket and gave a displaced look at the bus. The burnouts were still working in the engine compartment while the cheerleaders and football players got ready for a group hike Chase had arranged to calm everyone down after waking up to the slashed tires. She assigned Tera and Shawna to stay behind in case the Ranger came back, and to keep the burnouts from stealing anything from the tents (Chase only whispered that part to Tera). Darleen volunteered to stay behind, too, though Tera could tell it was to spend more time with Zack.

"Have you seen Sam?" Katie asked.

"She might still be in Bobby's tent," Tera replied.

"Which one is his? Time to get her cradle-robbing ass out of bed."

"Cradle-robbing or not, I think she made Bobby's year. Hell, maybe his whole high school career."

"I'll make sure she signs his yearbook," Katie said with thinly veiled disgust. Tera didn't understand what was making Katie so mad. She spent most of the evening staring at Tera and smiling the way Samantha had to Bobby. Only Bobby didn't have the conflicting emotions Tera had, keeping her from answering those smiles, so he got lucky off them.

Of course, Katie could have also been set off by the damage to the car and needed to vent. Tera didn't want to concern herself with it. Soon Katie and Samantha would be on the other side of the lake and Tera would be alone with Shawna.

Chase's party departed at the same time as Katie and Samantha. Amber changed her mind and left Chase's group to stay with the boys around the bus. Tera sat in a chair next to Shawna as she flipped through a magazine by the tents but in sight of the guys working on the bus.

Darleen took Zack's hand and convinced him to walk with her along the south path out of the campground. She told Tera they planned to walk around the whole lake and would be gone for the rest of the day. Amber convinced Nick and Tony to follow her to a different northern trail into the woods, away from everyone else. Nick brought some of his weed. Tera and Shawna placed bets on which grouping would get tired and come back first.

Ian tinkered with the bus engine alone. Tera wanted to help and keep him company while he worked to save all of their asses, but she hadn't been alone with Shawna since school ended. She stared at the girl she'd been pining over all year, her stupid mind holding out some hope that Shawna might one day return her love.

Tera thought about Katie's not-so-subtle glances at her the night before, when the whiskey had all but run out. While everyone except her and Ian were having sex, Tera had nothing to stop her from hooking up with Katie since she had her own tent to keep it secret. Katie was a smoke show, and to have a woman seven years older than her taking such an obvious interest...

Tera went from staring at Shawna to watching the party boat shrink as it crossed the lake carrying Katie, Samantha, and the couple from the other campsite.

This is stupid, Tera thought. This was her vacation, and it didn't need to be ruled by fear.

"Yo, Shawn-ista."

"Yo, T-bag."

"You know you're my best friend, right?"

Shawna darted her eyes back and forth from the top of the magazine, as if it were a trick question.

"Of...course?"

"Nothing could break our bond, right?"

"What...is this? I don't like these questions already."

"Just...let me finish. I'm...not what you think I am. Peter and I...that's not real. It's a front."

"A front? Are you...?" Shawna looked over at Ian and gasped, then gave Tera a sly smile. "Did you hook up with Ian? You *dog!* I wish he would've come to my tent instead of Jason. He's kind of a—"

"—putz. I know. No, Shawna, I'm not screwing Ian. I'm not screwing Peter, or *anyone*, and it's because of you."

"What? Why would *I* have anything to do with—?"

"I've got it in my head that maybe, someday...you and I might... I mean... Fuck! This was easier to say in my head."

Shawna stared at Tera with her eyebrow arched.

"Are you finally coming out, T?"

"Fina—? You *knew?*" Tera asked, flabbergasted.

"Please, baby! Your chaste little pecks on the cheek with Peter in school? The hotel stays where you always choose the bed with a mirror angle? You think I didn't notice your lingering looks at me or the other girls in the locker rooms? Those excuses for your blushing during our workouts were cute as fuck, girl."

Tera's face burned deeper the longer Shawna talked.

"What was all that about Ian and acting like you didn't know what I was saying then?" Tera sputtered.

"It's not *my* job to declare your feelings. I was going to go along with it as long as you were willing to go along with it. I figured you'd wait until we were in college and away from that podunk town and tell me *then*."

"Okay, I'm relieved at how much you're taking this in stride, but... Do you realize... I'm in love with you?" It was the hardest five words Tera had ever had to say, and a lump in her throat nearly kept her from getting it out.

"I love you, too! I'm so happy you're unburdening yourself *finally*. You don't have to pretend around me anymore!"

"Shawna, *in* love with you," Tera burst. Only Ian was around to hear, and she needed to make the point as clear as humanly possible. If Shawna was ever going to reciprocate, the moment was nigh. Tera's body hummed with adrenaline, more than after any of their cheer tournaments.

"I heard you, Tera. I'm sorry I'm not that way, but you're going to be up to your hips in girls once we get to college. And I'm going to be there to hear all about it. It could even be as soon as this week, if you hook up with Katie."

Shawna's smile was as bright as the sun, and full of care for her friend. Tera's heart, so full of unrequited love, thumped painfully, one last time, expunging the longing and filling up again with Shawna's platonic love.

"What the—? What's with you figuring me out all of a sudden?" Tera said, a hint of amusement creeping into her voice, cracking with emotion.

"Girl, I'm your best friend. I *know* you! You were stealing glances at each other all night. Now there's nothing stopping you from acting on it! Go get her, T!"

They stood up and embraced. Tera's eyes leaked a little, disappearing into Shawna's beautiful curly hair as they held each other tight. She'd lost the love of her life and gained a stronger bond with her best friend in one short conversation. She wiped the remaining tears away with her letterman jacket when they parted, then took it off along with her shirt.

"What are you—?" Shawna asked, as Tera stood before her in a black sports bra.

"Take yours off, too, while we help Ian. You won't want to get oil and grease on that shirt."

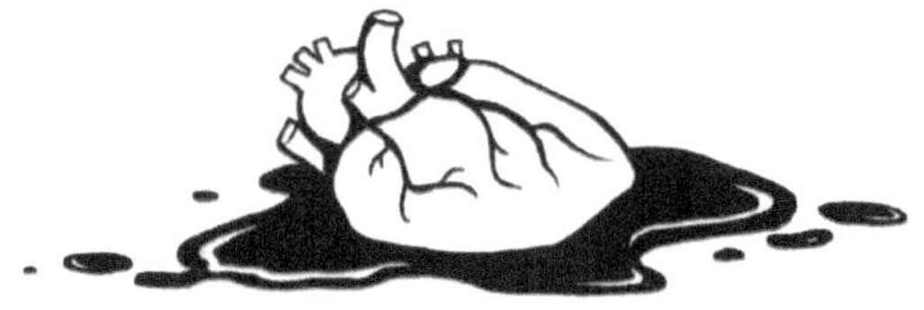

Tera, Shawna, and Ian worked tirelessly for hours, until their stomachs audibly begged for food. Tera milled around the camp and realized how poorly they'd planned the booze and food. It seemed all they had in abundant supply were Nick's drugs. She didn't feel like rooting through everyone's tents for hidden food. Yet.

Upon returning to the bus, she planned to suggest that they take the other party boat to the resort to pick up food when something pushed her from behind. The rush of movement made her stumble forward and fall to her knees in the dirt. Something sharp scratched across her back as the assailant landed on her.

"Maggie! What the hell's wrong with you?" a young boy cried.

At his call the dog pushed its weight down onto Tera's back as it hopped off and ran back to its owner. An unfamiliar hand reached down to help her up. A boy a couple years younger than her apologized profusely for the dog, admonishing his brother for not bringing the leash.

Shawna got down from the bus and knelt to pet the dog. She'd always liked them. Tera didn't, though, and every dog seemed to know it. They always pawed at her legs and never stopped jumping on her until their owners made half-assed attempts to pull them away.

The younger boy kept staring at Shawna's cleavage while she played with the dog. His older brother nudged him, but he only moved his eyes to stare at Tera's bra instead.

"Getting a good enough gander there, bud?" Tera asked. "Or should I pose for a pic?"

The older boy told his brother to knock it off and apologized again, his face turning redder the longer Tera looked at him. He broke the awkward silence with an observation.

"I guess they got you guys, too. Our tires were all slashed over there."

"Any idea who did it? Or why?" Ian asked.

The boy shrugged. "Our parents are at the resort. They said they'd make some calls, but they were really distracted by the state police. They talked with a whole lot of other adults before ordering us back to the camp."

"What are the police doing here?" Shawna asked. "I mean, *already*—if nobody called about the vandalism yet?"

"I don't know. They didn't want people near the laundry facility, though. Something must have happened in there."

"Jesus," Tera said as she shook her head and scanned across the lake. From where they were it was only possible to see the speck of tiny buildings. "What's your names, dudes? I've already met Maggie."

"I'm TJ. This is Corey," the younger one said, still directing his conversation to her chest.

"You guys...wouldn't happen to have any food you could spare at your camp, would you?"

The boys smiled conspiratorially. "Do you like veggies?"

"Sure," Shawna said. "You don't get bodies like ours without veggies."

TJ smiled and nodded, as if she'd just invited him to verify.

Tera rolled her eyes and grabbed her and Shawna's shirts before following the boys. Ian took a break from his work and came along, too. Maggie ran up the path ahead with TJ chasing after her.

"Say, Corey," Shawna said. "We're having a party tonight."

"I heard."

"Oh... Are...you coming? That didn't sound very excited."

Corey sighed and shrugged.

"Only if I can bring my friend."

"The more the merrier, I think," Tera chipped in. "As long as Chase approves..." She shared a knowing glance with Shawna. Chase didn't like wrinkles in her finely laid plans.

"Don't get your hopes up on booze and shit," Ian said. "We ran out last night and the clerk's watching us like a hawk. Gonna be a dry-ass party."

"Make it sound *more* unmissable, dude," Tera said. The burnouts were rubbing off on her; she'd never said 'dude' so often before the trip.

Ian shrugged as they helped themselves to leftover veggie lasagna and soup. It tasted great, not at all worthy of the boys' derision. Once full and having successfully saved the kids from eating their veggies, Tera noticed the fishing poles. She pointed and asked Corey if they could use them.

"I'm bored of looking at engines and tires all day, Ian. Let's try to catch tonight's dinner."

Tera taught Shawna to fish while TJ and Maggie played around between the shore and camp. Something about the two boys hanging out at the camp alone didn't sit right with Tera, especially after the tire vandalism. She wondered why that thought hadn't occurred to their parents.

After a couple of hours and the sun neared the peak of Mt. Bailey, Amber staggered into the camp from the northern path. Tera asked TJ to reel in the pole while she and Shawna ran over to Amber.

"Jesus, what happened?" Tera asked.

"I...I'm not sure. Nick offered me something stronger than the weed and we screw—"

Shawna shushed her, tilting her head at TJ and Corey within earshot.

"We...had a great time, but I passed out. When I woke up, they were both gone. I called out to them and searched around, but I couldn't find any trace of them. I came back here after— I swear I tried! I looked for hours."

Ian's eyes betrayed an anxiousness he hadn't shown before, even around the destroyed bus.

"Where were you? Can you take me?"

"Better get her some food and water, first. How do you feel, Amber?" Tera asked. "You still look a little...you know. Out of it."

"I don't want to go back out there. Everything was so...still... When I cried out to them...it fucked with my head. I don't want to be alone again."

"I'll be with you," Ian coaxed her. "Please, Amber. If Nick or Tony had come back here without you, we would go looking for *you*, too."

"Don't do that, you fucking *burnout*," Amber snapped. "Don't make *me* feel guilty because those guys thought it would be fun to play Hide & Seek after—after whatever they did to me when I was passed out."

"He's only trying to help his friends, Amber," Tera said, annoyed at her for throwing the word "burnout" around like that. "And I know you're scared Amber, that's just...a big accusation to make. Are you sure? I don't think any of them would—"

"How would you know, Tera? Just because they're all buddy-buddy with you since we got here doesn't make them good guys."

"I don't want to argue with you here," Tera said. "Let's go to the campsite and you can, I don't know, draw a map for Ian? Give us an idea where you went? I'll go with you, Ian. Shawna, can you stay with Amber until Chase or Darleen return?"

"Yeah, T. No problem."

"Corey, did your parents say when they'd be back?"

He shrugged and shook his head.

"Do you two think you can hang out on our side of the camp, with Shawna? It's getting dark..."

"Can I bring my game over?" TJ asked.

"Of course! Bring whatever you want."

Tera's stomach sank as they got closer to their camp. Some of the tents had been torn open, their contents strewn about the site. Shawna and Amber ran to their tents and cursed loudly over broken or missing items. Tera and Ian's tents didn't seem to have been touched. At first, they thought the damage could have been caused by a bear, but upon closer inspection, they'd been cut open clean, not torn.

"Amber, can you give Ian an idea where we need to go? Then help Shawna clean this up, I guess? Hopefully Chase and the others will get back before you have to do too much—"

"Who made you Queen Bee? Why are you telling everyone what to do all of a sudden?"

Tera bit her tongue to avoid a useless argument. "If you have better ideas—by all means. But you're at least going to help us find Nick and Tony, got it?

"*Got it?*"

Amber sulked and opened a map that detailed the hiking trails around the lake. Chase had picked it up before the trip and they'd found it, tucked away in a small side pocket of her luggage that hadn't been ripped open—the suitcase itself had been upturned and poured out into a bush. Tera dug around some of the bags that had been removed from the tents until she found a couple flashlights—one no more than a crappy keychain light.

Before she and Ian departed, Tera embraced Shawna; partially to calm Shawna down from having her tent destroyed, but more so because Tera had never searched a forest for missing people before, and her mind kept churning out worst-case scenarios. She'd hate to be at the end of one of those scenarios wishing she'd said goodbye to her best friend when she'd had the chance.

CHAPTER 8

DECISIONS

KILL COUNT: 9

KATIE FELL ONTO THE bed, her cheek pulsing from Randall's fist. Trent held Samantha back by both arms in the corner by the door. Kelly was high off her ass on the second bed. When Katie tried to get back up, Randall threatened to hit her with the butt of his gun.

"How can you blame Boyd's death on *me*, asshole?" Katie yelled. "I was on the other side of the lake!"

"We wouldn't have gotten thrown out of that bar, you goddamn dyke! You would have shut us up; curbed our drug use."

"What kind of fucked up logic is that? You might have killed me for stopping you! That's all you've been threatening since San Francisco! You're trying to scapegoat me for something that wasn't *any* of our faults. Will you calm down and put that gun away?"

Randall grimaced and stuffed it into his waistband. Then he backhanded Katie across the same cheek he'd punched. He forced himself on top of her as she hit the bed again.

"Randy, leave her alone!" Samantha screamed before Trent muffled her mouth with his hand.

Randall didn't protect the gun, too focused on slapping the shit out of Katie. She fought through his swings with one arm and used the other to pull the gun from his waistband. She jammed it up beneath his chin, just as he'd done to her on the day they'd arrived. He shot his hands up and awkwardly climbed off her with only his knees. She moved with him, not letting the barrel leave his flesh.

"Let Sam go, Trent," she threatened.

Samantha kneed him in the junk as soon as he let go. Trent writhed on the floor while Samantha gathered the money and drugs into the duffel bags around Kelly.

Katie locked eyes with Randall's while everything else moved around them. He gave her a knowing, malicious grin.

"You wouldn't shoot me, bitch. The pigs would hear you."

Katie reached behind and grabbed a pillow. She pressed it into his face, pushing him against the wall with the gun jammed into the center of the pillow.

"Okay, okay! What do you want from me? I just lost my friend! I'm high as fuck. We're all—"

"I'm done with your sob stories. *All* of your sob stories. You're not the victim, Randy, and you're not blaming me for this. Got it all, Sam?"

"Yeah, Katie."

Samantha opened the door, hitting Trent with it and pinning him against the wall, still in no condition to get up. Samantha couldn't have cared less about adding insult to injured balls. Katie moved away from Randall, tossing the pillow on Kelly. She finally stirred enough to notice Samantha backing out the door with the duffel bags.

"Hey, where are you taking the drugs?" she asked, more curious than immediately pissed—the woman had no idea what was going on.

"These bitches are robbing us, Kelly," Randall said, never losing the evil grin that promised to haunt Katie's dreams.

Katie slammed the door behind them, then followed Samantha down the stairs. Katie put the gun in her waistband and hid it with her shirt. The cold metal tickled her lower back. Goosebumps covered her body from the altercation.

"Get to the trailhead to the camp, Samantha. I'm right behind you and I'll take one of those duffel bags when I catch up."

Samantha nodded and walked ahead. Katie tried to remain inconspicuous as she made her way down to the shore. If they were going to get away with the cash and drugs for a nest egg, they couldn't alert the police. She looked east to the docking area where Timothy and Jessica waited for them. Katie waved for a few seconds before one of them finally noticed her. She exaggerated her arm waving to indicate that they were going to walk back to the camp instead.

Whether they really understood her arm waving, she couldn't wait. She went back to the parking lot at the trailhead entrance and glanced behind at the motel before it would be out of view. Trent carried Kelly on his back with Randall a few paces ahead of them. Randall started running when he saw Katie.

She sprinted ahead to Samantha and grabbed one of the duffel bags. They jogged as fast as they could along the uneven, snaking path. When they made it around a curve and looked back, no one followed. They might have been held back by Kelly, but she knew Randall wouldn't stop, regardless. He would toss Kelly aside the moment she became too much of a burden to bear.

Katie cursed for forgetting to grab her phone from wherever Randall had stashed it in the room.

After two miles of keeping ahead of them enough to remain out of sight, Samantha complained about tightness in her sides. Katie felt the same, and they moved off the path into the forest. They found some large stumps to lean against and kept an eye on the path. The light disappeared quickly as the sun set over Mt. Bailey.

Katie considered ending Randall's threat with the gun if she could get a clear shot, but with a known police presence nearby it would be impossible to get away with it. Knowing the sound would carry across the quiet serenity of the lake and echo off the surrounding forest, Katie planned to save it as a last resort.

After some time, they heard Kelly whining and Randall telling her to shut up. As they passed the hiding spot, it occurred to Katie that she'd led them towards the campgrounds and her car. That was all they needed to throw into the increasingly dangerous situation—teenagers and a family with young kids. *Fuck.*

Katie shook Samantha and nodded that they'd need to start moving again. She didn't know how much longer she could worry about the volume of the gun versus the threat Randall might pose to innocent people.

Back on the path, they slowly followed behind the trio of junkies. After half a mile, they came upon a little dam that poured into the beginning of Lake Creek. Beneath the single light pole, Katie discerned the shapes of the three of them and...someone else? A large figure blocked the path across the small dam. Randall gesticulated wildly for the man to get out of their way.

Katie grabbed Samantha's hand and picked up the pace, the duffels dragging on the ground as they hurried.

The next sequence of events unfolded between blinks. Katie and Samantha froze in place as the large man punched straight into Randall's face and yanked back with lightning speed. Randall's body crumpled to the path in a heap. The man was on Trent before he could untangle himself from Kelly's rag-dolled limbs. He reached down to grab Trent's ankles and pulled them up violently. Trent's head hit the pavement. Kelly went stumbling across the ground.

Samantha shot her hands to her mouth and dropped the duffel bag as they witnessed the man whip Trent's body overhead like it was nothing. The monster swung Trent's head into the side of the concrete walkway along the dam, caving it in. The man let the body fall into the creek, then turned his attention to Trent's dropped baggage: Kelly, swaying on her feet, unable to understand the danger.

Katie abandoned her bag, pulled out the gun and ran towards Kelly. She got in range only a moment before the man took a swipe for Kelly's throat. Katie trained the gun on him and fired into his torso. It hardly moved him. The next caused him to stagger. A third shot brought him to his knees. A fourth put him on his back.

The gun reports echoed from the forest, but they were in a bit of no-man's-land between the resort and campground. She decided to keep the gun and turn it over if the police ended up catching up to her in the aftermath. Proving self-defense in the situation wouldn't be too difficult if it came to it.

They walked carefully around the man's body. Samantha gasped when they came upon Randall. The man had punched his hand through Randall's teeth, grabbed his spinal column, and pulled it partially out of his mouth. Samantha vomited off the path while Katie shuddered, extra aware of her own spine in the moment. Kelly was a burden to hold up alone. Katie didn't expect her to miraculously save herself, but it'd be nice if she could at least stand on her own.

After crying and vomiting, Samantha composed herself and gathered up their duffel bags, then returned to Katie's side. As they turned to head towards the campground, there came a rustling on the dam. They looked back to see the bullet-riddled man getting back up on his feet.

"Sam...run..." was all Katie could manage.

They about-faced directly into a brick wall of a man, just as large as the one that had murdered Randall and Trent. He didn't acknowledge them as he took slow, almost casual steps towards the dam.

"You do good work," he said to the murderer. "Had my eyes on those two since the bar. I assume the laundry was yours as well?"

The man Katie had shot only stood there, breathing deeply. Menacingly.

"I get it, brother. Believe me, I get it. Lot of lessons need to be taught up here. But see, I'm on vacation, and I promised the little woman and kids we'd refrain from teaching lessons all week. But you've destroyed my truck. My...friends' car. You're bringing your classroom too close to my campground. Think we can work out a deal where you leave off until Monday? I'd really appreciate it, brother."

Katie's mind raced at the insane conversation unfolding before her. She nudged Samantha to move away from the scene quietly. Kelly partially tripped over Randall's corpse, causing Katie to have to stoop to save her from a hard fall. She put her arms into Kelly's armpits and dragged her away, close behind Sam.

Before they moved away enough to lose sight of the giants, the one she'd shot lunged at the man "on vacation." They grappled into the darkness. Katie pulled Kelly to her feet and flopped her arms over both of their shoulders to guide her along the path between them as they each took a bag.

A quarter of a mile later, two flashlights made their way through the forest along the north corner of the lake down to the path. Unsure what to expect after what they witnessed earlier, Katie pulled out the gun to feel safer, though she distrusted its effectiveness after...

The two flashlights shone in their faces.

"Hey, guys! Bringing a friend to the boat par—? Oh damn, Katie! What happened to your face?"

Katie squinted and was relieved to see Tera and Ian, then concerned at what could be following them.

"Can you two help with Kelly here? We've got a lot of baggage."

"Sure, Katie," Tera said as she and Ian transferred Kelly's arms over their shoulders and took up behind them.

"What were you two doing off the path?" Samantha asked.

"Looking for a couple friends," Ian said, notably dismayed. "They disappeared this afternoon, probably high as fuck, and wandered off. We can't find a trace of them. So, we're hoping they show up tonight or tomorrow or we'll have to make calls at the resort, too."

"What's in the bags?" Tera asked.

"It's just..." Katie said, reflexively holding the bag closer, "...our stuff. We don't want to stay at the motel. I'll stay in my car again. Maybe Bobby will let Samantha stay in his tent. If not, maybe she could stay on the bus with Kelly?" Katie tried not to sound desperate for options, but she was.

"We're not sure how any of that's going to work," Ian said. "Most of the tents were destroyed this afternoon. Cut to pieces. There's either going to be a lot of people crammed in the few untouched tents, or we'll all be in our sleeping bags around the campfire tonight."

Any remaining warmth flushed from Katie's face. Things grew worse by the moment.

Trudging onward, a foreboding sense of something following close behind in the dark tickled Katie's neck, like whenever she got up to get water or go to the bathroom in a dark hallway. Her half-asleep mind conjured something reaching out for her—that goliath man snatching her ankles like he grabbed Trent's—and the fear kept her steps hurriedly paced ahead of the others. It took all her inner strength not to outright run from them when her skin crawled, or a stray branch brushed her leg. All she wanted was to be beneath the safe confines of her blankets.

Katie wished the terror-filled trip could be over. No, she wished it'd never begun in the first place. Was her old life really so much worse than this bullshit?

She'd been kicked out of her home by intolerant parents and turned to a life of drugs and shitty part-time jobs, crashing between various friends' rundown apartments. Never in a million years would she think she'd want to go back to that—just to be able to never have to see what happened on that dam.

The cold sweat coating her body from the miles of running with the heavy duffel bags and supporting Kelly brought on a headache. Even with Ian and Tera helping Kelly, Katie wanted nothing more than to fall down and sleep. The blood pounding against her swollen cheek synchronized with her headache, magnifying each. She couldn't shake the image of part of Randall's spine protruding from his mouth, or Trent's head being bashed into the side of a slab of concrete, which added a dash of nausea to the mix of unpleasant sensations.

Katie highly doubted sleep would come, no matter how exhausted her body was.

As they came into the campground, she hoped they could get past the Hunt's campfire without drawing their attention. Flashlights lit on them as they passed, and Timothy and Jessica came to their little group unprompted. Their younger son played a video game at the picnic table and ignored them.

"I can't believe you wanted to hike with those bags rather than take the boat back," Timothy commented before he'd taken in their appearances. "Oh jeez, Katie, what happened to your face?"

"Nothing. I'm fine."

"When you went to your motel room, you didn't look like that," Jessica said. "What's going on? Who's this girl that can't walk on her own?"

"Folks, I appreciate your concern, but we just need rest. If you're still concerned in the morning, come over to the other side of the grounds and we can explain."

Katie didn't see any good in inciting fear in the Hunts by mentioning what happened back at the dam. What if the man who claimed to be on vacation won their battle? They'd have nothing to worry about, then. But if he hadn't, they'd probably have been dead already. The worst-case scenario was driving her crazy. While she *might* have safety in numbers, soon, the Hunts wouldn't. Was it going to be worth having such a long, drawn-out conversation at night? Would they even believe her?

Ultimately, if that man that she'd filled with lead won the battle, they would all be dead anyway. What could any of them do against a monster like that, even if they knew it was coming? Their transportation was damaged. The boats couldn't hold *all* of them. She returned to the thought that if the man on vacation had failed, they would have been caught well before reaching the campsite. She decided to hold onto that thread of hope and not mention anything to the Hunts. Samantha seemed okay following Katie's lead. Kelly was fucked either way and couldn't string the sentences together if she tried.

"Well, have a good night, then," Timothy said. "If you see Corey, tell him we're expecting him back no later than midnight."

Once they reached the campground, the cheer squad rushed to Tera to see if she was alright, except for Amber, who sulked by the fire. Katie and Samantha took on Kelly as Tera and Ian updated their friends on their situations. They dragged Kelly to Katie's car and laid her in the back seat. Katie cursed at the idea of having to sleep upright in the passenger seat. That was never comfortable, but maybe it'd be worth it for the vantage point. Besides, she already imagined it was going to be hard to sleep anyway.

Samantha sighed and stuffed the duffel bags in the trunk. Then she and Katie sat down next to the campfire, staring into it blankly, trying to forget what happened to their companions. Hated though they may have been, it was difficult to reconcile what they deserved with what happened to them. Katie lost herself in the fire for an eternity. The heat did no favors to her swollen and bruised cheek.

A hand on her shoulder brought her out of her daze. She looked up at Tera's concerned face.

"This is...such a fucked-up situation, Katie. Darleen and Zack aren't back yet either, though they should have been back hours ago. We've got four people missing. Half of us aren't in the mood for a boat party, and the other half wants to get their minds off shit and do it anyway. Well, most of us are on edge because of what happened with the tents, so...our compromise is to lay out our sleeping bags on the two boats and sleep offshore. There's enough room for you three if you want to join us."

Samantha nodded without moving her eyes from the fire. She'd be near Bobby either way, and probably feel safer. Katie figured anything would be better than trying to sleep in her car. She hadn't even noticed when the tires were slashed—how could she count on waking up for another attack? She went to the trunk, pulled out a needle, and placed it on the center console so Kelly would see it if she woke up—better for her to remain passed out in the car than to wake up screaming for more drugs and find no one in the camp.

Four couples pushed off in one party boat, while Katie, Samantha, Bobby, Tera, Ian, Shawna, Amber, and Corey took the other one. Corey mentioned that he wished his friend had joined, but he couldn't find her anywhere. The sleeping bags were stacked neatly and safely against the railing of the wide, flat surface. They went out a few dozen yards from shore and dropped anchor.

They shared small talk for a while, but it was pretty boring without alcohol according to some of the teens. After about thirty minutes, a canoe with a single dark figure approached the party boats from the direction of the resort. Katie reached back to the gun in her waistband to feel its safe, metal handle.

"Lynn!" Corey exclaimed.

Flashlights from both boats illuminated the homely girl with the lovely body paddling a canoe carrying various boxes and caddies of beer. Several kids from both boats cheered as she unloaded half on one boat, and half on the other. Once emptied, she tied the canoe to Katie's boat and climbed aboard with help from Corey.

It was pretty cute—a good-looking boy like Corey embracing a girl clearly out of his league, but, then again, in the dark, everyone looked the same.

A cool can helped soothe Katie's swollen face. She downed it once it got warm.

The kids drank into the night, livening up conversations and pressing their bodies closer than they would otherwise. Ian rejected Amber's advances at first, but after a few drinks, he let his guard down and she had him. Shawna seemed content to shoot the shit with Tera for the time being. Corey and Lynn couldn't keep their hands off each other and they didn't seem to remember other people were on board as they escalated to making out sloppily and openly.

Eventually, Shawna asked Lynn if she could borrow the canoe, said good night, then paddled to the other boat to hook up with one of the boys who wasn't part of an established couple. Soon the pairs set up sleeping bags. Katie felt stupid for not asking for one before they set out. Samantha simply shared with Bobby.

Lynn and Corey broke up their heavy make-out session with a conversation they both didn't seem to want to have, then Lynn dove into the water and swam to the canoe tied to the other boat. She returned and helped Corey in, then they paddled to the shore.

It was a good thing one of them remembered Corey's curfew, because Katie had completely blanked on Timothy's request to remind Corey to get back by midnight. In her buzzed state she almost didn't register Tera pulling at her arm, pointing at Shawna's unused sleeping bag. Tera had set it up next to hers.

Katie's preferred side to sleep on happened to coincide with Tera's so they faced each other. Tera's drunken "good night" and brushing her fingertips on Katie's palm might have pushed her to act on her lust any other time, but someone had to be an adult in their situation. At least that's what Katie told herself, like she wasn't drunk as a skunk, with the sound of Trent's bones snapping and echoing against the dam replaying in her ears. Katie said "good night" and rolled over. The sleeping bag welcomed her, but didn't relieve the cold...

CHAPTER 9
PRIDE AND VIRTUE

KILL COUNT: 13

SLATER BROUGHT HIS FISTS together and slammed them down on the large man's back, knocking him to the ground. The upper hand in strength went to Slater. He pushed the man off the dam and into the lake with his foot. After a few moments, the body sank. He watched until no air bubbles escaped to the surface. Slater stayed at the spot for several more minutes, to be sure. Though his vision was keener in the dark than most, it was impossible to see into the water well enough to know whether the man's body sunk there or drifted to another part of the lake.

Bloodlust rose in Slater's chest with the adrenaline of the fight. He hadn't exerted himself that much in a long time. It felt good. He trekked to his family's campsite but found no one there. Lynn had wished to stay behind at the resort, looking for tires to steal off vehicles for their F-350 and the Hunt's SUV. He didn't know where Killian would have gone, but he had an inkling toward Murdock's absence.

At that thought, Killian emerged from the darkness and embraced him.

"Our little girl has grown up," she said with great pride.

"...In what way?"

"Like a shark in the womb."

"Ah. That's great to hear. Did you find him?"

"Found and buried, for the most part. Part of me wishes she'd waited until after the vacation, but our timetables won't always line up with her changes."

"I'm...concerned that she did it over something so stupid. If he'd attacked her, that's understandable. But to do it over that boy's game? Feels unearned."

Killian started a fire, then produced their son's beating heart from a bag. She speared it and positioned it over the pit. The heart cried out like an oyster burning alive in the shell. After it was charred to perfection, they ate two thirds of it, saving the last third for Lynn.

Over dinner Slater informed Killian of the other teacher stalking the lake—the one responsible for crippling their rides and ending three of the assholes from the bar that'd harassed their friend.

"*I* wanted to do that on Monday..." Killian muttered.

"The girl's still alive. But she was out of it. Barely reacted to her friends' deaths. There'd be no point going after her, except to teach her not to take drugs."

"That's a good enough reason for me. How do you feel about that bus—are they making progress in escaping their cage?"

Slater lay back on his palms and stared into the twinkling purple sky.

"Let them be the masters of their own fates this week. If they get the bus moving before Monday, we'll leave them alone. If not..."

Killian sidled to him and kissed him, caressing his cheek with her blood and mud-stained hands. She was the most alluring being he'd ever seen, and the stench of decay on her body only intensified his attraction. They took each other by the fire several times throughout the night. Exhaustion was rare for either of them, but as they came close to hitting it, they finally broke apart to lay on their backs.

"Lynn's not back yet..." Slater commented.

"If she found the tires, getting them back to our truck will take a lot of time. Let her work."

Slater inhaled the smoky air as the campfire died. Killian's stench overcame it. He wasn't offended, but...

"Sweetheart, I think we need to bathe tomorrow morning."

Killian swatted his arm.

"That's rude."

"Not for me. For the Hunts. If *I'm* noticing the smell, it's sure to alarm them. They already look at us oddly with all the dirt stains. Adding blood into the mix will scare them off."

"Point taken. I will bathe for the sake of our friends and pretend it's not because you find disgust in it."

"I'll show you I find no disgust in it," he said as he pulled her back on top.

The F-350 didn't have four new tires on it in the morning, much to Slater's disappointment. He'd trusted Lynn to take care of it when they parted at the resort, after she found the Hunt's dog. At home she didn't often listen to her parents' requests to do even the simplest chores. She displayed a few too many traits of the teenagers that needed lessons, but she never broke their most sacred rule—the one that could only be broken after marriage—so Slater remained amicable.

Although with the way he'd caught her looking at Corey, that may have simply been an obedience based on a lack of options at home. Slater didn't like her pining over those boys in the posters, but as long as one never went *into* her room, he could live with it.

Slater lamented to admit it, but Lynn was rapidly becoming the woman he and Killian had anticipated. Smart. Intuitive. Strong. Bold. Soon she'd shed her father's features and grow into Killian's otherworldly beauty, just as Killian had when she was Lynn's age. Lynn's lessons would become legendary in the annals of cold cases across the country. She might even become the first of their kind to teach abroad.

Killian left the campsite earlier to take a shower in the one facility down by the lake. They would have happily used the lake water at the shore, but the layer of algae that covered most of the lake would only draw more stenches than remove them.

Slater went to the facility for his own shower to find Tim exiting with a caddy and wet towel. His face was beet-red and he didn't look like he'd been touched by water. Tim saw Slater and a look of fear gripped him, though Slater hadn't even attempted to frighten him. Tim seemed like he was fighting in his mind whether to run or wait for Slater to get closer for a conversation.

Killian followed out of the one-room facility with a restrained smile on her face. Slater nearly snapped before Killian motioned to him to calm down. Tim shrunk from Slater's approach, but there was a resolve in his eyes. He'd made his decision to face the conversation head on, straightening his back and neck to look Slater in the eyes.

"It was an accident, Slater. I apologize—to you and Killian."

Tim turned and went back to his campsite without another word. Slater folded his arms and looked at his glowing wife for a more detailed explanation.

"It's alright, Slater. He didn't do anything. You know we didn't bring towels. I was standing in the stall, air-drying, and forgot to lock the door. Tim walked in and...saw me, but the poor guy almost had a heart attack. He turned away to apologize immediately. He let me use his towel. He wouldn't stop sputtering and stuttering, much like our students when they realize the end of their lesson is near. It was rather cute, actually."

"Did you...tempt him?"

"No! If he was a stranger, I would have relished that, and held him for you if he succumbed so we could teach an adulterer a lesson, but Tim's our friend—*and* we're on vacation! Give me a little credit, please."

Slater's temperature decreased rapidly, and he unclenched his fists. More than being angry at the exposure of his wife, he felt an unfamiliar sense of dread before her explanation; fear that he might have to teach a lesson to his new friend. He was surprised to find that he didn't want that. No one in his life had ever given him pause—to even *consider* belaying his punishments—except Killian.

If Killian's account of Tim's reaction and courtesy was true, their friendship had deepened even more.

"Your turn, big man," Killian said after reaching up to kiss him.

Her fresh scent pleased him. They only bathed at home before going into town, and depending on their situations, that could be a weekend or a week at a time. Only Lynn bathed every day. Her desire to appear clean and wear expensive-looking clothes to impress her non-existent friends puzzled him and Killian, until they realized that habit would make it easier for her to teach abroad, so they stopped questioning it.

"Did you grab any clothes for me from the laundry facility?"

"It was hard to find anything in your size," Killian said, "but a group of bikers parked outside the bar and I snuck some stuff from their saddlebags. I left them in a heap on the bathroom sink in there."

"I like this dress you took for yourself. You don't wear them often enough."

"Thank you, darling. Now get in there so we can meet the Hunts for breakfast."

After his shower and air-dry, Slater and his wife ventured to the north part of the site. Tim's face glowed red again upon seeing Killian. Jessica saw Tim flush and apologized to Killian and Slater, too. Tim must have shared the experience. *Good.* Slater didn't like a couple that hid things from each other, especially those that were most tempting to hide.

"Sorry for the strange question," Jessica said as she laid out a hobo hash that had too much fish and not enough fish guts, "but did you see Corey this morning?"

Slater's hackles raised immediately.

"Why, no, dear," Killian said. "He's not in his tent?"

"No," Tim replied. "His brother says he never came back from the boat party like we asked him to. His curfew was midnight."

"Maybe he's still on the boat?" Killian said while leaning back to peer out at the lake. "Those two boats look full of people. Perhaps they decided not to come back to shore and Corey got stranded?"

"Makes sense, I guess," Jessica said. "I can't say I'm not disappointed he wouldn't make a better effort to come back. He doesn't usually disobey us. He complains a lot, like most teenagers, but he's a good kid."

"I'm sure he'll turn up," Killian offered. "This is so good, by the way. You're a great cook, Jessica. It *almost* tops that lasagna."

Slater smiled inwardly at how well Killian hid her true feelings behind a mask of over-complimenting. He knew how much she didn't like anyone's cooking but their own. Her subterfuge skills aroused him whenever he got the chance to witness them for himself. She was one of the greatest teachers in the country for so many reasons.

After breakfast the four of them took a walk around the site. The teens' camp was devoid of life, and most of the tents were trashed.

"What the hell happened here?" Tim asked. "You think it was the same person who slashed all of our tires?"

"Undoubtedly," Slater said. The only question in his mind was whether the mess was before or after their scuffle at the dam.

A rustling came from one of the still-intact tents. The zipper flap opened and out came Lynn, followed by Corey.

Rage nearly blinded Slater. Killian's sharpened nails dug into his arm to hold him back. Tim and Jessica looked like they couldn't contain their fury, either. Corey saw them and shame spread across his face. Lynn looked at the adults defiantly as she walked towards them. She addressed all four of them with confidence.

"I know how this looks, but please let me explain. Corey tripped getting out of the canoe. We left shortly before midnight to meet the curfew but we thought he might have twisted his ankle. This site is closer to the dock. We didn't want to wake up TJ, and the dog would have reacted badly to me again, if I had to help Corey walk home. Daddy, I know you wouldn't have wanted me to carry him anyways. I promise you we had separate sleeping bags and we slept on opposite sides of the tents. *Nothing happened.*"

Tim and Jessica looked as unimpressed as Slater and Killian.

"I am so sorry for this, Slater. Killian," Tim said.

He pushed his son roughly by the shoulder towards their campsite with Jessica close behind. They yelled at him as they walked, until they were out of earshot. Slater's eyes vibrated with anger at his daughter, who wasn't dropping the bullshit façade to save face, even without Tim or Jessica there.

Killian tore into Lynn, lecturing her on the power her virtue had in their line of work for the hundredth time. Lynn continued to deny anything happened. Killian got so fed up with the lies she threatened to physically verify that nothing had happened. Slater winced at the image that brought forth, but he wanted Killian to do it. He had no desire to teach Corey a lesson on Monday if their car wasn't fixed, or make hunting the Hunts to their home Slater's first priority after their vacation.

"Lynn, look into my eyes," Slater said as he and his wife loomed over her. "I've looked into thousands of eyes in my lifetime. I know when I see a lie, even when the truth might have saved someone from learning a lesson.

"Did you sleep with Corey?"

"Yes, Daddy. In the same tent, in *separate* sleeping bags, *away* from each other." Lynn then looked into her mother's eyes. "I...wanted to, though. I like him so much, but... I knew if anything happened, you would both punish *him* for it, even if it was *my* idea."

Her eyes didn't waver under either of her parents' intimidating eyes. Her voice didn't pause or shake except to admit her desire. Slater believed her honesty and virtue remained true. Killian relaxed her stance and embraced Lynn. Slater put his hand on her shoulder when they parted.

"You and your mother are going to apologize to the Hunts. I'm going to walk to the south shore and see if I can find any tires for our truck and their SUV. I need to clear my head.

"Oh, and Lynn, your share of your brother's heart is waiting for you at the campsite. Eat it before you do anything else today. Don't let that power go to waste."

Killian put her arm around Lynn's shoulders and walked her to the Hunts' camp. Slater poked around the teens' campsite to see if he could learn anything about the attacker's patterns or habits. Disabling the vehicles throughout the campground and stealing all the phones had been a nice start. Herding those three girls from the resort to the campsites through attacks was inspired. They'd think twice before going back that way, and trying to get to the resort from the south would be an eight-mile trek. Plenty of time to catch any escapees. Plenty of empty space, away from roads and campgrounds.

The tents were sloppy, though. And he was greedy. He should have listened to Slater's good-natured offer to wait until their family vacation was over. They were only in the beginning of the summer season. There weren't many people flocking to the lake immediately after graduation, but it would be more crowded in the coming weeks. Plenty more lessons would be needed—if the stranger had only waited. Instead, there was already a police presence after the creative, but exposed, aftermath of the laundry facility.

Slater was pretty sure the Ranger met a similar fate, since his vehicle had been abandoned. He'd threatened to cite him and Murdock for fishing without a license. The attacker robbed Slater of the pleasure of ending that annoyance on Monday. He'd planned to share that fatherly moment with his son—to catch a much bigger fish—but Lynn's blossoming ended up taking precedence over that possibility in the end.

As he moved on, he noticed the third vehicle parked at the site with destroyed tires, broken back window, and an open trunk. He peered into the back seat to find a woman with white foam crusted around her mouth. Her deformed body lay in the backseat with ten needles sticking out of both arms. She'd had violent seizures during the overdose and broke her back with the convulsions.

He'd taught many lessons to drug users over the years and seen them in many states of overdose, but she was the worst he'd ever found. The creativity of the attacker leveled up again in Slater's mind. He would love to shadow the man once their vacation finished. As long as he didn't get close to his family, or the Hunts again, he could've done whatever he wanted with the degenerate teenagers and junkies.

Halfway along his walk to the south shore campgrounds, in the southwest area of the lake, he found more of the man's handiwork: A heavyset but pretty girl and her burnout boyfriend, impaled with a long, thick branch slightly off the beaten path. The bodies were propped, sitting mid-kiss on a fallen log. As Slater suspected—the man was an artist as well.

The attacker was no slow-moving slouch—he'd covered ground efficiently. His body-hiding game needed work, though. If one was attempting to take out a whole group of people, having them find early victims and panic was a sure way to lose one's students. It had to be drawn out. They had to believe it was plausible their companions weren't returning to the group quick enough. Such a large project took more careful planning than Slater's adversary showed.

Slater did admit those kids still hadn't panicked and fled to the resort, though, so maybe the man knew what he was doing, after all. With the two kill zones established between the camp and the dam, he only needed to find a way to cut off their access across the lake.

It was too bad the bastard didn't get to complete his artwork. The teens had made it so easy for him, too, climbing onto those party boats all at once... While Slater hiked on, for his own personal edification, he pondered whether he would have tried to get the teens at the same time or only take one or two of them from the boats. During those periods of contemplation, he always wanted to hear Killian's thoughts on the matter.

Slater brightened up when he realized it would be a perfect question to pose to Lynn. He couldn't wait to get back to her once he finished searching for tires.

Chapter 10
That's All Done Now

Kill Count: 15

AFTER LYNN APOLOGIZED TO Timothy and Jessica, she and her mother left for their campsite across the highway. The way Lynn looked back at Corey over her shoulder and the way he returned it gave Timothy a sinking feeling their excuses were all bullshit. What sixteen-year-olds, alone in a tent with everyone else out of earshot, would be able to willingly resist the flood of hormones that opportunity inspired?

Corey's lack of a limp sealed the deal on the twisted ankle lie. As disappointed as he and Jessica were in his decision-making, Slater and Killian's demeanors worried Timothy more. Out of view of the other campgrounds, would they punish Lynn more harshly? They said they'd grounded Murdock at their campsite after he stole TJ's game. What would they do if they perceived Corey to have stolen Lynn's virtue? After all that talk about Lynn ever coming into contact with a boy before marriage, were they the type that would disown their child? Guilt over the thought alone nearly killed Timothy; *his son*, responsible for destroying a family...

Corey sat in a chair by the ashes of the previous night's fire and stared out at the lake while TJ fished from the shore with Maggie.

Thankfully, Jessica seemed just as awkward and unwilling to pry more answers from Corey as Timothy. She defaulted to making something quick for breakfast instead. When she brought Corey a plate, he only set it aside.

"I think those guys are stuck out there. They're waving their arms around wildly. And not in the fun way."

Everything in the surrounding forest had grown silent. Timothy zeroed in to listen to the lake, and sure enough, picked up shouting. Corey started to walk to the dock when Timothy stopped him.

"You stay here. I'll go out there. I think you've had enough fraternizing with other teenagers for the week."

"You guys *encouraged* it!" Corey shouted. "Chase told me last night it was *your* idea to invite me! God!"

Corey ran off towards the dock. Timothy made eye contact with Jessica and shrugged, then hurried after him. He caught up to Corey as he untied the canoe from the dock.

"I'm going out there, Dad."

"That's fine, son. I'll go with you. Glad to see your ankle is all better."

Corey pretended to focus more on getting into the canoe than answering the accusation. Though Timothy intended to have a frank talk with Corey about the night before, awkward silence was all he could manage as they rowed towards the two party boats drifting towards the center of the lake. The kids had tossed ropes between the vessels and tied them together.

"What's going on, guys?" Timothy asked. "Run out of gas?"

Katie shook her head.

"Something cut both of our anchors. The motors' wires are cut, too. We're not sure how this happened. We were all asleep..."

Several of the kids had been crying all morning. Katie answered his unspoken question.

"Two sleeping bags were gone when we woke up. Their friends Sarah and Teddy were in them. No one heard splashing or crying out—not enough to wake us up. The sleeping bags aren't floating anywhere, either. There's a chance they decided to swim to shore and they're in one of the tents. That's what I keep telling them."

Timothy panned to his son, asking with his eyes whether there were others in their camp last night. Corey gave a shrug in response.

"Maybe," Timothy said, not wanting to ruin what little hope the teens still had. "So, there're no oars on these things?"

"If there were, they were taken when the boat got sabotaged. There's nothing in the compartments. Of all things, we'd see *them* floating around, *right?*" Katie's voice cracked, clearly nearing her logical breaking point. She shook her head and changed the subject. "You both look a little tired from rowing out here. Sam and I can trade off with you while we tow back to shore."

"Yeah, right, Katie," Chase said. "You and Sam aren't stronger just because you're older. There are five football players and a mechanic here. They'll take turns towing. Darren, Garrett, you're up first."

They rolled their eyes at being involuntarily volunteered, but did as she instructed. Timothy and Corey sat down on the flat party boat deck while the other boys made a strong tow line with the remaining anchor ropes. Any delusion that it would be easy to paddle two boats four times larger than the canoe were dashed when the sweat-drenched boys traded off with two others after only covering a hundred feet.

Timothy frowned at the open boxes, cans, and bottles of beer scattered across both boats. Corey avoided eye contact. Timothy caught himself before he made a scene. They weren't *his* kids. He and Jessica *had* encouraged Corey to come, but that was because of Chase's assurance there would be no drugs or alcohol.

He caught Chase's eye and she admirably intuited his thoughts by sitting next to him.

"I'm so sorry, sir. I wasn't lying about the drugs and alcohol. There was nothing aboard when we left the shore. Your son's girlfriend brought this all in her canoe. If it makes you feel any better, neither of them drank anything. They were so wrapped up in each other—"

Corey kept his head turned away as if he wasn't listening. As bad as Corey proved to be at keeping secrets, Timothy grew concerned with the amount of them piling up. Chase noticed Corey's feigned ignorance, too, but a little too late to take back what she'd said.

"Um, again, I'm sorry. There were zero drugs, anyway. Small consolation, I know. Maybe this is a bad time to ask, but...do you have any extra food? I don't know if you saw our campsite but it was ransacked by bears or something, or whoever the fu— I mean, whoever's been screwing with our vehicles. We'd walk around to the resort but none of us have eaten or had any water since yesterday. The sun's been beating down on us for—"

"Alright, alright. I get it. We'll see what we have, but it's going to be pretty thin. When we get to shore and feed you what we've got, we'll take the canoe to the resort and bring back more."

"Thank you, sir. I'm sure you're angry at us stupid teenagers on an illicit boat party influencing your—"

"It's okay, Chase. I appreciate your honesty."

Chase nodded and went to the other boat to massage Darren's tired muscles. The third round of boys brought them to the dock and tied them up. The guy who Chase had pointed to as 'the mechanic' jumped onto the dock. Timothy remembered seeing him carrying Katie and Samantha's friend across the campground.

"Alright, guys, I can either try to work on these motors or keep going on the bus."

"Motors," Katie said before anyone else could answer. "Even if you fixed the bus, we're not finding tires for it up here. Better to get us across the lake to the resort where we can start hailing rides."

The boy nodded and walked off towards the site to get the toolset Timothy had lent them. One of the girls made to follow him. He yanked his arm away from her and picked up his pace. She came back sulking and helped the others off the boats.

"What the fuck's Ian's problem?" she pouted.

"You might have screwed over his relationship with his girlfriend, Amber," the auburn-haired girl said as she gathered the empty beer vessels for the recycling bin.

Timothy wasn't interested in their drama and pulled Corey's arm back to their site.

"You boys hungry after all that work?" Jessica asked without looking up from a new paperback.

"No, but we need to get some food into those kids. Then we're going to make a trip to the resort to replenish for the rest of the week. I think we're going to need to pay the extra fees to get someone to deliver our tires quicker. In hindsight we should have paid that exorbitant fee when we called yesterday."

"I didn't think so, Tim. We planned to be here all week, so what's the rush? Spending more would have been a waste of—"

"The tires, the tents, the disabled boats, that man Slater went after the other night, the Ranger that still hasn't come back to his car..." Timothy got close to Jessica and whispered, "...and I'm worried about what Slater and Killian might do when they realize—"

"Okay. I hear you. Maybe you're right. Plus the way Katie looked, and that girl who was strung out... Alright, I'll gather food and take it to the kids with TJ. You and Corey head to the resort. Maybe you should take one of the kids over there, too, in case you get tired from rowing."

"What makes you think I'd get tired before Corey?" Timothy smiled and kissed her.

He and Corey helped her and TJ carry food to the other side of the campground. While everyone else was preoccupied, Katie put her hand on Timothy's arm and nodded for him to step off to the side for a private talk. She shook and tried holding back tears. The brave face she'd been wearing around the younger group was cracking.

"I'm so sorry, Tim. I don't mean to make my problems yours, but something fucked up is going on. That girl we were dragging with us last night overdosed in my car."

"Oh jeez, I'm sor—"

"She was *murdered*. Stuck countless times in both arms. They broke the window and pried open the trunk—she wasn't capable of that, you saw her. Two of my other...friends...were killed last night. When we stumbled into your camp, we were running from the murderer. As of now, six of those kids are missing, and their friends are getting panicky. They're looking to me and Sam because we're older but..." her voice broke and trailed off. Tears flowed but she held back from sobbing.

Timothy stood in the way to protect the kids from seeing her breakdown. Behind a tree, he offered his shoulder to wet with her tears. He put his hand around her back reflexively and brushed against something metallic at her lower back. She sniffed and pulled out the gun before he could question it.

"Please, take it, Tim. I don't want it. It belonged to one of our dead friends. You probably heard me firing it last night."

"We thought it was some jackass kids setting off illegal fireworks... Anyway, maybe you should hold onto it while we head to the resort. In case you see that man again."

"It doesn't do anything to him."

Katie explained what happened. He couldn't believe what he heard, but there was no lie in Katie's voice or demeanor. Her reactions were genuine; she simply didn't know what to do. Not that Timothy knew any better. The best course of action seemed to be accessing a phone and getting everyone home sooner than later.

"Katie, can you be strong for a little while longer? Don't tell my wife. If the kids are listening to you, don't make them panic any further by mentioning any of that. I'm going to talk to the police and call for either tow trucks or tire delivery services. Police first. I'll get them to come over to our side of the lake."

Timothy squeezed her shoulders to reassure her, then found Corey and walked down to the dock.

"Sir, wait a moment, please," Chase said. "Darren will come with you. Whatever you need. He can help carry and paddle."

Darren shook Timothy's hand and nodded. He thanked both of them for the help and they all climbed into the canoe. Chase sat down on the dock and hugged her knees to her chest as she watched them paddle away.

A quarter of a mile from the dock, Timothy couldn't believe his horrible parenting skills: he forgot their life jackets. His mind had been racing with Katie's news and blanked on it in the rush to get to the police. He measured the distance they'd covered in his head. Chase was still seated on the dock, so they could yell for her to fetch some, but turning back would do nothing but increase the amount of time it took to get to the police and tire them out quicker. He decided to get more life jackets at the boat shop once they hit the resort.

Darren offered to take Corey's paddle and traded places.

"Chase seems like a real take-charge gal," Timothy said in order to break the uncomfortable silence since they'd launched.

"Yeah, that's her alright. Ever since middle school other girls have looked to her for leadership, even when she wasn't seeking it. She's got a real selfless quality that I love. She could work on sounding less 'bossy' but I think everyone understands where it comes from."

"Are you both going to the same college?"

"Yep. We've been together for five years..."

Although he didn't seem like the crying type, Darren's mouth twisted.

"This fu—Sorry. This crap going on now... We planned to hike to the top of the mountain tomorrow, just me and her. I was going to... Well, that's all done now. Knowing Chase, she'll be so preoccupied helping the police and Rangers find our friends, she'll forget all about spending time with me until they're found. Not that I won't help. That totally sounded like I didn't care... It's just unfortunate, is all."

"I hear you. You seem like a good match," Timothy said.

They were close to a half mile from the dock. Darren waved at Chase, and she waved back.

It took Timothy's mind a moment to understand what he was seeing: how a large hand from outside could suddenly grasp the side of their canoe, all the way in the middle of the lake. Another hand came out of the water and yanked the paddle out of Darren's hands. It swung the paddle up and cracked Darren in the side of the head. The blow knocked him unconscious, and his body flopped over the opposite side of the canoe.

Corey cried out as the canoe tipped over. The coldness of the water surprised Timothy's nervous system, especially in contrast to the sun beating down on them. His heart barely had time to recover from what he'd witnessed; adding the shock of cold didn't help. He swallowed some of the water before he surfaced for breath.

He emerged coughing and sputtering, putting his hands on the belly of the canoe. He nearly panicked when he couldn't see Corey, but after a frantic swim around the canoe, he found Corey clinging to the other side, scrambling to keep a grip on any part of the canoe.

Timothy grabbed him from behind. Corey swung around and punched Timothy in the face.

"Oh shit, Dad! I'm so sorry! I thought you were—!"

"It's okay. I'm going to boost you up. See if you can balance yourself in the center."

Corey nodded. Timothy kicked his legs as hard as he could to lift his son out of the water. The thought struck him—when had Corey grown into such a young man? Timothy spun around in the water but couldn't find Darren.

"Just a sec, Corey. I'm dipping below to see if he's under the canoe. I'll be right back, I promise."

Corey appeared scared, but Timothy had no time to reassure him. He ducked under, careful not to bump against the boat and knock his son into the water again. Darren wasn't in the air pocket of the canoe, either. Timothy dove a little ways down to see if Darren might be slowly sinking, but in the limited visibility of the murky lake, he saw nothing.

Timothy resurfaced and put his hand out for Corey to help drag him onto the overturned canoe, too, but the weight and imbalance caused Corey to slide off the side into Timothy's chest. The longer they remained in the water, the worse the feeling grew of something grabbing his feet from the darkness below. He remembered the seaweed was worse at the southern end according to the fishing guide at the resort, but it wasn't seaweed that worried him anymore.

His subconscious forced him to remember a video he watched in middle school that gave tips for how to survive falling out of a boat, among other catastrophes in the wild. The first rule was to wear a life jacket. The second rule was to not fall out of the boat. The third rule was to never go into the water to save your dog. The video morbidly showed a floating hat in the water, then pivoted to how to survive the hypothermia *if* you managed to get out of the lake alive, no thanks to your dog.

"Son, help me flip the canoe."

They kicked hard and managed to flip it. A part of the video did show how to roll into a boat sideways rather than trying to climb in perpendicular like most people are wont to do.

"Hold onto the side, son, I'm going to get in, then I'll pull you in. I'll be quick."

Once on board and while Corey scooped water out of the inside, Timothy heard a commotion nearby.

Three of the girls from the camp were swimming towards them, each wearing and towing an extra life jacket. One of the girls bobbed violently at the surface, as if something had her leg and the life jacket was the only thing keeping her from being pulled under.

Chapter 11

Breathless

Kill Count: 18

Tera didn't understand why Chase wore only her pink and white underwear and shouted for Misty. Her eyes shot out to the water where the boat carrying Darren, Corey, and Timothy had flipped over. Misty pulled off her clothes as she ran to Chase.

As members of the swim team, they showed no hesitation in responding to the littoral emergency. Tera's other friends were too shocked to move. Timothy's wife dropped what she was doing and ran after the girls. Tera followed her.

"Chase, what are you doing?" Jessica asked, halting her before she could dive into the water.

"What does it look like?"

"I know, I mean that's too far to free swim *and* deal with those three. They might be panicking when you get there. Take the life jackets!"

Tera ran past them and jumped on the party boat. She tossed two jackets to Chase and Misty, then put one on herself after stripping to her underwear. Tera threw two more to them and clipped a third to the strap of the one she wore.

She dove off the boat towards the men, knowing her head start meant very little. She wasn't on the swim team like the other two, but no one else acted with any urgency, and only Jessica had a clear-enough head to remember the life jackets.

Chase and Misty swam past Tera with speed and efficiency. Misty once bragged about swimming a mile in less than 35 minutes. Tera guessed they were about a half mile away. The drag of towing the other life jacket would probably slow her down. Chase explained before that open-water swimming was very different from swimming in the pool. However, their school couldn't afford a pool of its own, so they practiced against the flow in the South Umpqua River.

Without a current to slow them down in the lake, they seemed to be making good time ahead of Tera until Misty stopped for no reason. Suddenly she bobbed straight down. The two life jackets brought her back up. Chase lowered her head down several times, trying to find what grabbed Misty. When Tera reached them, she put her head under, too. *What the fuck?*

A hand had a hold of Misty's ankle, pulling her into the deep. When Misty resurfaced, Tera made out the shape of a large man at the end of the arm. He melded into the blackness below the sun's rays as he tried to pull her down again.

Even through the murky water, Tera saw the determination in Chase's face. Chase waited for his arm to come closer to the surface, then she lunged, scratching and digging her nails into it. Tera joined her. The muscles of the arm were thick; they were likely only tickling him. The life jackets made it harder to get any further; to kick his head or pull his hair. Tera changed tactics and tried to pry the man's fingers off her friend's ankle, but his grip was vice-like.

When Tera resurfaced, she put her arms around Misty, hoping the four life jackets would better keep Misty's head above the surface. Chase came up and cursed. She horrified Tera by unsnapping her life jacket. Chase slipped the two jackets over to Misty's flailing arms, further bringing the man closer to the surface. Before Tera could scream at her to put it back on, Chase dove hard, her feet coming fully out of the water before kicking down.

Tera put her face down to see Chase's back. Her movements suggested she was doing something to his face. Her right arm tore away, and the man's eyeball squirted out from her splayed fingers. The man let go of Misty's ankle to grasp at his face, sinking with the eyeball into the darkness. Tera reached her hand out for Chase to grab. She kept imagining the arm shooting out and grabbing Chase's ankle; no life jacket to save her.

Their hands came together, and Chase breached. Misty sputtered and shivered in panic. Tera didn't want to imagine how Misty would react if she actually got a look at what had tried to kill her. Tera handed Chase's jacket back, then noticed the canoe coming towards them. Timothy and Corey used cupped hands to reach them, but it was slow going.

Tera wanted more than anything to be away from that spot in the lake. *He's still down there—right below us!*

The thought sent a shockwave from her spinal column into her brain. She kicked and splashed aggressively forward, thankful to have a destination closer at hand than the shore. In combination with the exertion of saving Misty, it tired her arms out, and she knew cramps wouldn't be far behind if she didn't calm down. *But he's* right *there!* All she thought was *swim*; to escape a watery tomb. *Swim. Faster. Harder. Move!*

"Stop thrashing, girls!" Timothy shouted. "We're almost there!"

The canoe finally made it to them. Timothy switched places with Corey to keep more weight on the opposite side. Corey reached out his arm for one of them. Chase helped Misty up and in. Timothy switched with Corey again once Misty's weight evened things out. Timothy helped Chase in. Chase and Timothy reached out for Tera's hands but something tugged her back into the water. The life jacket she'd been towing disappeared below the surface, and the nylon clasp of the one she wore pulled taut against her neck. Her upper torso got dragged backwards into the water. Her feet flew out and kicked away Chase's hand.

Tera opened her eyes underwater to see from an upside-down perspective the man tying the loose life jacket to a frayed rope—the rope that held their anchors before they'd been cut, the one with the blue line woven into it. As the weight pulled her down, she made out another shape tied further down the line. Sarah's sleeping bag! And it was...still full.

Tera's entire life didn't flash before her eyes, like she expected, as the realization hit her: *I'm going to die.* One particular moment came to the forefront, though. She could almost feel the warmth of Shawna's embrace, enveloping her against the cold of the lake and the panic rising in her chest.

Tera blinked and Shawna's face changed. It was—*Corey?* He grasped at her neck. The tautness disappeared as the life jacket slipped off her arms and jerked away from her body. Corey put his arm around her waist and pounded his legs to bring them back to the surface. Chase, Timothy, and Misty pulled them into the canoe. More concerned with speed than delicacy, Tera's leg scraped against the edge of the canoe, leaving a long, raw stretch of thigh.

Her arms, legs, and lungs were on fire. Chase clasped her into the last remaining life jacket while Timothy put on Corey's. Only Timothy didn't have one. Tera did the math on the jackets they pulled with them, now with two lost, and the remaining people in the boat.

Chase held a stoic resolve that slightly cracked when Tera reached her hand out to touch her cheek. Tera would have loved nothing more than to hug her Queen Bee in her grief, but the life jackets made everything awkward.

Tera pulled herself up to a seated position and held Chase's hand tight while Chase returned its intensity. Misty did the same with the other hand.

Timothy hugged his son at the other end of the canoe, tears flowing.

"I've never been more proud of you, son. Or *angry.*"

Either nothing fazed Corey, or he was playing it cool for the three sopping-wet cheerleaders in their underwear sharing the canoe. He turned his gaze away to Mt. Thielsen overlooking the lake from the east. Tera noticed that at least the back of his ears were bright red; he wasn't made of stone.

Timothy looked each of the girls in the eyes and thanked them for their rescue, and stuttered apologies for losing Darren. Chase's resolve returned at the mention of his name. It gave Tera chills to witness her strength in the wake of such tragedy. Darren wasn't there, but Chase couldn't let herself be any less than the woman he'd fallen in love with.

"Sir, it's closer to camp than to the resort. By another mile, if not more. I suggest we go back to camp and spend less time on this lake than we have to. That...*monster* can breathe underwater."

"The police are over there, Chase," Timothy said. "We need their help."

"I agree. But there'll be safety in numbers, and I think we should all walk to the resort together."

"We can go straight to the north shore right now and walk the rest of the distan—"

"Sir, do you really want to leave your wife and child alone at the camp with this *motherfucker below us* around?"

Timothy thought about it, then nodded his agreement.

Despite the fear of having their wrists grabbed and pulled into the water again, they all took turns rowing with their cupped hands. During her rest, Tera watched the dock lined with their friends; eagerly awaiting their return as it got closer and closer. For some reason, it didn't make her feel all that much safer.

Tera laid in Shawna's arms next to the fire while Shawna stroked her hair with concern. The rest of the girls consoled and helped warm Chase and Misty. Their eyes transfixed to the fire, as if they couldn't hear a single word said. Timothy and Corey received their treatment from Jessica, TJ, and Maggie.

Based on Sarah and Darren's demise, they figured Darleen, Teddy, Nick, Tony, and Zack had all met with similar fates. Seven of their friends—gone for no reason. Katie was beaten up and the woman that Tera and Ian had helped to the campsite was nowhere to be seen. Not to mention the missing Ranger. The crippled vehicles and cut up tents all fell into place.

Katie put the kibosh on the group walking around the north of the lake to the resort by vaguely describing the deaths of her traveling companions along that route, and the possibility of there being a second dangerous man in the area. The apprehension Katie had about sharing her experiences evaporated alongside the appearance of the lake monster—no one would doubt her anymore. Timothy suggested they make the eight-mile trek to come to the resort from the south, and they all agreed that was the best course of action.

Garrett, Jason, Luke and Bobby either helped Ian fix the motors of the party boats or kept watch for the man that Chase and Tera described to them. Not that descriptions were really necessary if one were to witness a one-eyed man emerging from the depths...

Tera looked to the dock when she heard voices raised, right before one of the motors caught fire. Ian yelled at Luke to get away, then grabbed the small fire extinguisher from one of the boat's side pockets and put the fire out. He spiked the extinguisher into the deck, then shoved Luke. The other three boys got between them as Amber and Molly ran down to the dock to help break them up.

Luke pushed away from everyone, then threw his hands in the air. He stormed off the dock and took a walk towards the bathroom facility. Misty followed her boyfriend.

"Bring him right back, please," Jessica said. "Don't go far and don't be gone long. We're about to leave."

Misty nodded and picked up her pace.

After they returned, everyone gathered water bottles and set out on the south path. Their journey was cut short by Samantha's scream as a large man emerged from a bend in the path. The scream frightened most of the girls and they sprinted back to the campground without a second's hesitation. Tera stayed back upon seeing Timothy's lack of fear. He approached the man as if they were friends. Then Tera noticed the man at least had both his eyes.

Timothy motioned their intentions to the man, who looked back to the south, then shook his head. Timothy's shoulders slumped, and he guided his family back to the camp with the large man following.

Multiple conversations started up around the fire as everyone regrouped. Corey was tasked with watching over his little brother away from the upsetting circumstances, but not too far off. Tera didn't feel like her input would be heard or valued over Chase,

Timothy, Katie, Jessica, and now the big man Slater weighing in, so she reluctantly broke from Shawna's tight handhold to approach Corey.

He straightened up and cleared his throat when he noticed her, still trying to act cool. TJ sat in the grass, scratching Maggie's ear and watching his older brother silently.

Tera had never had anyone save her life before. She recounted all the things people say in movies and books to thank their heroes. It all seemed inadequate to verbalize, and if she said something that sounded like it came straight from a movie, she feared it'd seem like she didn't truly appreciate what he did for her.

She broke the awkward silence, grabbing his hand out of his pocket and squeezing it.

"Thank you, Corey."

She pulled him close for a tight, heartfelt embrace, like the ones she and Peter faked for their peers, nowhere close to sexual, though it all must have looked the same to TJ, who hooted at them. Maggie jumped between them and barked.

As annoyed as she was at dogs for jumping on her, she appreciated Maggie for making it easier to break away. She didn't want anyone to get the wrong idea. She squeezed his hand one more time and smiled, then went back to the campfire where the arguments picked up in volume and intensity, even though no one could come up with a solid plan.

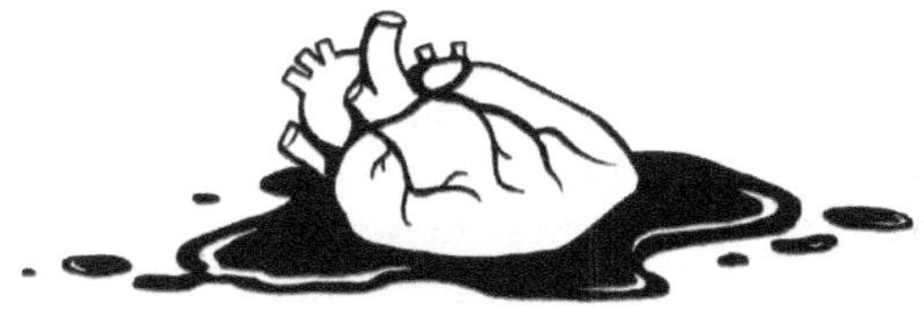

The closer it got to dark, the less anyone wanted to risk the walk to the resort. They reached a consensus to set up the camp with the remaining tents, brought the Hunt's tents over, and rotated shifts of four people watching each direction—the north and south paths, the highway, and the lake.

The people that'd been in the canoe took the first rest. They exempted Corey from guard duty so Tera, Misty, Timothy, and Chase earned the second guard shift. Tera positioned on the south path.

Memories of the dangers from the day replayed in her mind; often and unwanted. The feeling of her lungs desperate for air wouldn't go away. She had to keep reminding herself to breathe. It felt so good as she let the evening air in and out. She focused on breathing normally for a while, hoping it would bestow a meditative quality and the memories might leave her alone.

Footsteps approaching from the south startled her out of her meditation. She shone her flashlight on the advancing figure—Lynn.

Tera hardly got out a greeting before Lynn had her by the throat. Her hands were much stronger than she expected from a girl wearing upper-middle-class clothing.

"You come near my boyfriend again," Lynn growled, "and I'll gut you with my bare hands."

"You—you don't...understand," Tera choked. "He—"

"I don't care about your excuses, bitch. We claimed each other last night, and again this morning. I'll be *fucked* if I'll allow you or your slutty, druggie friends to distract his attention from me. You'd better goddamn pray your bus is running again before Monday, or I'll make you my first student."

"Student...of what? I don't...un—"

"Don't go near him, and you'll live. Otherwise..."

Lynn snaked her hand beneath Tera's shirt and pushed her sharp nails into her stomach. She left no doubt in Tera's mind that she had the strength and armaments to make good on her bare-handed threat. Lynn let go of her neck. Tera hadn't realized she'd been two inches off the ground until Lynn let go. She fell to her knees at the unexpected drop. Lynn shoved her hip into Tera's shoulder as she passed, knocking her onto her back.

By the time Tera stood up again, Lynn was nowhere to be seen. Puzzled more than hurt, Tera finished her shift, then went back to camp to shake Katie awake. Katie's fist shot out of the sleeping bag and hit Tera in the stomach, knocking the wind out of her.

Katie gasped and whispered apologies as she rubbed Tera's back. Once Tera caught her breath, she sat down hard on the ground next to the sleeping bag that she'd loaned to Katie.

"Sorry again, Tera. I was having a nightmare," Katie whispered as she tucked loose strands of hair behind Tera's ear.

"No doubt," Tera said, pulling her head away from Katie's hand. It might have only been a maternal gesture, but if it wasn't, Tera wasn't prepared to deal with that implication. That was the last thing on her mind.

"Where am I going?" Katie asked as she stood up.

"South."

"I'm so sorry, Tera."

She put her hand on the top of Tera's head lightly before leaving. Tera got into her sleeping bag and smelled Katie's stress sweat in the fabric. It was tolerable enough to ignore. What wasn't tolerable was the movement and moaning coming from a nearby tent. Tera tucked the sleeping bag over her head in hopes of drowning out the noise, but laying so close to the fire quickly made that insufferable.

Tera climbed out of the bag and stalked to the tent quietly to avoid waking the rest of the camp. Her shadow elongated and illuminated the tent from the light of the fire behind her, taking on a witchy, evil quality. Gasps came from inside the tent, followed by hushed insistences on who should be the one to check on the approaching shadow.

Tera leaned against a tree just outside of the tent flap and folded her arms. Garrett poked his head out. Tera rolled her eyes. He and Molly were the farthest removed from any of the day's violence so it was no wonder they were so goddamned clueless.

Tera bent down and grabbed his ear, pulling him up and covering his dumb mouth with her other hand to stifle his whining. Since he was shirtless, she grabbed his biceps, hauling him up and pressing him into the tree.

"You two *assholes* need to shut the *fuck* up, or take your bullshit elsewhere," she hissed inches from his face. He was taller and much stronger than her, but she had a day's worth of near-death adrenaline surging through her. Tera pressed him harder into the tree despite his attempt to shrug away from her.

"We're just—"

"There are kids and adults here. People are trying to sleep. Oh, and not to mention, your *friends* are *dying!* What the *fuck* is wrong with you two?"

Molly crawled partially out of the tent to check on the harsh whispering. Tera put her hand on Molly's forehead and pushed her back into the tent. She turned back to Garrett's eyes, burning with rage.

"I don't want to hear you two again tonight. If you're so turned on by all this, take it to the fucking shower."

She jabbed her finger into his hard chest.

"Don't forget, you're *both* on the next shift. If I find out you abandoned your posts to keep screwing around, I'll throw you both into the lake in the morning. Then you might get a sense for how three of your friends died today."

She didn't listen to his sputtering apology as she stormed back to her sleeping bag. A little while later, she heard the two of them leave the tent area. Even after all that, all he took from what she'd said was to take their party to the shower.

Fully awake and pissed, she sat back up and looked around. Everyone else seemed to be sleeping. Except Ian. He stared at her from the opposite side of the fire in his own sleeping bag.

"You ever going to finish rustling around in that thing?" Ian chided softly with a small smile.

Tera shrugged and smiled back, then hugged her knees to her chest. When she looked at Ian again, his smile morphed into a mischievous grin. He put his index finger and thumb together and brought them to his lips, then arched an eyebrow to her.

Chapter 12

Explosion

Kill Count: 18

KATIE LEFT TERA A sweat-soaked sleeping bag to go along with the punch in the gut, doubling her guilt. If some of the sleeping bags weren't destroyed or missing after the camp was ransacked, no one would've had to share—not that the couples seemed to mind. She sighed and went back to squinting into the darkness in an attempt to conserve the pathetic flashlight's batteries.

For the beginning of the shift nothing eventful happened. Fish plopped in the lake, and a light breeze rustled the various pines overhead. Their earthy aroma mixed with the campfire smoke but was soon overtaken by a skunky smell. She turned the light on and scanned around, though she had no idea what she could do to scare it off that wouldn't end with her getting sprayed.

That would be all she needed. After another sniff, she recognized it as something else; something from which she'd tried to distance herself since deciding to make her new life drug-free.

A hand on her shoulder nearly made her jump out of her skin. She swung the flashlight around at the same time as she reached for the gun, then relaxed upon illuminating Tera and Ian. Katie let out an angry sigh and flicked the flashlight off. A small red spark moved from Tera's mouth, then she passed the spark to Ian. He held it out for Katie after he took a drag.

"Maybe when I'm off duty, guys. Thanks, though."

"More for me, then," Ian said as he pulled in another inhale before handing it back to Tera.

"We're even now, Katie" Tera said. "Mini-heart attack for punching me like Houdini."

Ian took a deeper drag after getting it back.

"I wish I had something stronger, but Nick took the good stuff. I lost all three of my friends. I can't get anything fucking working. And I cheated on my girlfriend with the skankiest girl up here."

"Not to mention all the drugs and alcohol," Tera said through the side of her mouth as she held the smoke with her lips.

"I'm a little surprised Shawna isn't already dead," Ian said.

In the dark, though she couldn't see their faces clearly, Katie felt the rage behind Tera's quick turn towards Ian. The smoke blew out like dragon's breath.

"The *fuck's* that supposed to mean?"

"Nothing, Tera. It was a stupid joke. For all intents and purposes, *I* should be dead already. The stoners always die, regardless of first or last."

"I don't ever want to hear you talk like that again, fucking *burn*—," Tera snarled, but cut herself off. She dropped her head and sighed. "I'm sorry, Ian. That wasn't any better."

"I'd say we're even now, but, yeah, my joke was a thousand times worse. I'm really sorry."

Katie smiled at the two of them as they hugged it out. Nice to have a friend in such a shitty situation. She didn't want anything to happen to Samantha, but they weren't exactly friends that could joke around or confide in each other.

Conversely, it was terrible to have friends in their situation, too. Katie just wanted to survive. The man who killed Kelly had also taken the rest of the drugs and the duffel full of money. Katie had nothing—no future; no past to return to; no friends to ground her in the moment. She only had the gun sticking uncomfortably into her lower back and a mild interest in making sure Samantha also got out.

She liked Tera, but their timing was awkward, and the age difference was probably a bridge too far, despite the interest Tera showed on the boat. She was a nice girl and all, but...

Shut up, Katie thought. *Stop trying to justify it into existence. Focus on surviving.*

She tossed her head back and looked up through a gap in the forest canopy. When she stared long enough, she thought she could literally see the sky pinwheeling. It was like staring at a 3D poster long enough to finally see the whole picture.

Jessica divvied up their dwindling food supply, while Slater and his outrageously beautiful but strange wife brought ropes of small animals they must have killed near their campsite across the highway. Most of the girls made whiny noises about eating rodents, but the men were all curious enough to give them a try. Only Tera and Chase were brave enough among the girls to try it, and when their scrunched-up faces relaxed after the first bite, Katie tried it as well.

It tasted like survival.

While she helped Jessica and Timothy clean, a thought occurred to her—a thought so simple she hated herself for not thinking of it sooner.

"Guys, have you noticed there have been no cars passing along this stretch of highway for a couple days?"

Jessica and Timothy looked up in thought, then agreed it was out of the ordinary. Katie followed the line of thought further.

"You know, we haven't tried to get back to the resort via the highway. We've only tried the hiking trails and the lake. Maybe..."

"It's worth a shot," Timothy said. "I wish I could say I have the heart to try it after what happened on the lake."

"Oh, I wasn't suggesting you two go. You've got kids to worry about. I'll take Sam with me."

"Where are you going?" Slater's wife asked as she ambled to the picnic table.

"We're going to try the highway to get to the resort."

"I see. Well, if your plan was to go south, that part of the highway is a no-go. Slater says there are fallen logs about a mile down the road, blocking access both ways."

Katie's shoulders slumped.

"I guess that explains the lack of traffic… But wouldn't cars be passing this way still—those coming from the north— if only to turn around?"

Slater's wife shrugged. She didn't look at all concerned by the circumstances.

"I guess I'm going to check the north route, then."

"Are you sure, Katie?" Jessica asked.

"What else is there to do? If we wait here and a route was open all along that we never tried…" she shrugged.

"I'll go with you, dear," Slater's wife said.

"I don't see why we can't split up with one group going north and one going south," Jessica said.

"We don't know where that maniac is. Do you want to be in the group that chooses wrong?" Timothy said. "Even if we did survive… Knowing the other group didn't…"

"Okay, let me check the north first before we start handing out straws," Katie said.

Samantha whined as Katie pulled her away from Bobby. As much as Katie hated how clingy Samantha had become to an eighteen-year-old, she couldn't really blame her for seeking refuge in his athletic arms. Bobby made it easier for them by volunteering to come along. Jessica whispered Slater's wife's name to Katie before they parted, along with the knowledge that she was odd but fiercely protective. Jessica meant it to be encouraging, but after what Katie'd gone through with Randall, she wasn't about to put stock in other people's vouching for character. She'd see for herself who Killian really was if shit hit the fan.

Killian joined them at the highway, and they began their trek around the north loop. Killian didn't bother with small talk unless Samantha or Bobby asked her a question. Katie chastised herself for getting mesmerized by the perfect shape of Killian's butt whenever she walked ahead. Every part of her was *perfect*. Her proportions, her features, her confident posture... The only thing that seemed off was that she didn't bother to brush or even run fingers through her hair after sleeping. In fact, her clothes were dirty and disheveled. Killian was like a pristine plastic doll that some kid had slapped rutty, handmade clothes on; the contrast made her even more beautiful, but also took on a bit of the uncanniness all dolls possess.

Even more unsettling had been watching her gut the animals at the campsite earlier like a professional. There was an unexpected deftness and grace in her movements that couldn't come from practice alone. She would qualify for—and instantly win—Miss Backwoods America, for sure. Missus, actually. Katie couldn't believe a dime like her was married to that roast beef, Slater. He was either rich and they lived ironically, which would explain their daughter's outfits, or there was something else there that Katie couldn't see. Maybe he was really, *really* funny...

Nothing funny, though, about the fight he took on with Randall's killer when she and Sam had run into him at the dam. She replayed that scene begrudgingly, one detail growing more puzzling the longer she fixated on it: Slater's use of the word "brother" twice when he addressed the murderer. He'd seen the bodies... Surely, he understood what the guy had done...

"Um, Killian? Does Slater have a brother?"

"Not since he was a teenager, dear. Why? Figuring to get whatever piece of that you can get, knowing *he's* off limits?"

"Not at al—" Katie faltered at Killian's intense eye contact warning her to be careful how she answered. "I mean, no, that wouldn't matter anyway. I'm not...available, either. It's just that he mentioned 'brother' a couple times to the man hunting us, so I thought—"

"A lot of men like him call everyone 'brother.' Have you ever heard Hulk Hogan in front of a microphone?" Bobby added helpfully.

Killian silenced him with another warning look. Clearly, she didn't like anyone talking about her husband.

They walked past the dam. Either animals or the monster had dragged off Randall and Trent's bodies. Katie was mildly relieved, since she hadn't prepared herself mentally to see them again.

The sight a few hundred yards up the road stopped Sam, Bobby, and Katie in their tracks. Killian continued on as if there weren't several logs across the road and a disabled Caterpillar in the center of the highway. A black F-350 parked a short distance away on the shoulder with the Cat's trailer. Katie sighed and jogged to catch up to Killian.

Red smears and splatters colored the seat and windows of the Cat's cage. Katie recoiled as Killian ran her finger over the blood and put it in her mouth.

"Spilled about 36 hours ago, give or take a few hours. You'd think the pi—...that is, *police* would have been here by now," Killian said as she got out to look around for more clues.

Katie left her to it and walked along the highway to a bend in the road. Around it, orange construction barricades had been set up across both lanes. She went back to the Cat where Samantha and Bobby hurriedly talked to each other. Killian had left the highway to poke around in the forest.

"The keys are still in the Cat, Katie," Sam said. "Maybe we can get these logs off the road ourselves."

"Do either of you know how to operate this thing?"

"Can't be harder than driving my uncle's tractors on the ranch." Bobby shrugged.

While Bobby climbed up to the cage, Samantha stood dutifully by with her hands clasped, shaking slightly; with fear or hope, Katie couldn't tell. Katie went to follow Killian. Around a few trees and next to Lake Creek, she found Killian standing with her hands on her hips over a heap of gore with a construction safety vest. Katie vomited into the creek at the sight of it. Mid-spew, an explosion from the highway shook the ground. A rush of hot air blew past them.

"Well, that was a clever trap," Killian said, not having reacted other than to look in the direction of the highway.

Katie knew what she'd find before moving. She stopped after a few steps and dry-heaved. Her already-upset stomach revolted against the idea of running; her mind rebelled against having to witness the aftermath which surely awaited her. Killian put her hand on Katie's back and gave her a little push, encouraging but stern.

Though Bobby's fate was clear even before they emerged from the trees, Katie wasn't prepared to see Samantha with an iceberg-shaped hunk of glass sticking out of her neck. The explosion had thrown her body across the road, twisted and riddled with shrapnel.

Killian approached the smoldering wreckage, past the point that Katie couldn't bear the heat. Katie retreated from the inferno and went to check Samantha's body, even though she had no hope she'd still be alive. Katie had no idea what she could have done to save her anyway. Standing over the body with the heat of their potential salvation warming her back, Katie didn't know what to do to save herself.

She turned around to see Killian approaching, a slight char around her face, arms, and chest above the dress line, her hair highlighted by burnt orange.

"That was a bomb. Rigged to the cage. There's no way that thing could have exploded *that* severely otherwise, even if you threw a match into the gas tank," Killian said as she gave a glance around Katie to Samantha. "Poor sinners."

"W-what?" Katie managed. "Are you *that* religious?"

"Religious? Not at all, dear. Why?"

"You're judging my dead friend for no reason."

"I said 'poor,' didn't I? And I'm not wrong. Now, what do you want to do? Go back to camp or get to the resort?"

"I can't just leave her here."

"If you want to carry her body for miles, go ahead. I'm going to hunt down the man that's causing all this."

"Alone? Who *are* you?"

"No one to mess with. Slater warned the man to leave us alone until our vacation is over. Now it's time to teach *him* a lesson."

Katie didn't get whatever metaphor Killian used, nor how she could be so nonchalant about it.

"You sound insane. You know that, right?"

Killian flashed a deadly grin that made Katie retreat a couple steps.

"You're safer with me, dear. Until Monday."

"I don't get you. I'm...going to the resort."

"Suit yourself. I won't twist your arm off."

As Katie continued along the road towards the resort, she thought something kept passing between trees in her periphery. Each time she stopped to look, the movement stopped as well. Her heightened, fearful imagination had her seeing movements on both sides of the road the farther she went along.

There was an unmanned gas station at the junction of the highway loop and the main road. As she cut across the deserted lot, footsteps rapidly approached from behind. She turned to see a man with one eye moving straight at her, his hands outstretched in the air, fitted to be joined with her throat.

Before he reached her, a large object swung in from the side and smashed him across the face. The thick branch exploded in a puff of splinters and the man fell on his back. Killian stood over him and jammed the remaining jagged edge of the branch into the man's stomach. Katie came around and kicked him in the side repeatedly, then the side of his head. Killian put her left nails into his neck, drawing black blood, then hooked her right nails into a claw and thrust them into his chest.

As her fingers sunk through his shirt, into his flesh, the man swung his arm out and caught Katie's foot. He yanked her leg, sending her sprawling on her back. Katie rubbed her head and looked up to see him grab Killian's throat. She let go of his chest and clawed at his hand. Despite all her strength, he was able to keep his grip and stand up on his own, even as she tore away strips of flesh from his arms and face.

Katie got back to her feet and shoved the branch further into his stomach, twisting it in all directions, pushing past her squeamishness of splinters. He swung Killian's body into Katie, knocking her back to the ground. She remembered she had the gun the first time she fell, but had elected not to bother with it. She thought it'd be a waste of effort and bullets, considering the last time she'd encountered the man. This time, she decided to take advantage of his preoccupation with Killian to get a better shot.

She scrambled to her feet again, pulling the gun out. She ran to his blind side and shoved the barrel of the gun into his empty eye socket. Before she pulled the trigger she heard a snapping sound from Killian's neck. Katie fired, blowing the man's head back and releasing a puff of mist out the other side. He fell onto his back with Killian's limp body falling to his side.

Katie put the gun back in her waistband after touching the barrel to make sure it wasn't going to be too hot to touch her butt. She ran the rest of the way to the resort. The sheriff's presence that had been several cars strong earlier that week was down to only one—and the remaining car was empty. She went into the front office and demanded to know where the deputy was. The receptionist pointed at the store, then asked if Katie was alright. Katie left without answering.

She jogged down to the store to find the deputy shooting the shit with a fisherman, discussing the best sort of bait to use for the southeast end of the lake.

"Sir, we need your help."

"What is it this time? Another theft?"

"No, another— Can we talk outside please?"

After leading him to the dock, Katie gestured across the lake to the western campground and recounted all that had happened. He looked at her skeptically when she said the man got up after being shot four times in the chest.

"I'm not pulling your chain, sir. There are teenagers and a family with young kids over there. We're all scared to death. The man was doing everything he could to hem us in. Why haven't you looked into the blocked highway? Did you not hear that explosion an hour ago?"

"We've been a little busy with the murder in the laundry room and the theft of all the beer in the general store the other night. These sorts of things don't happen around here. We haven't been up here in decades—not for anything close to this, let alone all the stuff you're saying."

"Okay, well, can you call this shit in? Bring more cops back here? Get the highway cleared?"

"I can't just do that on your word, ma'am. Take me to the campground."

"Fine, whatever you need to believe me and help us get home. I'll show you up by the gas station something that will prove I'm not lying about *any* of this."

They got into his car and drove to the station. Katie couldn't believe *her* eyes. Neither the man nor Killian were there, only a black blood splatter on the ground. From the car it looked like oil from any leaking car.

"I don't understand! I shot him in the head!"

"You *what*? You're armed?" The deputy made for his weapon but Katie threw up both hands immediately.

"It's not what you think! Here, the gun is behind me. Take it! I don't want it!"

The deputy reached across, lifting the back of her shirt to get at the handle. Glass exploded from the driver side and showered across Katie's lap. An arm shot through the window and pulled the keys out of the ignition, then jammed them up into the surprised deputy's neck. The contents of his jugular veins sprayed all over the inside of the vehicle and Katie.

Katie grabbed the deputy's pistol from his holster and fired at the man's torso again. The police-issued gun had much more kick to it, nearly dislocating her shoulder when its unexpected force threw her arm back into the passenger door. The man fell, out of sight. Katie grabbed the deputy's shotgun lying close to her leg.

Upon exiting the vehicle, she slipped the deputy's gun into her front waistband, then clicked the safety of the shotgun off. She aimed it towards the ground as she walked around the vehicle. The man splayed out near the door. He'd pulled out the branch from his stomach and his clothes were soaked with black blood. Somehow, all the scratches from Killian's claws had healed.

Katie thought better of getting into point-blank range—that'd already backfired on her once she'd kicked him. Dozens of horror movies flashed in her mind. Although maddeningly unhelpful as she'd tossed and turned while trapped at the campsite, they helped her remember to pump the shotgun.

As if in response to her thoughts, his one good eye opened and he threw the bloody keys curled in his palm at her face. She shot reflexively towards him, but only tagged the side of his leg. She backed away from him, realizing how futile *any* guns were. He crawled to the keys and rolled back towards the vehicle before she pumped the forearm. She shot him in the back when he stood up, propelling him into the side of the car.

He opened the door and dumped the deputy out while she pumped again. At the sound of the engine revving, Katie backed away. The car lurched into motion. Katie had to choose between running or making a stand. She split the decision of not wasting another round on him: Nothing could slow *him* down, but—

Before it was out of range she shot the back tire, causing him to skid into the gas pump island and knock over one of the two pumps.

Katie pulled out the gun from her back waistband and shot at the growing pool of gasoline. Nothing happened. She shot again at the damaged pump. Still nothing. The man got out of the car and stared at her, breathing deeply, as if charging up before rushing her.

Someone crashed into her side, pushing her away from the scene back to the highway loop.

"This isn't a movie, dear. Fire wouldn't have stopped him, anyway," Killian said as she ran alongside Katie back to camp.

Katie wanted to ask what *would* stop him, but feared the answer and remained silent.

Chapter 13

Friday

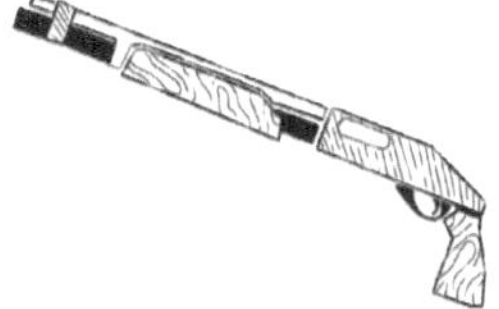

Kill Count: 22

Lynn cast out the fishing line so far Slater couldn't see the bait until it plipped into the water. She looked completely out of place, fishing in a black cocktail dress. Slater couldn't believe how inappropriately she'd packed for the trip. She'd already caught three above-average-sized trout, though, while the kids at the other end of the campground had only pulled in one. Slater kept his eyes out for any signs of the man terrorizing the lake and keeping them hemmed into the area.

An explosion from the highway worried him, but he would have felt it if Killian had become a victim. When they shared hearts of their kind, it bonded them in more than their delightful taste. Lynn might have felt it on a much smaller level, after they dined on her little brother's, but Slater and Killian had shared far more hearts together over the years; theirs beat as one.

The explosion caused the kids and the Hunt family to huddle up even more. To help distract them, Slater suggested they work on catching dinner since their food supply had dwindled. He could certainly send Lynn into the forest for chipmunks, squirrels, and racoons, but most of them hadn't appreciated Killian's wild rodent offerings the other night.

Lynn fished for hours, using all three of the Hunt's licenses so they didn't go over the total allowed of fifteen rainbows. Slater surveyed the area while Lynn reeled in another catch, dashing its head on a log before adding it to her collection. Two figures came into view from the north path into the campground. His hawk's vision immediately picked out his wife. The other had bathed in blood and carried a shotgun and a shiny Magnum in the front of her pants.

Killian embraced and kissed Slater. Her crispy eyebrows and bangs smelled wonderful. He frowned at the fading red marks around her neck. She pulled out of his embrace and loudly cricked her neck to both sides. He never tired of hearing that sound, but it usually came from his students.

The bloody woman rolled her eyes and pointed the shotgun at Slater's heart. It would be a simple matter to rip it out of her hands and impale her with it, and she could barely hold it steady. Killian's eyes kept him from breaking his vacation promise.

"What the fuck *are* you people?" she asked, pressing the barrel into his chest. It tickled.

"What do you mean, dear?" Killian asked.

"Stop calling me that! I heard your neck break. I saw you go limp and die. That man looks so much like you, Slater. I've shot him seven times—with *three different guns*. Your wife impaled him with a branch. He kept coming, and she says fire wouldn't have stopped him, either. So, I'll ask again," she said as she pumped the forearm," what *are* you people?"

Slater refrained from laughing aloud when his wife caught the unspent cartridge when it popped out of the chamber.

"You're obsessed with movies, aren't you, Katie?" Killian laughed and handed her the shell back. "You racked that back when we were at the gas station. And if you're trying to intimidate my husband, that's not going to work. Lower your gun, please. We're not your enemies this week."

"What the fuck does that *mean!* Slater said something like that at the dam. Are you both like *that monster?*"

Slater wasn't sure how much Katie needed to know. The fear in the campground had grown palpable, delicious, and at any other time it would have been a sheer delight to let it turn frenzied.

Except Slater had the Hunts to think about. He didn't care what happened to Katie and the teens before or after his family's vacation. In fact, they were valuable buffers between the killer's bloodlust and the Hunts surviving until help arrived.

"Do you need help, Daddy?" Lynn called from the shore.

"No, Lynn. Catch one more and take them to the others. Not a single fish more, though. You're about to max the licenses."

Katie lowered the shotgun. Her arms shook from holding it up too long. She handed it to Killian in defeat. "I don't know how to load this."

"You seemed to be working it pretty well from what I saw." Killian smiled as she released the magazine and pressed in the shell. She clacked it back into place and handed it to Katie with the barrel pointed towards Killian. Katie didn't seem to pick up on the magnanimous gesture as she yanked it back. "I don't think telling you what we are will help you in any way," Killian said. "But what I *can* tell you is that the key is removing the heart. Shooting it wouldn't do anything. Slater would have fallen down but gotten back up again after a few minutes, even at this range. The heart has to be fully removed. Even then, there's another step."

"Okay. And...? What's the other step?"

Before Killian answered, the auburn-haired girl came jogging to them. Her hand flew to her mouth in horror at Katie's blood-soaked appearance. She sputtered but couldn't get any words out.

"I'm...sorry about Bobby, Tera. He didn't..."

"Fuck! Did... Were you able to call anyone at the resort?"

Katie shook her head.

"Why don't you go clean up?" Killian said, gently guiding Katie towards Tera.

Katie gave Slater and Killian a reluctant expression, but Killian returned softness—an unsaid promise to continue their conversation later. As the girls dragged their feet off toward the bathroom facility, Lynn followed them with her trout. Killian moved closer to Slater and put her hands between his legs.

"Today was an *unbelievable* rush. I need you *right now*."

The girls headed to the shower facility, so that was out. He didn't want to stunt Killian's lust by hiking up to their campsite, either. Glancing towards the highway, he remembered the white F-350 and its big bench seat in the back, then swooped up *his* catch of the day.

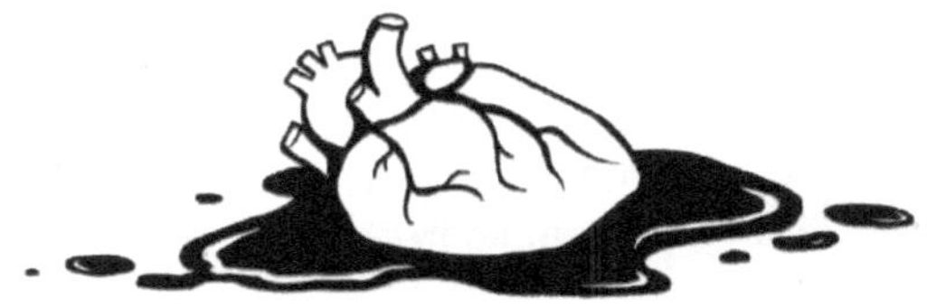

At the campfire before dusk, Killian cooked the trout guts for themselves and the filets for the rest of the group. Katie called a meeting to debrief everyone what they were up against as far as she knew. She'd given the magnum with its five remaining bullets to Timothy, the 9mm with seven remaining bullets to Ian, and held onto the shotgun with five shells and a sixth in the carrier.

Not a single one of those rounds would do any good. However, Slater considered the value the young sinners could provide as a buffer until he either neutralized the killer or they got the Hunt family safely on the road. If the expendables died too easily, though, it would be that much harder to outlast the killer.

"Hey, Tim," Slater nudged his friend's side. "How about your boys take the dog for a walk? Have any of the girls except Katie and the bossy one walk with them."

"Why not one of the guys? Or Ian with the gu—"

"In times like this, you want the shrill, unnecessary screams of a teenage girl to alert us to anything going on. Even if it ends up being over nothing, it's better than not knowing something's wrong."

"I'll go," Jessica said.

"No, you should hear this, too. But it's not for the boys to hear."

Tim talked to Tera, who convinced one of the girls to walk with them. The girl vowed to keep the campfire in sight at all times, but that was likely more for her own nerves than the boys. Lynn broke away from Killian and followed them. Slater didn't like her getting near Corey, but she would be a much better guardian; the other girl could be fodder.

"Alright, listen up, people," Slater began. "I'm going to tell you the type of man we're dealing with…"

He talked through dinner. Some of them lost their suspended disbelief while listening to him once he described what the man would likely do next.

"So you're saying this guy is being driven by something besides bloodlust?" Ian asked after Slater finished.

"It's definitely in the blood. He can't control it, though. He needs another half to temper him. Most of the men like him never find that half."

"Why is he being all clever and shit about all this?" Tera asked. "Why not simply come at all of us?"

"That's how they operate in the beginning. All blood and death, no nuance. There comes a time, if they live long enough, that boredom kicks in, but he hasn't reached the choosy stage, yet, where he decides who to kill and who to spare. That's also something temperance helps with. I'm afraid it will continue to be indiscriminate in his current cycle."

The fire crackled and sparked as each of them either stared into it, despondent, or into each other's eyes with worry.

"Something you should all understand is that this is *art* to him as much as it is a *need*."

"He's a sick *fuck*," the bossy girl spit. "I don't care how *he* feels about what he's doing. Just tell me how to kill him."

"I admire your guts, dear," Killian said. "But it's going to take a team to do it. Katie and I almost had him but it wasn't enough. Slater had his chance one-on-one and didn't finish the job."

"Hey now, wait a minute, sweetheart," Slater said as his blood temperature rose. "The *vacation* is what kept me from—"

"Alright, my love. I didn't mean you were incapable. If it helps in the next encounter, I grant you leave of your promise…"

Slater swept his eyes across the teenagers. He imagined how he'd end each of them. Wrap one in fishing wire and pull until they were nothing but discs of flesh and bone. Flay four of them and use their skins as tents and their bloody, skinless bodies as the poles. He'd pleasure himself near a tree while he watched Killian put her expert knife skills to use. He'd ravish Killian while they kept a teen's neck between their grips, fingers interlocked, and snap the toy's neck on climax. They'd save a few for Lynn to stalk and hone her burgeoning teaching skills. They'd take their time with—

"...for the killer *only*, Slater."

He scowled but he could see in her eyes that her imagination ran as wild as his own. It was difficult for them to hold back their pleasure at the circumstances, but Killian did a commendable job pretending like she had everyone's best interests in mind.

"Fine, so we work as a team," the bossy girl said. "What do we *do* to kill him?"

"Remove his heart," Killian said. "I see some of you girls getting squeamish. You knock that off right now. If he's immobilized near you, you do whatever you have to in order to get at that heart. Dig it out with a tree branch, rip his chest open, whatever. Then you bring it to me or Slater."

"Why to *you*?" Tera asked. "He still won't be dead at that point?"

"There's a ritual we need to perform to truly end his threat."

Fortunately, only a mild dissent came from a few of the kids who hadn't been involved in the fight so far. He appreciated that the ones who'd gotten close enough to death didn't ask more than essential questions. Tim and Jessica appeared calm and determined. They had the most skin in the game; the most to lose.

Slater put his big paws on each of their shoulders.

"Your family's safe with Killian and me. We promise."

Maggie came back to the campfire, growled at Slater and Killian, then dropped the attitude when she snuggled between Jessica and Timothy. TJ and the girl watching them followed close behind.

"Where's your brother, TJ?" Jessica asked.

"I don't know. I thought they were behind us."

Slater held his hand up for Tim to sit back down, then moved quickly out of the camp in pursuit. He tracked the footprints into the northern part of the campground. They weren't there. In the thicker part of the forest at the edge of the site, he picked up the sound of moaning.

He slunk into the trees and hid once he found two dark shapes in a well-hidden area, nearly pitch black. No normal human would have spotted the couple before stumbling into them. His superior night vision made out one figure leaning its weight into a tree with its hands while the other shape stood upright behind.

Lynn's moaning was clear, as was the boy's near-silent grunting. Slater squeezed the bark off the tree he hid behind. If they weren't on vacation the boy's back would be wrapped around a trunk. If he wasn't the son of his friend...

Slater gritted his teeth at hearing his little girl climax, followed shortly after by Corey. He planned to casually interrupt them by making rustling noises but got caught up in imagining the boy's torturous fate instead.

Lynn's rejection of her virginity would diminish her power. She could still be something great, but she'd never be as strong as her mother. Killian had strung Slater along for a decade with promises of what she would become if they waited. And waited. And waited. She'd been right to do it; her power almost eclipsed his own.

When they became one on their wedding night (and what a night that was), they were unstoppable as they took their lessons across the country to all the different lakes, cabins in the woods, haunted houses, banal suburbia, abandoned warehouses, cavernous high schools, college dormitories, frat and sorority houses...

Lynn had just thrown that all away for nothing, for a nobody. What was he going to tell Killian? That they needed to try again? As much fun as that would be, he'd put so much hope and pride into his little girl...

"Corey," Lynn said. "You're not into that *cheerleader* who hugged you, are you?"

Slater would have said 'cheerleader' with the exact same disgust as Lynn.

"What? How did you know about that?"

"It doesn't matter. Answer my question, please."

"No, I'm not into her. She was only thanking me for saving her life. She could have just shaken my hand or something, but I guess she wanted to do that instead. I'm sorry. I didn't ask her to do that."

Making out with cheerleader sluts. Lying to his and Lynn's parents about their night in the tent. Most-assuredly unprotected premarital sex. Taking his daughter's virginity and monstrous potential... Slater didn't like the idea of ending his friend's son's life, but come Monday, he wasn't sure he could live with anything less.

"I have something for you," Lynn's voice interrupted his brooding. "I saved this for us to share after our special night in the tent."

"Meat? Jerky? What is this?"

"Please eat it first. I have my own. We must eat it together."

Was she...? Was the meat...?

"Oh. This is really chewy... Okay, I swallowed it. What was it?"

"Its...spiritual. We're bonded now. We can sense things in each other. It will protect you."

No... She couldn't have...

"Thanks, I guess. Is it...laced with something? Sounds weir—"

"It's not, Corey. It's special. It will make you feel special, too."

"Okay. When does it—?"

"It might take a little while. But I can think of something to do while we wait."

Slater bit his hand as they started again. Murdock's heart... She was supposed to have eaten it when Killian took her back to their campsite. Lynn must have hid it while her mother's back was turned.

Lynn didn't actually understand why she had to eat the heart. It most certainly would *not* help the two of them sense each other. Slater and Killian's shared senses were earned through decades of deep love and bonding through good lessons and bad, not from eating the hearts of killers they took down together whenever their classrooms crossed.

Lynn was partially right, though, about the protection of ingesting such a heart; the near immortality of the being passed on that way, as well as some of their supernatural strength and regenerative properties. A tiny bit, like the half of a third Lynn gave Corey, wouldn't be all that much protection, but it would be better than nothing.

As much as it pained him, at least Lynn had done him a small favor in protecting Corey. Slater could concentrate more on protecting Tim, Jessica, and TJ.

Lynn's moaning picked up in volume and intensity. Slater thought again of Killian. What would she do? He never lied to her. He knew she'd control herself around Corey, at least until Monday, but what would she do to Lynn when she found out? She had put just as much stock into her daughter as Slater had. Would she—?

"I already knew," his wife whispered directly in his ear, her lips brushing against the lobe. She grabbed his hand and pulled him away from the tree as Lynn climaxed again into the darkness. Another couple of steps and Corey audibly followed.

At least Corey was attentive...

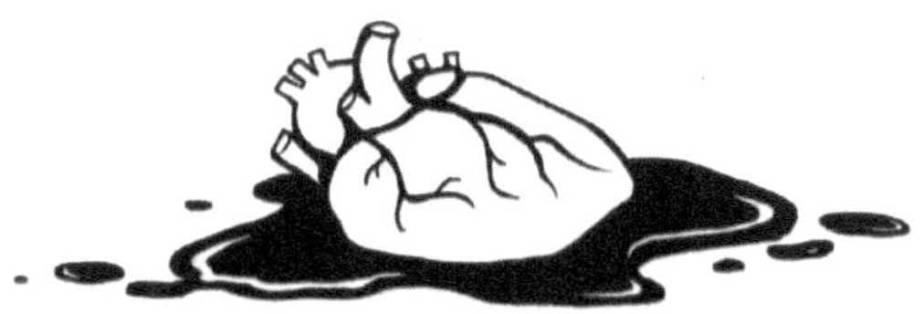

Slater and Killian stood watch to the south. Corey had been admonished by his parents for leaving his brother behind. Lynn came back to camp circuitously to avoid suspicion from the Hunts. Three of the teens stood watch at the other points around the camp site.

"So are you going to tell me how—" Slater started before getting interrupted by his wife.

"She couldn't keep that lie up with me when we got back to the camp. She thought for sure you were going to detect it. She hoped I'd help you go easier on her."

"She's taking advantage of my vacation promise."

"She sure is. Well, after she told me, it didn't matter explaining to her what she'd given up alongside her virginity. Once it's gone, it's gone. That doesn't mean she can't still go abroad like we dreamed. If she were to marry that boy, it would even make travel easier. She'd have to be extra, *extra* careful, but when I proposed that idea to her, there was a gleam in her eye, like she welcomed the challenge."

"I can't believe she lied to me so convincingly. Maybe... Maybe we have less to teach her than we thought. Can you imagine one of our kind living with a normal guy? I've heard of wives not realizing who the monsters they live with are until they get caught out, but not the other way around. It's...unique, anyway."

"There you go, my love. We still have reasons to be proud of her. I don't fancy trying for another, anyway. Those two were hard enough to pass, and I hate tiptoeing around them whenever I want to have you around the house."

Slater slid his hand up Killian's thigh, beneath her dress. It was difficult to control himself when she talked like that, and she knew it. He pulled her behind a suitable wall of trees and let her have him to her heart's desire.

CHAPTER 14

PANIC BREWING

KILL COUNT: 22

A SHRIEK FROM THE middle of the campground sprang Timothy out of their tent. He motioned for Jessica to get back inside with the boys and Maggie, then ran towards the bathroom facilities. From a distance, he saw Shawna backing out, dropping her shower caddie and throwing up. Tera ran past him at amazing speed, with Chase not far behind.

While those two tended to Shawna, Timothy crept towards the door, unsure what he'd see even with Shawna's scream as preamble. He scanned around for Slater, but he wasn't anywhere to be found. Timothy opened the door, and the stench of death assaulted him. He had always wondered what that smelled like, since it was mentioned in movies and books without any actual descriptors of what made a stench "death-like." This was it, though.

The light switch didn't work, but the small vents near the ceilings let enough light in to see dimly. There was a toilet and sink to the left, and a shower stall to the right, which had the lockable door that Killian had neglected to use. She didn't even respond surprised when Timothy had inadvertently seen her fully nude... It was more like amused—even though he only saw her for a millisecond before he turned away in embarrassment. Despite that rushed, fleeting moment, he couldn't keep his brain from taking a snapshot of her clean, utterly unbelievable body. He thought of it way too often. Her visage came to him involuntarily, even unprompted—further haunting Timothy's already spectacularly-bungled vacation.

That odd, intrusive memory flashed to him, then flushed down the drain in the center of the room like the pool of blood seeping into it from the shower. Steeling himself, Timothy pulled the shower door open. It was the young couple that had kept to themselves most of the time and never introduced themselves. They were naked in each other's embrace. His stomach churned the closer he got to them.

Their heads had been smashed together. Timothy couldn't hold back his stomach any longer and dove for the toilet. Clamoring came from outside. Wiping his mouth on his sleeve, he exited to find all the remaining teens huddling around the door.

"What's in there, Tim?" Chase asked.

"Nothing you need to see. Please back away, guys."

Unsatisfied with his non-answer, Tera did a quick headcount of her friends.

"Where's Molly and Garrett?"

Everyone looked around.

"It was them, wasn't it?" Tera asked.

Shawna nodded.

"Oh fuck! This is *my* fault!" Tera cried. "I told them to stop screwing in their tent the other night and to come here instead."

Shawna embraced Tera to calm her down.

"Guys, I'm going to ask you all to move back to the camp site. I'll try and figure out what to do," Timothy said, not at all sure what to do.

Chase didn't depart, though. She took a few steps towards him and lowered her voice. "Someone wasn't doing their job last night on guard detail."

That hadn't occurred to Timothy, but it made perfect sense when she said it aloud. "You're right, Chase. But let's not go around pointing fingers yet. We don't need to stir up more panic."

She nodded and walked back to the site, while Slater and Killian approached from across the highway. They must have gone back to their site after their shift to check on Murdock.

"Mornin' Tim," Slater said. "Waiting to shower—? Whoa, did you see something *else* you weren't supposed to see in there? You're white as a corpse."

Timothy pointed to the door and shook his head. Slater and Killian went inside and came back out with the same neutral expressions.

"We'll clean this up, Tim," Slater said. "Keep everyone at the site until we let you know it's done."

"What are you going to do with the bodies?"

"We've got a spare tent we can wrap them in until authorities find a way to get to us. Don't worry about the logistics of it. I move a lot of bodies in my line of work. I promise not to put them someplace where any of the still-living kids could stumble upon them and spike the tension."

Slater had such an odd way of putting things sometimes. Had he mentioned his line of work before? Timothy couldn't remember it coming up, and since it was their vacation, he didn't pry. People wanted to get *away* from work on vacation, not talk about it with strangers. In their current predicament, though, Timothy felt he needed to ask Slater his profession.

After the cleanup, of course.

Back at the site, Jessica prepared what she could from leftover fish. As unpleasant as the forest's rodents were to eat, Timothy knew they'd have to request the Slater family get more. Fishing off the shore wasn't timely, and only Lynn seemed to have any luck.

Chase admonished her remaining friends for being babies and not "growing a pair." Timothy approached them. "Now, Chase, that's not fair at all. No one is prepared to handle anything like this."

It was tough meeting her eyes knowing she indeed handled things better than anyone could expect from a young woman who'd just lost her loved one and a lot of her friends. But yelling at her friends wasn't helping. Chase's anger didn't leave her face, but she stopped chiding them.

"I don't know about you all," she continued, "but I'm sick of waiting for this asshole to pick us off one by one. Either we lay traps around the site, or we go after him."

"The Slaters will help—" Timothy started.

"They're unreliable, sir. They disappear without notice, and they only look at us with contempt," Chase said. "I wouldn't bet on them helping unless it serves them."

"She's right," Katie said. "Killian keeps making snide comments about us 'sinners' and she didn't flinch when Bobby and Sam... Just because she and Slater are strong as fuck doesn't mean they'll use it to help. They're only interested in their 'vacation' time—which ends Monday, apparently."

"Lynn will help," Corey piped up, startling Timothy. He thought he was still helping his mother.

Tera barked a laugh.

"Lynn will only help *you*, dude. That's fine and all, but it doesn't do anything for *us*. I'm with Chase. We need to do something if we're going to survive, and we can't count on the Slaters to be part of any of it."

"Okay," Timothy said. "So what do you guys have in mind?"

"Ian, what all do you have in your toolbox?" Chase asked the boy Timothy always saw tinkering around with the bus and boats. He wished he knew more about engines so he could be of more use. The boy made slow progress.

While the kids schemed, Katie walked with Timothy back to Jessica.

"There're four tires up the road, near where the Cat blew up. The problem is they'll only fit the F-350. Regardless of what we think of the Slaters, do you believe they'd let us all get into the back and lift us out of here if we get those tires?"

"I don't see why not. They've been helpful to my family, anyway. I'm sure even if they didn't want to help any of you they would if we asked them to."

"Okay," Katie said resolutely, giving her head one sharp nod as if committing to the idea, body and mind. "So how do we get those tires? We'll need four people, obviously. Ian and I should go. We'll be the fastest at removing the tires."

Timothy knew what she was getting at: she needed volunteers. She wouldn't broach it herself, knowing what happened the last time Timothy tried to help. However, Chase's defiance had rubbed off on him.

"I'll go with you," he said while meeting Jessica's worried look. "That removes all three guns from the campsite, though."

"I'll take one," Jessica said.

"You've never touched one in your life, Jess."

"Neither had you until Katie put that one in your hands. Hand it over, Tim."

He handed her the magnum. Though feeling a little less safe without it, he heartened that at least Jessica would use it better, especially if she needed to defend TJ or Corey. She had a maternal protection factor that could never be discounted, whereas Timothy's testosterone failed him more than once.

Katie brought him to the group of teens again and addressed them.

"Guys, we need to take Ian and a couple more of you to get tires for the truck. I know where they are. We can probably be back in a couple hours. As soon as that F-350 over there is outfitted, we can get the fuck out of here together. Who else wants to—?"

"Hold on, Katie," Chase interrupted. "We need Ian *here* to remove the damaged tires while you're away. Who else knows how to change tires?"

Jason and Luke shrugged, causing Chase to roll her eyes at them. Tera raised her hand part way.

"I knew there was someone here with *balls*," Chase said, throwing a withering scowl at the boys. "I'll go, too."

"Settle down, Chase. I'll go," Jason said. "What would the rest of them do here without you?"

Chase didn't rise to the bait and simply nodded.

"I don't mean to be morbid, but I want one more for insurance," Katie said. "If something happens to one of us, it will make getting those tires back nearly impossible."

"I'll go," Shawna raised her hand.

"Where is everyone going?" Slater appeared from behind a tree, startling everyone.

"We're getting tires for your truck," Timothy said. "Want to—?"

"I'd prefer Slater help Ian or get us more food," Chase said.

As much as her bossiness got under everyone's skin, Chase had a point. It would also help ease Timothy's mind if Slater stayed around the camp to protect Jessica and the boys if something were to happen.

"I'd appreciate that as well," Timothy added when Slater didn't respond to Chase.

Timothy hugged his boys and kissed Jessica, then joined Katie, Tera, Jason, and Shawna on the road.

"Want me to hold onto that shotgun?" Jason offered.

"Does it look like I'm *struggling* with it?" Katie left no doubt with the edge in her reply. Unless one of them professed to spending their weekends at the shooting range, Katie had already proven herself capable of using the guns; she wasn't about to be conned out of her protection with dumb, masculine bravado.

"Why do you think we haven't seen any hikers this week?" Shawna mused.

"The crime at the resort probably sent a lot of people home. The killer set that up, just like he did with the roads." Katie sighed heavily. "We've been played since we got here."

"Katie, how do you know we're not walking into another trap?" Tera asked.

"I don't. And probably... Maybe we *are*. But it's better than sitting around doing nothing."

"I'm surprised you wanted to go out again after... When I helped you clean off all that blood, you were shaking like crazy."

Katie waved off the concern and grimly marched forward. She put on a convincing brave face around the kids. If she hadn't broken down in Timothy's arms the other day, he wouldn't have been able to tell how much of a toll the situation took on her. He imagined what he would do if Corey were in her shoes. He picked up his pace and fell in beside her, then put his arm around her shoulder as they continued walking.

She sniffed once but maintained her composure onward. Katie leaned into him, ever so slightly, signaling she appreciated the gesture.

When Timothy parted from her, Tera joined Katie's side and held the hand that wasn't steadying the shotgun over her shoulder.

Shawna joined Tera's side and held her other hand. Jason only rolled his eyes.

"Pretending to be above affection doesn't make you tough," Timothy whispered to him a few paces back from the girls.

"Not trying to impress anyone, sir," Jason replied. "Not going to set up a hug circle, either."

They walked for a mile, past the dam, until they came upon the smoldering carcass of the Cat in the middle of the road.

"Either he came back to gather Bobby and Sam, or their bodies were taken by bears or something," Katie said as she gave the Cat a wide berth.

A black F-350 parked a few dozen feet up the road on the shoulder with the Cat's trailer attached—tires still mercifully intact.

"Hold on, guys," Timothy said, mustering his courage. "Katie, stay back. I'll check it out."

Timothy approached the truck cautiously. The back windows were tinted, so he squinted to see if there were any dark shapes moving inside the cab. He went around to put a foot up on the back bumper and gasped. He flailed his arms and lost his balance, falling back onto the flatbed trailer. The teens ran to him, but he held his hand up.

"Don't! You don't want to see Bobby and Sam that way."

Katie cursed and booted a rock from the shoulder into the forest. It made a satisfying *thwack* against a tree. Timothy hopped down from the trailer and approached the passenger side door. The handle lifted but the door didn't budge. The same thing happened on the driver's side. Jason helpfully tried it himself, as if his football strength would be the key. Timothy gathered his breath, then climbed into the bed, trying hard not to stare at Bobby's charred remains or Samantha's dead-eyed stare into the forest canopy.

He moved carefully to the toolbox installed in the back of the bed. Inside he found the truck's jack and tire iron. Jason got to work on the back tire with Tera's help while Shawna stood close to Katie and the shotgun on lookout. Timothy scooted on his back beneath the bed to locate the spare tire, then asked Jason for the iron. Once removed, he handed the iron back and pushed the tire out. Shawna rolled it next to the trailer. Katie assisted Timothy back to his feet and he brushed himself off.

"Jason, Tera looks like she knows what she's doing," Timothy said. "Maybe you and I can move those logs off the road."

Jason shrugged and followed while Shawna fell in beside Tera. The logs had been stripped of all bark and branches and bleached white by the sun. They were too big to pick up, but easy enough to roll off to the shoulder when Timothy and Jason pushed the same end of the logs together.

They finished at the same time as the last of the five tires were propped up beside the trailer.

"Well, assuming we get Slater's truck up and running, we've now got a clear shot out of here," Timothy reassured them. "Or if nothing else, maybe people will start driving through here again."

"Won't matter with the road work barriers up the road," Katie said.

"How far up the road are they?" Tera asked. Shawna put her hand on Tera's shoulder and started to protest, but Tera interrupted her. "How far, Katie?"

"Quarter of a mile, maybe? Just around that bend."

"You guys start moving the tires, I'll go move the signs."

"Wait, Tera, it's not safe to split up," Timothy said.

"I run track. I'll be right on your tails. Start moving. I'll grab the spare tire on the way back. The sooner you get these on that truck, the sooner we can go home."

"This doesn't feel right, T," Shawna said.

"You're all wasting time talking about it. Go!"

Tera didn't wait for another word and jogged away. Timothy looked at the others and shrugged, though his jaw set tight. He grabbed a tire and rolled it along the road back towards camp. The others followed. One more look back, and Tera disappeared around the bend.

CHAPTER 15
CALM AND SOLACE

KILL COUNT: 24

TERA MOVED THE ROAD work signs off to the side, then looked in the direction of the resort, only a couple miles away. Why weren't they trying that route again? Katie seemed to think the killer watched it. Tera considered the fifty percent chance that he could be doing that, or he could be watching the camp. He couldn't be doing both.

Tera kept her eyes sharp through the trees for any movement whatsoever. She peered back towards the bend before picking up her jog again for the resort. An uneasiness settled on her when she realized she couldn't hear birds anymore. Her pace slowed, then she stopped to listen, allocating her focus to one sense at a time.

She took a couple more steps before the hulking shape of the killer tromped out of the forest ahead. He stopped in the center of the road and stared at her. His hulking shoulders rose and lowered while flexing his hands menacingly at his sides. Tera briefly considered running straight at him, then past him at the last moment. If he was going to chase her, it might as well be on the way to the resort.

Then she remembered the man's great strength in the water, and how he didn't seem to need to breathe. He survived having his eye ripped out and being shot by Katie numerous times. Outrunning him was a dumb, desperate hope she tossed from her mind.

Tera took a few steps backwards, then turned on her heels and ran when he took his first step. She looked over her shoulder every few dozen feet. He didn't run but his pace was brisk. She slowed to a quick jog, realizing she would tire herself out well before getting to the camp.

After rounding the bend, she almost felt confident in the distance between them. She nearly jumped out of her sneakers at the sight of the killer coming out of the woods between the lake and road. He had simply cut through the bend rather than following it directly. One more unexpected shortcut like that and he'd be upon her. She lost hope in getting to the camp before him. If she couldn't rely on her own speed, she'd have to cripple his.

Tera stopped at the truck and picked up the tire iron that she'd left on the trailer. There was nothing else that might help her that she could see. The spare tire Timothy had removed still leaned against the trailer. She pictured herself rolling it along beside her as she jogged, keeping an eye out over her shoulder, losing balance, tripping over it, the killer catching up... It was a good idea at the time, in case something happened during their desperate plan, but she couldn't think of any good reason to bother then. All she'd succeed in doing was dying before reaching camp, or bringing the killer to everyone before the truck could be fixed.

While those thoughts caused her to hesitate, the killer didn't relent in his frightening approach. Tera climbed onto the trailer and stood away from his side. Up close his threatening face terrified her. How could anyone survive all the wounds he'd endured? In light of that and the fact he seemed to have mostly healed, what good would the tire iron do?

He stared at her while rounding the trailer. Tera kept herself on the opposite side, out of his reach. She thought about jumping off and running again once he was blocked on the other side of the trailer, but that would only delay the inevitable. He would still get to the camp, and all the guns waiting there wouldn't do anything to really stop him.

She didn't know how much she could trust Killian's knowledge of removing the heart. She didn't trust that whole family. She had a suspicion they'd do the same thing as Lynn—protect the Hunt family and leave the rest of them to fend for themselves. Slater and Killian had a constant sneer whenever they had to talk to any of her friends but kept genuine-looking smiles around the Hunts.

Tera realized she could only rely on herself and her squad, and they weren't anywhere close by. A new desperate thought emerged as she continued circling around with the killer. If she ran, she might get caught and killed. But if she could keep his attention, her friends would have a better shot at getting the tires on without the killer interrupting. If she lured him into the forest, she could circle back to the highway and get picked up by the F-350.

The killer interrupted her thought process by climbing onto the trailer. It jostled enough for Tera to momentarily lose balance. He got close before she swung the iron around and connected with his face. He staggered backwards as Tera's legs failed her from the impact and increasingly unsteady footing. She fell off the trailer onto her back on the hard-scrabble shoulder. Dust kicked up around her. The killer dropped down from the trailer with a fresh cut on his face. Did the ground shake or did she imagine that?

When he got within reach again, Tera swung the iron on top of his foot as hard as she could. While he didn't cry out, he paused enough for her to get another swing into the side of his knee. He buckled and knelt while she scrambled to her feet and took another swing at his head, connecting with a satisfying *thunk* that knocked him down. She took a whack at his heart. He clutched at his chest like a heart attack victim.

A few more hits against his head and he stopped reacting to the blows, becoming stiff and motionless. Although he was notably unconscious, his muscles didn't seem to loosen. Tera hopped back, aware of how quickly he could have her ankle in his grasp if she stood too close. If she had a knife, she would have gotten to work carving out his heart. She backed up, scanning around for anything sharp. The glass that Timothy had smashed out of the truck was small and uselessly cubed.

Tera went to the Cat and climbed onto the side. Peering into the cage for a toolbox, she found nothing. Then she remembered the toolbox on the back of the F-350. She jumped down from the Cat and climbed into the bed of the truck, keeping an eye on the killer in the dirt to avoid the gruesome sight of Bobby and Samantha.

The tools clattered as she searched for anything that could do the job. All she found was a thick flat-head screwdriver. It would be nearly impossible to get through his ribcage with that, though. The back part of the hammer could work. She clutched its wooden handle and peered back to the ground. The killer wasn't there anymore.

Tera swung around frantically. She heard movement behind her when it was already too late to react. A large hand gripped the back of her T-shirt. He flung her out of the bed, over his head, and into the shoulder embankment. Rocks banged into her back and shoulders. She hardly had time to feel pain before he advanced on her.

Tera smashed the hammer into his knee, hobbling him again. The handle broke after a hard blow to his head, splintering into a thick stabbing weapon. Tera thrust towards his heart, but she only hit a rib. He grabbed the handle out of her hand and slashed at her. The splinters raked across the arm she raised to defend herself. She backed out of his reach, then ran to the tire iron again.

The fight was pointless; Tera knew that. There was nothing she could do to get at his heart, let alone remove it. Tera turned and ran into the forest, parallel to the road. The killer stalked after her, seemingly in no particular hurry. Somehow, despite the differences in speed, she couldn't create a large enough gap to lose sight of him. Was she dreaming? The blood on her arms and the pain in her back were real enough.

She came to Lake Creek from its beginning at the dam. Tera thought about running back to the campground again, but in order to buy the camp as much time as possible, she decided she'd run along the creek to the north. The killer also seemed to have a moment of reevaluation at the crossroads. He stopped up on the road, turning back and forth between the campground and creek. He took a step towards the camp.

"Hey! *Asshole!* Over here!" Tera waved and jumped.

He turned his head slowly to her but didn't move. Tera knew the saying about a bird in the hand being worth two in the bush—did *he?*

She took a few steps towards him to entice him to chase. It worked. He stormed towards her again. She turned and ran, this time keeping him within her sights rather than trying to outrun him.

Further up the creek, while checking back on the killer, she tripped into a mess of putrid red muck. An orange vest was the only identifying characteristic of the person she fell into. Her stomach rebelled and she vomited, adding to the horrid mess. The killer got close enough to grab for her before she swung the tire iron into his head.

As he staggered away, she stood and made to ram his good eye with the open socket of the tire iron's arm. He recovered in time to catch it and ripped the iron out of her hands by thrusting her weight away from him. She lost her grip, nearly dislocated her shoulder, and fell backwards into the creek. Sputtering and trying to keep her head above water to see what he was doing, she re-verse-crab-walked farther into the creek.

Her hand purchased a hefty but small-enough rock to throw. As the killer advanced into the creek she threw it at his head, hitting him above his good eye and rewarding her with a pitiful groan. Tera threw another. Then another. The killer moved towards her slower. As much as he could survive anything she threw at him, he obviously didn't *like* the pain. As he turned to get out of the creek Tera shotput a heavier rock, hitting him at the base of his skull and knocking him to the bank face first.

Tera pushed through the water, feeling like she was running in a dream again, then picked up the larger rock that had just felled the killer. She brought it down on the back of his head. He put his hands up to protect himself and she smashed his fingers until they jutted out in multiple unnatural directions.

"Why...won't you...*die!*" she screamed between blows.

As he rolled over, he used a mangled hand to dig into the bank and fling mud into her eyes. Tera threw herself backwards into the creek, opening her eyes beneath the shallow water as she swam to clear her face and put distance between herself and the killer. He splashed behind her, getting closer. On the other side of the creek she struggled to her feet. He was mostly submerged, splashing halfway across the waterway.

Tera's ankle caught fire as she stepped awkwardly between a rock and log. She collapsed on the bank and rolled back into the creek, unable to find purchase to stop herself. Beneath the water, a hand grasped for the back of her neck—she could feel the current from his action. He missed and his fingers caught the fabric of her shirt instead. He ripped it upwards. Tera's shirt choked her as he lifted her out of the water. Instead of choosing a new handhold, he slammed her back down. The threads of her shirt tore mercifully on the second slam, and she struggled out of the shirt and his grasp.

She kicked away from him as she tried to stand, but the pain in her ankle was so great that she fell backwards again. The killer stood over her and grabbed her neck with both hands, then held her beneath the water. She put her hands around his, but his grip was crushing. He pressed the back of her head into the rocky bed. She dug her nails into whatever flesh she could reach. Her strength waned the longer he held her under, but his stayed firm, unyielding.

Tera kicked her legs out uselessly, causing her ankle to burn more. Her limbs lost their strength and she stopped thrashing. She stared up through the water to the man's neutral expression. Couldn't he have bothered to *look* like she'd sufficiently wasted his time?

She should have gone back with Katie and Shawna. But then he'd be on them there, too.

A sense of calm and solace took over as she fooled herself into believing she'd accomplished something—she'd given the rest of them time to escape. Her hands let go of the killer's stranglehold and she opened herself to death.

Above the water's surface, a blurry, black object appeared next to the killer's ear. Part of his face exploded outward through his nose, dappling the water with black splotches. His grip loosened but all his weight fell on top of her, keeping her pinned to the creek bed. The water dyed opaque with the killer's blood. In the darkness, Tera accepted it as her last moment. Despite the contaminant gore swirling around her, she kept her eyes open, searching through the black for that pinprick of sun everyone's supposed to see at the very end. She felt light. So light.

She couldn't see who lifted her out of the water as she sputtered and sucked air back into her lungs. Whoever pulled her out, she hugged them tightly. Tera shivered uncontrollably, edging into shock. Her savior pulled one of their arms out of her embrace. She jumped when they fired a round into the killer's body. The sound threatened to rupture her water-logged eardrums. A high-pitched whine exploded through her head.

Too late she let go, put her palms to her ears, and screamed. A soothing hand grasped her bare shoulder, then Ian's face appeared before hers as he crouched down to her eye level.

"Are you okay?" his voice muffled through her damaged hearing.

She hugged him again, forgetting all about the killer. Ian struggled out of her grasp and fired. The crack didn't hurt as much but the ringing intensified. She faintly heard the killer fall into the water. Ian grabbed her shoulders and moved her away, then sloshed back to the killer and fired directly into his heart. The killer's stiff body floated down the creek.

Ian went back to Tera and offered his hand while averting his gaze from her black bra. She took his assistance, then leaned heavily onto his shoulder; she couldn't put any weight on her damaged ankle. They staggered out of the creek and up the bank. Ian turned back to keep an eye on the killer while removing his T-shirt. He handed it to her without turning around, his ears turning red.

Tera struggled to put the wet shirt on but finally managed it. She limped to him and embraced him fully from behind, clutching his bare chest with both hands. She didn't want to let go, but he gently took her hands in his and turned around. Ian offered his shoulder and they limped back towards the road.

"Thank you, Ian. How did you find me?"

"Heard you shouting from the dam. I was *this close* to running past it."

His voice cleared up as the ringing dissipated from her ears.

"Did something happen? Why are you here?"

"Once they got back with the tires and you weren't with them, I started running. Chase yelled at me to stop but I ignored her."

"We're almost done, right? Once they get those tires on..."

"I wouldn't count our chickens yet. Wait until we're on the highway and this goddamn lake is behind us."

"Do you think he's still a danger? I saw you fire into his heart."

"We can hope, but if Killian was right about needing to *remove* it..."

Though it provided no literal respite, Tera felt better being back on the road after Ian helped her climb up the embankment. Once on level ground, she sat down on the warm pavement and took her shoe and sock off gingerly to find her ankle swollen and red beneath.

Ian winced at the sight of it. The lightest touch sent lightning bolts through her foot. The injury was worse than freshman year when she stumbled out of the starting blocks, then tripped over the first hurdle right onto her face. Only Peter didn't laugh at her, and he was the only one who cheered her up. She developed a close bond with him from that day forward.

"If no one's got any pain meds back at the camp, I should still have a little bit of weed left. It might help," Ian said, standing and extending his hand.

Once she was up, Ian showed his back and bent his knees.

"Are you sure? It's like a mile back, isn't it?"

Ian nodded over his shoulder, and Tera climbed onto his back, hugging around his neck. For a scrawny burnout he didn't seem to have much trouble with her weight, but she still felt badly for burdening him. His adrenaline must have been spiking at the same time hers diminished. Every hundred feet or so Tera looked over her shoulder to make sure the killer wasn't coming after them.

Tera asked Ian to stop before they came into view of the campground. He let her down, then leaned back against a tree to catch his breath and recover his strength. Tera glanced around, satisfied no one was watching and there was no danger looming nearby. She put her hand on his chest and the other hand on his cheek as she drew in closer. She kissed Ian in a much less-chaste way than she ever kissed Peter.

Ian returned her kiss, but didn't put up any resistance when she pulled away from him.

"Don't get any ideas, Ian. I'm thankful for you saving me, but..."

"You have a boyfriend. And you hinted that you're not into guys. *And* you're on your period."

Tera snorted.

"Jesus, it must have sounded like I hated you; throwing out every excuse in the book."

Ian shrugged and smiled.

"Guys like me are used to it. I didn't think anything of it. You're allowed to not want to hook up with someone just because they're around. Besides, I wasn't lying about my girlfriend, either. Though that's doomed now that I've slept with Amber…"

"Well, if you're determined to tell her…"

"You think I shouldn't? What kind of scumbag would that make me? She doesn't deserve that lie hanging over us."

In another life, Tera could see herself taking Ian for her own, and probably punching Amber for trying to sink her claws into him. The idea fluttered her stomach and she leaned into the unexpected feeling, kissing Ian again. Tera was all too aware it might be the last chance she could ever thank him, and whether they survived or died, she may also never see him again.

Her second kiss was longer and more insistent. Ian only took what she gave, even when she pressed into him to take pressure off her ankle. Her arms squeezed around his neck. An unexpected warmth she'd never felt before blossomed from her chest and pushed her to seek out his tongue with her own. Though he didn't touch anything on her body but her upper hips, she would have let him touch elsewhere.

Perhaps out of respect for Tera previously expressing disinterest, perhaps in an attempt to avoid more guilt after his trespassing with Amber, or even that Ian had his head on straight and this wasn't the time or place to make out, her hero didn't take any further advantage of her. Ian was the one to pull away.

Without a word, Ian turned for her to climb on his back again, and they entered the campground to the sound of Chase arguing with everyone.

Chapter 16

Tailgating

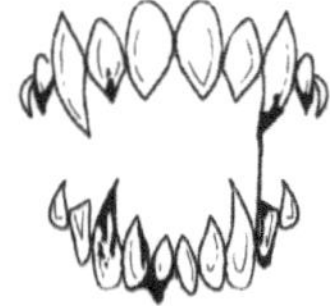

Kill Count: 24

Katie appreciated Ian not hesitating to run after Tera once Timothy explained what happened. Ian's help would have sped up getting the tires onto the truck, but Jason, Timothy, and Slater were enough. Chase yelled at Ian's back to not split up again, but he didn't respond or slow down.

"I want to help her as much as anyone," Chase said to the others. "But now there's *two* we have to wait for before we can get out of here."

"One step at a time, Chase," Timothy said. "Tires first. Maybe they'll be back before long, and it won't matter."

Katie kept watch around the truck with the shotgun at the ready while the men worked on the tires. Chase directed her friends to grab only necessities from the remains of their tents and put them into the back of the F-350. They laid out sleeping bags on the metal bed to ease the coming uncomfortable ride.

If they counted Tera and Ian, from the bus that once carried eighteen teens, only eight remained. Misty remained close with her boyfriend Luke, while Jason made himself useful helping Timothy and Slater. Shawna paced back and forth, obviously worried about

Tera. Amber didn't help much other than to do as Chase directed—after Chase had to repeat herself. The teens planned to sit in the bed of the F-350, and Katie would stay with them while the Hunt and Slater families took the cab.

Killian and Lynn came down from their camp across the road as the last tire was locked in place. Timothy and Jessica exchanged glances. Katie stood close enough to hear Timothy ask Slater where his boy was. Slater looked at Timothy gravely and explained they didn't want to alarm everyone further, but their boy had been a victim of the killer. Jessica and Timothy attempted to console the Slater family, but none of them seemed particularly broken up about it.

Katie didn't trust a single word that came out of any of that family's mouths. On top of that, she wanted to be as far away from them as possible to avoid finding out what their vague comments about what would happen on Monday really meant. It was late Saturday afternoon, and they planned to leave soon, so hopefully "Monday" would never come with them in the same vicinity.

The two families promised to drop the teens off in their hometown of Myrtle Creek on the way to California. Katie wanted nothing to do with them further than Myrtle Creek, and she planned to arrange her own transportation from there.

If anything, maybe Katie could stay at Tera's while she sorted herself out. Or at Chase's. She rubbed people the wrong way, but Katie recognized she'd only taken charge in a situation that no one else wanted. She dealt with the grief of her boyfriend's death and the deaths of most of her friends without letting it affect the job she felt she had to do in protecting the rest of them.

Katie barked at Amber to stop whining and either help or shut up. Amber continued sulking but stopped complaining. Everyone claimed their spots in the truck before Chase shouted for them to stop.

"Tera and Ian aren't back yet! We're not going anywhere without them."

"We'll pick them up on the way," Slater said with no conviction.

"What if they're not on the road and we pass them?"

"What if they're *dead*?" Amber sounded a little too much like she wanted that to be true.

Chase glared at Amber. "Tera would wait for *you*, bitch. And she'd *never* hope to find you dead."

"I'm so *sick* of listening to you!" Amber shouted, then made to lunge at Chase but Timothy got between them.

"That's enough, girls! We need to get on the road, but we'll go slowly and keep our eyes out for them."

"What if we don't see them, sir?" Chase said with her hands on her hips. "We'll just say, 'oh well,' and pick up speed? What if they're still alive and got chased into the forest? Or they're hiding? Or *something*?"

"Ian's got that gun. Maybe they can make it to the resort and get help there?"

"The resort is a lie, Tim," Katie said. "Bad things keep happening whenever we try to get there. I think we need to pass it like it's not there and get the hell onto the main highway to Roseburg. That said... If we're in the truck and moving, it's less likely the killer will come upon us and blow this whole plan up."

"Fine," Chase said as she folded her arms. "*You* can *all* go. *I'm* waiting for Tera."

Jessica came over to put her hand on Chase's shoulder.

"You're a good friend, Chase. But Katie's right. We're safer in the truck. I promise Slater will drive slowly. But we need to get moving before we lose the remaining daylight."

Chase shrugged Jessica's hand off and backed away.

"You chickenshits go. I'm waiting."

"What if we find them?" Timothy said. "Then we'll have to come back for *you*, complicating our escape. Come on, Chase. We're not leaving *anyone* behind. Get into the bed."

Shawna also attempted to convince Chase to get in. She had even more of a reason to want to wait for Tera, but preferred searching to waiting. Chase's expression remained stubborn, until they all looked up to see Ian carrying Tera on his back into the camp. Shawna and Chase ran to them and helped get Tera down. Her ankle looked broken, and she wore Ian's shirt for some reason. Her hair was a damp, disheveled mess, her eyes were red and puffy, and she had deep purple finger bruises around her neck.

They helped her into the truck bed while Ian ran to get his stuff. The Hunt family climbed into the backseat of the cab while the

Slaters sat in the front. Maggie became agitated and growled at the Slaters. Katie opened the back window for Maggie to sit in the bed with her and the teens, assuring TJ she'd be okay. The dog ignored everyone but Tera, much to Tera's annoyance. She tried to push Maggie away before quickly giving up. It didn't seem she had much fight left in her after whatever had happened out there...

Ian shut the tailgate and climbed over, then rapped his fist against the side of the truck for Slater to move out.

"Got anything left in that gun?" Katie asked Ian as the truck jostled them getting onto the pavement.

"Should have three shots left. Yours?"

"Five shells loaded, one in the carrier. Jessica's magnum has five."

"Fat lot of good any of them do permanently, but they're good at buying us time. The guy quit moving after I shot directly into his heart. He just floated down the creek and stopped chasing us."

Katie nodded. She thought he'd been dead before, too. She was tired of talking about it. Tired of thinking about it. She wanted to fall asleep like Tera had instantly once they got onto the smooth road. Shawna huddled into Tera's side and Maggie curled up against her other side. Katie determined to keep alert. Jason or Luke might handle the shotgun better than her, but the layer of invulnerability it provided simply from holding it wasn't something to relinquish.

Slater drove them past the dam, around the wreckage of the Caterpillar, and past the roadblocks that Tera had moved. Katie's fear didn't dissipate even as they passed the gas station. A construction crew had set up equipment to fix the damaged pump island, but it was early evening and their shifts must have been over. She cursed under her breath that the killer had the foresight to remove the murdered deputy and his car.

She peeked through the back window to check on the fuel gauge. Slater noticed her in the rearview mirror and said they had more than enough fuel to get to Roseburg in a couple hours.

Katie breathed a sigh of relief that was matched by the teens as they pulled onto the main highway.

Home free.

The highway traveled north for a tenth of a mile before curving around to match the bend of the lake. They drove a few miles in satisfied silence. Katie turned her attention from Tera's serene, sleeping face to movement in the corner of her eye. Through the windshield, something moved up along the highway.

"What is that?" Timothy asked Slater.

"That's the creek overpass..." Ian said, fear rising in his voice. "Slater, run him over!"

The teens and Hunt family murmured as Slater pressed down on the accelerator. The hunched, heavy-breathing, hulking form of the killer was unmistakable, even in the rapidly decreasing light of sunset.

"That's not going to do anything," Killian said to no one in particular and without raising her voice. To her, it seemed like a boring fact.

The killer's body disappeared below the F-350's grill with no impact. His body wasn't smeared across the pavement behind them, either.

"Do you think it was a ghost the whole time?" Amber whispered.

"Definitely not..." Chase replied.

"Things would make a lot more sense if that were true," Luke said.

He and Misty sat against the tailgate opposite Tera and Shawna's corner. Katie jolted as a hand reached up over the tailgate onto Luke's shoulder. Before anyone reacted, the hand clamped down, then pulled Luke up and over, sending him crashing to the pavement in a way that guaranteed a broken neck. Misty screamed for Luke, then leapt over the side of the bed and rolled through her landing along the shoulder of the road.

Slater swerved and slowed but didn't stop, despite Chase's protests to do so. The killer reached over the tailgate again and grabbed Tera's shoulder. Shawna cried out and held onto Tera's hands while Ian wrapped his arms around her waist. The killer tore violently on Tera's shirt. He'd dislocate her shoulder if he wasn't stopped.

Katie had no idea what the spread of the shotgun at that range would do. She could hit Tera, Ian, and Shawna if she fired. Steadying herself, she rose to get closer and be certain the spread wouldn't be a factor. The killer nearly had Tera up and over the tailgate before Maggie jumped onto his shoulder and tore at his neck. He let go of Tera and tumbled off the back of the truck. The dog landed on his chest and continued attacking his neck as Slater put distance between them.

TJ cried for Slater to turn around, his voice shrill and cracking. Jessica and Timothy tried to console him and explain why Slater shouldn't stop. Chase raged at Slater to turn around, drowning out TJ's cries. She wanted to go back for Misty. Slater and Killian insisted it was too late.

"Fuck all of you!" Chase screamed and jumped out the side as Misty had done. She picked herself up and ran with a hitch in her step after a tumbling stop.

Katie wanted to survive. She could sit safely in the truck and be free soon. Ghost or not, the killer couldn't keep up with the truck, and he'd be occupied by Misty, Chase, and the dog. But Chase and Misty risked their lives to save Darren, Timothy, and Corey without hesitation when their canoe was attacked on the lake, and the dog just saved Tera. Chase had adamantly demanded to wait for Tera, and she was proven right in waiting; the truck would have passed Tera and Ian without seeing them on the hiking path into the camp if they hadn't.

Chase, Misty, and the dog didn't deserve to be left behind, but Katie was okay with Slater's decision to prioritize saving the families in the cab. Katie made sure the safety was still on the shotgun, then dove off the side, rolling violently along the shoulder while trying to remain cognizant of the barrel's direction relative to her head.

When she stopped rolling, she felt like she'd been beaten for several minutes by sticks and stones, though it had only been a couple of seconds. She looked up to see the F-350 with no brake lights and shook her head. She heard grunting and skidding a few dozen feet further up the road.

Katie stood with some difficulty, the dizziness leaving her body slowly. She staggered cautiously towards the grunts. Jason had also jumped from the truck and was recovering a bit further on. Katie helped him up, then they jogged back to where Chase and Misty bailed.

The sun had nearly set, and there were no streetlights. They didn't have flashlights. Katie second-guessed the course of action, if only because blindness wasn't going to be much help to the girls. She would have threatened Slater with the shotgun to turn around, but she'd tried that once before, and they didn't seem fazed by a barrel pointed in their faces.

Jason didn't complain, but he limped along. He scoffed at her concern when she slowed down.

"I played an entire football season with worse injuries. Don't worry about me."

Katie nodded and kept her attention on seeking out movement. She clicked off the safety, then thought better of it and clicked it back on. In the dark she was liable to shoot Chase or Misty as much as the killer. They approached the general area Chase jumped from, but she had been on her feet and running to Misty almost immediately. Further along the road, they came to the spot that the dog attacked the killer.

Katie squinted down the highway as the last of the dull orange-blue faded from the sky. She found some spots of black blood trailing off the shoulder and into the forest. Jason walked past and Katie took up behind him, covering their six until they heard crying ahead.

Chase was hugging Misty a few paces away from Luke's lifeless body. Hoping not to startle them in the dark, Katie called out that they were approaching. Jason moved Luke's body from the center of the road to the shoulder while Katie shielded Misty from watching.

"What's your plan, Chase?" Katie asked, not at all eager to have to figure everything out herself.

"Back to the resort. It's the closest civilization to us. The next town in the other direction is too far on foot."

Katie agreed with Chase's decision and they started walking. "We'll come back for him," Chase said in a low voice to Misty. They walked for a mile, each with a limp, holding their thumbs out to any passing vehicle, though at that time of the evening they were scarce. None of them stopped anyway, even when Katie tried to hide the shotgun at her side.

Quick movements from the forest made the three kids huddle together while Katie clicked off the safety and stood between them, aiming into the trees in the direction of the noise. Her heart pounding out of her chest, she readied for the angry killer to burst from the darkness.

Katie pulled the trigger in a near-panic as something crashed into her legs. All she shot was the forest canopy as she tripped backwards onto the pavement. She looked between her legs to see whatever had knocked her down skitter off into the darkness. She sighed in relief when Maggie trotted back and rubbed against her arm, wagging her tail without a care in the world.

The teens swarmed Maggie while Katie clicked the safety back on and loaded the last shell from the carrier. After another quarter mile of walking, a pair of headlights slowed as it came upon them, though it was traveling on the other side of the road, heading to Roseburg. It stopped on the shoulder and the driver rolled down the window, but they could only make out the silhouettes of whoever was inside.

"Where you kids headed?" a youngish man asked with a drawl.

"Roseburg, sir," Chase answered.

"Nice weapon, there. Looks like what the poe-lease carry," the man nodded at Katie, then spat out the window at their feet.

"In case we come across a bear or something," Katie responded hesitantly.

"What're you kids doin' out at night walkin' on an empty highway?"

"Our car broke down and our phones don't work up here," Chase said without missing a beat.

"Well, we ain't goin' to Roseburg 'til next week. But we got us a cabin up the road with a landline. Hop in back and you can call you a ride from there."

Katie wanted to get the fuck out of the goddamned forest, not cozy up in a stranger's cabin, but what was the other option? Keep walking along the road until the killer inevitably showed up? The kids rounded to the tailgate and climbed in. Katie noticed a Confederate flag bumper sticker and it made her skin crawl. She weighed the pros and cons and was about to ask the kids to get back out when the driver called that he would leave if she didn't climb aboard.

After another second of hesitation, she unlatched the tailgate and helped Maggie up, then climbed in herself. The kids all huddled as close to the cab as possible after what they had experienced in the last truck. Katie kept the barrel of the shotgun aimed at the tailgate as the truck sped up. Maggie seemed to be on full alert, as well. Misty sobbed quietly while Chase continued to console her, but she didn't last long before breaking down into tears, too. She must have been thinking about Darren. Jason put his hand on Misty's shoulder as it shuddered.

The road bent around after several miles, putting them a further distance away from that damned lake.

Not long after, the truck turned up a dirt driveway that increased in elevation far higher than Katie liked. They jostled and rumbled over the pot holes in the rough road that only barely qualified as such. The truck eventually, mercifully flattened out and they came to a stop.

Katie clicked the safety off as a shiver went up her spine.

"Be on your toes, guys," she whispered.

The driver and passenger doors opened and two men got out.

"The fuck?" the driver said.

Katie looked over the side of the truck bed, shotgun at the ready below the rim. She was both relieved and angered to see the white F-350 parked in front of the cabin.

Chapter 17
Retirement

Kill Count: 25

Slater had enough of the kids behind him yelling at him. He had enough of TJ's crying over that stupid dog. Before he even had the inkling to turn around and yell at them all to shut up, Killian's hand rested on his thigh to soothe his rage.

If Killian had told him before their vacation started that she would continuously lesson-block him every day, allow their teenage prodigy to lose her sacred virginity to some random kid, not punish Tim for seeing her nude, all while someone *else* had the time of his life knocking off these stupid teenagers, he would have bet part of his heart he'd have strangled her by then.

But, for reasons he couldn't fully explain, her temperance only attracted him to her more. It helped that the week had featured some of their most memorable and gratifying love-making following the times she stopped him from acting on his nature. Maybe it was simply the realization that they were so intimately linked that she knew what he thought a second before he even thought it.

He never assumed he'd like that invasion of his psyche. He turned to her dark silhouette, the shape of her profile exquisite in the dying light. Her lips pulled back in a beautiful smile, calming him further. He put his hand on her thigh.

Lynn sighing and turning away from her parents affection struck a pang in his heart. She would never be able to attain such a level of intimacy with her future husband—thanks to the foolish tainting of her gift.

Slater noticed a dash light blinking suddenly. The fuel gauge dipped to Empty. The killer must have done some damage to the tank while he worked his way beneath the chassis to the tailgate.

"Sorry, everyone. Looks like we need to find a place to park."

"What's going on?" Tim asked.

Slater pointed at the gauge in answer. Tim sighed and relayed the information to his wife and the remaining teens in the back.

"Probably a good thing, anyway," the Black girl said. "Tera's burning up back here."

Slater didn't care about that, but he didn't like the idea of sitting along the shoulder until morning. He kept his eyes out for the next driveway. He turned off and rode up a steep one, towards a single light peeking through the trees on a pole outside a cabin.

Lynn and Killian exited the vehicle and circled the cabin before the others even opened their doors. He almost joined them when the Black girl tugged at his shirt.

"Sir, I'm sorry, can you please help Tera? Her ankle's swollen and she's shivering too much to walk."

Slater sighed and rounded the tailgate. The boy who worked on engines and the whiny girl helped Tera to the edge. Slater picked her up beneath her knees and shoulders and she put her arms weakly around his neck. Her skin burned, even through her clothing. He brought her to the cabin door where Killian opened it from the inside.

"This is wrong," Jessica said. "We can't just walk into someone's house uninvited."

"There's no one home, dear," Killian said. "And if anyone returns, we'll tell them about our dire straits. Slater and I will handle it. Whatever we eat or use, we'll leave some money behind before we depart."

Slater enjoyed the easy way she lied. They didn't have any need for money and never carried it, and even *he* believed her.

Tim hugged TJ and sat him down in a recliner. Jessica sat next to Tera as she lay on the couch and instructed the other three teens to look for medicine, towels, and blankets. Slater very much wanted to follow Lynn into the kitchen where Corey had walked a moment before, but at the last moment decided to hold back. She'd already screwed up her future and there was no changing that.

Slater stood near the door, watching Tera shivering. She'd been in a hell of a fight with the killer, that much was sure, and she somehow lived through it. Slater begrudgingly respected her; the same as Killian spoke of Katie's heroics once they returned from the gas station brawl.

Slater searched the cabin to determine the number of beds. There would definitely need to be some sharing. There was only one bathroom. The whiny girl locked herself in and had the shower running immediately. The Black girl stood outside, jangling the door.

"Amber, we're looking for medicine. Can't you unlock the door? No one's going to see you!"

Slater reached across the girl and squeezed the round doorknob tight, then twisted it until a snap came from inside the mechanism. He opened it a crack for the girl to slip in. She smiled up at him and closed the door behind her. He heard the mirror squeal while the girl argued against Amber's protestations.

Further down the hallway, another door wouldn't budge. His hand raised to break it open, too, when a headlight casted from the front window down the hallway. Another truck crunched over the rough driveway, then pulled to a stop with noisy brakes.

Slater startled Tim as they both reached the front window. Two men in trucker hats walked cautiously towards the F-350. He heard muffled voices, including a woman's. Soon Katie and the three idiots who'd jumped out of the moving truck came out from behind the smaller truck and were talking to the two men. That damn dog ran out from the darkness and scratched at the front door.

Killian was about to go outside when Slater put his hand on his wife's shoulder.

"I'll go."

"Slater," Killian whispered, "they have no phone here. We'll have to steal that truck..."

Slater nodded and walked down the porch. He was greeted by two handguns from the males who had gotten out of the truck. Katie pumped the shotgun and aimed it at the males' backs. Slater didn't stop walking towards them, despite their loud threats. He stopped a casual couple of feet away to address them.

"Guys, we're sorry to break into your house, but we're out of gas and we have a sick girl inside. I respect property rights, *believe* me. We'll pay for the night if you'll allow us the use of the cabin until morning. We really only wanted to use your phone but it appears you don't have one."

Katie put the barrel of the shotgun in the back of the more threatening male.

"What the *fuck* were you two planning to do with us? No fucking *phone?* Drop your goddamn weapons before I drop *you.*"

The men cursed and put their weapons on the ground. The male teenager left the two girls and picked up the guns, then held them out for Slater. Slater smirked and shook his head. The kid looked confused, then walked into the cabin, followed by the girls. Slater heard TJ's rejoicing over the return of his dog as the door opened.

Slater loomed over the two men as they scowled at him.

"Fellas, there's no reason this can't be civil. I know it's a huge imposition, but we'll be gone before you know it. Like I said, we'll make it worth your while. We just need to figure a way to get some gas in our truck and we'll be on our way."

"You know, I ain't heard a single request here. You's imposin' and dictatin' but you ain't askin.'"

Slater put his hand on the man's shoulder and squeezed in a threatening manner.

"It's how it's going to be, junior. I do apologize again. It behooves you to treat us well. We won't steal anything, we'll pay you for 'rent' if you like, we'll leave your house just as we found it. Hell, we'll even cook dinner for ya. My wife's an amazing cook. You won't regret it."

The two men muttered as they walked into their cabin. Katie lowered her shotgun and sighed. She brushed by Slater and sat down hard on the porch. She frowned out at the driveway beneath the light pole, scanning as if on self-imposed guard duty.

Fully trusting that Killian would back his threats if the men decided to cause a ruckus inside, Slater sat next to Katie and watched for the killer with her.

"You're such a prick, Slater," she said without looking at him.

"If you were driving, you might have weighed things differently. Family and friends in the cab. You think I should have stopped and put my family and the Hunts in even more danger?"

"There *is* no danger for your family. I watched your wife die. You're just like that man chasing us. Only for reasons I don't understand, you're helping some of us. I wish I knew why you always look so contemptuously at those kids, though."

"Force of habit."

"Most of them are pretty amazing. I hate teenagers sometimes, too. But sometimes...they surprise you."

"Tell me about it..." Slater mumbled, thinking of Lynn's behavior over the last week.

"I meant that in a good way."

"Mm. You look exhausted. Find a place to lay down inside. Killian and I will take up guard duty."

"I trust you two about as far as those rednecks," Katie muttered.

"Until Monday, we're your best protection."

"Killian said something about that, too. Your vacation. You're both creeping me out. I don't know what you keep threatening about *Monday*, but I'll take you both down if I think you're going to hurt those kids."

Slater unexpectedly found himself hoping that he wouldn't have to hurt Katie or Tera on Monday. He nodded at her useless threat and stood up to go inside. Tim greeted him and put his hand up on Slater's shoulder as he peered outside at Katie.

"Does she need a guard swap?" Timothy asked.

"Not from me, anyway. You're welcome to ask her yourself."

"Okay. Keep an eye on those two, please. They look...dangerous."

"I'll be the judge of that. You have nothing to worry about, Tim."

Tim ventured outside and sat next to Katie. Killian joined Slater's side and whispered that the two men had locked themselves in their room. He nodded and she went into the kitchen to prepare food with Jessica. Lynn came to him a few minutes later.

"Daddy, one of those men wouldn't stop staring at my chest. The other leered at the other girls. Can I teach them a lesson tonight?"

"If we're stuck here until Monday, sure. Leave them alone until then. Hopefully they'll remain locked in their room and we won't have to think about them. Your mother and I are taking care of it."

"Okay, Daddy."

Lynn went to sit close to Corey, causing Maggie to growl. TJ pulled her outside to stand with Tim. The teens huddled around Tera, trying to make her as comfortable as possible. The mechanic of the group noticed Slater watching and sidled next to him.

"You think that man's still chasing us?" the boy asked.

"Not sure. It would be pretty hard to pick up our trail, being on the road for miles before we got off."

"Not if we were dripping gasoline the whole way."

Slater cocked his eyebrow. The killer would have excellent night-sight, almost a hound-like sense of smell, and gasoline takes hours to evaporate.

"What would be your next move, uh, kid?" Slater asked.

"Ian. I say we steal that truck. Maybe they'd even appreciate the upgrade to the F-350 if you left it here."

"Dangerous to move your friend, at least until her fever breaks."

"We could go straight to the hospital in Roseburg. Keep her bundled in blankets. We need to get moving, or that man's going to find us soon. I also don't like the two guys we're stealing from. I'm willing to bet they have more guns in that bedroom."

"You have one. Katie and Tim have the other two. That boy that came in with them took both of their guns. Killian and I are watching for those two to make a wrong move."

"Why *are* we waiting? If you're so confident in stopping the rednecks from intervening, we could jack the truck, get to the Roseburg hospital with Tera and immediately send help back here for the rest of you."

"Ian, the killer isn't going to stop coming just because you drive to a new town. He has an urge to finish what he started. It's as sacred as the vow I made to my wife not to ruin our vacation. He's not going to come after my family, but he'll go after the rest of you until he's done. For now, you've got me and my wife for protection;

another twenty-four hours. If you're lucky, we can finish him before it's too late. It's best not to drag this anywhere else."

"If this was all you had planned we could have waited at the camp. Set traps. Tera wouldn't have been hurt trying to help get those tires. If that's all true, when you planned to drop us off—" Ian cut himself short. He was a smart one. He could see the realization settle in, followed by a tempered rage Slater knew all too well.

Yeah, kid. He'd have picked you off in Roseburg just the same, and we'd be long gone.

Slater redirected the focus away from speculations on his previous intentions. "You all came up with your own plan. I'm just going along with what you think is best."

"You know what I think?" Ian jabbed Slater's chest with the barrel of his handgun. "You and your wife are *studying* us. All that vague talk about knowing what the killer is and isn't going to do... Asking what I'd do... 'Going along' with our plans... You never finished telling us how we can kill him—if removing the heart isn't the end, then what the *fuck is?*"

As if on cue, Killian came out of the kitchen and announced dinner.

"Don't concern yourself, Ian. If you're lucky enough to be the one to remove his heart, you bring it to me or my wife. That's all you need to know. Now go eat."

Slater walked down the hallway and knocked on the bedroom door, informing the two men they could come out for dinner. He heard metal clinks and slides, then silence. He steeled himself for the burning impact of bullets, but the men opened the door with empty hands. Slater trailed them as they made their way to the kitchen.

Everyone ate in awkward silence, scattered in huddled groups throughout the living room and dining area. Slater noticed one of the men constantly eyeing the teen girls, and the other made Lynn his object of desire. He considered saying something once dinner ended, but Ian surprised him instead by standing and displaying his gun in front of the men.

"I know we're the trespassers here, guys. But I've had enough of you two looking at my friends like that. Keep it up and see what happens."

"That's the second time we've had a gun flashed at us on our own property. And we ain't touched none of your friends, junior. Sit back down before you hurt yourself."

Ian's expression didn't change so Tim got between them.

"Ian, we don't need to add gunfights to our list of dangers right now. Put it away, please."

Mumbling to himself, Ian left instead and relieved Jason of guard duty on the porch.

"Such bullshit we got to put up with in our own house," the man muttered.

The tension and stress were deliciously palpable; powder keg situations were quite fun. They tended to result in lessons being handed out by the students as the teachers merely watched and stoked the flames. Once he and Killian cornered a drug gang in a house and didn't have to teach a single lesson. All they did was arrange a few cats to jump out at perfect high-tension moments, and after the gang's paranoia resulted in a few dead bodies, they'd placed the corpses in all sorts of random places to pop out and fuel their fear. The only disappointing part of the evening was how quickly it took the gang to completely turn on each other; the entertainment ended far too soon.

The hardest part had been wrangling the cats.

After dinner, Tim helped Jessica clean the dishes. The two men went back into their bedroom and locked the door. The teens took turns in the shower, speeding through in an attempt to preserve hot water for each other. Slater could tell Lynn was getting antsy. Not being able to shower infuriated her, no doubt already growing more self-conscious around her boyfriend, though Corey gave no signs that he minded.

Even so, Lynn allowed the Hunt family to take their turns before her as a courtesy. When Corey exited, he apologized to Lynn that the hot water had run out. She sighed and said she'd wait a few hours, even though it would be well into early morning by then.

By one-thirty AM, they all slept save for the Slater family. Lynn kept an eye on the inside while Slater met Killian outside during her guard shift. She held his hand and laid her head against his bicep.

"I'm so proud of you, honey. A whole week... Only one more day and we're free."

"Thanks to you, sweetheart. I was considering... What do you think about retiring? Let Lynn take over? I've never felt closer to you since this vacation from teaching..."

Killian sighed, deep in contemplation.

"You like having friends, don't you?" Killian asked after a moment.

"I'm not the only one. The look in your eye when you stood up for Jessica was unlike anything I've ever seen in you before. If there wasn't a bar full of people watching..."

"I'll admit our sex life hasn't been like this since the first year of our marriage. If retiring is what it takes to keep it going... Let's do it. We'll make more friends, and Lynn will be out of the house soon."

"An empty house for us. Anywhere. Anytime."

"A lovely dream. First, though, I want to hear how those two men make you feel."

Slater's heartbeat picked up in strength and speed. "The one that keeps staring at Lynn... I want to stuff his hat down his throat and hang him like a coat on that set of deer antlers on the wall."

"Mmmm... What about the little one?"

Slater's heart pounded and he began to see red.

"I'd snatch that shotgun out of Katie's hands and shove it up his..."

Killian kissed him deeply, cooling his rage perfectly. She pulled him out to the bed of the F-350 and laid him down, taking him as she had all week.

After an hour and several more imaginary lessons were brought up and defused, Slater got down shakily from the bed. Killian remained, sleeping peacefully. He sat back down on the porch and sighed. He'd never been so happy before. In truth, Slater couldn't wait to retire on Monday.

Through the partially open front door, he heard Lynn finally take her turn in the bathroom. While the shower remained running, the bathroom door opened and closed again.

Slater frowned and stepped inside, ready to go in and break up the two lovebirds, but Corey slept next to Jessica on the floor of the living room. Down the hallway from the front door, a sliver of light peeked out of the bedroom.

A gunshot came from the bathroom.

Chapter 18

Changes

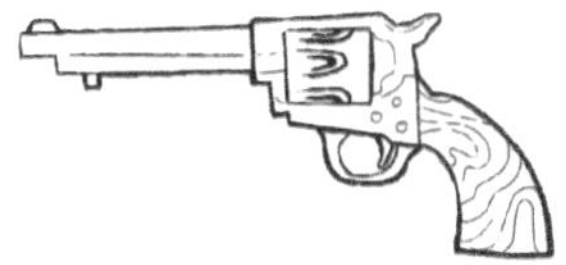

Kill Count: 25

Timothy startled awake from a *pop* in the bathroom. Then came another. Katie had the shotgun pointed down the hallway when a handgun came out of the shadows. Ian stood up and pointed at the man, too. A shot came from behind them and Slater fell face first through the front door, the back of his head spurting black blood.

While everyone's attention pulled to the commotion behind them, the man in the hallway shot Ian, sending him backwards against the living room wall. Both cabin owners yelled at Katie to put the shotgun down. Timothy wanted to reach for the magnum he'd placed on the side table, but he couldn't see what both men were doing at the same time. He feared for Katie's life as the three of them shouted at the top of their lungs for the other party to drop their weapons.

The teens held their heads down while Shawna put her body over Tera, who neared delirium from her fever and likely didn't understand what was happening. Timothy breathed in a small relief when Ian stirred. Jessica shielded TJ while he held Maggie by the collar. The dog growled but thankfully didn't bark to add to the tension-riddled cacophony.

Timothy turned slightly to see where the magnum lay in case he needed to dive for it. It wasn't on the table anymore.

Katie wouldn't back down, seemingly determined to take the hallway aggressor with her if the man behind her fired.

"You drop that weapon before I do for you what I just did for that ugly bitch in the bathroom!" the man yelled.

Timothy couldn't believe his eyes as a pair of slender white arms materialized from the shadows of the hallway behind the man. They grabbed him around the throat and lifted his gun arm towards the ceiling. The rest of Lynn's naked body came out of the shadows, two streamers of blood flowing down her torso and legs.

"Drop your gun, asshole!" she snarled at the man at the front door.

"I'll kill this bitch if you don't let him go!" he yelled, readying to fire into Katie's back.

"Hey!"

Corey shouted from behind Timothy, then one of the loudest sounds he'd ever heard exploded next to him. The shot missed the man in the doorway. Corey fell into the side table from the kickback of the magnum. The hallway man shook out of Lynn's grasp, pushing her back into the shadows, then fired at Corey.

Katie got caught up in indecision at Corey interrupting the standoff. She had wheeled around to the man at the front door, assuming the hallway man was incapacitated. The man who'd killed Slater was too busy feeling himself, amazed that he hadn't been hit by Corey, when Katie fired into his torso, sending him staggering backwards out the front door and down the porch steps.

The hallway man had the back of Katie's head in his sights when three shots came from the living room. The impact knocked him into the hallway threshold where he slumped down and stopped moving. Timothy followed where the shots had come from to find Ian, clicking through an emptied clip.

Jessica shrieked over Corey's limp body. Timothy remained frozen in mortified confusion at all that happened in the span of only a minute. His boy...

Movement came from the hallway as the man grunted, though he didn't seem to be able to lift his arms. Lynn came out of the darkness and reached down for the man's throat, then tore it out in one swift, bloody motion. Timothy expected her to run to her dead father, but instead she joined Jessica's side. She picked up Corey's hand while Jessica hugged him tight. He couldn't believe how effortless Lynn made that kill look. Why was that his first thought; not marveling that she wasn't dead herself?

The teens all cried in a spectrum of shock, relief, and sadness. Chase was the most composed as she went to check Ian's wound. Katie went outside to verify the man she'd shot was dead. Timothy approached Jessica and their boy slowly, not wanting to see what he feared most in the world. Tears blurred his vision as he reached shakily for Jessica's shoulder. TJ bawled against Maggie, refusing to look upon it himself.

In unison, Katie cursed outside, and Amber and Misty screamed inside. Before he could turn around a big hand rested on Timothy's shoulder with a familiar grip.

"Is he...?" Slater asked.

Timothy's mouth dropped open at seeing his friend fully upright as if nothing happened. He walked around to find the same gaping bullet wound he'd seen when Slater's face hit the floor.

"What in the name of God...?" Timothy started.

"Daddy!" Lynn exclaimed and left Corey's side to hug him.

Timothy was just as shocked to see up close—and not only because she wasn't bothering to cover up—that Lynn really had been shot twice, but she moved as freely as Slater.

"He shot my Corey! Where the hell were you? How could you let that man get the drop on you?"

"I was...a little fuzzy. I'm sorry, Lynn."

Timothy's mind snapped as loud as the gunshots ringing in his ears. In a desperate bid to delay the truth of what happened to his son, he spun on Slater.

"What the *fuck* is going on with you two? How are you *alive*?"

"We just are, Tim. We're fine."

"I see that! That's the problem! You were just shot in the head! Your daughter was shot twice, center mass! How is this possible?"

"I can't explain it to you and have it make any sense. But in a few minutes, I have a feeling you're going to be thanking my daughter."

Timothy shook his head in disbelief. He huffed and sputtered. It didn't change anything, though. He wasted his breath and thoughts trying to figure out something that seemed impossible. He turned to his boy again.

Jessica recoiled, releasing her tight embrace of Corey and backing up. She shouted joyfully as Corey's arms and legs began twitching. Corey groaned as he sat up. Jessica threw her arms around him, inspiring another groan that sounded more like embarrassment than pain; painfully embarrassed, the Corey special. Lynn pushed past Timothy to hug Jessica and Corey giddily. Blinking a few moments at the reanimation unfolding before him, Timothy got down on his knees to take his turn at hugging his son as well. Corey moved as easily as Lynn and stopped groaning at the stiffness and consequent affection at being alive. He said he felt normal despite the bloody wound in his chest.

Slater took his daughter by the shoulders and guided her back to the bathroom, but she kept looking back at Corey with a big smile until they disappeared down the hallway. As Jessica continued to fuss over their boy, Timothy went to check on Ian. Chase had already wrapped a towel over his shoulder where he'd been hit and was applying pressure.

Katie returned from outside and sat in a recliner, shaking her head in angry silence. He raised his brow when their eyes met.

"We're never getting out of this *fucking* forest," Katie whispered.

"Katie, I know a lot has happened, but don't talk like that. We can use their truck and get to Roseburg."

Katie laughed. It wasn't good-natured in any way. It verged on the maniacal.

"The tires are slashed—all eight of them. We're fucking *trapped* in an even smaller space than that campground. Ian just emptied his clip out. I'm down to four shells, and I believe that magnum only has four left, too. And it doesn't even matter, because *we can't kill that motherfucker*. At least now you've seen the Slaters for what they are. I don't get to be the only one that's going to meet the end, having seen it coming: we're going to die by the killer's hands, or theirs."

Timothy didn't like the way Katie held the shotgun. With that laugh, he could easily imagine her pointing the barrel below her chin and pulling the trigger. He knelt down cautiously in front of her and reached for the gun, gently tugging it away from her.

She laughed again, but let it go.

"What, you think I'm going to off myself? I don't want to die, Tim. I'm just accepting that that's what's going to happen. Doesn't mean I'm going to make it easy for that son of a bitch."

"Okay, Katie. I get it. I'm just going to hold onto this for a little bit, okay?"

Katie lost the suicidal mirth in her eyes and they seemed to glaze over. She reached and grabbed the shotgun back from his grasp, yanking with unexpected strength, then hugged it close to her chest, like it was her last friend in the world.

"Alright, Katie," Timothy said as he got back to his feet. He put his hand on the top of her head to show she still had real friends. Whether the gesture worked or not didn't register in her blank expression.

TJ asked Corey what it was like to be shot while Jessica turned her attention to Tera, who shivered in Shawna's arms. Shawna whispered affirmations to her, but it was impossible to tell if Tera registered any of them. Chase and Misty removed Ian's temporary bandage to check whether the bullet went all the way through or not. Amber and Jason sat on the floor away from the action, still in shock. Timothy brought each of them a blanket.

Slater came out of the dark hallway rubbing the back of his head. Timothy frowned at that.

"It'll heal up after a week or so. Corey's might take a little longer, but at least it won't hurt while it's healing."

"Did you or Lynn do something to my son?"

"She did, Tim. Again, it wouldn't make sense if I explained it to you. I'll give you more details when things settle down."

"I'm holding you to that. Don't think I'm going to let you sweep this under the rug."

"Wouldn't expect you to, my friend. Hey, has Killian come in yet? She's a heavy sleeper, so I wouldn't be surprised if she slept through all of that, but was just wondering if she poked her head in."

"I haven't seen her," Timothy shrugged.

Was it really possible someone could sleep through that much gunfire and shouting? Interested to know, he followed Slater outside.

"Something's wrong," Slater said, picking up pace as he rounded the F-350.

He peered over the rim of the bed and shook his head. Before Timothy asked, Slater only said "she's gone."

"Where would she go?"

"She wouldn't."

Timothy poked at the tires, losing the logical part of his brain that believed what his eyes were seeing in real time. He feared Killian might have been the next victim... Could she even *be* a victim? Timothy supposed that if the Slaters knew how to end the killer, he must be capable of the same to them. He put his hand up to Slater's shoulder, ignoring the wetness of his black blood soaking the top half of his shirt.

"I'm sorry, Slater."

"She's not dead. I would know if she was."

Slater peered into the surrounding darkness. Timothy realized the light pole no longer illuminated the driveway; everything was only visible from the light of the cabin. *Why is the killer still dragging it out? Why not cut the electrical wiring altogether?*

Timothy turned to find Slater no longer at his side. He hadn't even heard retreating footsteps. He scratched his head and walked around both trucks, then did a circle around the cabin. Slater was gone.

Back inside, no one seemed to know what to do with themselves. They were too scared to sleep, and there were still several hours of darkness left. Shawna tended to Tera's needs, Chase and Misty to Ian's, and Jessica and TJ continued marveling over Corey's miraculous survival. Timothy shuddered when Corey pulled his shirt up and Jessica tentatively touched the bullet hole. Corey didn't wince, only shrugging at her increased probing. Finally he exclaimed when she got a little too deep with her finger, searching for a bullet.

"So you can still feel pain, but you're healing is like...like..."

"Wolverine," a raspy Ian said.

"Like, from the X-men movies?" Misty asked.

"X-men *comics*. I guess to people like you it would only be the movies," Ian scoffed weakly.

"I'm aware they were comics first, jerk," she said with a small smile.

Chase had been holding pressure on Ian's shoulder. She grabbed Misty's hand and replaced it with her own, then stood next to Katie.

"Those men just gifted us two more guns. They probably have more in that bedroom. Look with me?"

Katie continued staring into space, but her grip on the shotgun audibly tightened. She didn't respond. Timothy walked to the mouth of the hallway and nodded back at Chase. She and Lynn followed him deeper into the cabin. Inside the bedroom the closet doors were open. There were several rifles lined up against the wall.

Timothy found a bag of grenades and claymores and set it aside. Boxes of various caliber ammunition were stacked on the shelf at eye level. Chase shuffled through the rifles as if choosing the perfect bowling ball.

"None of that is going to stop him," Lynn said. "He'd survive the explosives, too, unless they blew out his heart. You'd have to hold it on his chest when it blew. That's not happening."

"What do you suggest?" Chase asked as she put the rifle back.

"Blades. That would require letting him get close, but that's your only chance to end this. What Katie and Jessica are carrying have stopping power to make the blades easier to use. These rifles are too low-caliber and would be hard to hit anything in close-range. You risk killing yourself or others if you bring the explosives into it."

"How do you know all this?" Timothy asked, digging deeper in the closet, hoping to find a machete or ax.

"I need to be aware of all weapon types. My future job will be dangerous."

"You already know what you're going to do?"

"Family business."

"I don't see any blades in here," Chase announced. "I'm going to the kitchen."

Lynn tore through dresser drawers while Timothy searched under the mattress and in the night table, but found nothing helpful. Slater told him that he'd have Lynn to thank for saving Corey's life, but when it all happened, she hadn't done anything remarkable besides hold her bloody hands in his.

"Lynn, what exactly did you do to my son?"

She stopped digging into one of the drawers but didn't turn around.

"What are you referring to?"

Red flags flew that there could be more than one thing.

"The bullet wound! How is he alive? How are *you* alive?"

Lynn turned but stared at the floor, unable to meet his eyes.

"I…I don't know how to explain it. Mom told me about it but not the why's and how's. It's a kind of…family bonding. I shared something with him that changed him."

"In what way?"

"Pretty much the way you saw. Nothing else changed about him, though. He's still himself, just more like those *X-men* they mentioned."

"What *else* did you do to him?"

Her face turned red as she continued studying the floor. Timothy then understood. She'd changed Corey in another way; a way with less supernatural bullshit surrounding it. He sighed, imagining how Slater and Killian would react when they found out. When should he tell his wife? What would he say to Corey now that "the talk" couldn't be delayed any longer?

Timothy took some solace in knowing there were far more pressing concerns to deal with in the moment.

"My mom already knows. But…could you not tell my dad?"

He didn't need to be asked, but nodded to put her mind at ease. He feared the big man's reaction, especially after seeing him survive that gunshot to the head.

A bone-chilling, primal scream came out of the nearby forest. It reverberated through the cabin and shook the thin-paned windows. Timothy ran to the living room to find their group cowering. Katie was already on her feet and standing near the front door.

Lynn staggered out of the hallway behind him, hand to her head as if she'd been struck by an unexpected migraine.

"Mom…" she whispered and fell, hitting her head against a table and crumbling to the floor. Corey ran to her.

The lights cut out. After a few moments of startled murmuring as the kids huddled closer together, Timothy smelled smoke. Flickering orange light grew outside the living room window, on the porch. Katie tested the door knob and hissed.

"Of course it's a fucking fire..." Katie muttered.

CHAPTER 19
SPLITTING UP

KILL COUNT: 28

HANDS WITH UNBELIEVABLE STRENGTH squeezed Tera's neck. Water rushed around her, muffling her struggle. *Where's Ian?* The assailant pulled her out of the water but didn't release an ounce of tension. Her eyes bugged out of her skull as she frantically searched for help.

Ian lay on the bank of the creek in a pool of blood. Chase and Misty ran for her, but they were far away and though it *looked* like they ran, they never got closer. Timothy and Slater stood protecting their own families in the distance, though one from each of their broods was missing. Shawna hid behind Katie as she raised the shotgun from the bank. There was no way its spread would do anything more than tickle the monster choking Tera out—not from that range.

A figure came out from behind the killer. The sun shone directly overhead, casting only shadow over the killer and the figure's faces. The sun disappeared and all the water around them turned to fire.

Lynn was killing Tera, and Corey stood over her shoulder. As Tera's vision darkened, a little smile formed on his lips.

Tera came to consciousness as Timothy carried her down a hallway. It took her a second to get her bearings once they entered the back bedroom. Where were they again? Tera seemed to have swapped one nightmare for another. Jason pushed the window screen out and helped Chase and Misty get Ian through. Why did Ian need so much help? Corey and Amber carried Lynn across the room, though Corey shouldered most of the burden as Amber cried and complained.

"Where's my... Where's Shawna?" Tera whispered to Timothy.

"Outside with my family and Katie already."

Tera had a piercing headache, but her fever seemed reduced; they must have given her something while she was out.

"Sir, I think I can manage. You don't need to carry me like a baby."

"Those must have been some pretty strong pain meds if you can't feel your ankle."

"I'll hop. Or... There—in the closet. I'll use one of those rifles for support. Look after your own family."

"Tera, you're in bad shape."

"Let me down, please."

Timothy did as she asked. Tera hopped one-legged to the closet, like the ramp up to the triple-jump, her favorite event in track. She picked out the longest rifle and checked that it was empty of a chamber round to avoid shooting her foot off. Before turning around, she noticed an open bag full of grenades and claymores. She grabbed the bag and slung it over her shoulder.

All the movement wasn't doing her headache any favors. She leaned against the door frame while Timothy helped get Lynn out the window. Tera peered down the hall where smoke billowed towards her from an inferno behind it. She pulled Ian's shirt over her nose and kept watch while the others struggled out of the window.

"Tera, come on!" Timothy called to her.

She was last. She didn't hear any screams from outside. Why did the killer start the fire if he wasn't going to pick them off as they escaped? Tera had a feeling: in her mortal battle with him in Lake Creek, she detected that the killer enjoyed the chase. He didn't want to kill all of them at the same time. *He'd had plenty of chances.* Why else would he have taken her bait to follow her down the creek when the rest of the group was occupied with the truck at the campground?

Tera hopped to the window, then heavy footsteps came from the hallway, sending a jolt through her spine. It had to be the killer. The fire had already made it to the bedroom entrance. Tera pulled a grenade out of the bag as she swung her good leg out the window. She pulled the pin, tossed it towards the door, then fell out the window into Timothy and Jason's arms. An explosion and a cry came from the bedroom. Smoke streamed out of the cabin, stinging Tera's eyes.

Jason took the bag and the three of them fled into the forest behind the others, Timothy guiding Tera as she hobbled on her rifle crutch. After a quarter mile of slow progress, they came to a little area of fallen logs where the rest of the group had stopped to rest and gather themselves. Shawna bolted up and hugged Tera tight, then offered her lap for Tera's head as she laid down on one of the logs. The headache pulsed heavily behind her eyes as she closed them and tried to control her breathing.

"We need to get back to the highway," Chase said. "If we run into the woods randomly we'll never get out."

"Which way is that?" Amber asked.

"We can go back to the driveway to be sure. If we go downhill from *here* we could miss the highway. It's not a straight line."

"Running is useless," Ian said weakly. "Didn't you all hear Slater? He's never going to stop hunting us."

"It's only useless if we run off together..." Tera said, her arm draped over her eyes. "He'll waste time chasing one of us at a time, given the option. He *likes* it."

"What are you suggesting?" Jessica asked as she hugged TJ tighter.

"Let me—" Tera started.

"...*us* hold him off," Ian finished.

"I'll help," Lynn said, startling Corey. She got up out of his arms to address the group. "He killed my mother."

"How do you know that, Lynn?" Timothy asked.

"I felt it. So did my dad. You all heard it when he screamed, didn't you? No physical pain could make us cry like that..."

"I thought you couldn't die?" Timothy said. He seemed to have a difficult time wrapping his head around everything and it was noticeably annoying Katie, who pinched the bridge of her nose at the question.

"Unless the heart is eaten," Lynn continued. "The killer will have gained strength from it. My mom was one of the most powerful in the world..."

Tera sat up from Shawna's lap and addressed the Hunt family.

"I don't give a shit about any of this. Sir, take your family to the highway. Ian and I will keep his attention as long as we can."

Shawna put her hand on Tera's shoulder to protest, but Tera shrugged it off, hoping the rude gesture would make her next words easier to say.

"You too, Shawn-ista. Go with them."

Shawna frowned, then put her arm around Tera's shoulders and squeezed tight so she couldn't be brushed away again.

"You're not as tough as you think you are, T. I'm staying with you."

"Yeah, Tera," Chase said. "I'm not leaving you or Ian, either. Come up with a better plan than stupidly sacrificing yourselves for little to *no* gain. Something that involves this..." Chase pulled out a long bowie knife. "Found this in their kitchen. This is how we'll end that motherfucker who took Darren away from me."

"He killed our friends. He—Luke," Misty stuttered, then found her resolve and declared, "I'm with you guys."

Jason pulled out the two handguns he'd taken from the rednecks and nodded. When they looked to Amber she shrunk back and shook her head. That didn't surprise anyone, and, if anything, it was a relief that her whining wouldn't somehow end up getting them all killed. There could be no hesitation; no cowering.

Katie stood up with the shotgun and nodded at the Hunts.

"I'll help your family get out."

Timothy started to protest, but Tera cut him off.

"Get ready to move out, sir. Your family *and* Lynn."

"I said I'd help!"

"*Fuck you*, Lynn," Tera spat. "I don't want your help. Protect Corey and his family."

The rage and pleasure flashed across Lynn's face, as if Tera needed any more reasons not to trust the bitch. She worried a little over what Lynn might do to the family, but her protection of Corey at the very least was genuine. Perhaps that would be enough to ensure their safety as a unit.

"We'll get help," Jessica said as everyone stood up from the fallen logs.

They walked back towards the burning cabin cautiously. Katie sidled next to Tera and put her hand on the small of Tera's back, then whispered.

"I'll get them to the road and in a car. Then I'm coming back for you."

Tera put the rifle on her strong side, then draped her arm over Katie's shoulders and leaned on her.

"You should *stay* with them. Lynn is too dangerous. We'll find our own way home."

"I don't *have* a home, Tera. I *will* come back for you."

"I can't stop you. I...appreciate it, though, even if all you come back to is more death."

Katie stopped and turned to face Tera as the others moved past them.

"Don't talk like that. You're fuckin' tough. I wish I had half of your courage."

"Courage is overrated. Most of the time it's just indecision and not having a better plan."

"That's my whole life in a nutshell."

Tera enjoyed how closely Katie held her; it was warm but, more so, reliable. They got caught up gazing into each other's eyes, inches away. She'd believed Katie wasn't into her after ignoring her back on the boat. Because of that, Tera'd only offered her hand in comfort when they went to get the tires from the F-350 near the Caterpillar. Somewhere along the way, Katie had simply become another "adult" like Timothy and Jessica.

Sharing that moment together, heading back into the mouth of danger, Katie turned human to her again; vulnerable. She seemed damaged. Katie hadn't been beaten up as badly as Tera, but her eyes betrayed that she'd *seen* the worst things any of them could imagine.

"Did you ever see the movie *Speed*? The ending with Keanu and Sandra?" Katie asked.

A smile curled on one side of Tera's mouth. Her brother, ten years her senior, was a huge action movie fan and it was one of his favorites. They watched it together a lot when he still lived with them. But she shook her head so Katie would make the first move of a bad decision in the intense situation.

Chapped lips and close, imminent danger didn't allow them to fully enjoy the quick peck, but Tera would cherish her first real kiss with someone like her for as long as she drew breath.

They caught up to the rear of the group as they came into the small clearing around the burning cabin. Timothy shook hands with each teenager—except Amber who huddled behind Jessica and TJ. Katie let go of Tera's hand reluctantly as she parted to follow the Hunts down the driveway.

Chase sprang into action, going through the grenade bag. She divided them up, handing a pair to each of them—Tera, Shawna, Ian, Misty, Jason, and herself, leaving three claymores in the bag. She handed the bag to Shawna. Jason kept one of the handguns in his waistband and handed the other to Ian. Ian shook his head.

"I'm getting weaker. You don't want the gun in my hands."

Tera hopped to him and put her palm on his forehead. His skin was clammy and cold, and the color didn't look right in the orange glow of the cabin fire. They needed to finish things as quickly as possible to get him to a hospital.

Jason handed the other gun to Misty, while Chase practiced a few swings and stabs with her bowie knife.

"How are we going to draw him to us?" Misty asked.

"Let's spread out up the hill. Then we'll fire off a couple shots," Chase said.

"What then?" Shawna asked as she provided support to Tera.

"You need to subdue him," Ian said through gritted teeth. "He'll be knocked out if he's really hurt. Probably needs that time to regenerate or heal or whatever. When he's down, Chase needs to be nearby with that knife, so nobody run off out of earshot."

Shawna helped Tera up the hill from the burning cabin while Jason did the same for Ian. Chase and Misty ran ahead, sure-footed and fearless. They spread apart in the dark. The girls called out ahead of them, yelling insults and taunts at the killer. Jason and Ian joined in as they moved away.

Tera's head pounded. She wanted to do her part, but her ankle continued to burn as the meds' effectiveness waned.

"Why aren't you calling out, Shawna?"

"My bravery only goes so far, T. I don't want anything to happen to us."

Tera parted from Shawna, sat on a log, and handled one of the grenades while Shawna did the same.

"You should have gone with Amber, then. I don't intend to hide out here. *Hey, asshole! Remember me?*" Tera yelled.

She held her temples after her outburst. Shawna put her hand on Tera's thigh.

"Fine, just...conserve your energy. *We're over here, cocksucker!*"

Shawna's breathing picked up as her attention heightened to their surroundings. She gripped Tera's leg a little harder. Tera stared at Shawna in the dark, illuminated only by the faint glow of the cabin and the moonlight peering through small holes in the forest's canopy.

"Shawn-ista, do you think, when we get to college, I'll get you drunk enough to..."

Shawna laughed and kissed Tera's cheek. Tera felt a resurgence as Shawna's lips touched her skin.

"If we survive this, T-bag, the first night you get your roommate to leave your dorm room, you'll be my 'college experiment.' Promise."

Tera chuckled and hugged her. "I was just kidding. I'd never do anything to jeopardize our friendship, but the fact that you'd even entertain the thought is enough to give me something to live for right now. I love you, Shawna."

Shawna kissed Tera's other cheek, then pulled away and screamed out to the killer again.

"What's left in that bag?" Tera asked.

Shawna opened it and pulled out the three claymores.

"Whatever these curved things are. What can we even do with these?"

Tera handled the wires and found the clacker at the end of each.

"Let's set a trap. Maybe we get him to go after one of us and catch him between two of them. This wire is really long, so we wouldn't need to be that close to set them off. And before you ask which one of us does that, it's obviously going to be me since I'm hobbled."

Shawna sighed and let Tera hold the clackers as she unspooled the wire of one. Shawna ventured into the darkness and set one up, then did the same with the second claymore.

"Did you make sure to point the business side towards the enemy?" Tera asked when Shawna came back.

"So simple TJ could have done it."

Their friends yelled out in the night. Shawna scanned around, then crouched down in front of Tera. "I'm going to draw him into the trap."

Tera nodded and let Shawna break away. As she disappeared into the dark, a gunshot rang out from the direction that Jason and Ian had gone. More shouts came from that area. She recognized Jason and Ian's voices, though Ian's cracked under the volume. Their shouts were interrupted by an explosion from one of the grenades, then another shot.

Heavy footfalls came from Tera's left. The grenade weighed heavily in her hand as she put her finger on the pin. She barely made out Chase's silhouette running from left to right towards danger, followed a few feet back by Misty.

"Misty!" Tera called.

She skidded to a halt and rerouted to Tera. Tera told her where the claymores were and to try to get the killer to fall into their trap. Misty nodded and took off. Tera stayed seated, focused on her surroundings. It took everything she had—all the patience and discipline she'd accumulated in her lifetime of athletics—to stay put and not try to help her friends.

Another explosion—closer that time. Two more shots. A bullet ricocheted off a tree uphill. Tera's palms dampened with sweat. Rapid footsteps came towards her. She put the grenade down and picked up the two clackers.

Chase sprinted into view, then vaulted behind the log and put her hand on Tera's shoulder.

"He's coming towards Jason and Ian. Misty got your message to Jason. Shawna's at the killer's flank, keeping his attention and angling him to the trap."

Soon Misty joined them, handgun raised into the darkness. Another shot rang out, close to the trap.

"Jason must be a terrible shot," Tera muttered. "All he needs to do is hit him a couple times and he'll be down."

"Whatever, it's working," Chase said, her grip tightening. Shawna came into view from the trap area with Ian leaning on her. They crashed to the ground in front of Tera.

"Jason's doing it," Ian said, almost too quiet to hear over everything else. "Get the detonators ready."

Another shot came from directly ahead of them, then Jason came into view.

"Now!" Chase yelled.

"Jason's not clear!" Tera yelled louder, more for Jason's benefit than to admonish Chase.

Chase ripped a clacker from Tera's hand and detonated one of the claymores. Jason dove forward from the explosion behind him. Tera faintly made out a hulking silhouette staggering down the hill, then squeezed the clacker to trigger the second explosion. They heard a cry and a heavy thud somewhere beyond Jason's prone back. Shawna and Misty hurried to Jason and picked him up while Chase ran to the figure on the ground.

She raised the bowie knife high and stabbed into the killer's chest twice before his hand thrust up and grabbed her by the neck. Chase didn't panic, stabbing a few more times where she could. The killer threw her away. Her head hit a tree and she fell to the ground face first, the knife still in her hand.

Tera shot up. Misty ran in his direction, firing down at his body. He threw a branch at her, hitting her in the face. In the blink of an eye the killer stood and advanced on her. Jason fired his gun until it clicked silent. Tera prepared to throw a grenade when a hand touched her shoulder and held her back from hobbling any closer.

"I've got this, Tera," Ian wheezed. "You're amazing."

He smiled and squeezed her shoulder, then pushed her to the ground and ran straight at the killer. He had wires wrapped around his back.

"Get back! Don't forget to eat the heart!" he yelled at Misty and Jason, then rammed into the killer, wrapping his arms around him and holding their torsos together.

The killer squeezed his arms around Ian's back, folding him in a horrible position. As Ian's arms splayed out, Tera recognized the clacker of the third claymore in his hand. Her scream drowned out as the explosion ripped him in half.

CHAPTER 20

JERKY

KILL COUNT: 29

KATIE WATCHED THE HUNTS' six while they marched along the road to a straightaway that wouldn't be quite so dangerous to flag down drivers. Cars passed every few minutes, but none ever stopped for the group of people walking along the side of the road in the middle of nowhere in the dark, as if that was something normal to do.

A truck downshifted from around a bend, so she walked into the road, waving her arm while holding the shotgun behind her. The truck skidded a little to go around her and barely missed her. When the next truck came into view, she pointed the shotgun at the driver, but he only increased his speed. She couldn't blame him. He had a lot more stopping power than her little shotgun.

She dove to the shoulder as the truck barreled past her. Jessica picked her up.

"Someone will stop, Katie. You don't need to put yourself in danger like that."

"I just need them to *stop!* The longer I'm down here the longer those kids are up there in the forest with *him.*"

Timothy came up to her and put his hand on her shoulder.

"Look, you got us down here like you promised. If you want to go back, go ahead. We'll keep walking and hitching. Thank you, Katie."

Katie nodded and jogged back towards the driveway about a quarter of a mile up the hill. She took a drink from one of the water bottles they'd packed away from those rednecks' supply. By the time she got to the beginning of the steep driveway she had to slow to a walk or succumb to cramping. Halfway up the hill, gunshots rang out, then two explosions. She picked up the pace with a passing thought that she would have never imagined running towards those sounds instead of as far away and as fast as possible.

When she got to the burning cabin, a third explosion echoed through the trees along with a scream. She stumbled up the slope in that direction. She came upon the teens in disarray. Chase lay face down next to a tree. Shawna stood over Tera as Tera sobbed over half of Ian. Jason and Misty searched desperately over the ground for something. The killer lay a short distance from Ian's body with a giant hole in his torso, not moving at all.

Katie knelt next to Chase and shook her by the shoulder. She moaned and woke up slowly, then thrust the bowie knife outwards in reflex. Katie fell backwards and skidded down the slope a few feet.

"It's just Katie, Chase," she said.

Chase took a second to get her bearings, then apologized. Katie shook her head and pointed towards Jason and Misty. Chase got up on legs that wobbled, ready to buckle, but managed to stay upright and run after them. Shawna helped Katie get up, then Katie put her arm over Tera's shoulders.

"I'm sorry, Tera," Shawna said. "But we need to find that fucking heart or Ian's sacrifice meant nothing."

Tera sniffed and laid Ian's torso down gently while Shawna split to search for the heart. Tera kissed Ian's forehead, then limped away from the corpse. It was such a tender gesture that Katie almost envied him. Would anyone cry over her when she died? Katie embraced Tera tight, letting her get everything out. When Timothy hugged Katie in her distress, it had been a miraculous lift. He was the only one to understand how much she was struggling. Katie felt the same connection to Tera.

Tera broke apart after sniffing away her sorrow and joined the others in the search. Katie approached the killer and pointed the shotgun at his face, waiting for him to pop back to life. When his lips twitched, she fired point blank, putting a hole in his head to match his torso.

"That was just me!" she shouted so the kids would keep searching.

Katie breathed a deep sigh of relief. *Could it really be over?* She didn't let the thought keep her from aiming the shotgun at what was left of the monster. She took a quick glance at the teens fanning out, combing through the gore that had burst from his back.

"I think this is it!" Misty cried.

They huddled beneath a beam of moonlight to verify the shape of the thing in her hand. They jumped back when it beat, and Misty dropped it. It rolled down the hill towards Katie and the killer's body. His hand reached out for it, as if summoning it, but the bowie knife halted the heart inches from his fingers. Chase picked it up and kicked away the hand. The killer used that momentum to grab the end of the shotgun and rip it out of Katie's hand, sending her tumbling over his torso to the ground.

He swung the butt of the shotgun around and tripped Chase. She held onto the knife though, and removed the heart from the blade, tossing it to Misty. Tera used the barrel of her crutch rifle to pin his wrist to the ground. Jason tried to take the shotgun out of the killer's ironclad grasp.

Misty handed the heart to Shawna, then pulled the last loaded handgun out of her waistband. She fired three shots into the killer's wrist. The tendons controlling his fingers disconnected, forcing him to let go of the shotgun. Jason rolled away with it, then tossed it to Katie. She motioned for the kids to get away and kept the shotgun trained on the killer after pumping the forearm.

"We need to eat this heart!" Tera cried.

"*We?*" Misty said, then vomited at the mere thought.

"Don't chicken out now," Chase said as she took the heart from Shawna. "Come on. Down to the cabin. I'm not eating this shit raw."

Katie supported Tera down the hill to find Chase had already skewered and cooked the heart near the fire on the front porch. While the kids mentally prepared themselves, Katie kept her eye on the darkness up the hill, fully expecting the killer to run full speed at them despite missing most of his organs and brains.

The heart made pitiful sounds like screams as it sizzled. It could have been the blood boiling out of the valves, for all they knew, but it was no less eerie. Suitably charred, Chase walked it over to the hood of the smaller truck and cut the heart into six strips.

"This is going to change us, like Corey, isn't it?" Jason asked.

"I don't care what it does to me," Tera said. "As long as that motherfucker is dead forever."

She ate hers quickly. Misty, Shawna, and Jason only stared at their strips. Tera grabbed Shawna's and ate it, but chewing through a second helping was noticeably tiring her jaw and she went much slower. Chase made to bite hers but hesitated, then threw up off to the side.

"I'm so sorry, Tera," Chase said when she came back. "I'm afraid I'm not going to be able to keep this down."

Tera waved Chase to bring it to her. She sighed and strained to get it all down.

Misty looked at Tera sheepishly. *Oh, so that's how it's going to be,* Katie thought before stepping in and taking it, then Jason's. As she ate her strip they noticed movement from the edge of the darkness. Like in her brief waking nightmare, the legs ran towards them. The torso hung uselessly behind them, dragging on the ground, but that didn't slow him down.

She handed the shotgun to Jason and stuffed the second strip into her mouth. Disgust crept up on her the longer she chewed, and the longer she chewed, the weaker her jaw became. She backed away from the kids and the legs angled towards her. Jason aimed the shotgun and fired it into the right knee, sending the flailing body to the ground at Katie's feet.

It dragged itself towards her, pathetic and slow, but she knew its grip wouldn't be either of those things if it reached her. It *was* dying; she was killing it with every bite. She backed away as she prepared her mouth, throat, and stomach to force down the last strip. Misty and Chase held the killer's ankles, stopping its pursuit altogether.

"Finish it," Chase barked.

Katie almost laughed at Chase's renewed bossiness. She wished the stakes weren't so high, or she'd have goosed Chase's demand for all it was worth. But Chase was still *trying*, despite it all, and Katie respected her. Chase grunted and struggled against the legs trying to kick free of the girls' grips.

Katie forced the last strip down to her stomach, only chewing as much as she had to that it wouldn't choke her. She watched in satisfaction as the killer's thrashings weakened. When her stomach suddenly signaled that it intended to revolt against its contents, she washed it down with the rest of her water bottle, then burped.

The final tension released from the killer's body at Katie's unceremonious belch. Chase and Misty collapsed on the ground hard after letting go of the legs. They hugged each other. Jason hugged Shawna. Tera ran at Katie and jumped up on her hips unexpectedly, bringing them both to the ground, rolling in each other's arms. When they stopped, Tera kissed Katie deeply, passionately. Her hands touched Katie in places that should have been saved for a warm bed.

She had a brief thought that she should protest and push Tera away, but something in her egged her to return Tera's passion. Katie grasped Tera's butt, then dismayed that her pants were too tight to get her hands under the waistband. Their lips didn't part as Katie fumbled for the snaps of Tera's front buttons. Before they could enter any state of undress, four loud throat-clears came from a few feet away. They broke their kiss and looked up together at Jason, Shawna, Misty, and Chase with their arms folded and looks of horniness, amusement, disbelief, and annoyance.

Tera got up spryly, then lifted Katie up effortlessly.

"I feel so fucking *great!*" she exclaimed. "My ankle's all better! My headache's gone! What the *fuck!*"

She embraced the other four excitedly before coming back to Katie and hugging her tightest of all, spinning her in the air. Now that they'd survived, all Katie wanted to do was get Tera into a bedroom so she could get all the weird energy out. For *her* benefit, of course.

Shawna came up and hugged Tera from behind. The other three came in for a big hug as well, as they all nervously giggled out their survivors' relief.

"Can we go now, boss?" Katie teased Chase.

"Let's wait until morning. I'm fuckin' exhausted," she replied, then lowered the tailgate of the small truck and crawled in.

Misty followed. Shawna and Jason went to the F-350 and did the same. Tera never let go of Katie until Katie, against her will, pushed Tera to join the F-350 and get some sleep. Katie leaned against the smaller truck with the shotgun resting on her shoulder.

"You can sleep next to us, Katie," Misty said.

"In a little bit. I'm going to stand watch."

Chase peeked over the rim and clicked her tongue.

"When was the last time you slept? I think you've taken every guard duty over the last three nights *and* longer than anyone else. I'll stand watch for you."

"I appreciate it, boss. But I'm wide awake right now."

Chase laid down, grumbling for people to stop calling her that.

Katie ambled to the corpse of the killer. Feeling petty just looking at the remains, she dragged him to the cabin and pushed his body into the fire. She stood back out of the flames' heat radius and watched it burn. After a few moments she swayed on her feet. Her eyes grew heavier as the warmth wrapped around her like a blanket.

She dreamed of Tera lying on top of a waterbed, her curves syncing with the bed's movements. Katie stood on the frame's edge, ready to dive into the middle, but when she started falling her arms and legs wouldn't move. A painful belly-flop awaited her. Tera disappeared as Katie braced for impact.

She startled awake as her face hit something hard, standing between her and the fire. The morning's cold sent a fierce shiver up her spine. She trembled as she looked up to see the full, unburned, undestroyed features of the killer in front of her. She backed away while bringing the shotgun and its last two shells up, but the killer grabbed the barrel and yanked it out of Katie's hands.

She thought she might still be sleeping and slapped the underside of her forearm. It stung and, to her dismay, signaled she was indeed awake. She startled herself again as she backed into something even harder—the grill of the small truck. The killer didn't advance on her or do anything with the shotgun other than hold it by the barrel. He turned and looked down at the smoldering pile on the porch.

After regaining her breath, Katie realized it was *Slater's* slumped back. She approached him with caution. He dropped the shotgun to the ground. Katie picked it up, then shuffled a couple steps to his side. His cheeks were grimy with rivulets of mud coming from his eyes.

"Lynn said... Is Killian really gone?"

Slater nodded. Katie couldn't help feeling sorry for him, no matter what she thought about their strange, dangerous family before. Of all the things she'd distrusted about the man, there was no doubt how much he'd loved his wife. That unexpected acknowledgment of his capacity for true compassion carried her closer to Slater. She put her hand in his. Her normal revulsion for men, and Slater in particular, didn't keep her from hugging him, or stop her from a horrifying drive to pull his head down to her level and kiss him on the mouth. He looked hard into her eyes after pulling away from her.

"You... Did you eat—?" Slater asked as he switched from her eyes to the corpse on the porch.

When he broke eye contact, she shook her head and came back to her body. Katie let go of his hand and backed away in horror. Something had possessed her to kiss him.

"What...the *fuck?*" Katie whispered as she wiped her lips in disgust.

"You've..." Slater started, "he ate my Killian's heart... Now you..."

Katie's eyes widened in terror at the implication. A ruckus came from the back of the F-350 as Shawna cried out "Tera, stop!" Katie turned to find Tera strangling Jason. Chase and Misty jumped out of their truck and pulled Tera away from him. After a moment, she shook her head as Katie had, then apologized profusely to Jason.

"What the fuck is happening to us, Slater?" Katie asked loudly as she backed away to the truck, holding her hand out for Tera to get down.

Slater looked at them sadly.

"Were you the only two that ate the heart?"

They nodded in unison.

"Your bodies absorbed the essence of his heart, as well as the hearts *he* consumed. You've got my wife in you. That's why you kissed me. The killer's heart is why Tera tried to kill the boy. I don't know what else will happen to you—whether he consumed other hearts like ours other than Killian's. But we're all different. You'll feel all the essences at some point."

"How do we stop this?" Tera asked as her grip tightened around Katie's waist. Tera's little burst of inappropriate passion before made much more sense.

"You won't be able to. If you're anything like Killian and me, you'll learn to deal with it and lean on each other to file down the edges."

"That...doesn't sound so bad..." Katie whispered, unsure if that was her thought or Killian's.

Slater stepped to them, his hands curling into claws. Katie backed away with Tera holding tight. "However, I won't let that happen. I *will* have my Killian back."

"If you mean...going home with you, I'll kill myself before I'd—"

"That's good. I can take your hearts with less effort. I...like both of you. I wish it didn't have to be this way."

Katie scrambled to think of a plan, but all that came to her was planting the shotgun over his heart and hoping the spread blew it out the back. but he wouldn't let her get that close. She still raised it, though, hoping the threat would stop him from taking another step.

Chase stood in the back of the F-350 and pulled a pin on a grenade, then tossed it at Slater's feet. He kicked it beneath the smaller truck's chassis and it blew on the other side.

"I'll deal with you kids in a moment," Slater said matter-of-fact-ly.

Chase and Jason prepared to leap on his back from the tailgate, but Katie shouted at them to stop.

"Slater, you still have a promise to keep," Katie said, causing him to finally stop in his tracks. "We have a full Sunday ahead of us. Your vacation doesn't end until Monday."

"You damn bitch. How dare you hold my promise over me?"

"Are you willing to break it? You still have a daughter. She's waiting for you in Roseburg by now. Killian...she's asking you to keep your promise for her sake. For your daughter's sake."

Luckily it was still dark; he might have seen Katie's face burning bright red through her bluff, but he seemed to buy it. She didn't hear Killian's thoughts so much as feel her impulses. She wanted to kiss Slater *and* bond permanently with Tera. Katie's mind felt like a marionette with Killian's lovely, slender, clawed fingers controlling it. It was everything Katie could do to fight through that invisible influence, but she realized she could use that against Slater for the time being. His hands had lost their strangling quality and his shoulders slumped again.

"Guys, I want you to get to the highway. Hitch your way into Roseburg," Katie said. "The Hunts went to the sheriff's office. They'll probably be there for a while as they work to get people up here. Meet them there."

The four of them got down from the truck and gave Slater a wide berth.

"What are you going to do?" Chase whispered into Katie's ear.

"I'm going to hold this man to his promise while you prepare the sheriff for our arrival. Tell them to get blades ready. See if you can get them to lock up Lynn before we get there."

Chase nodded and put her hands on Katie and Tera's shoulders, giving a reassuring squeeze. Misty and Jason followed her down the driveway. Shawna hugged Tera, then ran down after them.

"What do you plan to do with me for a whole day?" Slater asked.

"I'm getting you to your daughter. I just...needed to be sure everyone else was going to be safely away from you, no matter what happens between us."

Though he didn't make any aggressive moves towards the two of them, anger and frustration showed in his face. She felt pangs of sympathy for him that weren't her own.

Killian was going to be hard to suppress.

CHAPTER 21
FULL UP

KILL COUNT: 30

A week's worth of contained instincts escaped from Slater's body through a blood-chilling roar at the sight of his Killian, splayed on the forest floor with a gaping hole in her chest. All because of those rednecks. The more he thought about it, the angrier he got. Why had he bothered to see what the gunshots were about? Lynn would always be safe. The other people in the cabin had been armed. He should have let the chips fall as they may, or, at the very least, awakened his wife to investigate the gunshots together.

That son of a bitch out there... Having the time of his life in the mountains, playing their remote location beautifully, killing indiscriminately without *a promise* to hold him back. Slater was fine with all that, except when it came to the Hunts and his own family. Yet...

The trip had robbed him of two of his own while the Hunts remained intact. Despite the unexpected friendship, Slater would trade all of them to get Killian back. He could live without his son, but he needed his wife. The only way to get her back would be unsatisfactory to the real thing, but better than letting her essence reside forever in the killer's heart.

Slater searched around the cabin's perimeter for a while un-til the only thing he could see were his own tracks. The killer proved to be too strong, too cunning for Slater to keep up. Even if he came across the killer, he had doubts for the first time in his life that he would be powerful enough—Killian was near-ly Slater's match, and she had been dispatched too easily... Of course she'd been sleeping at the time, but that did nothing to quell Slater's increasing despair—an unfamiliar feeling.

He watched the cabin go up in flames and the group of un-worthy fools he'd been protecting too much as they carried his daughter into the forest. Hoping to catch the killer follow-ing them, Slater sat on a log and waited. Tera's gambit with the grenade bought them plenty of time to escape. The killer's charred body eventually climbed out of the window, but before Slater could even stand up to run after him, he disappeared around the cabin. Slater chased but lost the trail just as he had before.

Fed up with the futility of it all, he returned to Killian's body and carried her further up the hill to search for a suitable resting spot. After a decent hike he startled a mountain lion near its den. It tore off into the night as he approached.

They'd never made plans for what to do with their bodies. There was no need for wills when the only thing they had to pass on was their beating hearts, and it was unlikely they'd get to pick who ate it. The thought that hurt Slater the most was knowing that, if they had been careful, they could have lived together for centuries more. They weren't *quite* immortal like vampires, but their bodies' deterioration was slow, and they could add centuries of renewal by consuming more hearts of their kind. With their children still less than two decades old, Slater and Killian hadn't even remotely *considered* their ends would be near.

Burying her body without its heart meant nothing in the long run. Her essence wasn't with it. But Slater remembered how much Killian loved the natural world. He imagined she would have been okay letting her body feed nature, so he laid it near the mouth of the den, then stripped off her clothes.

Something he never thought he'd feel hit him as he looked upon her one last time—sadness.

He would never find another like her. Any other female from their species could never replace Killian. She had been perfect in every conceivable way.

As he trudged back down the hill toward the cabin, he had a desperate thought—what if the killer consumed *Slater's* heart and reunited his essence with Killian's? It would leave Lynn alone, but she was headstrong and ready to take on the world despite her lack of training. She dragged Corey into the family, so she'd have someone even when both her parents were gone. Slater didn't care to wonder how the Hunts would handle any of it.

All he wanted was his Killian.

Explosions and gunshots rang out from below. Slater might have run down to end the killer before, but in his grief he only wanted to reminisce on his great love. He prepared himself mentally for what he'd allow the killer to do to him—after the killer finished off the teenagers, of course. Slater passively wondered if he would see Killian's signature in any of the kills.

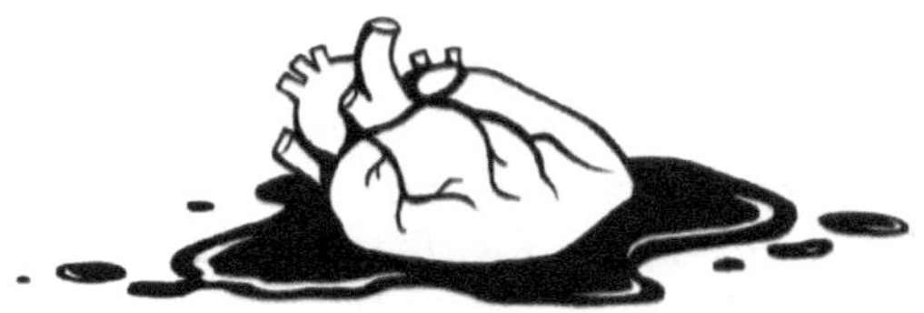

Katie kept the shotgun pointed at Slater's chest, using the hood of the small truck to steady her elbow while Tera slept in the back. Katie wouldn't let herself sleep, and although Slater hadn't started a fight, she wasn't convinced of their relative safety. Her eyes were puffy and dark, and her eyelids kept fluttering closed as the very first light of dawn brightened the sky.

Slater thought over his options. He had prepared to offer his heart to the killer, but the young lovebirds shit all over that. Killing them and consuming their hearts was the first thing that came to mind, but they just *had* to remember that fucking promise... Knowing Killian could sense him through the girls, he couldn't bring himself to break it, though. He'd made such an effort to follow through for her sake...

Another option was to let them kill *him* and consume his heart as he'd planned for the killer to do. Ultimately that would give him what he wanted—a reunion with Killian's essence. But he realized that neglected Lynn in his plans, when previously he'd have never considered abandoning her before formally passing on the family business. He had felt such pride for her during the trip, then utter disappointment, then a growing indifference.

That wasn't a one-way street. Lynn was angrier at Slater for what happened to Corey during the shootout in the cabin than for his getting sloppy and shot in the back of the head. She clung to the boy. She was willing to give up centuries of the most legendary teaching the world would ever see, all because her self-control didn't exist... Except for when she lied to her parents, Slater thought bitterly.

Maybe he'd looked at his little girl through blood-smeared glasses for too long. They made a mistake by delaying her training when she so clearly wanted to start. Then she might have understood what she gave up; her full, unrealized potential.

If they'd taken her to work, Lynn would have discovered how powerful abstinence could be, even to mortals. She would have witnessed many of the final girls escape their lessons thanks to *their* self-control. It wasn't *always* like that—*of course* there were exceptions. But Lynn's behavior didn't fill Slater with hope that she would be one.

Only her mother had been exceptional... Truly.

Tera startled Katie awake by hopping out of the truck. Slater expected the shotgun to go off, but Katie maintained control even though her eyes had been closed. How much longer could that last?

With no sense of modesty or wariness of the company in front of her, Tera wrapped Katie up and kissed her, a few seconds from tearing off their clothes. Katie resisted for a second before leaning into it just as hungrily.

You're overdoing it, sweetheart.

Slater cleared his throat pointedly. The girls stopped and looked sideways at him without parting their lips. They slowly peeled away from each other when Slater made it clear he wasn't going to avert his eyes. The girls stared at each other before coming to their senses.

"Wha—why did…?" Tera sputtered.

"Did you get a sense of…disgust, too?" Katie asked.

"Yeah! But it wasn't *mine*! I…I really— I like you a lot, Katie. But it was like an invasion of my mind… I didn't start all that but, well, *I* certainly didn't want to stop it, either."

"Your choice in orientation seems to have tempted my wife," Slater guessed. "She probably always wondered what it would be like to try, but couldn't get past it."

"It's not a—! Oh goddamn, I am *not* getting into that argument with *you* of all people. But…the *passion* in her… Jesus Christ, Slater," Katie said as she held her hand to her forehead. "Until she showed her *preference* at the end there, I've never felt such a surge of… Love seems like too mild a word for it."

"Killian's love is strong enough to make me not kill you two and kept me from killing every person in this forest all week. I wish I could convey to you how deep and meaningful that is for someone like me."

"So, we have your wife's libido now?" Tera asked as she leaned against the truck next to Katie.

"For a brief moment you did. If she felt displeased after indulging in the vicarious curiosity, it probably won't be as easy to sync up with her desires again going forward."

"How do we get rid of her? I don't want that feeling coming up when Katie and I… Well, when I…do that later… You know?"

Slater sighed and leaned next to Katie's other side. Their tension dissipated as they reflected on their options together.

"I don't know how we could rid you of her without killing you. And…if we don't think of something by tomorrow, I'm not waiting to find another solution. In a way, I'm sorry it's you two standing in my way. I'm not sorry for anyone I have to go through to get my Killian back, though."

"Thanks for your honesty, I guess," Katie scoffed.

"Well, you'll both prove difficult to subdue. You killed the most powerful one of us the world's seen in quite some time, and now you have his and Killian's essences, as well as those he may have killed before. I've got my work cut out for me." Slater almost tried to joke, but the girls weren't in the mood.

"I don't feel all that proud of any of this," Tera said, staring off into the dying fire of the cabin. "We just went through so much shit and I lost so many of my friends but it's… It's messed up that this is the first time I've ever *wanted* to be myself." She quickly glanced over to Katie and blushed. "And now I'm less myself than I started."

All three of them turned towards the driveway at the sound of a vehicle approaching. Slater smiled a little bit. Their hearing already improved. When they scampered off to hide, they moved almost as gracefully as Killian. Given a few days' practice, they'd be naturals. Slater moved to the trees and hid.

An old rural fire engine with a big water tank parked next to the small truck and a couple of volunteer firefighters got out and prepped the hose for the cabin. The smoke must have been spotted as soon as the sun came up. Slater saw an opportunity to steal the truck and drive to Lynn. He only took a single step before stopping. He watched in amusement as Tera came out from behind the F-350, sneaking up to the back of one of the firefighters.

She pulled a bowie knife out from her waistband a few feet from her target, transfixing Slater. Tera reminded him of Killian when she was the same age, her slender, athletic body, and lithe, cat-like movements. Pulling out that knife excited him in a way he thought would be lost forever.

She dowsed his arousal by stopping at the last moment. Tera stood up straight and examined the knife in puzzlement, like she had no idea how it—or she—had gotten there. She scratched the back of her head until Katie came up behind her and pulled her away. The firefighter never noticed anyone behind him.

Come on, Slater thought. *Embrace it!*

While the hose shot out and created enough noise, the girls snuck into the firetruck. Slater closed the distance between the trees and the truck and climbed into the passenger side.

"Leaving without me?"

"Figured you could see us," Katie said as she turned the engine over and backed down the driveway, ripping the hose out of the firefighter's hands.

The truck bumped and jostled violently on the way down the driveway—Katie didn't take it slow. Slater wished he'd put on the seatbelt like the girls. His head smashed through the side window as a particularly large bump threw him into it. When Katie slid the truck out onto the highway and put it into gear, Tera put her hand on his head where it bled. He felt Killian's concern through her touch.

Why *would* she be concerned, though? Killian would have known that was nothing more than a scratch. It'd heal in no time. And Tera had no reason to be concerned about his health... He watched their psyches clash across her face before she shook her head and asked Katie to stop.

Once the truck pulled over, Tera climbed out over Slater and cut the trailing hose with the knife, then climbed in and tapped Katie's thigh to get going again.

"Where did you get that?" Katie asked. "I thought Chase took it with her."

"She slipped it in my waistband as we hugged goodbye."

"Probably insurance against leaving you two alone with me," Slater mused.

A few miles on, the truck nearly hit an oncoming minivan before Tera tore the wheel from Katie and steadied them. Katie had slumped back in the seat and snored softly. Tera scooted Katie to the side and pulled the truck over, then swapped her zonked-out weight to the middle with Slater's help. Tera adjusted the shotgun next to the door and got them moving again, grinding gears for a ways before Slater's annoyance forced him to give her instructions. She got the hang of it after a few miles.

Once all the lurching and grinding finished, Katie nuzzled into Slater's side. She fully succumbed to a deep sleep that had been a *long* time coming. Her pungent stress sweat smelled *wonderful*. Katie hadn't found much time to sleep, let alone shower over the last week. It was *almost* like Killian's musk when she didn't shower for a while, despite their daughter's lectures on "proper hygiene."

A tear nearly came to his eye as Katie's arm hugged around his waist and she sighed blissfully, purring like Killian would.

A dozen sheriff's cars, several ambulances, and two news vans passed them about halfway between the lake and Roseburg.

"Little fuckin' *late*, assholes..." Tera muttered.

She sniffed, then a few sobs burst forth, causing the truck to swerve. Slater told her to pull over and they switched places. She placed the shotgun against the passenger door and positioned herself with Katie so they resembled perfect beings of love and comfort. Slater once again got them moving in a positive direction. For all the mishaps the girls caused during their turns driving, Slater found that he wasn't much better, routinely glancing away from the road to the pair with envy.

In the town of Glide, Slater pulled over at a gas station. The girls woke up after the rumble of the old truck came to a stop. They stretched and climbed out once the weapons were hidden beneath the bench seat.

"How are we paying for the gas, hon—goddamn it—*Slater?*" Katie said.

Katie held onto herself remarkably, Slater thought. *Killian must be tearing her proverbial hair out.*

"Get the pump ready," Slater said to Katie as she yawned. "I'll handle the cashier."

Slater started towards the minimart when Tera came to his side and put her hand in his. Tera, in contrast to Katie, proved much more malleable. A few feet shy of the door she ripped her hand away. The same look she'd had when she almost killed the firefighter spread across her face—this time, a hint more horrified.

"Tell your wife to leave me alone, Slater," Tera scowled and went into the minimart ahead of him.

Inside, Tera busied herself around the warmed-over food that'd been spinning for over a week while Slater leaned on the front counter. The cashier stuffed a pinch of dip behind his lower lip. Slater gave the young man his warmest, fakest smile.

"Howdy, son. I don't want to bore you with a long-winded story about how we came to your gas station in desperate need of your product. Suffice to say, I'm going to need you to allow that beautiful young lady out there to start pumping. *Now.*"

The young man smirked and peered out at Katie, who thrummed her fingers on the hood of the truck.

"Sorry, *dad*. You gotta pay, or you gotta move on. And she's a six, *at best.*"

"He's giving you a polite chance to go along, dude," Tera piped up from the food corner. "Believe me, you need to take the olive branch."

"Are you two threatening me?" the cashier spit into a tin can that looked like it hadn't been cleaned since he was born, then pulled a sawn-off shotgun from beneath the counter.

Tera nonchalantly brought an armful of food and drinks to the counter and looked at the shotgun with the same look of amusement Killian would get whenever one of their students thought to stand up for themselves.

"Look, dude, let my girlfriend fill up our…family heirloom truck and bag up this food, before I—"

Tera slapped her forehead and leaned on the counter, grimacing at the battle playing out inside her mind.

"What the *fuck?* How is she *doing* this?"

"Alright," the cashier said as he picked up his phone, keeping the shotgun trained on the two of them, "I'm calling the cops on you dykes, and Bigfoot here."

Before Slater moved, Tera thrust her hand out and snatched the end of the gun. She yanked it out of the young man's hand, causing him to drop his phone over the counter at Slater's feet. Slater stepped on the screen and enjoyed the satisfying crunch of the glass.

Tera pointed the gun at the man and forced him to get the pump flowing. Slater looked at her sideways and raised an eyebrow.

"Sweetheart?"

"No, that was *me*. Killian let that 'girlfriend' comment slip, opening me up for the first time in this podunk county to judgment that I've lived in fear of my whole life, and he *immediately* goes for the D-word! I was going to get the address and mail him the money later, but now…"

Tera thrust the barrel closer to the young man's face, making him flinch back.

"…you're going to give me your stash of weed, you little *shit*."

Slater and the young man shared a look. Slater shrugged that the young man had better get with the program before Killian *or* Tera started getting violent.

CHAPTER 22

SELFLESSNESS

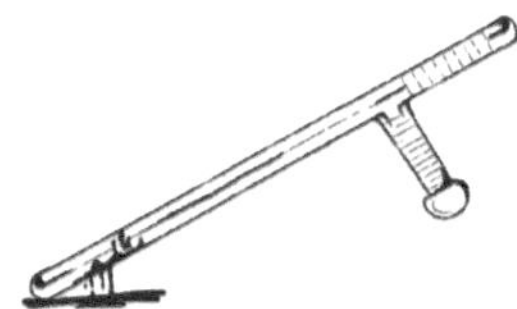

KILL COUNT: 30

TIMOTHY AND JESSICA LISTENED to Chase, Misty, Jason, and Shawna recount the final battle. The kids' ingenuity and sacrifices for one another floored them. The sheriff's office allowed them all to stay in the conference room while the deputies worked on preparing a force to cover the resort area. Chase had told the sheriff all she could from the kids' perspective while Timothy shared all he knew to supplement it.

Amber sat in the waiting room with Corey, TJ, and Maggie. Corey was moody and got threatened with being cuffed and thrown in a cell when he protested Lynn's temporary separation. They questioned her after Chase spoke with one of the deputies.

Only a few miles from where Katie had left them, a semi with an extended living cab pulled over and offered the Hunts, Lynn, and Amber a ride the rest of the way into Roseburg. Corey and Lynn couldn't keep their hands off each other, even in the presence of his parents. Timothy and Jessica had to separate them to opposite ends of the cab. Corey mumbled to himself that he was going to go home with her anyway. Not wanting to make a scene for the nice man who'd gone out of his way to pick them all up, Timothy held his tongue, but he could tell Jessica was at her wit's end from the lack of sleep and the harrowing events that transpired within the cabin.

With the attention shifted to rescue efforts, Chase detailed to Timothy how Katie and Tera were still trapped up there with Slater, and Slater had threatened them. Those girls had risked their lives for all of them more than once. Timothy hoped the deputies would get there before something awful happened to them. Slater had shown himself to be a friend a number of times, but only to Timothy and his family. With Killian's death, it was anyone's guess how he would react, especially after hearing that mournful, devastated howl upon finding her dead body.

A deputy came into the conference room, shaking her head.

"That girl in there is a real piece of work. All she wants is to be with her boyfriend. Doesn't care what happened at the lake at all, it seems."

"She's dangerous, ma'am," Chase said. "I wish I could tell you why, but it would sound more insane than everything you've been told this morning already."

"Care to humor me on that?"

Chase looked at the surviving teens, and they nodded. All four of them followed the deputy to an interrogation room, leaving Timothy alone with Jessica.

Timothy rested his head on the table. His family was safe. He could rent a car *right now* and they'd be home in about twelve hours, but... He feared how Corey would react. Timothy had no idea what to do with Lynn. If his family wasn't there, Timothy would go back for Katie and Tera. He'd take Amber and the other four kids home personally. He'd give Slater a chance to explain himself without the killer's ominous presence keeping them from having a real conversation. He'd help the sheriff's deputies piece together the entire sprawling crime scene. He'd—

Jessica put her hand on his back and rubbed, bringing him back to the present. She smiled weakly and they embraced for a few moments. Timothy's eyes welled up at the sound of his wife's soft sniffling. It was odd—feeling "safe" after all that; and he still couldn't relax thanks to all the future complications running through his mind.

"I..." Timothy started.

"Before we do anything, you need to talk to your son."

It felt good having a direction in that moment. He nodded and kissed her, then they left the conference room. Jessica went to sit with TJ and Maggie while Amber stared off into space next to them. Timothy took Corey outside and sat down on a nearby bench.

"I know what you're going to say, Dad," Corey said.

"Well, that's a relief. I've been dreading this talk for years, and you went ahead and learned everything there is to know in a few nights."

"I don't know everything. I know that I love her, though."

Timothy refrained from chuckling at his son's blissful naïveté. He had fallen in love with Jessica early, too, but never acted on it. He had no experience to pull from while he was still in high school. His love for Jessica hadn't been muddled by the burst of hormones and emotions that came along with a first-time sexual encounter. Or so he heard...

"Look, son, I can't pretend to know what you're feeling. You nearly drowned, you saved Tera and Katie's lives, you've had *sex* for the first time, you were *shot* for the first time, and you rose from the *dead* for the first time—all within a few days! Before I tell you how you *should* feel, why don't you tell me how you *do* feel? What's going on inside?"

Corey didn't betray too much outward emotion, as teenagers are wont to withhold, but it seemed like he hadn't even considered anything outside of his new "girlfriend" who consumed his every thought.

"I don't know how to describe it, Dad. I feel...violent! I wanted to kill that deputy that dragged Lynn away. But her love...it *soothed* me. Something strange also happened when... Before you and Mom separated us... I felt this insane love for her, but in the back of my mind, something spoke up, like...a little voice separate from my own... It even sounded kind of like TJ—saying what we were doing was disgusting and I was better off 'whapping it' than making out with such an ugly girl."

Timothy had a hard time digesting any of that. None of it made sense.

"You really think she's ugly?"

"Jesus, Dad! *I* don't think she's ugly. And she's...changing really fast. Haven't you noticed? Ever since... Never mind. But it was the *voice* calling her ugly! And I would never say 'whap it.' After... Hmm... After she and I shared something...*not that*...but, she had me eat something. It was dark so I didn't see what it was. It was meaty, though. She said it would protect me. I remember getting these weird thoughts after I ate it—like the one I just described—like, really far in the back of my mind."

"Why didn't you—?"

"Why didn't I say anything? 'Oh yeah, Mom, Dad, by the way, I'm hearing voices now on top of everything else that's going on.'"

Timothy remembered something Shawna had said in the conference room. After Tera and Katie ate the killer's heart, they made out in front of everyone, and likely would have had sex if they hadn't been interrupted. Shawna had known about Tera, but Chase, Misty, and Jason hadn't, and Tera lived in fear of anyone else knowing about her orientation to the point that she'd chosen a double life with her best friend Peter as a cover.

"Son, did Lynn ever say how her brother died?"

Corey shrugged.

"She doesn't talk about him. Didn't her dad say the killer got to him?"

Timothy sat back in deep thought.

"Dad?"

"We'll continue this conversation later, but *before* you and Lynn are alone together again. Go back to sit with the others. I need to check something out."

Timothy asked a deputy if he could see Lynn in one of the interrogation rooms. They let him inside and he sat down across from her. It was a strange thing to fixate on, but Timothy studied her face for a moment before either of them spoke. She really had gotten prettier, hadn't she? Lynn raised her eyebrows and took on a shy glow, but didn't say anything. Timothy cleared his throat, attempting to take the position of authority.

"Lynn, what happened to your brother?"

"Daddy said it was—"

"No. When you came back to the campground with TJ's game console, it was bloody. You left bloody handprints all over Corey's shirt. You fed my son something after you two...you two..."

"Made love?"

Timothy let his hand drop on the table and he stared at her in exasperation.

"I didn't need *that* part of the sentence finished for me! What *really* happened to your brother?"

Lynn looked around while scratching her arm.

"No one's watching right now. This is just between you and me."

Lynn stared down at her hands, then mumbled something.

"What was that?" Timothy asked as he leaned in.

"He was going to kill your son..."

"Corey?"

"No, TJ. When I confronted Murdock about the game console, he threatened to kill TJ if I gave it back to him."

"So, you...*killed him?*"

"I didn't mean to. I *literally* didn't know my own strength. I haven't had a chance to practice anything yet! My parents were really close to letting me join them. They probably would have started teaching me...after the vacation... Anyway, I...got a little rough with him and...broke his neck. If it makes you feel any better, that was always destined to happen. It would have been me or him eventually."

"Why on Earth would that make me feel better?"

Lynn shrugged and looked down at her hands again.

"What *are* you people?"

"I don't know that there's a name for what we are. There are many of us, though."

Timothy's gut sank as all the pieces that'd been dodging his understanding all week finally fell into place.

"You've made Corey one of you, haven't you?"

Lynn didn't look up, but she nodded slightly.

"It's more than the miraculous healing. Did you know he can hear Murdock's voice?"

She was finally surprised about *something* and met his eyes. "What? Daddy never said that would... I mean, I can hear Murdock, too, a little bit, but I never thought someone outside the family would..." Lynn took a second to organize her thoughts into something comprehensible. Timothy knew how hard it was to understand something so outside of the realms he'd previously thought possible, but here they were. Lynn continued. "Eating hearts—they only told me I would gain the others' strength. I always thought it would forge a strong emotional connection after sharing the heart with my love, like my parents have. Had..."

Lynn sniffed, likely thinking about her mother.

Great, Timothy thought. *She's not* evil, *she's just misguided.*

He cleared his throat, cementing his resolve for the unpleasant news he meant to deliver next. "Look, Lynn, I don't know what's going to happen with your father. I'm assuming you would have felt it by now if something happened to him? Like you did with your mother?"

Lynn nodded.

"If he comes down from the mountain, *safely*, you need to go with him. I don't want to entertain any thoughts you or Corey might have that my family will take you in if Slater doesn't come back, though. I'm sorry to sound cold-hearted, but you're going back to *your* home, not ours. Call relatives, call others like you, live alone—I'm sorry, but you can't stay with us. You and Corey are too young. You aren't ready for...*all this.*"

Lynn's shy glow disappeared rapidly, and, alarmingly, the room's temperature rose. She furrowed her brow, only slightly, and yet Timothy was shocked to find that simple change in expression *scared* him.

"You're not taking my Corey from me," she whispered.

"He's not *your* Corey. He's still a child. Do we *really* need to have this conversation?"

Lynn frowned at him before folding her arms and looking away.

"If I was '*normal*' like any of those *slutty cheerleaders* you wouldn't be saying that."

"I can see why you'd think that, but... They're not...whatever *you* are. All I'm learning about your family..."

"You know, *I'm* a child, too! I just lost my mom! My crappy little brother is gone. Who knows what'll happen to Daddy? I don't have any other family. Like it or not, Corey and I are...connected thanks to that heart I gave him. The heart that *saved his life*, by the way.

"Let me tell you, Corey is going to *need me* to help guide him through his changes. I saved both of your sons. I saved your dog even though it attacked me. And I...*I need him*... My...urges are tempered when I'm around him."

Timothy didn't trust her enough to believe that, despite the good points she raised. There was too much unknown about her...species? Race? Branch of monsterdom? Still...

"Alright, Lynn, we'll talk about this later with Jessica. If Slater makes it back to you, that's the answer. If not...we'll discuss it further. I'm inclined to tell you to learn how to deal with a long-distance relationship until Corey graduates, but...you've given me plenty to think about."

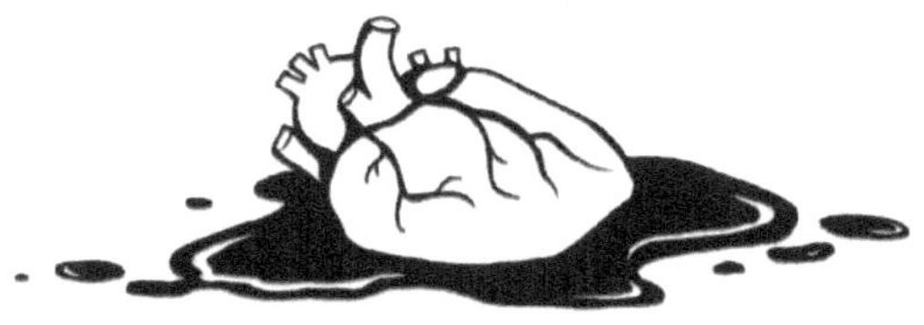

In the early afternoon, all the teens' parents swarmed the parking lot of the sheriff's building. While the survivors' parents smothered them, the parents of missing kids demanded answers from the deputies who hadn't left for the resort. Voices raised, and eventually the deputies had to rely on the large wooden separation to keep them from the parents as they pushed aggressively into the lobby.

Thirteen families had been contacted about their children missing—twelve with rumored fatalities confirmed only by Chase, and one belonging to Tera. Timothy had no idea what he could possibly say to assure any of them, so he kept his family tucked away from the mob of forlorn parents. It proved to be a good decision—some of the parents tipped beyond furious to *dangerously* furious in their search for answers.

Soon some of the families started pointing fingers. Whose idea was the trip anyway? Weren't the kids supposed to be visiting their new colleges? Practicing with their college football teams? Staying the night at their best friends' homes? Cheering for charity?

All were excuses they'd been fed by their kids, adding to the endless confusion and despair. To Timothy's horror, Chase gathered them all and admitted her part in orchestrating the lies and stealing the bus. She stood strong and never wavered through the admission. The remaining deputies had taken the lull in the families coming after them to don riot gear and came out to separate Chase and her family from the near-riotous families of the presumed deceased. Misty, Shawna, and Jason stood next to Chase in solidarity. Though it seemed to torture her at first, Amber eventually joined them, protecting their Queen Bee from the worst of the families' fury.

By the late afternoon the vitriol died down as reality sunk in for many of them. Timothy's heart hurt as he imagined how he'd feel if Corey or TJ had been one of the departed. Lynn's words struck him properly then, as they hadn't when she said them—she had protected his boys. Murdock could have murdered TJ. Those rednecks murdered Corey. The killer might have murdered Maggie.

Were it not for Lynn, Timothy and Jessica would have been another pair of enraged parents coming to grips with their children never returning home. Would he be able to hold back from going after Chase, not knowing how strong and fearless she'd been during the whole ordeal?

He remembered his fear when Corey jumped into the water selflessly to save Tera—a person he didn't know. Someone was in trouble and he acted immediately. He did the same thing in the cabin when he picked up the magnum to save Katie. Corey didn't know he'd be safe from the returned bullet—it was another selfless act to protect a stranger.

Timothy hugged his son tight, much to Corey's annoyance.

The parents with kids presumed dead were eventually told by the deputies to go home, and that they'd be contacted the moment more definitive news reached them. The parents of the surviving children didn't hide their desire to go home as well, but their kids refused to leave, holding out hope that Tera would be rescued by the caravan of deputies that had made for the resort earlier in the day. Chase and Shawna were adamant they wouldn't leave until they knew for sure either way.

Timothy bought a dozen pizzas for the remaining families and the deputies holding the fort while they waited for more information. As the sun set, a deputy who'd been working the phones for hours with no break pulled Tera's family aside to speak. There were reports of a girl matching her description traveling with an older woman and large man. There were also indications she was more than a mere hostage in their little crime spree. Worse, by the look in her parents' eyes, Tera and the woman seemed to be romantically linked.

"She's not herself! There's something going on with—" Chase interjected, only to be turned on by Tera's parents. They'd had enough of Chase's interference.

Not even Shawna could soften the double blow or convince them nothing was going to be as it seemed, and Shawna and Chase hedged away from discussing the supernatural aspect of it all. Timothy couldn't blame Tera's parents for not believing the jarring news presented to them, but he *could* blame them for taking the rumor of Tera's orientation on par with how many of the other families had learned their children were likely *dead*.

Timothy pulled the deputy that had interviewed the teens aside and asked what she thought of their stories. She scanned around, then lowered her voice before telling him she thought the kids were either on hard drugs and alcohol for the whole trip, or they were in on the deaths of their friends. She wasn't holding them because she needed more information from the deputies combing the resort. She knew where they all lived anyway, and they were already keeping themselves nearby for the sake of Tera so there was no need to escalate their containment...yet.

Timothy prepared to lay things out clearly for the deputy, but, in that moment, he realized he had only seen one death by the killer—Darren's on the canoe. He could clear up the redneck snafu—at least everything aside from Lynn, Slater, and Corey's recoveries... The more he thought about it, there would still be too many questions begetting more questions, and he was liable to say something that would give the deputies the same cause to distrust him as the teens.

Tera's fate was in her own hands—if the reports were to be believed. Timothy had nothing left to contribute but comfort to his family. He worried that he'd never see Slater again, not only as a friend, but that the unfortunate circumstance would force him to make a decision on Lynn. Banishing her wouldn't feel right—he knew that—but unconditionally welcoming an unknown entity into his family didn't hit the mark, either. He pulled Jessica aside and discussed their options. Once they came to a decision, they braced for the fight ahead.

CHAPTER 23
TAKING CHARGE

KILL COUNT: 30

TERA PUT HER ARMFUL of food, drinks, and weed into the cab, then handed Katie two shells from the gas station cashier's sawed-off. When their hands touched Tera felt another surge of attraction, too painful to suppress. She put her arms around Katie's neck and kissed her while she fumbled the gas nozzle back into its home. Slater pulled them apart by the shoulders.

"This... I can't... I thought she wasn't into it?" Tera whispered to herself as she climbed into the cab.

Katie and Slater discussed who should drive but Tera leaned her head out and said her hands were already on the wheel. Katie was too tired and there was no telling where Slater would take them. The closer they got to the end of his damn vacation, the less they could afford to trust him.

Back on the road and grinding the gears much less often, Tera realized they were in the most conspicuous vehicle in the county, and they just robbed a business at gunpoint. Killian drove too much of Tera's participation in the whole thing, making it hard for her to process how *she* felt about everything going on; were the butterflies in her stomach exhilaration from the robbery, anxiety over driving the stick-shift, or bursts of lust for Katie?

Tera slammed her fist on the steering wheel. She couldn't think of anything she could possibly say if they were pulled over, and the danger of Killian getting her own words in terrified her. Shitty possibilities piled up and their options dwindled. Katie put her hand over Tera's fist but said nothing as she drifted to sleep again. Tera glanced at the back of Slater's head as he gazed out at the passing hills.

"Hey, there has to be something we can do. I don't want your wife in me for the rest of my life. I have school in a few months. I have family and friends. What the fuck are we even doing right now? Where are we running to?"

"To get Lynn."

"Does she not know her way home, or can't she figure it out? I don't want to deal with the sheriff. That's where they went, by the way. They're the reason we passed that entourage of authority back there on the highway. Unless your plan is to kill a building full of cops?"

A surge of excitement filled her.

"Knock it off. I'm not killing anybody," she muttered to Killian. Or was it the killer?

Slater cocked an eyebrow at her and asked, "What do you suggest we do?"

"Is there anywhere we can go to learn more about...whatever the fuck you are? *We* are? You know how they have those Sasquatch 'experts' all over the place now? Are there any experts on *us*?"

Slater thought about it for a moment, then shook his head. They sat in an awkward, tense silence for another few moments until Slater perked up.

"At my house before the vacation, we were...visited by someone who claimed to belong to a group researching supernatural or paranormal activity or some shit. I'm one-hundred percent sure he left his wallet and phone behind. Maybe we can track down his group of friends and learn more."

"He was...*researching* you? They knew you were—"

"No, he only thought our house was haunted. But it's a start. Even if that group doesn't know what I am, they know other people who might. They were college-aged—probably connected to a professor in a field of study that might be able to help.”

Killian tried to push past Tera’s defenses.

“Your wife says she has a book in your house. Very old… It has information about you that might prove useful as well.”

“All signs point to returning to my house, then. With any luck, Lynn might have detached herself from the boy and be waiting for us there, too. Go south on I-5. We live in—”

“I know where you live. Killian is telling me.”

“Killian? Sweetheart? Can you hear me?”

It was strange hearing Slater’s voice turn so soft. Tera couldn’t tell whether it creeped her out more than it made her sad, but it definitely made her angry.

“Stop it! It’s bad enough what she’s trying to do to me. I don’t need *you* encouraging her!”

Katie stirred and frowned in her sleep, then talked in an unfocused manner without opening her eyes.

“Home...vacation over...finish painting...hook them up...fill belly...”

As Tera’s stomach churned with excitement from Killian the darker presence of the killer saw an opportunity to slip into her vulnerabilities and took it. He filled her with a dreadful bloodlust that nearly blinded her. It was much harder to control than Killian and she could barely control her at all. Tera veered the firetruck over into the median as the highway expanded into four lanes and came to an abrupt stop. She stuck the nose of the vehicle into the oncoming lane, causing a vehicle to swerve into the other lane to avoid them, almost hitting the car it attempted to pass. Both honked, and Tera honked and screamed out the window thanks to Killian’s sudden input.

Tera hopped out and waited until a sedan slowed down and pulled into the median to check on them.

“Engine trouble?” the good Samaritan asked while poking his head out of the window.

Tera approached the driver door and leaned over. “You could say that. We need to borrow your car.”

The presence that had produced the surge of bloodlust lent her its strength. When the man’s arm went to shift the car back into

Drive she thrust her hands in to grab his shirt and pulled him out of the window. Slater opened the back door and laid Katie on the seat before climbing into the passenger seat himself. Tera balled up the man's shirt, one arm holding him at length while she pulled back her other fist. The presence wanted to punch straight through the back of the man's skull. Her knuckles tingled in anticipation of the feeling of his brain stem snapping in her grip.

Tera gritted her teeth and tensed her muscles, holding them back. It wasn't going to work; she could feel herself slipping. She channeled the building energy into a strong shove, throwing the man to the ground. She fought against the presence as it turned her vision red. She closed her eyes and put her hands over them.

"Nnngh... Take the keys to the truck," she strained, tossing the keys at his feet. "I'm so...sorry about this."

"Is that man forcing you to do this? Did he hurt you?"

"Please, get away from me," she whispered. "I can't hold it back..."

The man tried to get up but she pushed him back down with her foot, then straddled him, cocking her fist back again. The presence was winning.

Tera screamed as she punched down, but shifted her hand to crush into the pavement next to his head instead. She rolled off the man in agony, clutching her wrist. Her whole hand had shattered. Strong arms picked her up and carried her to the passenger side of the sedan. They got moving again after Slater adjusted the driver seat to fit his large frame.

Tera's whimpering lessened as her hand healed rapidly before her eyes. An hour later and on the interstate, the pain disappeared, and she flexed all the fingers as if nothing had happened.

"Well, that's useful..." she muttered, though she would trade the ability if it meant she could be rid of Killian and the killer's essences.

Tera sighed and rolled the window down, then lit up a joint. She put her hand to her forehead and wiped loose hair out of her eyes as they welled up. She thought about Ian. In the short time they knew each other, she believed they could have become best friends. She regretted never once crossing paths with him in their four years of high school together. Hanging out with him and his buddies would have been fun, and could have provided much-needed re-lief from the high-pressure cliques of jocks and cheerleaders. Ian had been so understanding of her, even when she kissed him—she couldn't think of another guy who wouldn't have taken advantage of her vulnerability in that moment of con-fused gratefulness and passion for being alive. She would have felt safe to open up to him, and perhaps his other friends, who hadn't given a fuck what the world thought about them. If only...

"Ian got *you*, you mother-*fucker*," she muttered before taking another drag, flipping off the killer nestled in her heart.

Tera took her time with the joint while Katie slept the sleep of the dead in the back. Her snoring over the road noise was so cute. Tera's heart fluttered at the thought they would sleep together, probably soon. It would be her first time. She hoped she wouldn't disappoint someone seven years her senior and sporting a face that nearly guaranteed it would *not* be Katie's first time. She was a modest nine in Tera's book; that gas sta-tion clerk was a blind douchebag.

An image passed through Tera's mind of a large bed in a dark farmhouse. The blankets of the bed waved by a breeze through the window, as if beckoning her forward to Katie, seated on the edge. She wore black jeans with a loose button-up white blouse and a cowgirl hat that matched her short wolf-cut perfectly.

Katie pulled the hat down to cover her chest as she unbut-toned the blouse and shrugged out of it.

"Can you help me, my beautiful, sinful cheerleader?" Katie whispered as Tera knelt before her and put her hands on Katie's knees. "I can't take these jeans off one-handed."

The word "sinful" only bothered her for a second—the feel of Katie's thighs, both inner and outer, hypnotized her until her hands reached for the front door of the jeans. She relished the slow, clicking descent of the zipper teeth unlocking. She let her pinky and ring finger slide down the front of Katie's panties. Her heart quivered at the feel of the soft springy hair behind the fabric. Tera couldn't wait to—

"What are you doing, Tera?" Katie asked, but her voice came from behind Tera's head, not above it.

Tera opened her eyes to blackness, and a large presence by her left ear. Her face was inches away from unzipped jeans, but things weren't like the vision. A repugnant smell emanated up into her nose. She jerked her head away only to hit it against the steering wheel, which forced her face back to Slater's crotch. Tera pushed away from him and put her back into the door, breathing heavily as her mind squared what just happened with the dream that had forced her into that position.

"Did—did I—?" Tera stammered, wide-eyed and frightened.

Slater sighed and shook his head. Tera's sigh was louder and full of relief before rage overtook her hijacked heart.

"You fucking *bitch!*" Tera screamed, then smashed her head against the dashboard, trying to drive Killian out.

Katie put her hand on Tera's shoulder from the backseat but Tera shrugged it off, then drove her head into the console, hoping the harder structure would do the trick. It didn't. She heard cackling in the back of her mind after a cracking in the front of her skull.

"Why didn't you *stop* me, asshole?" Tera yelled at Slater. "You know I'm not your wife!"

Slater shrugged and kept his eyes on the road.

"I miss her."

"That's it? You *miss* her? So you were going to allow *that* to happen?"

"I'll admit I don't know how weed works, but I was hoping it was one of those things where you forget everything that happens while you're high."

"That's not how it fucking *works!*"

Tera lunged at him, pummeling his face over and over. She allowed the presence to feed her strength. She delighted in causing Slater pain—blood was all she wanted to get out of him. The car swerving at seventy-five miles per hour didn't bother her. If they got in a wreck, they'd all survive. Hurting Slater and making him regret taking advantage of her was all she cared about.

Katie tried to pry them apart, but Tera pushed her back hard before returning to punching Slater. When Katie came forward again Tera punched her nose.

"We're even now, Katie!" Tera cried as she let loose one last punch into Slater's lecherous heart.

Katie laughed unexpectedly as blood ran from her nose to her mouth.

"You're right! I forgot about punching you before."

Tera wedged her leg down to the brake, causing the car to spin out along the shoulder. Slater took his foot off the accelerator, bringing the car to a complete stop. The presence's strength coiled around her legs as she kicked Slater out of the driver side door. Tera thrust her hand over the console into the backseat, feeling around on the floor for the shotgun. She accidentally found Katie's leg and another surge flooded into her.

"Not *now*, Killian," Tera growled.

"Looking for this?" Katie asked as she held up the shotgun.

"Hold it on him!"

They both exited the vehicle. Tera straddled Slater and went back to pummeling him.

"What time is it?" she asked Katie without stopping.

"An hour to midnight."

Tera let go of Slater and stood up, using his stomach as leverage.

"Fuck! Do you feel Killian getting excited the closer we get to Monday?"

Katie nodded and put the barrel to Slater's chest to hold him down, though he hadn't fought back.

"Look, Slater," Tera huffed. "This is getting fucked up. Not all *that*, I know you're just going to heal through it. I'm fucking pissed at these two *things* inside me fighting to take control. Now, I'm all for finding a way to get them out of us without also killing you. You've been surprisingly non-violent through all this and that makes it really hard for me to want to kill you.

"That said, know that Katie and I can turn to the killer's presence, too. You've seen for yourself that I'm not in complete control, and neither is your wife, no matter how hard she fights for it. She was completely unable to stop the killer once I let him take over. The only thing that brought me out of it was punching this gorgeous cowgirl because that was, beyond everything else, something *I* didn't want to do."

"Cowgirl?" Katie raised her eyebrow.

"Trust me, you'll look amazing in the hat."

Slater put his hands up in surrender so Katie would back away. He picked himself up.

"What's your point in all this, cheerleader?" Slater asked.

"I *don't* want to kill you! But I think we've all heard enough ominous hints about what's going to happen when your vacation is over to know that you're going to try to kill us after midnight. Is there any way we can come to some arrangement to try and *not* kill each other until *after* we've learned there's no other possible way to reverse this? Can you convince your wife to play along? I can feel her anticipation..."

Slater rubbed his bloody face and looked at the two of them with a solemn, almost pained expression—something he hadn't shown once all through the beating Tera had given him.

"Killian, sweetheart, do you remember our last conversation before our final romp in the truck?"

Tera and Katie both shuddered as the memory of that romp played in their minds. They couldn't believe two people could bend that way—not even professional gymnasts.

"We talked about retirement... We were prepared to let Lynn take over. Well, she'll be home at some point. I'll teach her everything we know. But these two girls—they're brave. Strong. One's virginity makes up for the other's—"

"Hey!" Katie snapped.

Slater held up his hand.

"I'm talking to my wife, Katie. Please don't interrupt. As I was saying...I...already didn't want to kill them. Even if I don't retire, we need to find a way to get your essence out of them. If we have to use some other vessel so we can remain together, fine. If I kill them and consume their hearts, it puts you inside me, but that wouldn't be as freeing for you. We'll find someone—"

"Enough, Slater," Tera interrupted. "I won't stand here and listen to how you're going to find some unsuspecting girl for your dead wife to possess. I'm not humoring that shit, and if that's the only solution you're willing to accept, I'm just going to have Katie blow your heart out right here and now. All I want is an agreement to wait until we've done everything we can to see if there's even the *slightest* hope of getting them out without anyone else dying—you or us and *especially* not ruining anyone else's life with this bullshit."

Slater nodded. He didn't look particularly displeased but he didn't have many other options; he didn't hold the power anymore. Unfortunately, knowing that his first, *best* course of action entailed involving another innocent person didn't fill Tera with confidence. If she didn't find an answer, he certainly couldn't be trusted to come up with one himself. Tera held out her hand and he took it. She allowed the killer's strength to come through and they matched each other's grips. Slater and Katie did the same dance to extend the standoff.

"Alright, now that that's settled, I'm fuckin' beat and I need to sleep the last few hours to the house. Are you up for driving, Calamity Kate?"

"Ok, but I'm *not* sure I'm on board with all this cowgirl stuff. Let's let this breathe a little before we come up with pet names."

Tera agreed and gave Katie's hand a little shake, relishing the contact. Tera crawled into the backseat, laid down face first and fell asleep almost instantly, giving a passing thought to how in the world monsters lived in a "home" and what the Slater family's would be like.

CHAPTER 24

SYMPATHY

KILL COUNT: 30

KATIE REGISTERED KILLIAN'S EXCITEMENT as she drove up the long driveway to the farmhouse. The mental gymnastics required to keep Slater's wife at bay were exhausting. She handled it more gracefully than Tera, but it was still a battle. The killer didn't vie for supremacy so much as seethe in the background. He almost got the better of her when she tried seducing another hick gas station clerk into a full tank in southern Oregon, though. He pushed past Killian's cooing words to make Katie reach across the counter and twist the clerk's shirt in her fist. She pounded and broke the glass counter in an attempt to shift the killer's drive to inflict harm on the cashier.

"That resistance you two think you're somehow mastering?" Slater asked when they got back on the road and Katie pulled shards of glass out of her fist, "fight that for a week straight and maybe you'll understand a little bit of what I've been going through."

"Are you fishing for sympathy or trying to get us to stop resisting? You don't think I know Killian is trying to take me and Tera over? You'd have two Killians in even younger bodies. Is that what you want? To screw a girl only a couple years older than your daughter?"

Slater punched the dashboard and left a large imprint of his fist. Katie forgot for a moment that it was early Monday morning and technically nothing held Slater back from killing them anymore—morally, anyway. She flinched when he looked at her after the damage.

"I am *really* trying to control myself, Katie. I want Tera's deal to work out. Please...don't egg me on or say shit like that about my daughter. I know you feel the killer's presence... How do you think it feels for me to be of that same essence and have no one to hold me back but myself?"

"I apologize, Slater. I'll drive the rest of the way in silence."

Katie tried to keep that conversation in mind as she put the car in Park outside of the dilapidated farmhouse. The whole property was supremely unsettling. It was late morning, but the trees covered so much sunlight it created an ominously gray day that only grew darker the closer they got to the front door. Every crack and peel of the house's ancient paint was shadowy at the edges so that it seemed like the whole building had been painted in muddy evil.

Katie put her hand over Tera's as she huddled close behind and wrapped her arm around Katie's stomach. The house had no electricity, and most of the light that managed to get through the trees died at the windows and open doorway. Slater's large frame darkened the front hallway further as he came in behind them and slammed the door shut.

All the little hairs on the back of Katie's neck stood on end, and Tera tensed up as Slater's heavy footsteps creaked on the old wooden floorboards. That familiar feeling of something reaching out for her in the dark paralyzed her until Slater brushed past them.

"Has Killian told you where the book is yet? I'm going to see if I can remember where we put that frat-boy's wallet and phone after she taught him a lesson for trampling her flowerbeds."

Katie and Tera reluctantly split up to search the rooms. Something strange happened the farther inside they ventured and the darker the house became—her eyes adjusted at a remarkable rate, to the point that Katie could swear she could "see in the dark." Was it another perk of their new forms?

"Tera? Are you—?"

"I can see everything!" Tera cried from the other room.

Her hearing picked up, too—rats moving between walls, birds scraping their talons on the roof two floors above, Tera's feet scuffing along from room to room, a body dragging along hay in the outside barn...

Katie ran outside and skidded to a halt a few feet inside the barn doors. The smell of rotting flesh assaulted her senses so strongly it nearly knocked her down. There were chunks of body parts hanging from hooks, and whole bodies stuffed in the dark corners. Slater dragged and tossed them around casually.

"Here he is," Slater said, but he pulled a little too hard and the young man's arm ripped out of its socket.

Katie vomited into some hay off to the side. Tera ran in a moment later and dry-heaved over the same spot. Slater shrugged at them and handed Katie the man's wallet and cell phone. She bolted out of the barn to get as far away from the smell as possible, but it either followed her or her sense of smell had improved along with her sight and hearing.

Tera jogged past her to the car and pulled out the shotgun. She brought it to Katie and shrugged.

"This place is creeping me out. I'd feel safer if you have that and we stay close together."

Katie nodded, then sighed at the phone for being locked. If the wallet yielded no results, she'd have to brave the barn to unlock via facial recognition or fingerprint, whichever was least deteriorated. She set it aside and searched through the wallet to find the man's address and student ID from a central California university. There was also an amateurish business card for a paranormal and supernatural investigation unit that listed YouTube and podcast channels, plus the group's phone number and email address.

"Find anything?" Tera asked.

"Nothing we can do anything with here. No electricity, no Internet, no phones... We'll need to find another house and ask to use their service."

"I know I just said we should stay together, but I'll run to the neighbors while you keep searching for that book Killian mentioned."

"Leaving me here with Slater?"

"After that dream I had in the car..."

"Okay. You don't want to be alone with him. Like I do, either, but I guess with this shotgun..."

Tera reached for a quick kiss, not even reacting to Katie's vomit breath, grabbed the business card, then ran down the driveway out of sight. Katie enjoyed the view of Tera leaving, then returned to the barn. Thankfully Slater was in the middle of dragging the young man's body towards the house and she didn't have to go into that foul-smelling barn of death again.

"What are you doing?"

"Setting up the body."

"What?" Katie frowned.

"When those people come looking for him, they're going to find him. We can leverage their fear to get them to tell us what we want to know."

"What the hell are you talking about? Like you're setting up a *jump scare?*"

"Trust me, I know what I'm doing."

"I didn't say you didn't, I just don't get your...process."

Slater ignored her and dragged the man up the back steps and into the house. Katie shook her head and sat on the steps, focusing on one of the unwelcome guests inside her head.

"Where's this book, Killian? You've been awfully quiet since we got here. ... It's not, I already checked those rooms. ... I'm pretty sure Tera was in that room, but I'll double check. ... Why shouldn't I check Lynn's room? ... Is she *that* sensitive? That's pretty hard to believe. ... You're right, she's just a kid, but she's hardly sweet and naïve from what I've seen. ... Yeah, we figured with the way those two can't keep their PDA under control."

Katie rubbed her head as Killian seethed. The pressure of such strong emotions that weren't her own made her skin break out in a sweat.

"Virginal power? That's pretty dumb, Killian. ... I'm not saying you wrote the rules for your race or species or whatever the hell you...*we* are, but— ... What do you mean, there's still hope? That's not exactly something you can bring bac— Oh you heartless *bitch*! There *is* no book, is there?"

Katie shut Killian out of her mind to the best of her ability and ran around to the front of the farmhouse, abandoning hope in their stupid plan. She needed to get Tera away from there before—

A black shape materialized from around the corner of the house. Something hard smashed into her face. Her legs kept moving forward before her back hit the ground. Slater loomed over her, then reached down and tore the shotgun from her grasp.

He pointed it at her face.

"You'll live if I shoot you, but it will take weeks for that pretty face to heal back to normal. That's the *best* case. If it blows your head off, your body will live, and you'll be aware of everything. That happened to my old dad when I took his mantle. He cursed me up and down while I kept his head in a jar and tied his body to a tree. If you want to try it, though, be my guest."

"The *fuck* are you doing, Slater? You promised—"

"The only one I've ever loved enough to keep a promise to is trapped inside you two."

"You fucking—" The shotgun butt struck her in the head.

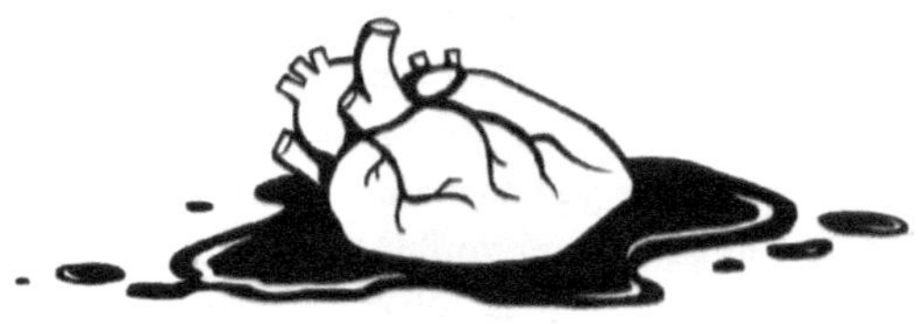

Katie opened her eyes to darkness and no night-vision. Slater had tied a black cloth around her eyes. She smelled him clearly, though, and heard his breathing only inches from her ear. She struggled against a hard wooden slab—a table or old door, it felt like. Her arms and legs were shackled to each corner with almost no give.

"No use struggling, but if you insist on it, I'll tear off your clothes and let loose my snake."

"You have a snake? What are you, a moody goth teen?"

Katie smiled after Slater struck her with his big, meaty fist. If she didn't know she would heal, she wouldn't have dared to say anything. Angering him didn't seem like the worst mistake anymore. Flustering him could just as likely make him clumsy. Katie'd put together over the whole week that whatever type of monster they were, it wasn't immune to mistakes.

"Why are you keeping me alive, asshole? All you have to do is take my heart, right?"

"I'm waiting for these paranormal idiots to get here so I can ask them one question: Should *I* consume your heart or feed it to the cheerleader? If it's the latter, it *will* be as fresh as possible."

Killian quivered with aching hunger for her man and the anticipation of being implanted into Tera's beautiful, young, *virginal* body. Killian stopped hiding her motivations since Slater had the upper hand.

"Are you there, sweetheart?" Slater whispered into Katie's ear, causing her to shudder in revulsion.

His big hand snaked beneath her shirt and rubbed her stomach, not indicating whether it was going north or south, but it threatened either way.

"Why don't we use her up before we kill her? If you plan on keeping Tera a virgin longer so you can cultivate all that raw power, it would be nice if I had something to make the wait easier..."

"You sick fuck—" Katie growled and received another blow.

His hand hooked down over her jeans; his fingers got between her skin and panties, tearing a few hairs out, before they both heard the front door open.

"Katie? Slater?" Tera called into the silent house. "They'll be here soon!"

"*TERA GET THE FUCK OU*—!" Katie screamed but Slater ripped his hand out of her jeans and punched her so hard she felt her skull fracture against the wood.

Her chin fell to rest on her chest, dazed. She heard Slater leave the room, but his normally heavy footfalls became softer—nearly silent—like a cat in stalking mode. Katie strained her improved hearing. There was silence followed by the sudden spring of Tera's jump and run, like the moment a gazelle realizes a lion is only a few feet away, bounding up and away at the last moment. The front door opened again, and Katie couldn't hear anything outside.

She tried to rub the cloth off of her eyes using her shoulder but couldn't quite get the angle right. She thumped her head against the wood and thought while Killian cackled. Tera would be easy for Killian to take over if the two halves met—she had already lost control a few times, even if she found the strength to hold back at the last moment. Katie had a much easier time keeping things under control. She wondered if there really was anything to that virgin bullshit.

Come to think of it...

Killian's anger at Lynn losing her virginity suddenly made sense. Slater and Killian may have wished for Lynn to fly the nest, see the world, and kill the masses, but that had been plan A. Now that Killian was an abstract essence, Slater undeniably wanted the best possible substitute for his wife. With Lynn inheriting Killian's unearthly gorgeous face and body, who could be better as a grooming candidate?

Tera wasn't the only one in danger if their plan didn't work.

"Why am *I* expendable?" Katie laughed, momentarily forgetting her predicament in the face of such blatant irony. "Killian, *I'm* a virgin. ... Yeah, I've had sex, but never with a— ... It's not *defined* for— ... Fine! *Don't* use my body! You know my mom looked as good as me when she was fifty? We've got amazing genes in my family. ... They don't just *give* jobs to good-looking women anymore. It has nothing to do with— ... Yeah, okay! I *did* use drugs, and that's part of why— Look, my personal life is over! Done! Take me and leave Tera and Lynn out of this. They're just kids! ... Yes, I want to—... She's eighteen! You know what I meant when I said 'kids.' ... List my sins all you want—I'm not ashamed, bitch! I'm ten times the prize for you and your sick husband. I've been a virgin longer than Tera, and you've already lost Lynn. I'm the better play and *you know it.*"

Killian pondered while Katie felt the strain of having her arms being locked above her shoulders for too long. As she pulled weakly against the shackles, she realized she'd neglected the "other" inside her. He'd been so hard to control when she threatened that gas station clerk. Until a moment of true desperation, Katie would have never humored invoking him. Uncontrollably violent? Yes. But he had no hang ups or schemes or motivations other than to inflict death. If she let him loose, would she be able to aim that hostility towards Slater? Or would she accidentally hurt Tera? Tera had punched Katie in the car with unnatural force. They were able to laugh it off, but knowing how Tera felt about her, and she'd *still* unloaded that punch...

"Whatever. Get me out of here," she whispered and allowed his strength to course through her.

The right shackle loosened and yielded enough so she could get the cloth off her eyes. Seeing in the dark gave her new confidence and she put more power into ripping the shackle out of the wood. Once it tore away, she easily snapped the left shackle, then the two at her feet.

Killian raged against the back of Katie's mind, but Katie concentrated on slamming a door shut in her face and it worked to muffle her. Katie used the key on a side table to unshackle the metal around her wrists and ankles, then slunk into the hallway and searched for any kind of a weapon. She found nothing that wouldn't just bounce off Slater without doing any meaningful damage. It seemed the monsters enjoyed using their hands, or, perhaps, the fewer options they had to use on each other the better. *What a happy home.*

Katie found herself taken aback in Lynn's room for all the boy-band posters, unicorns, rainbows, flowers, and other girly milieu scattered around the room. Katie experienced pangs of sympathy for the poor girl—growing up in such an environment; yearning for simpler things, only to be bred to kill and to be taken over by her own parents eventually.

How many teenage girls had Lynn robbed to get such an extensive wardrobe of preppy, pretty dresses and other clothing? Some of it was luxurious material. Katie remembered her own painful childhood—wanting to show the world her true self, but so many external factors had forced her to retreat to her room; the only place she lived without fear of anger, disgust, hate, or anything else the world threw at her simply for being born "sinful." In her late teenage years, drugs helped her get through the depression all of that caused, but created a different downward spiral she only escaped by leaving her hometown, falling in with Samantha and her stupid friends.

Katie bitterly fumed over remembering Samantha. Drugs had changed her, too, but she'd been a good friend for a while—the only one Katie ever really had. She directed her anger at the killer for taking Samantha away so senselessly, and it managed to allow Katie to regain control, suppressing him as she had Killian. Her hands curled into her *own* fists and she ran out to the barn to pull down one of the giant meat hooks.

She wouldn't have believed the property could get any darker until the sun set. She exited the barn, distancing from the horrid smell, then attuned her hearing, listening for Tera. No footsteps anywhere, but she did detect tires crunching along the driveway. Headlights came into view and illuminated the house as Katie peeked around the back corner of it.

The car engine cut out and four doors opened simultaneously. Five college-aged students exited, then opened the trunk to gather weird-looking equipment. She picked up their excited chatter.

"Do you think we'll find Justin in there?" one of them asked.

"The girl on the phone said there would be enough material here for us to create a month's worth of content, regardless."

Katie almost yelled at them when she noticed a large figure among the trees a few yards away from the car—Slater stalking his prey. Katie tightened her grip on the meat hook. It was time she did the same.

Chapter 25

Heartless

Kill Count: 30

Slater approached the five co-eds—three men and two women—with a neutral expression. He purposefully stepped on a branch and cracked it, startling all five of them to turn and shine their flashlights on his face.

"For supernatural experts, you people frighten easily," he said to their horrified faces. "I'm the gardener and I heard some truly strange noises coming from inside that farmhouse over the last week. I sent my daughter to call you after I found your friend's wallet."

The co-eds turned on their equipment and thanked Slater for calling them. Blips, whirs, beeps and other nonsense sounds came out of the electronic devices that were simply LED bulbs housed in ornate plastic. Slater resisted the urge to laugh and watched them inch towards the farmhouse, all huddled together.

Slater approached the man with glasses and tapped on his shoulder, startling him yet again. The wannabe ghostbusters were going to be a *delicious* lesson to celebrate the end of his brief retirement...

"Hey, frat-boy, I've got a question for you."

"I'm not in a frat, sir. Pfft, no frat would ever allow guys like us to join."

"I should have guessed. The other two look like their only reason to be in your little club is to get close to the women, and *you're* probably the only one that knows what he's doing. Am I right?"

The man pushed his glasses up on his nose and huffed in arrogance—Slater hit the nail on the head.

"Everything was all going according to plan until Justin brought his friends into the group. Now we've had to drive all this way to find the jerk. He stopped answering our texts and calls about a week ago."

"Your plan being: you were going to take those two girls into haunted houses, scare them with fake effects, then comfort them from the safety of a hotel room once they're too frightened to sleep alone?"

"Yeah! Did you run a fake paranormal hunting squad when you were in college?"

"I didn't run one, no, but I've run *into* countless groups of them. Scared piss-pants, all."

"Interesting. There must be a lot of paranormal occurrences around you. Do you work exclusively at rundown places or do you have *the sense?*"

Slater shook his head then put his hand on the idiot's shoulder and smiled. "I have an important question to ask you."

Slater gave a vague description of a supernatural being similar to himself and asked about the heart consumption ritual. The man didn't have a satisfactory answer other than comparing him to beings infamous for cannibalism in other cultures and ending with, "but they don't really do that."

Angered at the man for wasting his time, Slater reached out to choke him one-handed when a hook curved around his elbow and pulled his arm back. Katie appeared by his side, keeping one hand on the hook and the other on her hips in a very congenial way, reminiscent of Killian.

"Hello, young man!" Katie said with a big grin. "I think you need to go find your friends and get the hell off my fucking property!"

"But we're just looking for our frien—"

"You think I wouldn't notice a stranger in my house? Get your friends, and *get out.*"

"Hey, lady, you people called *us!*"

Slater glanced at Katie side-eyed. Her confidence barely masked the pleading in her eyes. Katie tried not to let it show how much she wanted to get the club kids to safety, but she wasn't Killian—Slater could read her like a book, and the paranormal guy wasn't picking up on the hints.

Slater grabbed Katie by the throat and lifted her off the ground. The man screamed and ran into the farmhouse. Katie struggled and buried the hook into Slater's shoulder, forcing his muscles to let go.

He laughed as she struggled to get her breath back.

"Right into the barrel... Thanks, sweetheart."

"That wasn't her. Where's Tera, asshole?"

"I didn't expect a cheerleader to also be a track runner. She's fast, and her new form has made her faster. I couldn't keep up with her. I stopped chasing when I realized there was no way she would ever leave you here to die. Some students are easy to teach because they're too stupid or too scared. Some, like you and Tera, are easy to teach because you're too brave; willing to run back into a dangerous situation to save others.

"You know what I learned early on? Both types of students die all the same. Best to be patient and let them come to me. Just like you did to save that Poindexter."

Slater lunged for Katie but Tera blurred into view and pulled her away, into the house. He smiled and took his time walking in behind them. A remote rested above the door frame that he pulled down and pressed a button. All the doors and windows to the outside slammed shut and locked. He delighted in the collective gasps throughout the house. Slater was pleased at himself for re-membering to top up the batteries that powered his traps before the vacation.

He pressed another button which unlatched several cabinets and closet doors to invite the investigators to explore them. The door off the entryway was a coat closet. Slater eased in, then cracked it open and listened. Slight footsteps approached the front door. Katie and Tera crept to the door knob and turned it uselessly.

They flicked the deadbolt but the door remained locked. They took turns fumbling with the knob and lock to no avail.

"Are you fucking kidding me?" Tera muttered. "So many stupid horror movies make sense to me right now."

"All we need is a ring of keys to drop on the ground over and over," Katie replied, then led Tera farther into the house.

Slater came out of the closet and crept through the dark hallway. A light moved around the kitchen. He leaned around a corner, just a smidge.

"Ohmygod!" one of the college women cried as she held a camcorder in Slater's direction. "A shadow person! Just like that other YouTube channel!"

"That's so lame!" her boyfriend scoffed. "Those are *so easy* to fake. You know, Justin's probably been here all week setting this place up for us."

"Shut up! You know how annoying it is to edit out audio?"

The two stupidly ignored Slater's presence and rummaged through cupboards and drawers. The woman opened the pantry door and screamed. A black cat hissed and jumped on her shoulder, then ran away. The man laughed at her until she stormed into another room. Once he got control of himself, he resumed searching.

With the man alone, Slater slipped in close. He hovered at the man's shoulder, waiting for that wonderful realization that *something* was behind him. The man finally did sense it, just as Slater was about to cut his losses on the oblivious idiot. He stood up straight, doing a slow turn that gave Slater all the time in the world to think of how he wanted to end the lesson.

Katie slammed into Slater's side and pushed him through the dining room door. He heard Tera give a little "boo!" to the man once he turned around fully. Where there should have been the sounds of final, gurgling breaths came raucous laughter.

Slater seethed. He did not condone *fun* in his classroom if it wasn't him or his wife having it! He took a swing at Katie, but she ducked away and ran out of the room. Slater went back into the kitchen to find that Tera had led the man out. He took a deep breath and collected his poise before going into the living room. The other man without glasses poked around the fireplace, looking for a hidden latch or button that would open a secret passageway. His girlfriend trained her camcorder on him.

Slater blended into the darkness so well that the Poindexter ran right past him to alert the other two that he couldn't get any of the windows open.

"Why are you trying to escape, dumbass?" the fireplace guy said. "We *need* this footage, and it's amazing! That girl who called us wasn't lying."

"Guys, I'm serious. We can't get out. Everything is locked and there's some crazed nut outside! I saw him choke someone!"

"Did you check upstairs?"

"Umm. No. It…I don't want to go up there alone."

"Pissing your pants already? Jesus, there hasn't even been a skin-walker or *ju-on ringu* girl or anything yet. Instead of bellyaching, find some stuff to increase our subscriber count."

"Come on, Kyle, I'll go upstairs with you," the girlfriend said to the man with glasses.

Slater didn't need night-vision to know Kyle blushed as he followed her closely down the hallway, leaving the fireplace man alone to poke and prod the bricks. He pulled out a phone and started recording. Slater loved it when they used their phones. Students always got so wrapped up in staring at the screen instead of experiencing what was actually happening around them, which made it simpler to get close to them.

The dummy was so locked in on his phone that he thought he bumped into a wall when he swung his hand into Slater's chest, then moved on, whispering vaguely scary musings about his surroundings and how they made his colleagues piss their pants already.

Slater reached for the poker that the man gripped in his non-phone hand when an orange light illuminated the whole living room. Slater slipped back into the edges of the room near the hallway. He watched Tera and Katie move away from the fireplace into their own shadows, leaving behind a bottle of lighter fluid and a box of matches. A brief, unheard-of self-defeating thought entered Slater's mind—was he out of his league? How had he not heard them?

The young man marveled to the phone how the fire *magically* lit itself in his presence. Having lost the element of surprise, Slater skulked and sulked down the hallway, but perked up when he remembered those other two had gone upstairs. He found them in a bathroom near the top of the stairs, staring into the mirror, daring each other to say the name of a local killer legend. They giggled too hard to utter the name a third time—it would have been a perfect cue to scare them before the kill.

Slater decided to flip the script and greet them as they came *out* of the bathroom, filled with relief that they were safe from their dumb mirror scare.

Unfortunately for Slater, the idiots got caught in a charged moment from standing so close to each other in front of the mirror. Kyle began to lean in, and the girl seemed open to him doing so. Well, Slater was patient. He stood outside the bathroom in front of the stairs, refraining from tapping his foot like a parent with a schedule to meet.

Two sets of hands grabbed him by the ankles and yanked them back. His face hit the floor, then the hands dragged him down the stairs, his head smacking the boards rapidly. He heard the two upstairs gasp and break apart to check on the commotion.

"Who's there? Justin? Cindy? Greg?"

Tera and Katie rolled Slater away from the view upstairs. Kyle and his friend talked into their camera about the ghost that just ran down the stairs. Slater lost patience at the joy and art he longed to draw out of the situation being drained by his tormentors. He prepared to thrust his hand into one of their chests when he got up from the floor, but they were already gone.

Slater wrestled over the momentary split on which students to go after next, but the decision was made for him when he heard sinful, sensual sounds coming from Lynn's room. He opened the well-oiled door and slipped in, disgusted to find the kitchen couple mid-coitus on his daughter's bed.

In almost every classroom Slater and Killian had taught, from lakeside camps to schools to hotels to warehouses, and even abandoned mine shafts, there was always at least one absurd couple that either got off on the intense, fearful situations around them, or had libidos that far surpassed their survival instincts. It was always a young man, comprised of ninety-six percent hormones, that somehow—for reasons Slater and Killian could never understand—would manage to talk a bimbo into interrupting their search for a way out of the deadly situation for a meaningless quickie.

Well, if they didn't value their lives over sex, Slater wasn't going to give half a second of thought to ending them, especially when they made it so easy. He reached into the corner for the lacrosse stick Lynn liked having around to compliment her dreams of being a normal, upper-middle class schoolgirl. He raised it over the young man's bare back, ready to send the stick to its final destination in the floorboards beneath the center of the bed.

As Slater made to stab down, it suddenly became heavy, then got ripped out of his hands and cracked off the back of his head. The stick gave way against his skull, snapping the fiberglass shaft in half. It plunged through his back, narrowly missing his heart.

"Hey assholes! Get the fuck out of the room!" Tera yelled from the doorway.

Katie grunted as she pushed Slater away from the bed while the students scrambled out with their clothes. Slater swung his body around and backhanded Katie. Tera ran into the room, slamming the door on the asses of the couple for extra emphasis. She threw her body into Slater's stomach, crashing him against the wall and sending the pole further through his chest. They both turned to run away but Slater grabbed Katie's wrist and ripped her to his chest, impaling her through her stomach with the bloody, jagged edge of the stick.

Katie cried out as he put his arms around her, pulling her closer, ready to break her spine. Tera wedged herself between them and pushed against the wall to slide Katie off the stick. He would have squeezed them both to pulp but froze when Tera kissed him on the lips. After Katie slipped off, Tera broke the kiss and met his eyes.

"That was the last time you'll ever 'kiss your wife.'"

She grabbed the stick with both hands, twisting and churning it. It scraped his heart, and he fell to his knees in a pain he'd never experienced. Katie staggered out from Lynn's closet with a metal hanger she unwound, then poked the sharp end through his eye.

Damn it, Lynn, he thought in misery. He'd expressly forbidden metal coat hangers in their home for that very reason. He regretted not instilling more fear into Lynn for the many ways their kind could be stunned. He regretted many things as he knelt in agony while Katie and Tera tried their damnedest to get at his heart, pushing through the hole in his chest with their clawed hands. Through his remaining eye he spotted the stupid college students recording the whole scene with their phones.

Everyone flinched and froze as something crashed through Lynn's window, interrupting the scene. They all turned to find Lynn peeking her head above the sill, wide-eyed and furious.

"What the *fuck* are you all doing in *MY ROOM?*"

"Language, young lady!" Katie blurted, accompanied by a look of shock that those words came out of her mouth.

Slater took advantage of the surprise from his daughter's entrance to punch Katie, then grabbed Tera by the throat. Without letting go, he stood up and kicked Katie in the stomach so hard that she was sent tumbling into Lynn's closet across the room. He crushed Tera's neck in his fist. The ragdoll state he put her in wouldn't last all that long, but he wasn't going to let her get away to heal anymore.

The students screamed as he turned in their direction, dragging Tera behind on the floor. They ran back into the hallway and scattered. When he got to the door frame, a hand rested on his shoulder that he never thought he'd feel again.

"Daddy?"

The only thing that could have brought his fury down completely was his wife's voice, but his last remaining family nearly succeeded.

Nearly.

"Prepare the basement, Lynn Chelsea. We're getting your mother back. Take this sinful cheerleader and strap her down."

He handed Tera's limp body to Lynn. She hesitated, then took Tera in her arms and carried her to the basement.

Slater took a step out into the hallway, then a claw jammed into the hole in his back and grabbed his heart. He fell to his knees again as Katie grunted and pulled.

"Shut the fuck up, Killian. You both betrayed us. There's no more sympathy."

It was a strange feeling—his heart detaching and beating in Katie's grip. The rage that had been ever-present in his mind since he was a tyke was replaced by an overwhelming desperation to get the heart back into its proper place. He'd never felt so weak or vulnerable... Is that how Killian had felt, alone in her last moments, too? His poor love.

Katie raised the heart to her mouth and almost bit into it like an apple before Slater managed to grab a fistful of her hair. He swung her into the doorjamb, breaking her back. His heart ripped out of her grasp during the action, causing him supreme pain as the heartstrings pulled to stay attached. For good measure, he got up and stomped on her neck.

The hole in his back and chest were closing quickly. He had to re-open his wound in the front to jam the heart back into its home. The tearing of his skin and the flexing of his ribs was nothing compared to the agony of being heartless.

With Katie and Tera unable to stop him anymore, he slipped into the darkness once more to finish off the co-eds.

CHAPTER 26

EVIL THOUGHTS

KILL COUNT: 30

LYNN PROVIDED DIRECTIONS TO Timothy as they headed to her house. They dropped TJ and Maggie off at Jessica's parents' before the trip. Corey sat in the back with Jessica while Lynn sat up front, and the two kids sat diagonally so they wouldn't snake their hands between the front seat and the doors.

Timothy and Jessica couldn't cling to their outrage with the knowledge that Corey miraculously lived, but he changed forever in ways they may never understand. They talked through many scenarios before they rented the vehicle in Roseburg: abandon Lynn at her home, take her into their home, turn her over to the authorities, send Corey to military school or to a private school across the country and live with Timothy's brother... Jessica surprised Timothy when she suggested they kill Lynn. They'd laughed uneasily, not sure how hard to take that as a joke, but also knowing it wouldn't matter. They both watched her and Slater get shot in fatal areas, along with their son, and it was like nothing.

The one thing they agreed on was bringing Lynn to her home and crossing their fingers that Slater would already be there so he could be the key to separating the two lovebirds. Timothy did *not* look forward to the drive home after a forced separation, but preferred that to any other option. The iciness from Lynn and Corey during both legs of the trip grew unbearable. They clearly resented the physical separation in the vehicles, and the awareness that their relationship would come to an end in a matter of hours was palpable.

The situation agonized Timothy: if they were genuinely in love and not under some sort of spell or supernatural folklore bullshit, he knew that feeling all too well.

An hour from Lynn's house, Timothy tried a last, desperate attempt to soften the coming blow for both of them.

"Kids, when I was in high school, I was friends with this guy in our little IT club. Well, it was more like a Magic: The Gathering club, but we still spent some time... Uh, forget that part. Um, anyway, he pined after this girl—a really good friend of his—so much so that he thought he was suffocating whenever she wasn't around. She was everything to him. A goddess, that he could never—"

"Dad, Mom's told this story a dozen times before. You didn't hide your feelings as well as you thought."

Jessica covered her mouth as Timothy glared good-naturedly through the rearview mirror.

"Okay, moral of the story... I spent four years in physical proximity to the love of my life without acting on it, and a few years in college in *no* proximity to her, and look at us now. I got the woman of my dreams, and if I had the chance to go back, I wouldn't change anything about how we came together. I needed distance to appreciate her more; allow my hormones to take a back seat so I could love her as a person and not worship her as some ideal on a pedestal. Instead of lust, I was stuck with thoughts of all the romantic things I would do for her if only given the chance. So when I *did* finally get the chance, we could start from a deeper type of love than the purely physical."

"That doesn't sound quite like the way Mom described it..." Corey began.

"Jesus, Jess, how much did you share with him?"

"Hey, *I* was trying to have 'the talk' when *you* wouldn't step up—"

"Okay! I'm *trying* to say, we're not saying you two can't continue your relationship long-distance. Once you're eighteen, you can do whatever you want. But the two years until then won't be as bad as you think it will be, and you're both going to appreciate each other so much more after some distance."

Lynn only ever looked ahead, hardly speaking over the hundreds of miles traveled except to give directions. She seemed unmoved. Corey only smirked or scoffed at every other attempt to reach him.

Timothy felt a measured relief when they pulled in to find two cars at the end of the driveway of Slater's house... Although there were no lights coming from inside. They got out and began searching for others, peeking into different windows when the front door wouldn't open.

Timothy, Corey, and Jessica were halfway to the barn in the back when glass shattered, and Lynn shouted about people in her room. Corey turned to go to her when Jessica grabbed his arm. She gave her son a look of trepidation at Lynn's cry that said "stay together."

From the open barn doors, Timothy got a whiff of the inside. Curiosity won out over dread about what could possibly be making that smell. He approached the barn but stopped at the entrance—too dark to see clearly, and the smell overpowered him. He couldn't have gone further if he wanted to.

Timothy turned back to his wife and son, frozen stiff and waiting for a response from him—their own curiosity for the smell's origins not nearly as strong as their fear of the answer.

"Maybe they didn't feed their livestock while they were on vacation?" Timothy mused, then immediately regretted opening his mouth as the smell became a taste—the stench of death multiplied.

Timothy pushed Jessica and Corey back towards the house gently even though he fought with everything he had not to run away from the barn and throw up.

The back door wouldn't open either. They walked around to the broken window. Timothy laced his fingers together to make a step for Jessica to peer inside.

"Oh my God, someone's lying on the floor. Boost me a little more!"

Corey helped Timothy get her up, then he lifted his son up, too. If he didn't know Corey would survive mortal danger, he would have sent him right back to the car. Instead, Corey reached over and pulled his dad up with surprising ease. They walked over to Jessica as she cradled Katie's broken body.

Katie startled them by opening her eyes.

"Nnngh, what the hell are you people *doing* here? He's going to kill all of you!"

"Who is?" Corey asked.

"Slater. There are more people in the house, and he's trying to kill them. You're all in danger!"

A scream from a room upstairs punctuated Katie's warning.

"Stay with her," Timothy told Jessica and Corey, then ran upstairs.

He looked through a couple rooms before finding a young woman and man with glasses shrinking away from a body that had fallen out of a closet, the smell similar to the barn but on a much smaller scale.

"It's Justin!" the girl cried and hid her face in the guy's chest.

To Timothy's horror, the two of them sniffed, then took pictures of their dead friend.

"At least he died doing what he loved..." The man sighed.

"Jesus Christ, people, you need to get out of here. Come on!"

Timothy turned hard into a large figure in the door frame. He looked up, unable to see the man's face. The two people behind him shined flashlights on Slater and screamed at his bloody eye socket.

"Oh, Slater! I'm so glad we ran into you!" Timothy said, barely able to keep his voice under control. "We brought Lynn back! Maybe you already saw her?"

Slater's hulking form breathed heavy, and his hands curled into claws. When he looked down at Timothy's face with his good eye, recognition slowly came over his expression.

"Tim, I need you to step aside."

"Uh...yeah, you know there's a dead guy on your floor here? And your barn is full of other dead *things*? How long have you been home? I think all your livestock died during your vacation."

Was Slater rolling his eye? Or searching the room? He took a step forward and Timothy backed up with him, keeping himself between Slater and the young people he kept staring at.

"Oh! Lynn is willing to try a long-distance relationship with Corey. Isn't that great? Yep, we can even leave right now and they'll be super cool about it. Who would have thought? She just needs a phone or laptop to stay in touch. Hey! I think my company has a couple older generation laptops I can wipe and hook you two up with. How about it?"

The anger on Slater's face lessened at each question. He kept looking back and forth as he inched further into the room, unable to completely ignore Timothy, but unwilling to fully engage in a conversation at the moment.

"Uh, jeez, those laptops won't do much good if this place doesn't get some electricity. I know a contractor—great guy—I could get you hooked back up to the grid. I'll pay for it. Or I've got connections to secure you a great, really nice generator. Won't that be great for Lynn?"

Slater tensed at the sudden presence of another college student happening upon the scene. The two already in the room ran to the door and they all disappeared down the hallway together. Slater sighed and put a grip on Timothy's shoulder that nearly brought him to his knees.

"Stop interrupting me, Tim. I...need to teach these students a lesson. They don't respect another man's property."

Slater let go and turned to the door. Timothy put his hand up on his shoulder but Slater pushed him back. Timothy tripped over the corpse and hit his head against the wall. When he picked himself up Slater was gone. Slightly dazed, Timothy staggered into the hallway and downstairs. He retraced his steps back to Lynn's room but his wife, son, and Katie weren't there anymore. He peeked outside the window and didn't see anyone, though in the dark that didn't mean much.

An idea occurred to him as he noticed the cars. He climbed out and ran to the rental, then positioned it so its high beam headlights would illuminate all the windows on the front of the house. He looked into the other two cars. One still had the keys in the ignition and he positioned it to provide even more coverage.

Back inside the house after setting up a crate below Lynn's window, he wanted to call for Jessica, but feared Slater finding her because of it. Timothy wasn't sure if he could hurt Slater even if he wanted to, but knew he'd feel better if he had a weapon in his hand. He went to the kitchen and found a long carving knife and a butcher's blade.

Whimpering came from beneath the dining room table. Timothy startled two different college students when he lowered himself down to their hiding spots. They gasped at the sight of the knives once they turned their phone lights on.

"Hey, why aren't you guys escaping through that bedroom? Or breaking open windows? They may be locked but that doesn't change their breakable properties."

The two looked at each other, then shrugged. "Each second of footage in this house is another dozen subscribers."

"How are you getting that footage hiding beneath a table?"

"We'll edit up to the point where you poked your head down here—leave it ambiguous for the viewer. Now that we have this footage we'll go to a different room. We're pumped you had those blades in your hands!"

"Do you two realize there is an *actual* killer here, actively *hunting* you?"

"No risk, no reward."

"And the reward is faceless people clicking a button on your YouTube channel?"

They scoffed at his old-man questions, crawled out from beneath the table, and scurried out of the dining room. If they didn't *want* to escape, Timothy felt less responsibility to help them and re-focused on finding his wife and son.

He found them in a room scattered with broken, torn up toys. Murdock's bedroom, he assumed. They had Katie laid out on the floor. Corey snapped a toy in half and threw it across the room, then scratched his head for a moment as if he'd come back to himself after a lapse. Timothy wanted to ask what that was about, but Katie's arm moved.

"Did you find Tera?" she asked.

"No, but I found plenty of co-eds with no sense of self-preservation. How are you doing? Can you move your legs yet?"

"Almost. It's really strange feeling my body heal itself so quick-ly."

"Do you still have that shotgun somewhere?" Jessica asked.

"Last time I saw it Slater smashed its butt in my face. That was before he threatened to rape and kill me with his goddamn wife."

"Killian's alive?" Timothy asked. "I mean, that's not as impor-tant as what they planned to do to you, I'm just—"

"She's not alive in any way that matters to you. I need to find Tera and get out of here."

Timothy had just about *had it* with all the vagueness surround-ing the week's events. He persisted in finding out Katie's meaning when a couple of small animals ran down the hallway outside. He peered out at the tail ends of two black cats running into Lynn's room, presumably escaping through the window.

"I'm going to look for Lynn," Corey said.

"Absolutely not, young man," Jessica grabbed his wrist.

He pulled out of her grasp and escaped. Jessica ran after him.

"Tera and I almost had him, Tim," Katie said before he could fol-low. "Not because we've changed. We worked together and didn't split up. Go to your family. Get them the fuck out of here. Put all this behind you."

"We're not leaving you two."

Katie stretched out her back and sat up.

"Slater was right—bravery is stupid."

"Huh?"

"Nothing. Let's go be stupid."

They searched the rooms for the shotgun while ignoring the ridiculous, filming co-eds they came across. Katie moved remark-ably quietly, let alone for someone who'd just recovered from a broken back. After the fourth room Timothy took her quiet for granted and didn't realize she wasn't following him anymore until he did a full turn around the room.

"She smelled me in here," Slater said as he emerged from a clos-et.

Timothy backed away towards the door.

"Slater, were you really planning to kill Katie?"

"You don't understand what's going on, Tim. Stop worrying about them. Take your family and go home."

"I can't do that. Those girls saved us. Several times. I won't let you hurt them anymore."

"Nothing you can do will ever make them safe, even if I stopped pursuing them. They can't escape what they've become. Regardless, they both have something I need."

Katie bulled past Timothy, sending him to the floor. She raised an axe above her head but Slater caught the handle on the downswing, thrusting the end of it into her chest. He grabbed her by the neck, ripped away the axe, and tossed it behind him. Timothy crawled towards it but Slater stuck his foot out to block him.

"Tim, this is the last time I'm going to warn you; the last time I'm giving you the chance to save your family. When I get my wife back, if you're *still here*, none of you will be spared. No more games."

While Katie struggled to get Slater's hand off her neck, Timothy noticed her give him a quick glance and nod like she gave him permission to abandon her. He got up and ran to the axe, then swung it at the back of Slater's head. Slater spun around and the axe buried itself in Katie's shoulder before Timothy could stop his momentum. She couldn't scream with Slater's hold around her throat. Slater grabbed the axe out of Timothy's grip, dislodging it from Katie's shoulder blade, and cracked the handle across his face.

Timothy had never taken a hit like that in his life, but truth be told, it hurt more that they'd turned on each other. Timothy had hoped Slater would see reason through his madness. But who was Timothy to talk? He had no idea what he'd do to get Jessica back. He supposed he'd kill Slater in a heartbeat—

"Daddy! She's ready for you!" Lynn called from another part of the house.

What stunned Timothy even more than his friend turning on him was Slater thrusting his other fist into Katie's chest, ripping out her beating heart. Timothy couldn't move. He had failed her with his weakness. Katie'd put herself through so much to help in all their survival, and what good had it brought her? Her life ended in a second of unbelievable violence.

Timothy's shock intensified as Katie continued to struggle. Slater dropped her to the ground.

"What are you going to do with that?" she growled before he pressed his foot into her stomach.

"Split it with your girlfriend. Get my wife back."

"Why can't you let kill—Killian go?" Katie asked through her useless straining for her heart.

Slater left the room without answering. Timothy helped Katie up, trying to ignore the hole in her chest.

"Are we done sympathizing, Tim? Can we finally kill these freaks?"

Timothy grabbed the axe but didn't know what he'd do with it. It hadn't helped either of them. As they moved slowly down the hall, searching for wherever Slater went, the college students emerged from nearby rooms and followed them with their phones.

"We're going to earn so many paid advertisements for this shit," one of them whispered.

Timothy resisted the urge to grab each one of them by the back of the pants and toss them out the window to their safety. He was alarmed by the next thought that crossed his mind unbidden—to use them as murder fodder so he could get his family and friends out of the goddamned house.

CHAPTER 27
PRICES OF FREEDOM

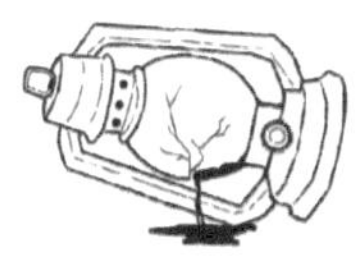

KILL COUNT: 30

LYNN LAID TERA ON a table in the basement, then lit a kerosene lantern and hung it on a hook overhead. She leaned over with a frown, holding Tera's head firmly in place. A little bit of feeling came back to her arms and legs. She tried lifting her hand but Lynn stopped her from moving it.

"Don't struggle. If you move your neck too much while it heals you'll risk altering your voice."

What did Lynn care about her *voice*? Lynn caressed Tera's face with her fingers, but in an unthreatening manner.

"You lucky fuckin' cheerleaders—people risking their lives to save you without even knowing you. Before he knew me, I wonder if Corey would have saved *me* from the lake."

As the numbness dissipated from Tera's other hand, she put it on Lynn's cheek.

"Lynn Chelsea, you stop bonding with this lezzie *slut* and start cutting open her chest."

"Mom?"

"Yes. There should be a good knife over in that cupboard. Chop-chop, young lady!"

"But...I *can't*. Corey saved her. That can't be for nothing. He might never forgive me..."

"That *boy* is *nothing*! You'll be travelling the world soon, teaching lessons for centuries, long after he's dead. You'll find 'the one' out there. Don't settle for the first boy you ever touched. You might even kill Corey later on, if you keep him around—once you realize he's wasted your prime years and potential. Do you really want that? Let him go home to his family."

Tera fought against Killian's power while searching Lynn's eyes. Conflict played out behind them that Tera never imagined possible. Did Lynn really love Corey so much that she'd defy her parents' expectations? Tera couldn't fathom doing such a thing against her own parents.

"Lynn, this is Tera now. You need to know, your parents' plan for you was to eventually take over your—"

Killian raged and pushed forward.

"Don't listen to the slutty cheerleader, Lynn! She's desperate to escape. She'll say anything! She thinks you're ugly and pathetic, and you'll *never* be as popular as her!"

Lynn broke away from their eye contact and paced around the basement. Tera pushed Killian from her mind as she sat up and hugged her knees.

"They're going to take your heart eventually. Or feed you mine. The goal is the same—for your mother to live in one of us. She and Slater only care about themselves. Maybe it wouldn't be for decades or even centuries, but that's always been their plan. They were going to do the same with Murdock."

Tera smiled to herself at a new idea. It wasn't a nice thought, but it was exactly what she needed to convince Lynn to listen to the possibilities: "Without Murdock, who do you think Slater will go after to get into a younger body? Who would make a finer couple than one that's already—"

"I *get* it! Let me *think*, cheerleader!"

"Would you stop calling me that? That doesn't define me any more than your family defines you."

"Stop manipulating me! I can think for myself."

Tera took in her surroundings. The orange glow of the lantern stopped before reaching the edges of the basement. She could smell that she wasn't the only human to have been laid on the table against their will. Was she even human anymore? Could she consider herself that? She scooted to the end of the table to get down.

"Stop, Tera!" Lynn pointed, which froze her in place. "If I help you kill Daddy, what's your plan for his heart?"

"I hadn't thought that far ahead... I guess Katie and I would do the same thing as we did for the other killer—split it and live with the consequences."

"You think you can handle a third being inside of you, raging to get out? I'm having a hard time keeping my brother contained sometimes."

"There's no alternative... Is there?"

Lynn shook her head. "Not that I know of."

"Then why did you ask—?"

"If there's *any* hesitation, Daddy could kill me. Easily. I just want to make sure we're on the same page."

"You'll help me, then?"

When Lynn nodded, Killian broke through again, stronger than before. Tera moved against her will. She ran to the cupboard and pulled out the large aforementioned knife. Footsteps clomped down the stairs and Tera looked up to see Jessica and Corey. Lynn ran to Corey's embrace like it was the only thing that mattered in the world.

Killian took advantage of the distraction and plunged the knife into Tera's chest. The pain helped Tera regain some control. It became a tug-of-war to keep Killian from sawing through the large veins around the heart. Tera fell to the ground on her back, wrestling with her own hands.

"Help me!" she cried to anyone.

Jessica tried pulling Tera's hands away, but they were getting slick with arterial blood. Killian took one hand off the blade and pushed Jessica's face away, knocking her back against a wall. Corey and Lynn hooked their arms through Tera's elbows to restrain her and forced the knife out. Tera became woozy from the rapid blood loss. Lynn pried the knife out of Tera's hand.

"Kill the slut!" Killian forced out of Tera's mouth. "Kill her, Lynn! Save your family!"

Lynn threw the knife into a cabinet on the other side of the room, then got on top of Tera to hold her down.

"Find some rope or anything else to tie her down," Lynn requested. "And something to gag her," she added, giving a cold stare down onto Tera's face.

Tera didn't like that idea, but if it shut Killian up, she would roll with it, as she did while they wrapped her up. Lynn lifted her easily as if Tera weighed nothing. Tera discerned satisfaction from Killian—she seemed to believe Lynn went along with the last thing she yelled. Tera almost believed it as well when Lynn laid her back on the table and used more rope to secure her to the table.

Lynn pulled the knife out of the cupboard and handed it to Corey.

He gave Lynn and Tera a little smile. Maybe they were truly as in love as they seemed, Tera thought as Killian fumed like a helicopter parent behind her shoulder. Corey wasn't just attracted to Lynn for making the decision, he was *proud* of her.

"He won't expect you," Lynn said, then took the kerosene lamp off the hook. "Hide behind some of those loose boards, Mrs. Hunt. He can see in the dark. Do you still have that magnum on you, or did you leave it at home?"

"We handed it over to the sheriff. It belonged to the state."

"Damn. Well, my Corey and I will do what we can. Maybe you can get to your husband while we attack and you two can escape."

"You think I'm going to leave Corey down here while—?"

"He's safe from dying, remember? And...Daddy won't want to kill Corey, if this cheer— If *Tera* was telling the truth..."

Tera had only guessed that part, but she nodded to alleviate Jessica's worried expression. Jessica hugged Corey, then hid herself behind the boards. Standing there, "alone" together, Lynn kissed Corey for far too long. Tera's voice was too muffled with the gag to tell them to knock it the fuck off. Jessica came back out and smacked them both on the back of their heads, then hid again.

"Sorry, Mrs. Hunt, it was just in case things go bad."

"What?" Jessica cried, having been lulled into a false sense of security by a sixteen-year-old monster.

"Mom, get back there," Corey chided.

Lynn went up the stairs and yelled from the door: "Daddy! She's ready for you!"

She came back down and pointed for Corey to hide beneath the table. After a few minutes Slater entered the basement, holding something in his large hand. Tera heard it beat and felt Killian's satisfaction and anticipation swelling in her own heart. She struggled against the bindings but was placated with a touch of assurance. Lynn put her hand on Tera's forearm while keeping her eyes on Slater. His dangerous, looming form filled the entire basement with foreboding darkness—there was *pressure* from his presence.

"Daddy, did you get that druggie's heart already?"

He nodded and displayed it next to the kerosene lamp Lynn held up at eye level.

"Who's going to eat it?"

"I'm splitting it with Tera. She won't be able to keep your mother at bay any longer with that added fraction of essence, and I'll gain an even deeper connection with her. Between us, we'll also share the strength of the killer from the lake. We'll become the greatest teachers in the history of the world."

"What about *me*, Daddy?" Lynn asked, her voice dripping with hurt. Tera couldn't tell if it was affected or genuine.

"We'll accelerate your training, but you'll never reach the potential you once had—thanks to the sinful loss of your virtue. Killing the boy and consuming his heart will help reacquire some of that, but you've lost the chance to ever be as powerful as your mother."

"Neither of you believed I wanted to live a normal life, but, you know, you're the ones that pushed me towards that..."

"You were practically begging us to train you before the vacation," Slater stated. He clearly *still* didn't believe Lynn had wanted that.

"Only so I could leave the country and live away from you two. I don't want to kill people."

"You killed your brother."

"He was going to kill TJ! And you would have encouraged it! Why not get Murdock's training started early, so you could make him consume your heart earlier—take over his body. Just like Mom was planning to do to me."

Slater seemed unaffected by the admittance being spoken out loud; he had no shame of the reality. Lynn controlled her voice so it didn't expose her rage, but Tera could feel her clenched fist shaking ever so slightly next to her head, beside the table.

"That was *originally* the plan, but your mother really wants this cheerleader's face."

Lynn put her hand to her own face, feeling it with a look of distant shock. Slater put a hand on her shoulder.

"It also frees you up to live your life. You should be grateful, Lynn. Tera is your ticket out. Now ungag her so she can eat this heart."

Lynn pulled the gag out. Killian rushed to control Tera's mouth.

"Oh Slater, the things I'm going to let you do to this body in a few years... Hurry and stuff that sinner's heart down her throat!"

Slater held the heart over Tera's face, covering it with blood dripping from the ragged valves. Katie's heart touched her lips before Lynn pulled back on Slater's arm.

Lynn spoke just as Tera registered Katie sneaking down the stairs. Slater was too distracted by Lynn to notice Timothy, too, although he was far noisier.

"Daddy, if you're freeing me from my daughterly duty—to sacrifice my whole body to carry Mom's legacy—can I still please have one bite? That way I'll always have a piece of her with me wherever I go. I don't want to be like you, but that doesn't mean I don't always want to have my family around."

Slater nodded and handed Katie's heart over to her. In the same motion as accepting it, Lynn tossed it over her shoulder and into Katie's surprised hands. Katie changed her path once she hit the bottom of the stairs and skidded into a dark corner of the room. She screamed in agony as she forced it back through her barely open, still-healing chest cavity.

Instead of going for Katie, Slater took Lynn's neck in his grasp and lifted her off the floor. She swung the kerosene lamp into the back of his head, catching his clothes on fire. He took a step forward but fell to the ground with a grunt, taking Lynn with him. Tera peered over the table as far as her neck would allow to see that Corey had sliced through both of Slater's Achilles.

Timothy brought an axe down on Slater's wrist, cutting it cleanly off. Lynn dug her nails into his other wrist, tearing at the tendons in an attempt to release herself. Corey climbed out from beneath the table and cut Tera loose. He handed her the knife and got in front of Jessica who had shimmied out of her hiding place. Tera pried Lynn's bloody fingers away from Slater's wrist and sawed through his tendons to the bone. He finally let go of Lynn's neck and she crawled backward on the floor, coughing.

The fire spread over his clothes as he attempted to push himself up, but with his damaged ankle and hands, his body wouldn't cooperate. Timothy made to swing the axe again but hesitated. Lynn got up and took it from him, then chopped off Slater's other hand, followed by both of his feet. Timothy joined Corey and Jessica.

Tera made to stab into Slater's heart, but Killian restrained her with all her might, freezing Tera's hand from plunging downward mid-strike. Slater rolled over and swung his arm like a club, tripping Tera and sending her back into the wall. She let go of the knife to avoid the possible struggle with Killian taking another stab at her heart.

While Lynn chopped, Katie appeared before Tera. Katie picked up the knife, then offered her a hand to stand up.

"You bitches will never be rid of us. We'll find a way to—"

Katie punched Tera. Tera thanked Katie for shutting that murderess up, then they knelt next to Slater's smoldering body.

"Are you ready?" Katie asked as she put Tera's hand over her fist, holding the knife at a downward angle together. They thrust the knife into his chest and carved out his heart, then cooked it over the flames, using the knife as a skewer.

Tera peered at Lynn, who breathed heavily while holding the axe poised in case Slater's body did anything unexpected. Katie slid the heart off the knife and tossed it at Lynn's feet. She chopped the heart in half, then flicked each side to Tera and Katie with the flat of the blade. Slater's body flopped around but it posed no threat. The Hunt family worked together to cover his body with a large board, holding him down and avoiding the flames.

As Katie and Tera took their first bites into the heart, Slater's disembodied hands skittered around the floor. One grabbed Timothy's ankle and clasped down tight, causing Timothy to cry out and fall down. The sickening snap of bone echoed in the small space, over the low sounds of Slater's body struggling. Lynn and Corey pried at the fingers to release Timothy. Taking advantage in the shift of attention, the other hand skittered across the floor and leapt up to Jessica's wrist, breaking that as well. Lynn left Timothy to Corey and tried getting the hand off Jessica instead.

The room filled with white light as the five college students huddled on the stairs, recording Tera and Katie eating a heart, a mutilated, struggling body beneath a charring board, and two disembodied hands crushing an ankle and wrist.

All parts of Slater stopped moving when the last of the heart entered their stomachs. Tera pressed her palms into her eyes, fighting back Killian's rage which was joined and intensified by Slater's. Katie writhed next to her, fighting her own battle. Tera hyperventilated, in fear that if she stopped fighting—for even a moment—she would lose her identity forever.

Something grabbed Tera's hand, then guided it to Katie's. Lynn knelt between the two of them and pressed their hands together until they managed to intertwine their fingers on their own. Tera discerned the raging couple pull back inside her as they touched, and Katie seemed to be regaining control as well. Lynn helped them both move closer together so they could embrace.

Lynn grimaced as she had when her mother had died, shuddering before getting up to rejoin Corey, who supported Timothy on his good leg. A couple of the college students put their phones away and helped Jessica up the stairs as she cradled her wrist. The other three students backed up the stairs, leaving Tera and Katie alone with no light but for the dying embers of Slater's corpse.

"Katie?"

"Maybe." Katie's tone had a hint of a smile.

"Heh. They're—"

"Having sex in your mind? I know."

"Fuckin' hypocrites."

Tera put her hand on Katie's cheek in the dark. "They're making me want to...not wait to get out of this goddamn place. But..."

"We could steal some more weed from gas station clerks. Muddy their influence..."

"I hope you have a better idea than drugging us up."

Katie shrugged and sighed, "That was a fucked-up idea, any-way. Old addictions coming to the surface. I'm not opposed to channeling their energy like Lynn just implied, if you're...ready for it, and...only if you want to. Killian's libido was strong, but Slater's has doubled that now. They've nearly drowned out the killer, at least. The longer I hold your hand..."

"That sounds *much* more fun than drugs, Katie," Tera whispered, then pulled in closer to kiss Katie's ear. "But before we find a hotel room, we need to stop at a farming supply store. I *really* need to see you in a cowgirl hat."

Chapter 28

Much Better

Kill Count: 31

THE SMELL OF THE forest and lake were pleasing, the air clean and warm. But everything around the resort and campgrounds reminded Katie of the summer's carnage. Whiffs of iron crept into her sensory memories. Her hands shook whenever she pulled them out of her pockets, tingling as if they had fired that shotgun only moments ago rather than months before.

The killer in her heart grew quiet and distant as Killian and Slater pushed his essence to the far recesses of her mind, but during her revisit to the camp killgrounds, she experienced a sense of satisfaction coming from that recess, like a painter making one last brushstroke before standing back a few feet to take in the whole canvas. The thought filled her with revulsion and she sneered inwardly.

The sheriff's office closed the investigation with frustration since there was no one to arrest. It took them longer than anyone would have liked to find the three bodies in the lake and the two that had been lost deeper in the forest, but once they were all found, Chase wasted no time in gathering the families of all the victims to the lake to christen a memorial she commissioned in their honor.

The memorial only covered the twelve kids who came to the lake in the bus. Katie wasn't sorry for Randall, Kelly, Trent, or Boyd, but she brought a bottle of whiskey to the campground to drink to Samantha and Ian. Far away from Chase's ceremony, she sat on a large fallen log and took a swig for each of them. Katie tipped the bottle to empty it, but a voice from behind startled her.

"Can I have some?"

Katie twisted around to find Lynn, pointing sheepishly at the brown liquid.

"How in the *hell* did you follow me?"

"You should know by now how quiet I am. Hiding in the back of your car was only a *little* difficult because I had to go to the bathroom with two hours left before we got here."

Katie smiled a little and patted the log. Lynn sat down and gazed out at the lake.

"I can't believe I didn't smell you. You're supposed to be at home, Lynn, studying and catching up on two years' worth of high school."

"The more I cram in the more falls out the other side. And it's hard to study with—"

"With you facetiming Corey every day? Yeah, I imagine it would be." Katie poked fun at her, but there was kindness in it.

"No, he's the only reason I'm pushing myself. I was going to say it's hard to study with Murdock on my mind."

"I thought you were getting better at suppressing him?"

"It's not that..." Lynn trailed off and a little tear fell down her cheek.

"Yeah..." Katie gazed at Mt. Thielsen, its jagged peak stabbing the blue sky. "You haven't had the best influences in your life. You're a different person now. Have you tried apologizing to him?"

Lynn sniffed and shook her head.

"I talk to your mother sometimes. She's mellowed out since Slater joined her. She's almost pleasant when she's not taunting me about being a lesbian or getting pissed that I took you in. Why don't you try talking to Murdock?"

"Okay. Can I have some of that first? Maybe it will help me get it all out."

Katie handed the bottle over and laughed when Lynn did the same thing Tera did the first night they'd talked, spitting it right back out. Lynn coughed and wheezed.

"How does anyone drink that stuff?" Lynn twisted her mouth in displeasure after collecting herself.

"It doesn't get better," Katie lied, "so my advice is to never drink again."

Lynn stood up and smirked. "Okay, '*mom.*' And...later, Mom."

"Say 'hi' to your brother for me, dear," Katie allowed Killian to say.

Lynn half-smiled and waved awkwardly, then wandered away from the campgrounds, talking to herself softly, a bonding walk in nature with her brother. Katie went to tip the bottle again, but another voice gave her a jolt.

"Can I have some?"

"Jesus Christ, you damn minors!" Katie shook her head and offered the bottle up to Tera.

Tera straddled the log, then sipped a tiny amount and winced. She smiled and handed the bottle back. "Much better than last time."

Tera's cheeks were red, puffy; still wet from crying. She laid back on the log and stared up at the forest and sky.

"I miss all of them. Even the jerks and airheads. I wish I could smoke with Ian again... And thank him. I don't even know how I would. I just... Why can't *he* be stuck in my heart instead of these three fucks?"

Katie let Tera vent. She wasn't away from her family often or long enough to do so. Only when she drove up to visit Katie and Lynn's house in Corvallis had she been able to get everything off her chest about what was *in* her chest. Her control improved—she only scared her parents a couple times earlier in the summer, though they all chalked it up to PTSD—but she was still a few years from catching up to Katie's tolerance.

"Do you think...if I'd eaten Ian's heart...?"

Katie shrugged. She did sometimes find herself wondering what the origin was of...whatever they were. Did it start from simple cannibalism? If they were to eat more hearts, would they absorb those essences as well? Or was it only their species? Katie shuddered to imagine more personalities in her head, even a benign one like Ian.

"I'd much rather Ian was inside me when you and I are, you know... Instead of *them* watching... Oh dude, that sounded weird. I didn't mean..."

Katie laughed and laid on her side, resting her head on Tera's thigh. Tera sat up and moved Katie's head off gently.

"I'm sorry, my parents... Things have calmed down on that front, but they still don't completely approve. I don't want another argument to flare up if they see us together."

"Okay, babe. Only a few more weeks until you move up to OSU. Did you get your dorm assignment yet?"

"It's just a few blocks from your house, and Shawna is down the hall on the same floor. I can't wait! Are you and Lynn really going to be okay with me staying with you whenever I—"

"You have to ask me that? I'm giving you a *key!*"

Tera stood up, then helped Katie off the log. Tera looked around for movement of any kind before she grabbed both of Katie's hands and pulled them into her chest, gazing deeply into Katie's eyes. "I love you, Calamity Kate. I'll see you in a few weeks, okay?"

"I love you, too. Call me anytime you feel yourself slipping."

Tera peeked around again, snuck a quick kiss on Katie's lips, then headed back to the memorial.

"I'm sure it'll be nice when you guys won't have to hide that from people," Lynn said, startling Katie yet again.

Katie put her arm around Lynn's shoulders and directed them towards the car, pouring the rest of the whiskey onto the ground as they walked. "You're going to need to teach me how you do that. I don't know how you're so quiet when you move."

"Do you think that will come in handy for lacrosse tryouts?"

"If it doesn't, your strength will carry you through. A couple years from now, you'll earn a scholarship to whichever school Corey goes to. I'm sure of it."

"I hope the girls at school like my outfits. I've been planning them for weeks."

"Is that what you're doing in your room when you're not studying? You'll have to show me what you've got lined up."

Lynn paused a few feet from the car. She wore a skeptical look. "Katie, I'm not...entirely sure when I'm talking to you or Mom, but...thank you. For everything."

Katie smiled and offered Lynn the keys to the car.

"I don't have my permit yet!"

"And you're not twenty-one yet, but that didn't stop you from drinking that whiskey. Besides, what's the worst that could happen if we crashed? We'll be *fine*."

"I'm not worried about myself. I don't want to hurt anyone else. You know—if it wasn't just us in the crash."

Katie tossed the keys in the air and caught them herself, then walked to the driver's side.

"You continue to surprise me every day."

Down the road Katie asked how the Hunt family was doing, and Lynn gave an update on their injuries, which were close to being fully healed after some intense rehab.

"Do you want to visit them the week before school starts?" Katie asked, to which Lynn nodded enthusiastically. "Great! One last road trip before our lives really begin."

Two Years Later

Tera rested her hand on Katie's shoulder as they watched the exterior of an abandoned warehouse—a warehouse outside of Salem, Oregon hosting a meeting between drug gangs. Lynn crouched close to them, holding a large remote in her hand.

"You know what fuckin' sucks about this, Lynn?" Tera asked.

"That we can't kill them with our bare hands?"

"No, dude, that we can't watch your Rube Goldberg invention tear those assholes apart. Can't you set up cameras next time?"

"Hey, I'm doing this to satisfy our bloodlust, not run a peepshow."

Katie kissed Tera's fingers and shushed them. "I can't hear the screams," she whispered.

"Mom?" Lynn asked.

"Nope."

When the last of the screams emanating from the large warehouse doors died out, the three of them laid back in the grass and shared in a collective sigh. Tera rolled into Katie's side and hugged across her torso.

"Thank you, Lynn," Tera said. "Are you going to major in robotics at Stanford? Or will you be too distracted by Corey to go to class?"

"Mechanical engineering. And...I want to be with my Corey but... He's going to have to get in line to my studies and lacrosse team," Lynn said resolutely.

Katie reached out for Lynn's hand. "I know I've been pushing you hard the last two years, but you're an adult now. Feel free to slack off on an assignment here or there if it means you need to spend a night out with him every once in a while."

Lynn squeezed Katie's hand before letting go, then leaned up on her elbow.

"I checked the schedule already. We'll be playing OSU in late February. Will you both watch me play?"

"Definitely," Tera said. "Even though I'll be cheerleading for *my* school, just know I'll be cheering in my heart whenever you score a goal."

Lynn clicked her tongue and rolled her eyes. "So fucking cheesy."

Tera chuckled and buried her face in Katie's armpit. Lynn helped both of them to their feet. Katie tossed the car keys to Lynn.

"Careful on the drive back. I thought I saw a police car camping out on the way here."

"Yes, Mom."

"That wasn't her."

"I know."

Lynn got into the car and drove off. Tera smothered laughter as they strapped on their helmets and climbed onto Tera's motorcycle.

"What's so funny, babe?"

"If Corey knocks her up, you'll be my GILF."

"My parents always thought I'd make something of myself. I think if they had to choose between a druggie, a lesbian, and a grandmother before thirty...they'd *still* disown me."

On the motorcycle, Tera caressed Katie's thighs wrapped around her hips. "My dearly departed friend Ian once said that he didn't give a fuck what others thought about him. That's a much better way to live."

Katie wrapped her arms around Tera's waist, and they rode off into the night.

THE END

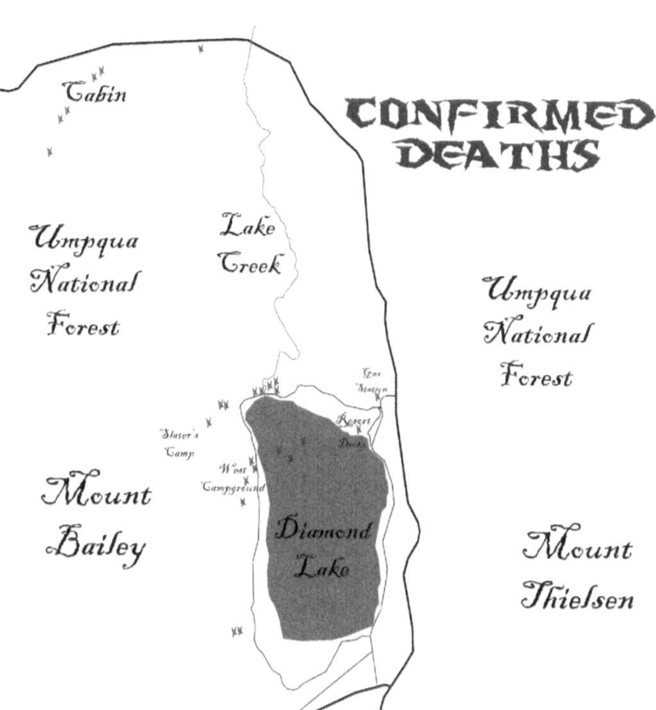

Cabin
CONFIRMED DEATHS
Lake Creek
Umpqua National Forest
Umpqua National Forest
Gas Station
Resort
Dock
Slater's Camp
West Campground
Mount Bailey
Diamond Lake
Mount Thielsen

SPECIAL THANKS

As an extension of the Dedication, I want to thank Diamond Lake. My family has spent a week up there nearly every year for over half a century. We've seen it sold and changed, but nothing has ever taken away its quiet serenity, its gorgeous views, and dazzling sunsets that defy photography.

I've never felt unsafe at Diamond Lake—not from animals, people, or anything. Well, that's not *completely* true. I've always been terrified of the seaweed gripping my feet and pulling me down, stronger than any life jacket.

Should you ever find yourself at the resort, I invite you to walk around the north of the lake to the west campground, and you'll appreciate how much care went into respecting the geography of the area to create the plausibility of hemming in dozens of people to pick off one by one.

It's a pleasant coincidence that Diamond Lake shares a similar name to Crystal Lake. The idea to write this slasher parody wasn't born from that idea alone—no, that was born from watching countless slashers from the 80s and 90s, absorbing every ridiculous cliché and trope, and reflecting them back in a way that doesn't quite deconstruct or admonish (except for the family values stuff. Slasher politics can fuck all the way off, and I find myself increasingly agreeing with the late Roger Ebert's extreme distaste for the genre outside of *Halloween*).

Thank you to my friend Lou, who, more than anyone else, I wanted to make laugh since he's probably the only one I know personally who would get every slasher reference littered throughout these pages.

Thank you to my amazing editor Ollie Ander at Acidic Ink Publishing, who helped ground all the references into a coherent, accessible tale that even a genre-neophyte could appreciate.

Thanks to my alpha, beta, ARC, and all other readers—you're literally the reason I want to keep writing, even at my lowest points.

About VB Scott

I'm an unassuming horror fan, metalhead, and Japanophile, all wrapped up inside a Pacific Northwest elder millennial.

I write in several genres and would love nothing more than for you to follow me as I release more stories that I hope you'll enjoy.

My handle is vb_scottwrites on Threads, Instagram, Facebook. Subscribe to my Substack at vbscott.substack.com

Feel free to contact me through my email address at vbscott.writes@gmail.com

ALSO BY VB SCOTT

Revenge of the Bakeneko

A historical fiction, action-adventure novel set in the early 1700s of Japan's Edo Period

A dice game in the hands of Takana Gozen is anything but a matter of chance. Takana covets golden *ryō* coins almost as much as she hates yakuza, and she is a master at manipulating both as she hosts backroom gambling events to pay off her deadbeat father's debt. She's spent the last eight years wandering the *Nikkō Kaidō* highway, living the life of a homeless vagabond—stealing, cheating, and killing—all in the never-ending pursuit of coin.

Instigated by the lowliest of prostitutes in the brothel Takana's mother runs, a series of brutal, deadly events break Takana out of debt, and she earns the power to oppose the very structures that bound her. The found family she collects along the way looks to her for leadership, and together they form their own *yakuza* clan—the most prosperous and feared in all of Eastern Japan: The Bakeneko Clan.

Takana has trained her whole life to survive deadly encounters, but the risks that come with being a clan head come in more forms than *katana* and *kunai*. Protection, love, compassion, friendship, and sacrifice will all be necessary if she is to survive her new life—a life that proves to be more dangerous and unfulfilling than the old one.

Black Aura

A horror/metal mashup novel that will take you straight to Hell.

Led by the sibylline Auranna Korpela, the world-famous metal band "Black Aura" is soon rendered infamous. Devoted fans vanish at every show. Auranna's inaction stuns the community and raises suspicion, birthing a stained reputation which precedes them. And through it all, Auranna suffers increasingly dark and perverse dreams of the netherworld.

But Auranna's visions morph into a hideous reality. Her foremost fan has contacted her from the abyss, and Auranna can no longer ignore her deepest fears taking root. As her bandmates and unlikely allies unite at her side, she must contend with a corrupted girlfriend, doorways to damnation, and a soul contract she never signed.

Despite the threat of Hell itself, most painful of all lurks the threat of dissolution: Black Aura disbanding at the height of their glory. Must Auranna sacrifice herself to win their salvation, or has their grim fate already been decided?

A masterful celebration of sixty years of metal, Black Aura's vivid characters and horror-rich immersion pave the road to Hell like never before.